A CATALOGUE
OF THE WORKS OF
Ralph Vaughan Williams

A CATALOGUE
OF THE WORKS OF
Ralph Vaughan Williams

MICHAEL KENNEDY

Revised Edition

London
OXFORD UNIVERSITY PRESS
NEW YORK   MELBOURNE
1982

Oxford University Press, Walton Street, Oxford, OX2 6DP

LONDON   GLASGOW
NEW YORK   TORONTO   MELBOURNE   AUCKLAND
KUALA LUMPUR   SINGAPORE   HONG KONG   TOKYO
DELHI   BOMBAY   CALCUTTA   MADRAS   KARACHI
NAIROBI   DAR ES SALAAM   CAPE TOWN

© Oxford University Press 1964

This edition published 1982

ISBN 0 19 315452 8

British Library Cataloguing in Publication Data

Kennedy, Michael, *1926-*
    A catalogue of the works of Ralph Vaughan Williams.
    1. Vaughan Williams, Ralph – Bibliography
    I. Title
    016.780'92'4   ML134.V/
ISBN 0 19 315452 8

Printed in Great Britain
by Ebenezer Baylis and Son Ltd.
The Trinity Press, Worcester

To
ROY DOUGLAS
*In memory of our friendship
with R.V.W. and
in gratitude*

INTRODUCTION

THE list of works by Vaughan Williams which forms the major part of this book first appeared as Appendix One of the first (hardback) edition of my *The Works of Ralph Vaughan Williams*, published in 1964 and reprinted, with some corrections and revisions, in 1966. The biographical and critical text of that book was issued separately, in hardback and paperback, in 1980, with a condensed list of works. In this new edition of the list of works (which has again been revised) I have also included a slightly expanded version of Mr Peter Starbuck's bibliography of Vaughan Williams's own writings. This first appeared as Part I of Appendix Three of the first edition of my book, and additions have been made from Mr Starbuck's 1967 thesis for Fellowship of the Library Association. Space and the need for financial economy have compelled me reluctantly to omit the second part of his bibliography – writings about Vaughan Williams. For Appendix Four (a list of recordings up to 1963 which of course is now considerably out of date) interested readers are referred to the 1966 impression of *The Works of Ralph Vaughan Williams*. I wish to express my gratitude to Mr Starbuck and the Library Association for permission to reprint the bibliography here, and to renew my thanks to all those people, too numerous to mention, who helped me originally in tracking down facts for the List of Works.

My views on Vaughan Williams's position in English music have not changed to any marked degree since I wrote my book twenty years ago. But it is still necessary, I believe, to counter the often-propagated picture of him as a composer who achieved his best effects almost in spite of his deficiencies, a primitive musician wrestling interminably with his lack of technique and somehow, with immense effort, emerging with a rough-hewn masterpiece ready for the publisher. Cecil Gray expressed this view amusingly nearly sixty years ago, describing Vaughan Williams as like 'a vast and ungainly porpoise' floundering about 'in the sea of his ideas'.

To be fair, no one did more to foster this view of Vaughan Williams than Vaughan Williams himself. 'I wish I didn't dislike my own stuff so much when I hear it – it all sounds so incompetent.' That was written to a friend in 1933, while he was at work on his Fourth Symphony. In 1942, at the time of his seventieth birthday, he wrote to another friend: 'I've tried all my life for clarity and never achieved it . . . the more I hear my own tunes the more I dislike them.' In his brief autobiography he wrote: 'Over-scoring has always been one of my vices, and it arises, I am convinced, from the fact that I am not always sure enough of myself, and have not the courage of my convictions, and that I must hide my nakedness with an apron of orchestration.' At the final rehearsal of the Eighth Symphony in 1956, when he was eighty-three, he said to me after one passage: 'That's not a silly tune, is it?' I said I didn't think it was. He thought for a moment and added: 'Rather silly, perhaps, but not too silly.'

Now, what was the cause of this self-disparagement? We can safely absolve him from any charge of mock-modesty. It arose, I think, first from his early years when he was struggling so hard to forge a personal and distinctive style and to avoid becoming merely an English version of some German or Austrian composer. For many years he remained acutely dissatisfied with his music, withholding much of it from publication, constantly revising it (as he did to the end of his life) and subjecting it not only to severe and ruthless self-criticism but inviting criticism and comment from friends, particularly Holst. It was the quality of his musical invention that most concerned him, not the manner in which it was presented. He became suspicious of brilliantly scored and 'effective' music, suspecting that the 'colour' was used to conceal lack of real ideas and dreading lest he should fall into the same trap. Yet in 1908, at the age of thirty-five, he realized that he could not be an ascetic in these matters and went to a younger man, Ravel, for lessons in orchestration. The result was at once plain to see and hear: significantly, his real emergence as a composer with an individual voice dates from 1909 with *On Wenlock Edge*.

Thenceforward, it seems to me, Vaughan Williams commanded the power to say what he wanted in the way he wanted to say it, which was not always in the same way. To do this, one must be formidably equipped technically, and I maintain that he was. (It is simply untrue, by the way, to say that he abhorred the solo virtuoso artist, but he put the stress on 'artist'. Consider how he admired, and composed for, the artistry of Lionel Tertis, Jelly d'Arányi, and

Larry Adler, among many.) Consider, for example, several works written in the fifteen years between 1910 and 1925 (from which one can exclude nearly five years of war when he was in the Army and wrote hardly any music). The *Tallis Fantasia* is rightly accepted as one of the finest examples of writing for a massed group of strings, contrasting (as Elgar had done) a string quartet and two string orchestras, extracting from those forces an extraordinary range of colour, dynamics, and the subtlest nuances, exploring to the utmost the capabilities of the instruments for melodic and contrapuntal effects, and successfully gauging all this to the sonorous acoustics of a great cathedral. No 'ungainly porpoise' wrote that music, nor did it arise from some lucky accident of unconscious genius. It arose from inspiration combined with practical knowledge, as did *A London Symphony* of a few years later, opulent, raucous, brooding, and rumbustious by turns and all by intent, the music itself vibrant with its creator's affection for the subject.

In 1922 came *A Pastoral Symphony*, which gave rise to some of the most asinine contemporary comments, e.g. Hugh Allen's 'it suggests V.W. rolling over and over in a ploughed field on a wet day'. Does it? Where? This is perhaps the most truly original of all his symphonies and technically one of the most daring and accomplished. Most of it is slow-moving but it avoids monotony by an astonishing display of orchestral resource in the use of tone-colour that is just as 'virtuoso' in the highest sense as anything by Strauss or Debussy. No 'clumsy amateur' could have devised the coalescing of woodwind and string solos with the sustained and massive harmonic tension of the rest of the orchestra in the first movement, nor the fleet-footed coda to the scherzo, nor the sudden fierce climaxes, as swiftly subsiding, like gusts of wind across the landscape.

At almost the same time Vaughan Williams wrote the *Mass in G minor*, which is the vocal equivalent of the *Tallis Fantasia*, a solo quartet being contrasted with, and merged with, the double chorus. Sir Richard Terry at once recognized its importance: 'In your individual and modern idiom', he wrote to Vaughan Williams, 'you have really captured the old liturgical spirit and atmosphere.' In 1925 *Flos Campi* was performed, for solo viola, wordless chorus, and small orchestra, an exercise in exotic and skilfully calculated sonorities. I could continue with many later examples: the amazing *Serenade to Music*, written for sixteen solo voices and capturing the individuality of each of the original soloists; the ruthless power of the Fourth Symphony, as deliberately harsh as the *Pastoral* is mellifluous; and the striking – and truly virtuoso – orchestral and choral effects which make the *Five Tudor Portraits* such an extraordinary achievement.

There are still those who – not having read his *National Music* carefully – blame Vaughan Williams for the 'parochialism' of British musical life in the 1930s and hold him to account for almost everything, from the public's continued unwillingness to like Schoenberg to the Royal College of Music's refusal in the mid-1930s to let the young Britten study with Alban Berg. These are side-issues, however – if fascinating ones – of Vaughan Williams's musical achievement. The tendency today, now that the first trough in the decline in appreciation of him has levelled off, is to confirm what has always been self-evident: that there are wide variations in the quality of his vast output listed in this volume, that the best is unique and the lesser peaks highly refreshing and often original. What is likely to continue to provoke debate and controversy for many years to come is the violent – and stimulating – critical diversity of opinion on just which works are the peaks and which the lowlands. And surely that is a sign of the vitality of the music.

M.K.

CONTENTS

List of Works

Arranged in chronological order

THE following is a list, as complete as possible, of all Vaughan Williams's compositions and arrangements in a creative period lasting eighty years from the age of six to his death within seven weeks of his eighty-sixth birthday. I have made each entry as detailed as I can, in the hope that this will be of interest and use to musicians, authors, students and the general reader. Where date of composition is known, the work is listed in that year, or, if composition was spread over a long period (as often happened) the relevant dates are given—again, if known. Otherwise, dates of first performance or of publication govern chronology. Vaughan Williams gave no opus numbers to his works, and no useful purpose would be served by trying to supply them now. All unpublished MSS. are the property of Mrs. R. Vaughan Williams except where otherwise stated. In the case of MSS. now in the British Library, catalogue numbers are given in parentheses. I have also reprinted in full all Vaughan Williams's programme notes about his own works.

1878

THE ROBIN'S NEST. A four-bar composition 'by Mr. R. Williams', and containing some fearsome-looking chords in the bass part.

First public performance: B.B.C. North of England Home Service, 16 November 1964, by Michael Barton (pianoforte).

Whereabouts of MS.: British Library (54186). This MS. is illustrated in *The Works of Ralph Vaughan Williams* (1964 and 1966 impressions only).

1882

A musical exercise book dated 5 June 1882 by 'R.V. Williams' has a motto in a childish scrawl

'If you play music play in time and tune, for what is music without time and tune?!'

This book contains some of the overtures the boy wrote for his toy theatre at Leith Hill Place. The first is

Overture to The Major,

and there is a note: 'This overture is copyright except to some few persons, viz. Misses Sophia Wedgewood [*sic*] and Williams and Mrs. Williams.' The work is plentifully sprinkled with 'crecendo', spelt thus.

Pianoforte Sonata in F. 'Respectfully dedicated to Miss Sophy Wedgewood.' Inspiration failed after six bars.

Chant du Matin.

Overture to the Ram Opera.

This has the inscription 'Ent. Sta. Hall', a sign of observation on the part of a boy of ten.

How doth the little busy bee.

This appears to be the first attempt to set words to music.

Sonata in three movements.

Marked 'op.4'. The first indication of tempo is spelt Algerreto non troppo. There is a fierce bass part.

Overture to The Galoshes of Happienes [*sic*].

Part of this is scored more fully, with parts for first and second violins, viola, first and second cello, and sidedrum.

Chorale, op. 9.

Grand March des Bramas, op. 10.

Song 'Here I come, creeping, creeping, everywhere,
　　　By the dusty roadside
　　　On the sunny hillside
　　　Close by the mossy brook.'

Note: 'The other verses of this song will be found in "Selections from the Poets", Vol. II, p. 207.'

Sketches for a Nativity Scene.

It was to be seventy-two years before this early interest in Christmas music came to full flower, apart from the *Fantasia on Christmas Carols* of 1912.

Whereabouts of MSS.: British Library (57265 and 57294A).

1888

PIANOFORTE TRIO IN G MAJOR. Performed at Charterhouse, Godalming, 5 August 1888, by H. Vivian Hamilton, pianoforte; B. K. R. Wilkinson and R. Vaughan Williams, violins; Stephen Massingberd, violoncello.

1889

A relic from Charterhouse days is three neatly and even floridly written *Kyries.* They are marked on the title-page:

'Fecit Ralph Vaughan Williams.
　　Schol: Carth: Dom:
A.D. III. Jun. Anno Domini MDCCCLXXXIX.'

Whereabouts of MS.: British Library (57265).

1890

Some of the surviving manuscripts from R.C.M. days are of interest solely because they give us a clue to the kind of work which students undertook for Parry, Gladstone and Stanford. They tell us little about Vaughan Williams except to show his obvious difficulty in finding his natural voice. The influence of Brahms is often all-pervasive.

Christmas term
1. SONATINA IN E FLAT
2. ORGAN OVERTURE

Whereabouts of MS.: British Library (57266–7).

1891

Spring term
1. FINALE OF A STRING QUARTET
2. 'MUSIC, WHEN SOFT VOICES DIE'. Performed at the Cambridge University Musical Club on 18 November 1893, by W. R. Gurley, R. W. Broadrick, R. S. Trevor and A. M. Moss.
   Part-song for male voices (TTBB) unaccompanied.
3. TUNES 'FOR A BALLET'
4. THEME WITH VARIATION, for pianoforte.

Summer term
5. Versions of a GLORIA IN EXCELSIS 'done with Dr. Parry'.
6. ANTHEM for tenor and chorus: 'I heard a voice from heaven saying unto me, write: From henceforth blessed are the dead.' Rev. XIV. 13.

Christmas term
The *Gloria* was completed and 'shewn up for R.C.M. exam'. It is an eminently respectable setting, with nothing to surprise Dr. Parry. For example:

Whereabouts of MS.: British Library (57266–7).

1892

Spring term
1. SUPER FLUMINA BABYLONIS. Setting for Dr. Parry.
2. ARRANGEMENTS FOR ORCHESTRA of Beethoven's Sonata op. 7 and of the Largo Appassionato of Beethoven's Sonata op. 2, No. 2. On a page of the latter Parry wrote: 'Cellos too often separated from basses.'

Undated but probably 1892

Whereabouts of MS.: British Library (57266–7).

3. VARIATIONS on a Ground Bass by Lully.

Whereabouts of MS.: British Library (57269).

4. SETTING OF 'CROSSING THE BAR' (Alfred, Lord Tennyson, 1809–92).

Whereabouts of MS.: British Library (57270).

5. HAPPY DAY AT GUNBY, scored fully with parts for violins, violoncellos, pianoforte and organ (needed for a thunderstorm). One section is marked 'Old country dance'. A note to the copyist after an illegible muddle says 'Don't copy this bar till you have asked for explanation'. Plus ça change. . . .

Whereabouts of MS.: British Library. Full score and parts (57268).

6. FIVE VALSES FOR ORCHESTRA

Whereabouts of MS.: British Library. Condensed score (57268).

7. FANTASIA A LA VALSE (orchestra and arrangement for piano-forte duet).

Whereabouts of MS.: British Library. Short score and piano duet (57268).

1893

1. WISHES. Setting to words by 'T' printed in the *Cambridge Observer* of August 1893. This is a ballad-ish love-song whose second verse seems to indicate a personal experience of the composer:

> 'Would that the love which in me lacks expression
> Might speak in every gesture, every act;
> So should I be transfigured in those eyes
> In which I would appear most excellent!'

Whereabouts of MS.: British Library (57270).

2. SUITE for four hands on one pianoforte. Dated 4 October. Remarkable only for a diminished seventh.

Whereabouts of MS.: British Library (57269).

1894

1. REMINISCENCES OF A WALK AT FRANKHAM, for pianoforte dated 28 August 1894.

The programmatic nature of this piece is clearly indicated by notes on the score, thus: 'A steamy afternoon (andantino languido)'; 'Little River Hall'; 'Anxiety on the Way Home'; 'Grinham's cottage appears in sight'; 'Evening comes on'.

Note at end of score says: 'Miserable failure, not to be taken seriously.'

Whereabouts of MS.: British Library (57269).

2. THE VIRGIN'S CRADLE SONG (S. T. Coleridge, 1772–1834). Song for voice and pianoforte, sung at Cambridge University Musical Club on 3 November 1894, by W. J. L. Higley, accompanied by R. Vaughan Williams. (See 1905, No. 3.)

3. VEXILLA REGIS. Hymn for soprano solo, mixed five-part chorus (SSATB), string orchestra and organ. Submitted as exercise for degree of Bachelor of Music.

    I. *Vexilla Regis.* Allegro. For soprano and chorus (includes canon between solo violin and soprano, and a canon 4 in 2 for four-part chorus).

    II. *Impleta sunt.* For chorus.

    III. *O Crux.* Andantino. For soprano and chorus.

    IV. *Fons salutis* (Fugue). Allegro. For chorus.

Whereabouts of MS.: Anderson Room, Cambridge University Library (Mus. B., 103).

1895

1. TRIO IN C MAJOR for pianoforte, violin, and violoncello. Completed 28 June 1895.

This is a 'manufactured' piece, quite lacking in characteristic fingerprints.

Whereabouts of MS.: British Library (57269).

2. TO DAFFODILS (Robert Herrick, 1591–1674). 3 July 1895.

3. LOLLIPOPS SONG; SPINNING SONG. Settings from Rumpelstiltskin.

4. PEACE, COME AWAY. Setting for four voices, flutes, clarinet, oboe, bassoons, horn, trumpets, cellos and basses of Canto LVII of Tennyson's *In Memoriam.* This is dated 27 September 1895.

Whereabouts of MSS. of 2, 3, and 4: British Library (57270).

1896

1. SPRING. Vocal valse for voice and pianoforte. Words from 'The Window' or 'The Song of the Wrens'[1] (No. 5) by Tennyson. *Unpublished.* 44 bars. Dated 17 February 1896.
2. VINE, VINE AND EGLANTINE, Vocal valse for soprano, alto, tenor, and bass with pianoforte accompaniment. Words from 'The Window' (No. 2) by Tennyson. *Unpublished.* 71 bars. Dated 12–16 March 1896.
3. WINTER, Vocal valse for voice and pianoforte. Words from 'The Window' (No. 4) by Tennyson. *Lento-allegro. Unpublished.* 69 bars. Dated 16 March 1896.

Whereabouts of above MSS : British Library (57270).

The following vocal works are undated, but were almost certainly written between October 1895 and March 1896.

A. RONDEL, for contralto or baritone, with pianoforte accomp. Words by A. C. Swinburne (1837–1909).
Andante. 66 bars.
Unpublished.
First performance (probable): London, Bechstein Hall, 28 May 1906. Gregory Hast (baritone), Henry Bird (pianoforte).

B. SONNET 71, for six voices (SSATBB) unaccompanied. (Motto, 'A poor thing but mine own.') Words by William Shakespeare (1564–1616).
Unpublished. Andante maestoso. 56 bars. Second copy exists incomplete.

C. ECHO'S LAMENT OF NARCISSUS. ('Slow, slow, fresh fount'). Madrigal for double chorus. Words by Ben Jonson (1573–1637).
Lento. 51 bars.
Unpublished.

Whereabouts of above MSS. : British Library (57270).

1897

1. THE WILLOW SONG. Traditional English tune, arranged for voice and pianoforte. *Andante* 3/4. 32 bars. Dated 19 February 1897. *Unpublished.*
2. STRING QUARTET IN C minor.
   Unpublished. Composed winter, 1898.

I. *Allegro*	197 bars
II. *Andantino*	135 bars
III. *Intermezzo* (allegretto)	92 bars

[1] Written in 1870 for Sullivan to set to music.

IV. *Variazione con finale fugato* 170 bars
(Thema: Moderato; Var. I: Moderato; Var. II: Adagio;
Var. III: Presto; Var. IV: Andante; Var. V: Maggiore: con
moto ma non troppo; Var. VI: Allegro (minore) marcato;
Finale: Fugato, allegro moderato.)
This is one of the most significant of the early unpublished works.
There is more than a hint of folk song in the Andantino, a reminder
that the elements of this style were bred in the bone.

The Intermezzo has a madrigalian flavour, and its principal theme is a
forerunner of 'Linden Lea':

First performance: Oxford and Cambridge Musical Club, 30 June 1904,
by M. W. Dawson, E. Chetham Strode, Dr. Jordan and A. K. El-
worthy.

Whereabouts of MS.: British Library (57271).

1898
1. SERENADE (word SUITE scored out) for small orchestra, in
A minor. Composed 1898.
Unpublished.
Instrumentation: 2 flutes, 2 oboes, 2 clarinets in A, 2 bassoons, 2
horns in F, 2 trumpets in A, timpani, 8 first violins, 8 second violins,
4 violas, 4 violoncelli, 3 double-basses.[1]
   I. *Prelude.* Andante sostenuto   88 bars
  II. *Scherzo.* Allegro   205 bars
 III. *Intermezzo and Trio.* Allegretto con moto 88 bars
 IV. *Finale.* Allegro   185 bars
An alternative third movement, Romance, is also in full score,
Andantino, 160 bars. (Letter to Holst from Vaughan Williams, from
5 Cowley Street: 'I have written a new coda and a new movement for
my Serenade and most of my degree exercise.'
First performance: Bournemouth, Winter Gardens, 4 April 1901.

---

[1] In most instances under 'Instrumentation' where more than one flute is given, one
of the flautists doubles piccolo.

Bournemouth Municipal Orchestra, conductor Dan Godfrey. First London performance: Aeolian Hall, 3 March 1908. The Aeolian Orchestra, conducted by Rosabel Watson.

This must be the work which Stanford described to W. S. Hannam of Leeds in 1899 as 'a most poetical and remarkable piece of work'. Yet Adeline Vaughan Williams, writing in 1898 to Ralph Wedgwood, said: 'Stanford, after practising the *Serenade* diligently at three rehearsals, threw it up for no apparent reason, so now it is trying its luck at the Crystal Palace – we expect it to return with "not wanted" on it every day.' An American performance in 1980 showed that the work has much merit. The Scherzo has a country-dance flavour and vigorous horn calls as the main theme:

Whereabouts of MS.: British Library. Full score (57272).

2. QUINTET for clarinet, horn, violin, violoncello, and pianoforte, in D major. Composed 1898.
   Unpublished.
      I. *Allegro moderato*   207 bars
     II. *Intermezzo: allegretto* 109 bars
    III. *Andantino*   172 bars
   IV. *Finale: allegro molto*   418 bars
   A feature of the Andantino is the third bar of the horn's opening phrase

repeated for 19 bars as coda before passing to clarinet and violin to end the movement *ppp*.

First performance: London, Queen's (small) Hall, 5 June 1901, at a chamber concert in the series promoted by George A. Clinton, by Miss Llewella Davies (pianoforte), Miss Jessie Grimson (violin), G. A. Clinton (clarinet), A. Borsdorf (horn), B. P. Parker (cello).

Whereabouts of MS.: British Library, with extra piano part of 1st and 2nd movements with cues (57273).

1899

1. THE GARDEN OF PROSERPINE. For soprano solo, chorus and orchestra. Completed 1899; begun 1897 or 1898.

Unpublished. Words by A. C. Swinburne. Full score completed: 489 bars.

Instrumentation: 2 flutes, 2 oboes, 2 clarinets, 2 bassoons, 4 horns, 2 trumpets, 2 trombones, 1 bass trombone, tuba, timpani, harp, violins, violas, violoncelli, double basses.

It is strange that this work remained unperformed and unpublished in preference to the inferior *Willow-Wood.* It is typical of its period, but contains imaginative scoring. Some of the soprano's music shows Vaughan Williams's unmistakable fingerprint:

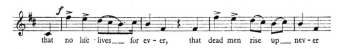

that no life · lives___ for ev - er, that dead men rise up___ nev - er

Whereabouts of MS.: British Library. Full score (57274).

The following vocal works were probably composed between 1896 and 1902; some were not published until many years later.

A. THREE ELIZABETHAN SONGS. Part-songs for unaccompanied chorus (SATB). Various dates have been given for the composition of these songs. In a bibliography of Vaughan Williams's music in the *Musical Times* of June 1920 Edwin Evans assigned them to 1895. Hubert Foss gives 1891–6, Percy Young 1893(?), James Day 1896 for (1) and 1891 for (2) and (3).

All the evidence of one's ears seems to indicate a much later date, say 1908, but we have the composer's words from his *Musical Autobiography*: 'Parry's criticism was constructive. He was not merely content to point out faults but would prescribe the remedy. The last two bars of my early part-song, "The Willow Song", were almost certainly composed by Parry.' This would seem to date this song at any rate at 1890–2, during Vaughan Williams's first spell at the R.C.M. The assurance and style of the music are far ahead of any other of his compositions of this time.

1. SWEET DAY. *Andantino tranquillo.* E minor. Words by George Herbert (1593–1632).

2. THE WILLOW SONG. *Lento.* E modal minor. Words by William Shakespeare, *Othello*, Act IV, Scene III.

3. O MISTRESS MINE. *Allegretto.* E flat major. Words by William Shakespeare. *Twelfth Night*, Act II, Scene III.
   First performance: (probable) Shirehampton Public Hall, 5 November 1913, by Avonmouth and Shirehampton Choral Society, conducted by Dr. R. Vaughan Williams.
   Duration: 7 minutes.

Publication: January 1913, London, Joseph Williams & Co. (J.W. 15360). Tonic Solfa edition 1924 (J.W. 15360 d, e, and f).

B. HOW CAN THE TREE BUT WITHER? Song for voice and pianoforte. *Andante non troppo.* C minor. Words by Thomas, Lord Vaux (1510–56).

First known performance: Magpie Madrigal Society concert, 5 June 1907. Francis Harford (bass).

Publication: London, 1934, Oxford University Press.

MS. in British Museum (50480). Probably composed in 1896.

C. CLARIBEL. Song for voice and pianoforte. *Andante.* F modal minor. Words by Tennyson from *Juvenilia.*

First performance: (probable) London, Bechstein Hall, 2 December 1904, Beatrice Spencer (soprano), Hamilton Harty (pianoforte).

Publication: London, Boosey & Co. 1906 (H 5026).

Whereabouts of MS.: British Library (59796).

D. COME AWAY DEATH. Part-song for five voices (SSATB). 45 bars. *Lento.* E modal minor. Words by William Shakespeare, *Twelfth Night,* Act II, Scene IV.

Publication: London, 1909, Stainer and Bell (S. & B. Choral Library No. 13).

Whereabouts of MS.: British Library (57270).

E. RISE EARLY SUN. Madrigal (words probably by Nicholas Gatty). *Performed* by Hooton Roberts Choral Society in September 1899 and 1901. Autograph MS. is lost, but in 1972 copies in Gatty's hand of the soprano, alto, and bass parts were found in Rotherham, among family papers, by Miss M. E. Glasbey, whose mother, aunt, and father had sung in the first performance. The missing tenor part was reconstructed by Roy Douglas and the work was performed again during the Hooton Roberts Vaughan Williams Centenary Festival, 1972.

F. MASS. For Soloists (SATB), mixed double chorus, and orchestra. Composed 1897–9. Submitted as exercise for degree of Doctor of Music, Cambridge University.

I. *Credo*— for soloists, chorus and orchestra.

Instrumentation: 2 flutes, 2 oboes, 2 clarinets in B flat, 2 bassoons, 4 horns in F, 3 trombones, tuba, timpani, strings, organ.

(*a*) Credo (*Andante maestoso*); (*b*) Et in unum dominum (*Un poco più mosso—alla breve*); (*c*) Per quem omnia (*Andante*); (*d*) Qui propter (*Adagio molto*); (*e*) Et resurrexit (*Allegro moderato*) (contains perpetual canon 4 in 2 for the four soloists doubled by strings to the

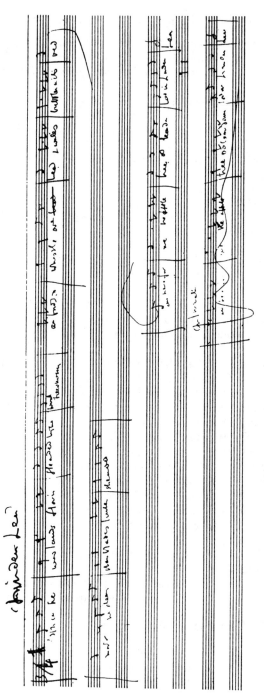

'LINDEN LEA.' THE FIRST SKETCH-BOOK DRAFT.

words 'Et unam sanctam'); (*f*) Et expecto (*Adagio molto*); (*g*) Et vitam venturi (*Allegro molto—tempo primo, allegro moderato*); (*h*) Amen (*Allegro—più mosso—molto più lento—tempo primo del Credo (Andante maestoso)*);

II. *Offertorium* for orchestra in G major. *Allegro moderato*.
Instrumentation: as above, except for 2 clarinets in A, and no organ.
III. *Sanctus*—for double chorus, brass, timpani and organ (no strings or woodwind). *Adagio*.
IV. *Hosanna*—for double chorus, orchestra and organ (da capo). *Allegro* (fugal).
V. *Benedictus*—for soloists, with 2 flutes, 2 clarinets, 2 bassoons, 2 horns and strings. *Andante sostenuto*.
Whereabouts of MS.: Cambridge University Library, Anderson Room (Mus. D., 26).

Fragments in a sketch-book kept from approximately 1897 to 1902 show that Vaughan Williams was toying with the following ideas for compositions:

(*a*) Setting of 'Dover Beach' by Matthew Arnold. Completed by April 1899, according to a letter of Adeline Vaughan Williams.
(*b*) Slow movement, scherzo, and finale of a sonata for horn and pianoforte.
(*c*) Dirge for orchestra. May have been incorporated in the *Heroic Elegy and Triumphal Epilogue* of 1900–1.
(*d*) Rhapsody. Possible sketch for the *Symphonic Rhapsody*.
(*e*) Dramatic March 3/4. May have been incorporated in the *Heroic Elegy and Triumphal Epilogue* of 1900–1.
(*f*) Cor anglais tune for 'Ozymandias'.
    There also survive portions of MS., one headed: 'Last movement of suite, 6/8 time. Notes for Ozymandias.' This has a part for solo singer. Another fragment says 'Notes for symphonic poem "Ozymandias" 1st desert tune, then pizzicato tune, then this—' followed by some barely decipherable notation.
(*g*) Words for Swinburne's 'Before the frost'.
(*h*) 'Viola piece'.
(*i*) Sketches for 'Let us now praise famous men'.
(*j*) 'Ballet tune'.
(*k*) 'Linden Lea'. Tune complete as song was eventually published with the exception of the line 'Now do quiver under foot'.

This sketch book is in the British Library (57294B).

1900

1. BUCOLIC SUITE for orchestra, in four movements.

Instrumentation: 2 flutes, (2nd doubling piccolo), 2 oboes, 2 clarinets, 2 bassoons, 4 horns in F, 2 trumpets in F, 3 trombones, bass tuba, timpani, triangle, cymbals, bass drum, harp, violins, violas, violoncelli, double basses.

I. *Allegro*	234 bars	A minor
II. *Andante*	101 bars	C major
III. *Intermezzo—allegretto*	164 bars	E minor
IV. *Finale—allegro*	332 bars	A major

Unpublished.

First performance: Bournemouth, 10 March 1902. Bournemouth Municipal Orchestra, conductor Dan Godfrey. Date of composition: The composer wrote on the score: 'Finished Nov. 29, 1900. Revised Aug. 30, 1901.' The revisions, in red ink, were slight.

The last-known performance of this work was at a concert of the Cardiff Orchestral Society on 30 January 1907, when the composer conducted. The music is worth detailed description. The first movement begins *sempre marcato* with four bars of open strings on the violins, forte, which continue as flutes and oboes play the first theme in the style of a country dance:

The second portion of the dance theme is taken up by piccolo, clarinet, and bassoon, accompanied by open strings on violas and cellos. The theme is afterwards continued by trumpets and horns. After a sequence of triplet arpeggios on the clarinet, the violins have a second dance theme.

After another theme descriptive of holiday gaiety on the country green, the key becomes F sharp major, for the oboe:

Both the tonality and the time are much changed during the rest of this movement.

The Andante opens with a quartet of strings in which the first violins have the following melody:

The harp has an effective part in this movement.

The Intermezzo opens with a clarinet melody over a sustained pedal note on the bassoon, accompanied by the violas divisi, and the cellos and basses pizzicato.

This melody is afterwards taken by flutes and oboes in extended form, and then by flute with pizzicato strings. With a change to 2/4 'poco più lento', the piccolo, clarinet and bassoon have a jaunty melody accompanied, pp staccato, by the three trombones and tuba:

which is afterwards continued by the trumpet to the accompaniment of strings col legno and scales on the woodwind.

The finale is the most elaborate movement and shows an advance in technical powers of orchestration. It opens with a solo on the flute, accompanied only by detached notes on the clarinet:

This passage is developed by the violins, and then by the full orchestra. It is checked by a change to C minor, when the oboe, bassoon and horn announce the following cantabile passage:

Conventional working-up of this material brings the suite to an end.

Whereabouts of MS.: British Library. Full score (57275).

1900–1901

1. HEROIC ELEGY AND TRIUMPHAL EPILOGUE, for orchestra. Revised in 1902.

First performance: London, Royal College of Music, 5 March 1901, conducted by Sir Charles Stanford.

After being lost for over 65 years, this score was discovered in the United States of America. The following analytical note appeared in the programme of the Leeds Municipal Orchestra's concert on 21 January 1905, and was probably written by the composer:

'The first section consists of a long melody given to the trombone, accompanied by a persistent syncopated figure on the strings. This melody is further developed by the horns and the section ends with a long-drawn cadence founded on the last bar of the melody. The theme of the middle section is given to the violins, divided into four parts, and repeated by the trumpets playing softly. After further development, the syncopated figure returns fortissimo, and the first section is repeated in shortened form. The coda is founded on the middle section, while the drum continues the syncopated figure of the opening.'

Whereabouts of MS.: Cornell University, New York. British Library has photocopy (MS. Facs. 736).

1901

1. LINDEN LEA. (Sometimes called 'In Linden Lea'.) Song for voice and pianoforte. (Although exact dating of the composition of this song is impossible, all the evidence leads to the conclusion that it was written in 1901, 'in one afternoon,' the composer said.) Sub-title 'A Dorset Folk song'. Arranged for voice and piano. Words by William Barnes (1801–86). Original words in Dorsetshire dialect are printed beneath the standard words in most copies. *Andante con moto.*

First published: London, The Vocalist Co. Ltd. in Vol. I, No. 1 of *The Vocalist*, April 1902, in version in G major. (Vocalist series No. 2.) Also published 1902 in 'Vocalist series of songs and ballads No. 2', with version for high voice in A major as well as G major version. A misprint on p. 1 of this publication gives composer's name as E. Vaughan Williams. This was Vaughan Williams's first published work.

The plates of The Vocalist Co. Ltd. were acquired in 1912 by Boosey and Co. who again issued the G major version in that year, under publisher's No. H.7549.

Other versions of this song:

(*a*) For male voice quartet (ATBB) unaccompanied. Arrangement by

Victor Thomas, published in Boosey's Choral Miscellany No. 73 (H.10244) in 1921. *Andante con moto.* D flat major.

(b) For mixed voices (SATB) unaccompanied. Arrangement by Arthur Somervell, published in Boosey's Choral Miscellany, No. 138 (H.12745). Publication, March 1929. *Andante con moto.* A flat major.

(c) For mixed voices (SATB) with pianoforte accompaniment. Arrangement by Sumner Salter, published in Boosey & Co.'s series 'Secular quartettes for mixed voices (SATB)' (2986-6). 1929. *Andante con moto.* A major.

(d) Melody and words only. G major, with tonic solfa symbols. Boosey & Co., 1931. (H.13507.)

(e) For unaccompanied three-part choir, SSC arrangement by Julius Harrison, published in Boosey's Modern Festival series, No. 219 (H.14922) in 1938. *Andante con moto.* G major.

(f) Pour voix moyenne et piano. A major. Version française de Lilian Fearn. Boosey and Hawkes mélodies anglaises (H.15842), probably 1946.

(g) Two-part arrangement by Alec Rowley, with pianoforte accompaniment (M.F.S. 158), Boosey and Hawkes, 1949.

(h) For male voices (TTBB) unaccompanied, arrangement by Julius Harrison. Boosey and Hawkes, Modern Festival Series No. 370, 1950.

(j) For voice, with accompaniment for full orchestra. Boosey and Hawkes. Orchestral parts available on hire. Orchestration by Leo Wurmser.

(k) For medium orchestra, without voice, arranged by Harold Perry (Boosey and Hawkes, 1950). Instrumentation: flute, oboe, 2 clarinets, bassoon, 2 horns, 2 trumpets, trombone, timpani, strings. Duration: 2¼ minutes.

(l) For pianoforte, arranged by Harold Perry (Boosey and Hawkes), 1954.

(m) For descant recorder and pianoforte, arranged by Stanley Taylor (Boosey and Hawkes).

———

First performance: Hooton Roberts Musical Union, near Rotherham, 4 September 1902, J. Milner (bass). First performance in London: St. James's Hall, 2 December 1902. Frederick Keel (baritone) accompanied by C. A. Lidgey (pianoforte).
Dedication: To Mrs. Edmund Fisher.
Duration: 2¼ minutes.
See 1943 for Fantasia on Linden Lea.

1902

1. FANTASIA for pianoforte and orchestra.
Instrumentation: 2 flutes, 2 oboes, 2 clarinets, 2 bassoons, 4 horns in F, 2 trumpets in F, 3 trombones, tuba, timpani, cymbals, violins, violas, violoncelli, double basses.
Single movement: *Moderato—andante sostenuto—allegro—allegro moderato—lento e maestoso—andante sostenuto.* 514 bars.
Unpublished. Note on score: 'Begun Oct. 1896. Finished Feb. 9th 1902, Revised June 27th 1904, Further revised Oct. 14, 1904.'

Whereabouts of MS.: British Library. Full score (57276).

2. RING OUT YOUR BELLS. Madrigal for SSATB unaccompanied. Words by Sir Philip Sidney (1554–86). *Lento.* D modal minor.
Dedication: To Lionel Benson Esq. & the members of the Magpie Madrigal Society.
First performance: Not known, but probably privately by the dedicatees in 1902, although there is no mention of any performance in their full list of programmes.
Publication: London, J. Laudy & Co. in Part Songs by Modern Composers No. 41, probably 1904–5. (J.961.L.) With optional accompaniment, published by Bosworth (P.S.42).

3. REST. Five-part (SSATB) song for unaccompanied voices. *Andante sostenuto.* E flat major. Words by Christina Rossetti (1830–94).
Dedication: To Lionel Benson Esq. & the members of the Magpie Madrigal Society.
First performance: London, St. James's Hall, 14 May 1902. Magpie Madrigal Society conducted by Lionel Benson.
Publication: In Part Songs by Modern Composers, No. 42, J. Laudy & Co., London, probably 1904–5. (J. 962 L). Re-issued, with optional accompaniment, by Bosworth (P.S.41).

4. BLACKMWORE BY THE STOUR. 'A Dorset folk song,' arranged for voice and piano. *Allegretto con moto.* E major. Words by William Barnes.
First performance: Hooton Roberts Musical Union, near Rotherham. 4 September 1902. J. Milner (bass). First performance in London: St. James's Hall, 27 November 1902. Campbell McInnes (baritone). C. A. Lidgey (pianoforte).
Published: The Vocalist Co. Ltd. May 1902, in *The Vocalist*, Vol. 1, No. 2 (Vocalist series No. 7). Also published separately 1902 in 'Vocalist Series of Songs and Ballads No. 7' in version for high voice in G major. G major version re-issued 1912 by Boosey & Co.
Date of composition unknown, but 1901 is likely.

5. ENTLAUBET IST DER WALDE. Old German Volkslied arranged

for voice and piano. English text by Walter Ford. *Andante maestoso.*
First performance: London, St. James's Hall, 27 November 1902,
Campbell McInnes (baritone), C. A. Lidgey (pianoforte).
Dedication: to Walter Ford.
Publication: London, Oxford University Press, 1937, in *Two Old German Songs* with 'Wanderlied'. *Andantino*, G major. German text also printed. First performance of 'Entlaubet ist der Walde' and of 'Wanderlied': London, Leighton House, 10 November 1905, by Walter Ford, in lecture on German Song.
Whereabouts of MS.: Both songs (*Entlaubet* being referred to as *Abschied*), with *Der Morgenstern* (unpublished) are in British Library (50480).

6. WHITHER MUST I WANDER? Song for voice and pianoforte. Words by Robert Louis Stevenson (1850–94), from *Songs of Travel* (XVI). *Andante.* C minor.
First performance: London, St. James's Hall, 27 November 1902. Campbell McInnes (baritone), C. A. Lidgey (pianoforte).
Publication: London, The Vocalist Co. Ltd. in *The Vocalist*, Vol. I, No. 3, June 1902 (Vocalist series No. 10). Also published in F minor in 'Vocalist Series of Songs and Ballads', No. 10. Reissued in C minor and D minor in 1912 by Boosey & Co. The original *Vocalist* publication has the first word of the title misspelt as 'Wither'.
For incorporation into *Songs of Travel* see 1904, No. 10. Date of composition was probably 1901.

7. BOY JOHNNY. Song for voice and pianoforte. Words by Christina Rossetti, text as in *The Poetical Works of Christina Rossetti* (London, 1882). *Andante con moto.* E modal minor.
Dedication: To J. Campbell McInnes, Esq.
First performance: Oxford, during Commemoration Week, 1902. First performance in London, St. James's Hall, 22 April 1903, by Francis Harford (bass) and Ernest Walker (pianoforte).
Publication: London, The Vocalist Co. Ltd. in *The Vocalist*, Vol. I, No. 6, September 1902, and as Vocalist series No. 21.

8. IF I WERE A QUEEN. Song for voice and pianoforte. Words by Christina Rossetti. *Allegretto grazioso.* E major.
First performance: Exeter, 16 April 1903, by A. Foxton Ferguson (baritone) accompanied by a Miss Wood. First London performance untraced.
Publication: London, The Vocalist Co. Ltd. in *The Vocalist*, Vol. I, No. 8, November 1902, and as Vocalist series No. 216. See 1905 for joint re-publication of 'Boy Johnny' and 'If I were a Queen'.

1903

1. TEARS, IDLE TEARS. Song for voice and pianoforte. Words by Alfred, Lord Tennyson, from 'The Princess', IV, 1.21. *Andante sostenuto*, C minor.
Dedication: To J. Francis Harford, Esq.
First performance: London, St. James's Hall, 5 February 1903, from manuscript, by Francis Harford (bass) and Evlyn Howard-Jones (pianoforte).
Publication: London, The Vocalist Co. Ltd. in *The Vocalist*, Vol. II, No. 15, June 1903, and as Vocalist series No. 53. Reissued 1914 by Boosey & Co. (H.8395).

2. SILENT NOON. Song for voice and pianoforte. Words by Dante Gabriel Rossetti (1828–82) from the sonnet sequence *The House of Life* of which 'Silent Noon' is No. XIX. *Largo sostenuto*. E flat major.
First performance: London, St. James's Hall, 10 March 1903, from manuscript, by Francis Harford (bass) and Philip L. Agnew (pianoforte).
Publication: London, Willcocks & Co., March 1904, in advance of the complete *The House of Life* cycle. Other versions for SCTB and SSC. Reissued with rest of *The House of Life* in 1933 by Edwin Ashdown Ltd. Arranged by Henry Geehl for SATB and pianoforte. London, Enoch & Sons, 1936, G major. Enoch Choral Series No. 91 (E. and S. 6511). Arranged by Henry Geehl for SSC with pianoforte accompaniment. London, Edwin Ashdown. © 1937 (E.A.36156).

3. WILLOW-WOOD. Cantata for baritone or mezzo-soprano solo and orchestra or pianoforte accompaniment. Words by Dante Gabriel Rossetti from the sonnet sequence *The House of Life* (Sonnets XLIX, L, LI, and LII). *Adagio quasi andante—andante con moto—adagio quasi andante—allegro quasi andante.* (The four movements are performed without a break.)
First performance: London, St. James's Hall, 12 March 1903, by J. Campbell McInnes (baritone) and Evlyn Howard-Jones (pianoforte).
This cantata and the song-cycle *The House of Life* were written at about the same time. The idea of setting a sequence of Rossetti sonnets occurred to Vaughan Williams in 1900. After writing 'Silent Noon' while staying in the Quantocks, he began *Willow-Wood*, intending it to be short. But during 1902 the work took on larger proportions, and the orchestration was completed in April 1903. The first performance, with pianoforte accompaniment, was given in the previous month. Vaughan Williams revised the cantata in April 1908, altering some of the scoring, and he added a women's chorus ad lib in 1908–9.
Instrumentation: 2 flutes, 1 oboe, 1 cor anglais, 2 clarinets, 2 bassoons,

4 horns, 2 trumpets, 3 trombones, 1 bass tuba, timpani, harp, strings. *First performance of revised version:* Liverpool, 25 September 1909, at festival of the Music League, by Frederic Austin (baritone) and Liverpool Welsh Choral Union, conducted by Harry Evans. As far as is known, this was also the last performance. The composer wrote on his MS. score 'Complete flop'.

Publication: Leipzig, Breitkopf and Härtel, 1909. (B and H 26255.) *Whereabouts of MS.:* Pianoforte score and full score in British Library (50434, 50435).

4. SOUND SLEEP. Trio for female voices (SSA) with pianoforte accompaniment. Words by Christina Rossetti. *Andante sostenuto.* E flat major.

Dedication: To Mrs. Massingberd. [Wife of Stephen Massingberd.] *First performance:* Spilsby, Lincolnshire, at the East Lincolnshire Musical Festival on 27 April 1903, as a test-piece. The festival was organized by Mrs. Massingberd, of Gunby Hall, whose choir, Gunby, were first in their class with this trio.

Publication: London, Novello & Co. Ltd., New York, Novello, Ewer & Co. Published in April 1903, as No. 349 of Novello's octavo edition of trios, quartets, etc., for female voices. Tonic solfa edition also published, Novello T.S. series, No. 1489, in April 1906. Version with orchestral accompaniment published by Novello. Material available on hire.

Instrumentation: 2 flutes (1 opt.), 2 oboes (1 opt.), 2 clarinets (1 opt.), 2 bassoons, 2 horns, 2 trumpets (opt.), timpani (opt.), strings. MS. score dated 7 October 1903, in British Museum (50436). Performance of this version with strings only was given by Penshurst Vocal and Instrumental Society, 30 December 1903.

5. ADIEU. German folk song, arranged for soprano and baritone duet with pianoforte accompaniment. Words translated from the German by A. Foxton Ferguson. *Andantino.* G major.

First performance: Exeter, 16 April 1903, by Kathleen Wood, soprano, and A. Foxton Ferguson, baritone, accompanied by Kathleen Wood's sister (Christian name untraced). First performance in London: Steinway Hall, 22 March 1904, by Beatrice Spencer, soprano, and A. Foxton Ferguson, baritone, with Ernest Walker, pianoforte.

Publication: London, The Vocalist Co. Ltd. in *The Vocalist*, Vol. II, No. 19, October 1903, and as Vocalist series No. 65. Reissued by Boosey and Hawkes, 1933, with 'Think of Me' under title *Two Old Airs* (H.13901).

6. THINK OF ME. German folk song, arranged for soprano and baritone duet with pianoforte accompaniment. Words translated from the German by A. Foxton Ferguson. *Allegretto.* E major.

First performance: London, Steinway Hall, 22 March 1904, by Beatrice Spencer, soprano, and A. Foxton Ferguson, baritone, with Ernest Walker, pianoforte.

Publication: London, The Vocalist Co. Ltd., in *The Vocalist*, Vol. II, No. 19, October 1903 and as Vocalist series No. 65. Reissued by Boosey and Hawkes, 1933, with 'Adieu' under title *Two Old Airs* (H.13901).

7. COUSIN MICHAEL. German folk song, arranged for soprano and baritone duet, with pianoforte accompaniment. Words translated from the German by A. Foxton Ferguson.
First performance: Exeter, 16 April 1903, by Kathleen Wood, soprano, and A. Foxton Ferguson, baritone, with Miss Wood's sister as accompanist. First London performance, with 'Adieu' and 'Think of Me' at Steinway Hall, 22 March 1904, by Beatrice Spencer, soprano, and A. Foxton Ferguson, baritone, with Ernest Walker, pianoforte.
No record of publication.

8. ORPHEUS WITH HIS LUTE. Song for voice and pianoforte. Words by William Shakespeare, *King Henry VIII*, Act III, Scene 1. *Andantino.* F major; also G major version.
Dedication: To Miss Lucy Broadwood.
First performance: London, Bechstein Hall, 2 December 1904, by Beatrice Spencer, soprano, accompanied by Hamilton Harty, pianoforte.
Publication: London, Keith Prowse & Co. Ltd. (1556) June 1903.
Other version: Arranged for SATB, in G major, by Frank Tapp. Keith Prowse & Co. Ltd. © 1937 (5597).
The date of composition of this song was 1902.
Whereabouts of MS.: British Library (50480).

9. WHEN I AM DEAD, MY DEAREST. Song for voice and pianoforte. Words by Christina Rossetti. *Andante sostenuto e mesto.* D modal minor. Version also in G modal minor.
First performance: London, Aeolian Hall, 28 November 1905, by Alice Venning, soprano, accompanied by Samuel Liddle, pianoforte.
Publication: London, Keith Prowse & Co. Ltd., June 1903 (K.P. 1554).

10. RÉVEILLEZ-VOUS, PICCARS. Song for voice and pianoforte. English adaptation by Paul England of French battle-song of fifteenth century. *Allegro.* E minor.
First performance: Eastbourne (Church Room, South Street) in a lecture-recital on the Songs of the Troubadours by Walter Ford, baritone, 19 October 1903. First London performance, St. James's

Hall, 11 February 1904, by Francis Harford, bass, accompanied by May Christie, pianoforte.
Publication: London and New York, Boosey & Co. 1907 (H.5155). English and French texts.

Whereabouts of MS.: British Library (59796).

11. THE WINTER'S WILLOW. Song, in the Dorset dialect, for voice and pianoforte. Words by William Barnes. *Andante con moto.* F major.
First performance untraced.
Publication: London, The Vocalist Co. Ltd. in *The Vocalist*, Vol. II, No. 20, November 1903, and as Vocalist series No. 68. Reissued by Boosey & Co. in 1914 (H.8394).

The following unpublished works also date from 1903:

12. Two of a projected *Four Impressions for Orchestra* to be called IN THE NEW FOREST. (See 1904, No.6).
    I. BURLEY HEATH.
    Instrumentation for whole series: 2 flutes, oboe, cor anglais, 2 clarinets, 2 bassoons, 4 horns in F, 2 trumpets in F, 3 trombones, 1 bass tuba, timpani, triangle, violins, violas, violoncelli, double basses. 169 bars of manuscript score; work incomplete.

    Whereabouts of MS.: British Library. Full score (57278).

    II. THE SOLENT (*Adagio molto*). Composed 1902–3.
    Inscription on score:
        'Passion and sorrow in the deep sea's voice
        A mighty mystery saddening all the wind
            —Philip Marston' (1850–87).
    184 bars of manuscript score, heavily revised and bearing Henry Wood's blue-pencilled markings.
    First (and only) performance: 19 June 1903. (This is a diary marking. Where the performance took place is not known. Possibly it was played through privately.)
    The opening of this work is a clarinet solo:

The connection between this theme and themes in *A Sea Symphony* and the Ninth Symphony (second movement) is obvious. This is the theme to which the composer refers in his analytical note of the Ninth Symphony. It also reappears in the 1955 film music for *The England of Elizabeth*.

Whereabouts of MS.: British Library. Full score (57278).

13. QUINTET in C minor for pianoforte, violin, viola, violoncello, and double-bass.
    I. *Allegro con fuoco* (384 bars).
    II. *Andante* (174 bars).
    III. *Fantasia* (quasi variazioni). Moderato (233 bars).
    MS. score is heavily revised. At end is written: 'Finished Oct. 27, 1903, revised Aug. 29, 1904. Further revised Sept. 28, 1905.'
    First performance: London, Aeolian Hall (Broadwood concert) 14 December 1905. Richard Epstein (pianoforte), Louis Zimmerman (violin), Alfred Hobday (viola), Paul Ludwig (violoncello), Claude Hobday (double bass).
    This quintet is one of the best of the early works, an outpouring, with a marked effort to control the flow rather than spin it out. The Brahmsian Allegro contains big gestures. The Andante has an expressive romantic melody which has a shape more recognizably Vaughan Williams. The finale, with its quiet ending and unusually sympathetic writing for pianoforte, is altogether more characteristic. Its principal theme:

    was used in the 1954 Sonata for violin and pianoforte in a slightly enlarged form as the theme for the finale's variations:

    The last-known performance of the work before it was withdrawn was on 8 June 1918.

Whereabouts of MS.: British Library (57277).

1904

1. JEAN RENAUD. French fifteenth-century song arranged for voice

and pianoforte. Words adapted for English by Paul England.
First performance: London, St. James's Hall, 11 February 1904, by
Francis Harford, bass, and May Christie, pianoforte, from MS.
Unpublished.

2. L'AMOUR DE MOY. French fifteenth-century song arranged for
voice and pianoforte. English version by Paul England. *Molto tran-
quillo.* C major.
First performance: London, St. James's Hall, 11 February 1904, by
Francis Harford, bass, and May Christie, pianoforte, from MS.
Publication: London and New York, Boosey & Co. 1907 (H.5156).
English and French texts.
Note. The programme of the Broadwood Concert on 11 February
1904, carefully describes the performance of the above two songs and
'Réveillez-vous, Piccars' as 'First time in London'. It is possible
that these two songs were given at or near the same time, but there is
no record. For first performance of 'Réveillez-vous, Piccars' see 1903,
No. 10.

3. SYMPHONIC RHAPSODY for orchestra.
Unpublished. Manuscript destroyed.
First performance: Bournemouth, Winter Gardens, 7 March 1904,
Municipal Orchestra conducted by Dan Godfrey.
The analytical note in the programme states that this work was
inspired by Christina Rossetti's verses beginning:

> Come to me in the silence of the night;
> Come in the speaking silence of a dream,
> Come with soft-rounded cheeks and eyes as bright
> > As sunlight on a stream;
> Come back in tears
> O memory, hope, love of finished years.

It was, therefore, complementary to the Rossetti songs and probably
summed up this period in the composer's development. Date of
composition was from 1901 to 1903. A letter from Holst in Germany
in 1903 (Letter XI in *Heirs and Rebels*, p. 19) refers to copying of
'the rhapsody parts' and says: 'I have only been able to correct the
two first flutes. On p. 6, last bar but one, surely you mean C for Fl I
and not E. But if so why have you scratched out C? I have *not*
corrected that but in other places I have filled in a few accidentals.'
At the Bournemouth concert the solo cellist in other works was May
Mukle, who became a friend of Vaughan Williams.

4. IN THE FEN COUNTRY. Symphonic Impression for Orchestra.
Manuscript score shows Impression as substitution for Prelude.
On last page of MS. occur the following inscriptions: 'Finished
April 10, 1904'; 'Revised Feb. 28, 1905'; 'Again revised Dec. 21st,

'1905'; 'Further revised July 29th, 1907'; 'Orchestration revised 1935'.
Instrumentation: 3 flutes, 2 oboes, 1 cor anglais, 2 clarinets, 1 bass clarinet, 2 bassoons, 4 horns, 2 trumpets, 3 trombones, bass tuba, timpani, solo violin, violins I and II, violas, violoncelli, double basses.
First performance: London, Queen's Hall, 22 February 1909, The Beecham Orchestra,[1] conducted by Thomas Beecham.
Dedication: To R.L.W. [Vaughan Williams's cousin (Sir) Ralph Wedgwood.]
Duration: 14 minutes.
Publication: Full score, London, O.U.P. (© 1969). Orchestral parts on hire.

Whereabouts of MS.: British Library. Full score and piano arrangement made by the composer with the title also in French, 'Dans les landes d'Angleterre, Impression Symphonique' (57279).

5. BALLADE AND SCHERZO. For string quintet (2 violins, 2 violas, 1 violoncello). Unpublished MS. Finished 22 May 1904; revised 1 October 1906. Ballade 181 bars; Scherzo 174 bars. The Scherzo is founded on a folk song:

The folk song concerned is 'As I Walked Out', which Vaughan Williams himself collected. Although the Scherzo is founded on this tune, for a large part of the movement only brief snatches are introduced and it is not until the penultimate page that the tune is played in a recognizable form.

Whereabouts of MS.: British Library (57281), Scherzo (57280).

6. HARNHAM DOWN. No. 1 of *Two Impressions for Orchestra.*
Unpublished MS.
Instrumentation: 2 flutes, 1 oboe, 1 cor anglais (or second oboe), 2 clarinets, 2 bassoons, 2 horns, strings.
Andante sostenuto. 120 bars. Score headed by following verse from Matthew Arnold's *The Scholar Gipsy*:

> Here will I sit and wait
> While to my ear from uplands far away
> The bleating of the folded flocks is borne
> With distant cries of reapers in the corn—
> All the live murmur of a summer's day.

---

[1] Beecham had just severed his connection with the New Symphony Orchestra, and had formed a new orchestra under this name.

Score is marked: 'Begun July 1904, finished 1907.'
First performance: London, Queen's Hall, 12 November 1907, New Symphony Orchestra, conducted by Emil von Reznicek. A second impression called *Boldre Wood* was also played. Nothing of this survives except the knowledge that it was a scherzo with Meredith's lines from *The Woods of Westermain*:

> Enter these enchanted woods
> You who dare

inscribed upon the score.

Whereabouts of MS.: British Library (57278).

7. ANDANTE SOSTENUTO, for pianoforte solo. 30 bars. 17 July 1904. Inscribed 'For your birthday' (Adeline Vaughan Williams). *Unpublished.*

8. TWO VOCAL DUETS. For soprano, baritone, pianoforte, and string quartet, with violin obbligato. String quartet ad lib. Words by Walt Whitman (1819–92).
   1. The Last Invocation—*Largo sostenuto.*

> At the last tenderly
> From the walls of the powerful fortress'd house
> From the clasp of the knitted locks, from the
>   keep of the well-clos'd doors
> Let me be wafted
> Let me glide noiselessly forth
> With the key of softness unlock the locks—
>   with a whisper,
> Set ope the doors, O soul
> Tenderly—be not impatient,
> (Strong is your hold O mortal flesh,
> Strong is your hold O love).

96 bars.
   2. The Love-song of the Birds—*Allegro ma non troppo.*

> Shine! Shine! Shine!
> Pour down your warmth great sun!
> While we bask, we two together
> Two together!
> Winds blow south, or winds blow north
> Day come white, or night come black
> Home, or rivers and mountains from home
> Singing all time minding no time
> While we two keep together.   (*Sea-Drift*)

42 bars.

MS. score of 'The Last Invocation' marked 'Finished July 23rd 1904 at North End Farm, Danby, Yorkshire'. These works were written for A. Foxton Ferguson and Beatrice Spencer who had already given performances of Vaughan Williams's folk-song arrangements.

First performance: Reading, Town Hall, 24 October 1904, by A. Foxton Ferguson, baritone; Beatrice Spencer, soprano; Miss Hedley, pianoforte; Maurice Sons and Dorothy Blount, violins; Alfred Hobday, viola; W. E. Whitehouse, cello. First London performance: 2 December 1904, at Bechstein Hall, by A. Foxton Ferguson, baritone; Beatrice Spencer, soprano; violin obbligato by Harriet Solly, pianoforte accompaniment by Hamilton Harty. The string quartet was not used in the London performance.

Whereabouts of MS.: British Library (57282).

9. THE HOUSE OF LIFE. A cycle of 6 sonnets, set for voice and pianoforte. Words by Dante Gabriel Rossetti. Numbers in square brackets refer to number in sonnet sequence.
    1. Love-Sight [IV] *Andante con moto ma non troppo.* A major.
    2. Silent Noon [XIX] *Largo sostenuto.* E flat major.
    3. Love's Minstrels [IX] Passion and worship *Lento* (*Il tempo sempre rubato*). D major.
    4. Heart's Haven [XXII] *Lento ma con moto.* E major.
    5. Death in Love [XLVIII] *Allegro maestoso.* C major.
    6. Love's Last Gift [LIX] *Andante con moto.* F major.
   First performance: London, Bechstein Hall, 2 December 1904, by Edith Clegg, contralto, and Hamilton Harty, pianoforte.
   It is likely that the whole work was composed during 1903. Figure in 64th bar of 'Love's Last Gift' at *poco più lento* was used as opening of *Willow-Wood*.
   Publication: London, J. Willcocks & Co. 1904. (Ward Co., 1760, except 'Silent Noon' which is 1714). Reissued 1933 by Edwin Ashdown Ltd. Available separately are 'Silent Noon' (see 1903, No. 2); and 'Heart's Haven' (Ashdown) in D, E and F.

10. SONGS OF TRAVEL. For voice and pianoforte. Words by Robert Louis Stevenson from *Songs of Travel.* Figures in square brackets refer to numbers in this sequence.
    1. The Vagabond [I] *Allegro moderato.* C modal minor.
    2. Let Beauty Awake [IX] *Moderato.* F sharp minor.
    3. The Roadside Fire [XI] *Allegretto.* D flat major.
    4. Youth and Love [II] *Andante sostenuto.* G major.
    5. In Dreams [IV] *Andantino.* C modal minor.
    6. The Infinite Shining Heavens [VI] *Andante sostenuto.* D modal minor.

7. Whither must I Wander? [XVI] *Andante*. C minor.
8. Bright is the Ring of Words [XIV] *Moderato risoluto*. D major.
9. I have Trod the Upward and the Downward Slope [XXII] *Andante sostenuto*. D minor and major.

First performance: The first eight songs above, in that (correct) order were first sung at the Bechstein Hall, London, on 2 December 1904, by Walter Creighton, baritone, with Hamilton Harty, pianoforte.

Publication: The history of the publication of these songs is rather complicated. Although first performed as a complete cycle, the publishers refused to accept them as a whole and divided them into two books.

Book I contained 'The Vagabond', 'Bright is the ring of words', and The Roadside Fire'. These were published by Boosey & Co., London, in 1905 and reissued 1907 with words Part I added to title-page. (H.4743.)

Book II contained 'Let beauty awake', 'Youth and Love', 'In dreams', and 'The Infinite Shining Heavens'. These were published by Boosey & Co., London, in 1907 and reissued later the same year with Part 2 added to title-page. (H.5557.)

After the composer's death the ninth song of the cycle, 'I have trod the upward and the downward slope' was discovered among his papers. This short song gives the work unity thematically: it begins with a quotation from 'The Vagabond', quotes 'Whither must I Wander?' during its course and in the coda quotes 'Bright is the ring of words' before ending with the tramping rhythm of 'The Vagabond'. The complete cycle was reissued in 1960 by Boosey and Hawkes, with the songs in correct order (B. & H. 18741). This, therefore, was the first publication to include 'Whither must I Wander' as part of the cycle. The following songs are issued separately:

(*a*) 'Whither must I wander?'—See 1902, No. 6.
(*b*) 'The Roadside Fire.' *Allegretto*. C major and D flat major. Boosey & Co., London, March 1910. (H.6606.)
(*c*) 'Bright is the ring of words.' Voice and pianoforte. Boosey and Hawkes, London.
(*d*) 'The Vagabond.'
    (i) Voice and pianoforte. Boosey and Hawkes, London.
    (ii) Unison, with pianoforte accompaniment. B. & H., Modern Festival series No. 701.
    (iii) Arranged by R.V.W. for male voices, TTBB unaccompanied, 1952. B. & H., M.F.S.374. (B. & H. 17178.)
(*e*) 'I have trod the upward and the downward slope.' Voice and

pianoforte. Boosey and Hawkes, London, 1960. A note on this
song says: 'This little epilogue . . . should be sung in public only
when the whole cycle is performed.'

Three songs of the complete cycle (Nos. 1, 3 and 8—i.e. the original
Book I) were orchestrated by Vaughan Williams in 1905, the
remainder by Roy Douglas in 1961-2.

Instrumentation: 2 flutes (1 doubling piccolo), 2 oboes, 2 clarinets,
2 bassoons, 4 horns, 2 trumpets, timpani, percussion (side drum,
triangle), harp, strings. [Mr. Douglas used only those instruments also
used by the composer.]

The first performance of the entire cycle as originally planned by the
composer was given on 21 May 1960, by Hervey Alan, baritone, and
Frederick Stone, pianoforte, on the BBC Home Service.

Duration: 23½ minutes.

Whereabouts of MS.: British Museum has full scores of Book I Nos.
1–3 respectively dated Nov. 10, 19 and 23, presumably the days on
which orchestration was done (50438 A and B);[1] MS. of 'I have trod'
and of 1952 arrangement of 'The Vagabond' (50480) and of 'The
Roadside Fire' (59796).

11. TWO FRENCH FOLK SONGS. Arranged for voice and pianoforte.
    1. Chanson de quête (May-day song). *Allegro moderato.* G modal
       minor.
    2. La ballade de Jésus Christ. *Andante con moto.* D minor.

Publication: London, Oxford University Press, 1935. French and
English words printed. Despite date of publication it seems certain
that these songs belong to 1904 when Vaughan Williams was arranging French songs.

12. FRENCH FOLK SONGS (arrangements).
    (*a*) QUAND LE ROSSIGNOL. E flat minor.
        Sung by Walter Ford, tenor, accompanied by Henry Bird at the
        first of eight lectures by Ford on 'The Songs of France' at
        Leighton House, London, on 18 November 1904.

Whereabouts of MS.: British Library (57282).

    (*b*) QUE DIEU SE MONTRE SEULEMENT. Huguenot battle-
        hymn. (Le Psaume des Batailles, Psautier Huguénot 1539.)
(Described by *The Times* as a 'wonderfully successful arrangement
. . . in the manner of Bach's organ chorales, with delightful imitative
passages in the accompaniment, and with the happiest possible
assumption of the old character'.

Sung by Walter Ford, tenor, accompanied by Henry Bird at seventh

---

[1] A is a rough score, B a clean score from Boosey and Hawkes.

lecture on French Songs by Ford at Leighton House on 30 January 1905. *Andante con moto.*

Whereabouts of MS.: British Library (57282).

1905

1. PEZZO OSTINATO. For pianoforte. *Andante sostenuto.* 46 bars.
   Unpublished, dated 27 January 1905.
   A successful, if slight, pianoforte piece.

   Whereabouts of MS.: British Library (57282).

2. YE LITTLE BIRDS. Song for voice and pianoforte. Words by Thomas Heywood (1575?–1650).
   First performance: London, Aeolian Hall, 3 February 1905, by H. Plunket Greene, baritone, accompanied by S. Liddle, pianoforte.
   All trace of this song has vanished. It is possible that the composer destroyed it because he preferred Holst's setting (1902) of the same verses.

3. A CRADLE SONG. For voice and pianoforte. Words by S. T. Coleridge (1772–1834), being a translation of the Virgin's Cradle Hymn, copied from a print of the Virgin in a German village in 1811. *Andante.* E flat major.
   Publication: London, The Vocalist Co. Ltd. in *The Vocalist,* April 1905, Vol. IV, No. 37, and as Vocalist series No. 112.
   A rather beautiful, unsentimental song. There is a hint in the accompaniment of the Lullaby in *Hodie* of 1954 and something of 'Sine Nomine'. It may be assumed that this song is the same work as Vaughan Williams's 'The Virgin's Cradle Song' sung by W. J. L. Higley, accompanied by the composer, at the Cambridge University Musical Club, 3 November 1894.

4. PAN'S ANNIVERSARY. 'A masque by Ben Jonson, music composed and arranged by R. Vaughan Williams. The dances arranged for orchestra from Elizabethan virginal music and English folk tunes by Gustav von Holst.'
   First performance: Stratford-upon-Avon, 24 April 1905. Chorus and orchestra of The Choral Union conducted by Dr. R. Vaughan Williams. Principal parts taken by Cissie Saumarez, Elaine Sleddall, Kate Cordingley, Edgar Waithman, and Henry Hickling, with the Bidford Morris Dancers.
   MSS. of this masque are in private possession.
   Its shape seems to have been as follows:
   I. Introduction: *Adagio molto.* (Full orchestra.)
   II. 'Loud Music' (scored for 2 horns, 2 cornets, trombone and timpani).

III. *Allegro.* Entrance of the Boeotians. (Folk song *Bristol Town.*) Piccolo, clarinet, side-drum.

IV. Hymn I. *Moderato.* 'Of Pan we sing—the best of singers, Pan that taught us swains how first to tune our lays.' *Instrumentation:* Flute, oboe, clarinet, bassoon, 2 horns, 2 cornets, 1 trombone, violins, violas, violoncelli, double basses, timpani. Voice parts for 2 sopranos, contralto and chorus.

*V. Dances. 'Masquers' Entry.'

VI. Hymn II. *Adagio molto.* 'Pan is our all.' *Instrumentation* as above.

*VII. Dances. 'Masquers' pavan.'

VIII. Hymn III. *Allegretto.* 'If yet Pan's orgies you will further fit.' *Instrumentation* as above with echo choruses.

*IX. The Revels. Galliard and Maypole dance.

X. Entry of The Thebans. *Allegro.* Folk tune 'The Jolly Thresherman'. Piccolo, clarinet, and side-drum.

XI. Hymn IV—*Moderato.* 'Great Pan the father of our peace and pleasure.' *Instrumentation* as above, plus triangle.

*XII. Repeat last movement 6/8 of the Revels. (This is note written on score by R.V.W.)

* G. von Holst's contribution.

A note on the programme stated: 'In the music to the choruses no attempt has been made to reproduce the Elizabethan style of music, but it is hoped that the music is appropriately simple. The music for the "Masquers' Entry", the "Pavan" and "Galliard" are taken from sixteenth-century dances (Rogero, Mal Sims and Spagnoletta), arranged for orchestra by Mr. G. von Holst. The entrances of the Thebans and Boeotians are two English folk tunes—"Bristol Town" and "The Jolly Thresherman". The Morris Dancers will be accompanied by their own music. The music for the Revels consists of four English folk tunes, "Sellenger's Round", "The Lost Lady", "Maria Marten" and "All on Spurn Point", arranged for orchestra by Mr. G. von Holst. Some of these traditional melodies are from the composer's own manuscript collection, others ("Bristol Town" and "The Lost Lady") are from the collection of Miss L. E. Broadwood, and are inserted by her kind permission. In the music of the choruses also, certain characteristic phrases from English folk music have been inserted. R.V.W.'

MS. short scores of Hymns I, II and III are dated respectively 15, 16, and 17 March 1905.

5. THE SPLENDOUR FALLS. Song for voice and pianoforte. Words by Tennyson, from *The Princess*, IV, i. *Allegretto con moto.* B flat major.

Publication: London, The Vocalist Co. Ltd. in *The Vocalist*, Vol. IV, No. 38, May 1905. Also as Vocalist series No. 116. Reissued 1914 by Boosey & Co. (H.8422).

6. BOY JOHNNY AND IF I WERE A QUEEN. Reissue by The Vocalist Co. Ltd.
   1. *Andante con moto.* F sharp modal minor.
   2. *Allegretto grazioso.* G major.
   See 1902 Nos. 7 and 8. See 1914, No. 1.

7. DREAMLAND. Song for voice and pianoforte. Words by Christina Rossetti. *Andante sostenuto.* D flat major.
   First performance: London, Aeolian Hall, 31 October 1905, by Gervase Elwes, tenor, and Frederick B. Kiddle, pianoforte.
   Publication: London, Boosey & Co., 1906. (H.5025.)

   Whereabouts of MS.: British Library. Copy (59796).

8. PURCELL SOCIETY. Volume XV of the *Works of Henry Purcell.* 'Welcome Songs', Part I, edited by R. Vaughan Williams.
   1. 'Welcome, Viceregent of the mighty King', on His Majesty's return from Windsor, 1680.
   2. 'Swifter, Isis, swifter flow', a welcome song in 1681 for the King.
   3. 'What shall be done on behalf of the man', on His Royal Highness the Duke of York's return from Scotland, 1682.
   4. 'The summer's absence unconcerned we bear', on the King's return from Newmarket, 21 October 1682.
   5. 'Fly, bold Rebellion', 1683, on discovery of the Rye House Plot.
   Publication: London, Novello & Co.; New York, Novello, Ewer & Co. 1905. Locations of the Purcell MSS. are given in the preface.

1906

1. THE ENGLISH HYMNAL, with tunes. London, Oxford University Press, 1906. This first edition contained the following original tunes by Vaughan Williams:

(*a*) 152. Come down, O Love Divine. (Moderately slow.)		Down Ampney.
(*b*) 524. God be with you till we meet again. (In moderate time.)		Randolph.
(*c*) 624. Hail thee, Festival day. (With vigour.)		Salve festa dies.
(*d*) 641. For all the Saints. (In moderate time.)		Sine Nomine.

   The following tunes, all derived from folk songs, were arranged by Vaughan Williams for the first edition and were his copyright:

Hymn No.

15.	O Little Town of Bethlehem.	Forest Green.
23.	Hark! How all the welkin rings.	Dent Dale.
186.	Come, let us join the church above.	Rodmell.
239.	Saints of God! Lo Jesu's people.	Sussex.
295.	'Tis winter now; the fallen snow.	Danby.
299.	When spring unlocks the flowers.	Gosterwood.
385.	Father hear the prayer we offer.	Sussex.
402.	He who would valiant be.	Monk's Gate.
525.	From Thee all skill and science flow.	Farnham.
562.	O God of earth and altar.	King's Lynn.
572.	I could not do without Thee.	Gosterwood.
594.	I love to hear the story.	Gosterwood.
595.	I think when I read that sweet story of old.	East Horndon.
597.	It is a thing most wonderful.	Herongate.
607.	There's a friend for little children.	Ingrave.
611.	When Christ was born in Bethlehem.	Rodmell.

The following tunes were arranged by Vaughan Williams, but were not his copyright. (Asterisk indicates English folk song):

7.	Lo! He comes with clouds descending.	Helmsley.
*16.	The maker of the sun and moon.	Newbury.
*20.	Behold the great Creator.	This Endris Nyght. (Carol.)
*29.	The great God of Heaven.	A Virgin Unspotted. (Carol.)
42.	O worship the Lord in the beauty of holiness.	Was Lebet, Was Schwebet. From the Rheinhardt MS. Uttingen, 1754.
*89.	Soul of Jesus, make me whole.	Anima Christi.
*90.	To my humble supplication.	De Profundis.
145.	See the Conqueror mounts in triumph.	In Babilone. (Dutch trad. melody.)
212.	I bind unto myself today.	St. Patrick. (Ancient Irish hymn.)
213.	Hail, O star that pointest.	Ave Maris Stella. (18th century melody.)
*221.	The winter's sleep was long and deep.	King's Langley. (English carol.)
249.	O Saviour Jesu, not alone.	Deo gracias. (Agincourt Song.)

268.	God, that madest earth and heaven.	Ar hyd y nos (Welsh traditional melody.)
*275.	Sweet Saviour, bless us ere we go.	Lodsworth.
*294.	The year is swiftly waning.	Devonshire.
308.	Father, see Thy children.	Adoro Te, No. 2.
317.	Laud, O Sion, thy salvation.	Modes vii and viii.
326.	(ii) Of the glorious Body telling.	Pange Lingua. (From the Mechlin Gradual.)
*344.	Thine for ever! God of love.	Horsham.
*355.	In Paradise reposing.	Hambridge.
*379.	'Come unto me, ye weary'.	Rusper.
*388.	Fierce was the wild billow.	St. Issey.
*389.	Fight the good fight.	Shepton-Beauchamp.
*390.	Firmly I believe and truly.	Shipston.
*417.	Jesu, my Lord, my God, my All.	Stella.
437.	Love Divine, all loves excelling.	Moriah. (Welsh hymn melody.)
*448.	O God of mercy, God of might.	Fitzwilliam.
*485.	Teach me my God and King.	Sandys. (Traditional (?) carol.)
*488.	The church of God a Kingdom is.	Capel. (English carol.)
490.	The King of Love my shepherd is.	St. Columba. (Irish hymn.)
*498.	There is a land of pure delight.	Mendip.
514.	Who is this so weak and helpless.	Llansannan. (Welsh hymn melody.)
*574.	I heard the voice of Jesus say.	Kingsfold.
579.	Rest of the weary.	Fortunatus. (Old English melody, not a folk song.)
*591.	Gentle Jesus, meek and mild.	{ Farnaby. Lew Trenchard.
*599.	Jesu, tender Shepherd, hear me.	Shipston.
*601.	Lord, I would own Thy tender care.	Eardisley.
*606.	Sing to the Lord the children's hymn.	St. Hugh.
*609.	Through the night Thy angels kept.	Horsham.
*638.	Jerusalem, my happy home.	{ i. St. Austin. ii. Southill.
*654.	God the Father, God the Son.	Farnaby.

*656. See Him in raiment rent. $\begin{cases} \text{i. Bridgwater.} \\ \text{ii. Langport.} \end{cases}$

Certain other arrangements may have been made by the Musical
Editor, but only those for which there is documentary authority to
attribute them to him have been included.

The following harmonizations were made by R.V.W., but not attributed to him until the 1933 edition:

18. From east to west, from shore to shore.	St. Venantius. Rouen church melody.
38. Why, impious Herod.	St. Venantius. Rouen church melody.
65. The fast, as taught by holy lore.	Jesu Corona. Rouen church melody.
123. The day draws on with golden light.	Solemnis Haec Festivitas. Angers church melody.
125. The Lamb's high banquet we await.	Rex Gloriose. French church melody.
129. Christ the Lord is risen again!	Orientis Partibus. Medieval French melody.
159. Be present, Holy Trinity.	Adesto Sancta Trinitas. Chartres church melody.
165. Father, we praise Thee.	Christe sanctorum. Melody from La Feillée, 1782.
181. O God, Thy soldiers' crown and guard.	Deus tuorum militum. Grenoble church melody.
208. All prophets hail Thee.	Diva servatrix. Bayeux church melody.
242. Christ, the fair glory.	Coelites plaudant. Rouen church melody.
480. Soldiers who are Christ's below.	Orientis partibus. Medieval French melody.
653. God the Father, God the Word.	Prompto Gentes Animo. Rouen church melody.

For additions and alterations in later edition see 1933.

2. NORFOLK RHAPSODY No. 1 in E minor, founded on folk tunes
collected orally in Norfolk and set as an orchestral piece.

Instrumentation: 2 flutes, 2 oboes, cor anglais, 2 clarinets (and optional
E flat clarinet), 2 bassoons, 4 horns, 2 trumpets, 3 trombones, tuba,
timpani, side-drum, harp, strings.

First performance: London, Queen's Hall, 23 August 1906, Queen's
Hall Orchestra, conducted by Henry J. Wood. First performance of
revised version: Bournemouth, Winter Gardens, 21 May 1914,

Bournemouth Municipal Orchestra, conducted by Dr. R. Vaughan Williams.

Duration: 10½ minutes.

Publication: Full Score, London, Oxford University Press, 1925.

This rhapsody is based principally on three folk tunes, 'The Captain's Apprentice', 'A Bold Young Sailor' and 'On Board a Ninety-Eight'. Snatches of 'A basket of eggs' can be traced. All these tunes were collected by Vaughan Williams at King's Lynn from sailors and fishermen on 9 and 10 January 1905. The work was written in 1905–6.

Part of the programme-note for the first performance, written by either Percy Pitt or Alfred Kalisch, probably the latter, is of importance, as it gives us a description of the Rhapsody before it was revised in 1914: 'This Rhapsody—two successors of which are already completed—is avowedly based on several Norfolk folk tunes collected by the composer. He affixes the complete list to the score. They are mostly printed, for the first time, in No. 8 of the Folk Song Society's *Journal*, and comprise: (1) "The Basket of Eggs"; (2) "The Captain's Apprentice"; (3) "A bold young sailor he courted me", (4) "Ward the Pirate"; (5) "On board a 93".[1]

'The composition opens with an introductory Adagio founded on the rhythm of the tune "The Basket of Eggs". At the sixteenth bar the solo viola introduces the melody "The Captain's Apprentice" ("freely, as if improvising"), lightly accompanied. Presently the original rhythm recurs in the horns, which later take up the tune of "The Captain's Apprentice". The tempo soon quickens, and the flutes in thirds have the theme of "The Basket of Eggs". The next song to be introduced is "A bold young sailor he courted me", which is given to the cor anglais, accompanied by the harp. After it has been handed over to other wind-instruments it finally makes its entrance on the strings. In this way we arrive at a climax, which culminates in a glorified version of the second tune. Fragments of this are now treated in various ways until the time changes to Allegro. We are now concerned with the first tune. When it appears in the oboe, it is accompanied by embroideries in the strings and wood-wind, which are an anticipation of the fifth tune.

'Presently, while these persist, the trumpets and trombones announce a version of part of the fourth tune, "Ward the Pirate", in augmentation; and this is succeeded by the fifth and last melody, "On board a 93", first heard on the strings. Eventually the whole orchestra joins in its treatment, and an augmented version of the third tune for cor anglais and horn, and then for bass trombone and tuba, is combined with it.

'As the tempo slackens the second tune enters in the strings, horns and trumpets, while the wood-wind and glockenspiel give out the fifth.

---

[1] 'On board a 98' is correct.

Its course is interrupted from time to time by suggestions of the fourth tune, which first appears on the trombones. Ultimately this is heard on the brass "brillante e marcato", accompanied by fragments of the fifth tune. This marks the beginning of the Coda, which is mainly evolved from the second bar of the opening melody, and ends brilliantly.'

In the course of revision the introduction appears to have been reconstructed. The flutes have the rhythm of 'The Basket of Eggs', but it is of 'The Captain's Apprentice' that the clarinet hints. 'Ward the Pirate' has disappeared, and the whole of the coda has been rewritten. There is no glockenspiel, and the 'brilliant ending' is now a slow fade-out by way of a return to the opening landscape. The noble and tragic beauty of 'The Captain's Apprentice' permeates the entire work.

Other version: Arrangement for wind band by Robert O'Brien.

(*Instrumentation:* flutes, oboes, cor anglais, bassoons, clarinet, alto clarinet, bass clarinet, contra-alto clarinet, contrabass clarinet, alto saxophones, tenor saxophone, baritone saxophone, trumpets, horns, trombones, baritones, euphonium, tubas, string bass, timpani, percussion, and harp (or pianoforte).) © O.U.P. 1973.

3. NORFOLK RHAPSODY No. 2 in D minor. For orchestra.
Unpublished. (2 pages of MS. lost).
Instrumentation: 2 flutes, 2 oboes, cor anglais, 2 clarinets, 2 bassoons, 4 horns, 2 trumpets, 3 trombones, bass tuba, timpani, triangle, harp, violins, violas, violoncelli, double basses. Folk tunes employed: 'Young Henry the Poacher'; 'Spurn Point' (collected by R.V.W. at Lynn Union, 9 January 1905); 'The Saucy Bold Robber' (King's Lynn, 10 January 1905).
First performance: Cardiff Festival, Park Hall, Cardiff, 27 September 1907, London Symphony Orchestra, conducted by Dr. R. Vaughan Williams. First performance in London: Queen's Hall, 17 April 1912. Balfour Gardiner Concert. New Symphony Orchestra, conducted by Balfour Gardiner.

The Cardiff analytical note by W. A. Morgan, after quoting the folk tunes, said: 'It opens with three bars of introduction *Larghetto*, when the tune of "Young Henry the Poacher" is heard by the woodwind played "andante sostenuto"; the last two phrases being repeated by the strings as a refrain. The tune is then heard in varied form by the violoncellos and violas accompanied by the following figure:

which is suggested by the tune itself. The tune does not at present reach its cadence, but is developed in animated tempo until the climax when a premonition of the second subject is heard, first by the strings, then by the horns and finally by the oboe. The second tune, "All on Spurn Point", now appears in its complete form, being played by the solo horn, after which it is repeated by a combination of instruments, and an extended cadence leads to the third tune, "The Saucy Bold Robber". This latter tune forms the basis of a short scherzo, which is first given in sparkling style by the piccolo and oboe, and afterwards by the full complement of woodwind, with an accompanying figure on the strings derived from the last bar of the tune. After a suggestion of canon, the scherzo gradually dies away, and gives place to a version of "Young Henry the Poacher", accompanied tremolando on the violas, but is interrupted from time to time by the figure given in the example above. The movement ends pianissimo with a reference to "Spurn Point".'

This work was written in 1906.

4. NORFOLK RHAPSODY No. 3 in G MINOR and MAJOR. For orchestra. *Alla marcia.*

Unpublished. MS. lost.

Instrumentation: As for No. 2, presumably. Folk Tunes employed: 'The Lincolnshire Farmer' (collected by R.V.W. at Tilney All Saints, Norfolk, 8 January 1905); 'John Raeburn' (King's Lynn, 13 and 14 January 1905); 'Ward the Pirate' (North End, King's Lynn, 9 January 1905); 'The Red Barn' (Tilney All Saints, 8 January 1905).

First performance: Cardiff Festival, Park Hall, Cardiff, 27 September 1907, London Symphony Orchestra, conducted by Dr. R. Vaughan Williams. First performance in London: Queen's Hall, 17 April 1912. Balfour Gardiner Concert. New Symphony Orchestra, conducted by Balfour Gardiner.

The Cardiff analytical note quoted the four tunes in full and continued: 'Rhapsody No. 3 . . . takes the form of a quick March and Trio, prefaced by an introduction of 29 bars founded on "The Lincolnshire Farmer", after which the tune is heard in its complete form by the oboe, as the opening theme of the movement, and then repeated tutti. Following on, the piccolo, clarinet and side-drum give the tune of "John Raeburn", which is repeated by the full orchestra; then, after a restatement of "The Lincolnshire Farmer" we come to the Trio, founded on the two tunes "Ward the Pirate" and "The Red Barn". The Trio bridges right into a passage resembling the introduction, when we have a recapitulation of "John Raeburn", but this time heard in conjunction with a syncopated figure on the brass. The strings continue the rhythm of "John Raeburn" while the horns play "The Red Barn", interrupted from time to time by the syncopated brass figure. A fortissimo climax is suddenly broken by the appearance of

"Ward the Pirate" pianissimo, accompanied by a long crescendo roll on the side drum. The crescendo is gradually contributed to by the whole orchestra, which finally joins forces and plays "Ward the Pirate" fortissimo and largamente. This brings the movement to an end, and leads to a few bars of coda, presto, founded on "The Lincolnshire Farmer".'

This work was written in 1906. The composer's original plan was that the three rhapsodies should form *A Norfolk Symphony*. As Edwin Evans explained in the *Musical Times* of May 1920, No. 1 was the first movement, No. 2 was a telescoped slow movement and scherzo, and No. 3 the finale. The idea was scrapped, and there is no record of the three having been played in one concert. 'Ward the Pirate' presumably acted as a kind of cyclic theme, reappearing in the finale after its first (now excised) appearance in the opening movement. Rhapsodies Nos. 2 and 3 were not played after 1914.

5. MUSIC FOR 'THE PILGRIM'S PROGRESS', a dramatization by Mrs. W. Hadley and Miss E. Onless of John Bunyan's book. For soprano and contralto soloists, mixed chorus (SATB) and strings. Music for twelve episodes was composed, with a Prelude and Epilogue for strings only, each founded on the hymn-tune 'York'. Manuscripts surviving are of music for:

(*a*) Prelude.

(*b*) The Arming of Christian: *Allegro moderato*. 'Founded on an English traditional melody.' The melody, as might be guessed, is 'Our Captain Calls', or Monk's Gate, the *English Hymnal* version to the words 'He who would valiant be'.

(*c*) Christian and Apollyon. *Marcato*.

(*d*) The fight between Christian and Apollyon. *Allegro*. After the fight, the contralto solo sings 'Whoso dwelleth under the defence of the Most High' to the tune which found fuller expression in *The Shepherds of the Delectable Mountains*.

(*e*) Vanity Fair. 'Down among the dead men', vocal quartet.

(*f*) Death of Faithful. *Andante sostenuto*. 'Adapted from an anthem by R. Farrant.' The anthem concerned is 'Lord, for thy tender mercies' sake', long attributed to Farrant (*d*. 1581) but now believed to be by another hand.

(*g*) Final Scene. *Andante sostenuto*. 'York' is used as the basis of this scene. A Chorus, 'Holy is the Lord' is followed by a soprano solo 'Blessed are they that are called to the marriage supper of the Lamb.' The alleluias in this setting derive from those in the hymn 'Sine Nomine'.

(*h*) Epilogue ('York').

First performance: Reigate Priory, Surrey, in December 1906, by anonymous cast. Produced by Mrs. W. Hadley and W. Nugent

Monck, with 'artistic tableaux' arranged by Frank Dicksee, R.A., Conductor, Dr. R. Vaughan Williams. First London performance: Imperial Theatre, 16 March 1907, with same cast and conductor. Two performances only, on same day, in which Southwark Cathedral choir sang.

Whereabouts of MS.: British Library (50418–9).

1907

1. THE ENGLISH HYMNAL, with tunes. Abridged Edition.
   In this edition Hymns 189, 195, 208, 213 and 250 of the first edition are transferred to a new Part III of the Appendix.

2. TOWARD THE UNKNOWN REGION. Song for chorus (SATB) and orchestra. Words by Walt Whitman, from the poem *Whispers of heavenly death*, first published 1870. *Grave, ma non troppo*. D modal minor.

   Instrumentation: 3 flutes, 2 oboes, cor anglais, 2 clarinets, bass clarinet, 2 bassoons, 4 horns, 3 trumpets, 3 trombones, tuba, timpani, 2 harps (or pianoforte), violins, violas, violoncelli, double basses, organ. This work may also be performed by an orchestra consisting of: 2 flutes, 1 oboe, 2 clarinets, 2 bassoons, 2 horns, 2 trumpets, timpani, harp or pianoforte, strings.

   First performance: Leeds Festival, Town Hall, Leeds, 10 October 1907, Leeds Festival Chorus and Orchestra conducted by Dr. R. Vaughan Williams. First performance in London: Royal College of Music, 10 December 1907, students' chorus and orchestra conducted by Sir Charles Stanford.

   Dedication: To F.H.M. (Florence Maitland, widow of the historian F. W. Maitland. She was Adeline Vaughan Williams's sister; her second husband was Sir Francis Darwin, whom she married as his third wife in 1913. She died in 1920.)

   Duration: 11½ minutes.

   Publication: Vocal score by Breitkopf and Härtel, London, Leipzig, etc., in 1907, No. 25791. Tonic Solfa edition issued 1907 also. Full score by Stainer and Bell, London (© 1924) (S. & B. 3121). Full score carries no dedication. Vocal score also available from S. & B. Work was slightly revised, 1919. Note on text: Vaughan Williams uses the phrase 'nor any bounds bounding us', as it appears in the 1888 Collected Poems of Whitman. In the 1930 McKay edition of *Leaves of Grass* it appears as 'nor any bounds bound us'. The work was probably completed in 1906.

   Whereabouts of MS.: British Library, Full score (50439), Vocal score (56086).

3. FAIN WOULD I CHANGE THAT NOTE. Canzonet for four voices (SATB.), unaccompanied. *Andante tranquillo*. F major. Words:

Anonymous. From Captain Tobias Hume's *The First Part of Airs*, 1605.
Publication: London, Novello & Co. Ltd.; New York, The H. W. Gray Co. (© 1907) in Novello's Part-Song Book, second series, No. 1030, and Tonic Solfa series No. 1600.
Version arranged for TTBB published by Novello & Co. 1927 in *The Orpheus*, new series, No. 603, *andante tranquillo*, C major, and in Tonic Solfa series No. 2548.
Version for trio of women's voices (SSA) Novello Trios No. 636.

1908

1. FOLK SONGS FROM THE EASTERN COUNTIES (*Folk songs of England*, Book II, edited by Cecil J. Sharp.) Collected and set with an accompaniment for pianoforte by R. Vaughan Williams.
Songs from Essex.
   1. Bushes and Briars. *Lento e molto espressivo.* A modal minor. Collected at Ingrave, 1903. Note on this song states: 'The first verse may with great advantage be sung unaccompanied, the accompaniment coming in at the bar marked †' [the 21st].
   2. Tarry Trowsers. *Allegretto.* D modal minor. Collected at Ingrave, 1904. (The accompaniment to the first verse may be used throughout if preferred.)
   3. A Bold Young Farmer. *Andante con larghezza.* E flat major. Collected at Nevinton, 1904.
   4. The Lost Lady Found. *Allegro commodo.* D modal minor. Collected at Herongate, 1904.
   5. As I Walked Out. *Moderato espressivo.* D modal minor. Collected at Herongate, 1904.
   6. The Lark in the Morning. *Moderato grazioso.* F major. Collected at Herongate, 1904.
Songs from Norfolk.
   7. On Board a Ninety-Eight. *Allegro.* D modal minor. Collected at King's Lynn, 1905. Note on score: 'The first verse may, with advantage, be sung unaccompanied, the accompaniment entering at † [19th bar]. The whole song may, with the exception of the last verse, be sung to the accompaniment of verse 1.'
   8. The Captain's Apprentice. *Lento.* D modal minor. Collected at King's Lynn, 1905.
   9. Ward the Pirate. *Moderato, alla marcia.* D major. Collected at King's Lynn, 1905.
   10. The Saucy Bold Robber. *Allegro.* C modal minor. Collected at King's Lynn, 1905.
   11. The Bold Princess Royal. *Moderato risoluto.* G major. Collected at King's Lynn, 1905.

12. The Lincolnshire Farmer. *Allegro.* E modal minor. Collected at King's Lynn, 1905.

13. The Sheffield Apprentice. *Andante con moto.* E modal minor. Collected at King's Lynn, 1905.

Songs from Cambridgeshire.

14. Geordie. *Andante con moto.* A modal minor. Collected at Fen Ditton, 1906.

15. Harry the Tailor. (To the tune of 'The Tailor'). *Allegro.* D modal minor. Collected at Wilburton, 1906.

Publication: London, Novello & Co. Ltd. © 1908. (12678.)

Dedication: 'These arrangements of Folk tunes are gratefully dedicated to those who first sang them to me. R.V.W.'

This book contains a 'general preface to the Folk-Song Series' by Sharp in which he puts his views on folk song as being 'the invention . . . of the community'. He also states that the tunes 'have not been editorially "improved" in any way'. In the matter of the words he admits that many have been altered for reasons which included 'the somewhat free and unconventional treatment of the themes of many of the ballads'. Notes in the score concerning the words are appended to the following tunes:

(a) *The Lark in the Morning:* 'The singer of the above tune remembered only fragments of the words. The complete words exist on a broadside, but in that form they were not suitable for this publication. In compiling the above text some of the broadside verses have been omitted and some of the lines transposed from one verse to another; nothing, however, has been added.'

(b) *Ward the Pirate:* 'The above words have been completed partly from a Sussex version (sung to another tune) and partly from a printed copy.'

(c) *The Lincolnshire Farmer:* 'A few lines have had to be supplied from a printed version and elsewhere.'

(d) *Harry the Tailor:* 'The words to which this tune was sung are unsuitable for this publication; other words, therefore (also traditional), have been substituted; they are taken from Bell's *Songs of the Peasantry.* The burden proper to the tune has, however, been retained.'

An introduction to the Songs by Vaughan Williams states:

'The 15 melodies which are arranged in this volume are part of a much larger collection made in the Eastern Counties. It is not to be supposed that they are the exclusive property of the counties to which they are credited; all that is claimed for them is that they certainly are sung in these counties, and that most of the melodies have not as yet been discovered elsewhere. It will be noticed that, while six songs from

Essex and seven from Norfolk are given, there are only two from Cambridgeshire and none from Suffolk. This means, not that these two counties are less rich in folk song than the others, but simply that time and opportunity have not yet been found to explore them. Nor do the songs collected from Essex and Norfolk represent an exhaustive search; all the Norfolk tunes come from King's Lynn and the neighbourhood, and the Essex songs from a small area near the town of Brentwood. It is to be hoped that an acquaintance with the melodies here given will incite others to explore those parts of East Anglia which are still unsearched.

'I wish to take this opportunity of expressing my grateful thanks to the singers of these melodies, and to all those who helped in the work of collection.'

For ease of reference, other arrangements by Vaughan Williams of the tunes included in *Folk Songs from the Eastern Counties* are given below:

1. *Bushes and Briars.*
   (*a*) Arranged for four male voices (TTBB). *Andante sostenuto.* C modal minor. Novello & Co. 1908, *The Orpheus* new series, No. 447.
   (*b*) For unaccompanied chorus (or solo voices) (SATB). *Lento.* G modal minor. Novello & Co. Ltd.; New York, The H. W. Gray Co. (Novello's part-song book, 2nd series, No. 1416). 1924. *Dedication:* To the English Singers.

2. *Tarry Trowsers.*
   (*a*) For voice and pianoforte. *Allegretto.* D modal minor. Novello School Songs series (No. 1472). 1927.

3. *Ward The Pirate.*
   (*a*) Arranged for four male voices unaccompanied (TTBB). *Allegro moderato.* G major. London: J. Curwen & Sons Ltd. (The Apollo Club series, No. 518). 1912.
   (*b*) For voice and pianoforte. *Moderato, alla marcia.* D major. London: Novello & Co. Ltd.; New York, The H. W. Gray Co. (Novello's School Songs, series No. 1473). 1927.
   (*c*) Version (*b*) included as No. 32 in *Folk Songs II.* (A selection of some less known folk songs, arranged by Cecil J. Sharp, R. Vaughan Williams and others, for voice and piano. Compiled by Cyril Winn.) London: Novello & Co. Ltd.; New York, The H. W. Gray Co. © 1935.

4. *The Saucy Bold Robber.*
   Original version as in 1908 publication issued separately by Novello and The H. W. Gray Co. in 1936.

2. THE JOLLY PLOUGHBOY. Sussex folk song arranged for four male voices (TTBB) unaccompanied. *Moderato.* B flat major.

Publication: London, Novello & Co. Ltd.; New York, The H. W. Gray Co. (© 1908) in *The Orpheus*, new series, No. 448.

(*a*) Arranged for unison singing with pianoforte accompaniment in *Folk Songs for Schools*, London, Novello & Co. Ltd.; New York, The H. W. Gray Co. (© 1912). (Novello's School Songs Book 232, No. 1128, edited by W. G. McNaught.) *Allegro risoluto*. G major.

(*b*) Version (*a*), for voice and pianoforte, included as No. 18 in *Folk Songs II* (A selection of some less known folk songs, arr. by Cecil J. Sharp, R. Vaughan Williams and others, for voice and piano. Compiled by Cyril Winn.) London, Novello & Co. Ltd.; New York, The H. W. Gray Co. (© 1935).

3. BUONAPARTY. Song for voice and pianoforte. Composed in 1908. Words by Thomas Hardy (1840–1928), from *The Dynasts*, Act I, Scene 1. *Allegro risoluto*. D minor.
Publication: London and New York, Boosey & Co. (© 1909.)

Whereabouts of MS.: British Library. Copy (59796).

4. THE SKY ABOVE THE ROOF. Song for voice and pianoforte. Composed in 1908. Words by Paul Verlaine (1844–96), translated by Mabel Dearmer (1872–1915) from the poem 'Le ciel est pardessus le toit'. *Lento*.
Note: Mrs. Dearmer, wife of the Rev. Percy Dearmer, wanted the Verlaine lyric set for her play *Nan Pilgrim*, her dramatization of her novel *The Difficult Way*. She asked R.V.W. to do it, but he pleaded that he was too busy. Later, however, he sent her this song.
Publication: London and New York, Boosey & Co. (© 1909)

Whereabouts of MS.: British Library. Copy (59796).

5. THREE NOCTURNES for baritone solo, semi-chorus and orchestra. Words by Walt Whitman. Unpublished. *Nocturnes* I and III are dated 18 August 1908. Text from *Drum Taps*.
   I. 'Come, O voluptuous sweet-breathed earth.' *Lento*. 62 bars.
   II. 'By the Bivouac's fitful flame' for unaccompanied chorus (optional pianoforte score provided). A version for string quintet exists. *Largo*. 83 bars.
   III. 'Out of the rolling ocean.' *Lento—andantino*. 120 bars.
These works are fragmentary and presumably had not reached final shape, as *Nocturne* II may have been written earlier for a choral society or group. They are the most important of all the unpublished MSS. up to 1914. The growing mastery which Whitman's verse precipitated is apparent. *Nocturne* III is of special significance, as it contains ideas which came to full flower in other works, notably *The Pilgrim's Progress, On Wenlock Edge*, the *Pastoral Symphony, Hugh the Drover*

and, most interesting of all, *Sancta Civitas*. The theme in *Sancta Civitas* which carries the words 'And I saw the Holy City coming down from heaven' appears in 'Out of the rolling Ocean' in this form:

It accompanies the words, 'Behold the great rondure, the cohesion of all, how perfect', and here one can perhaps trace a psychological link between the ideas of the Holy City and 'the cohesion of all' with the ocean, which in Whitman and in Vaughan Williams became a symbol for the exploration by the human soul of realms unknown to temporal man. And, of course, it was too good a tune to waste.

Whereabouts of MS.: British Library. Condensed scores of I and III, chorus parts with piano part of II (57283). String Quintet version of II (57280).

6. AETHIOPIA SALUTING THE COLOURS. *Alla marcia.* Unpublished sketch for setting of this Whitman poem.
There is a chorus part marked 'Humming' and, interestingly enough, the chief solo part is for a narrator, with Aethiopia's part given to a soprano and the final verse to a male voice. It was not until writing *Thanksgiving for Victory* in 1943 that Vaughan Williams again employed narration with music. This poem was a favourite with Vaughan Williams. At the end of his life he turned to it again, and half a page of very rough sketches for a completely new setting were found among his papers. These were probably done in 1957-8. The original setting is not dated, but I consider that it must have been 1908.

Whereabouts of MS.: British Library. Sketches of both settings (57283).

7. THE FUTURE ('A Wanderer is Man from his birth') for solo soprano, chorus and orchestra. Words by Matthew Arnold (1822–88). *Unpublished and incomplete.* MS (Vocal Score) of 32 pages.
It is quite impossible to date this work accurately, but to include it in 1908, after a study of handwriting and other factors of that kind which must be taken into account, seems reasonable.

Whereabouts of MS.: British Library. Imperfect condensed score (57283).

8. IS MY TEAM PLOUGHING? Song for voice and pianoforte. Words by A. E. Housman (1859–1936) from *A Shropshire Lad* (XXVII).
Unpublished in this form.
First performance: London, Aeolian Hall, 25 January 1909, Gervase Elwes (tenor) and Frederick Kiddle (pianist). The date of performance establishes that this song was almost certainly composed in 1908. Whether the other items of *On Wenlock Edge*, into which it was eventually incorporated, had also been written by this time is not known.

9. STRING QUARTET IN G MINOR. 2 violins, viola, violoncello. Revised 1921. I. *Allegro moderato*, II. *Minuet and Trio*, III. *Romance*; *andante sostenuto*, IV. *Finale, Rondo capriccioso*.
First performance: London, 8 November, 1909, by Schwiller Quartet at meeting of Society of British Composers in Novello's Rooms; first public performance: London, Aeolian Hall, 15 November 1909, by Schwiller Quartet. First performance of revised version: London, Contemporary Music Centre Concert, Russell Street, 6 March 1922. Artists unknown.
Duration: 28 minutes.
Publication: Miniature score, London F. & B. Goodwin Ltd., (© 1923) Reissued by J. Curwen & Sons Ltd. (C.E. 93011). Reissued by Faber Music (parts on hire).

1909

1. ON WENLOCK EDGE. Cycle of six songs for tenor voice, with accompaniment of pianoforte and string quartet (ad. lib.). Words by A. E. Housman from *A Shropshire Lad*.
  1. On Wenlock Edge (xxxi). *Allegro moderato*. G minor.
  2. From far, from eve and morning (xxxii). *Andantino*. E major.
  3. Is my team ploughing? (xxvii). *Andante sostenuto, ma non troppo lento*. D minor (Dorian mode).
  4. Oh, when I was in love with you (xviii). *Allegretto*. D modal minor.
  5. Bredon Hill (In summertime on Bredon) (xxi). *Moderato tranquillo* (a kind of G major).
  6. Clun (l). *Andante tranquillo*. A minor.
First performance: London, Aeolian Hall, 15 November 1909, by Gervase Elwes (tenor) and the Schwiller Quartet, with Frederick Kiddle, pianoforte.
Duration: 24 minutes.
Publication: Full score (46 pages) published (© 1911). London, Novello & Co. Ltd.; New York, The H. W. Gray Co. String parts published by Novello & Co. separately, also 1911 (Avison edition). Full score published by Boosey & Co. Ltd., London, in September 1942. This differs from 1911 Novello edition only in woodcut on title page.

String parts reissued separately, also score for voice and piano.

Other version: for tenor voice and orchestra.

Instrumentation: 2 flutes, oboe, cor anglais, 2 clarinets, 2 bassoons, 4 horns, 2 trumpets, 3 trombones, timpani, percussion, celeste, harp, violins, violas, violoncelli, double basses. (Parts available on hire.)

First performance of this version: London, Queen's Hall, Royal Philharmonic Society Concert on 24 January 1924, conducted by Dr. Ralph Vaughan Williams with John Booth (tenor).

It is not known when the orchestral version of the songs was made. The composer, in a letter to the author, said 'I do not remember'. It seems obvious, though, that 1921-3 would cover the likely date. Whereabouts of original MS, apart from sketches, not known.

Much has been said about the disagreement between A. E. Housman and Vaughan Williams over *On Wenlock Edge*. The impression is sometimes given that Housman was unwilling to allow composers to set his poems. Although he could not understand why they should wish to do so, he never refused permission. What he was difficult about was the reprinting of his poems in concert programmes. In most cases he refused permission, but he gave in on this point before the first performance of *On Wenlock Edge*. In a letter to his publisher, Grant Richards, on 11 November 1909[1] he said: 'The terms on which Mr. Lambert [Frank Lambert] may print my words with his music are that he should spell my name right. As to Mr. Vaughan Williams, about whom your secretary wrote: he came to see me, and made representations and entreaties, so that I said he might print the verses he wanted on his programme.[1] I mention this lest his action should come to your ears and cause you to set the police after him.'

The documented facts about the omission by Vaughan Williams from 'Is my team ploughing?' of the stanza beginning 'Is football playing?' are as follows: Letter from Housman to Richards, 20 December 1920: 'I am told that composers in some cases have mutilated my poems—that Vaughan Williams cut two verses out of "Is my team ploughing?" I wonder how he would like me to cut two bars out of his music. . . ."

Letter from Housman to Richards, 8 July 1922: 'I do not know what penalty the *Tatler* people have laid themselves open to [by printing, without permission, part of a poem], and anyhow I should think they had better be left alone. I am told that Vaughan Williams has mutilated another poem just as badly, to suit his precious music.' On 7 May 1927, Housman wrote to Richards: 'As to "Is my team plough-

---

[1] Vaughan Williams's only comment on this occasion occurred in a letter written years later to Mr. Frank Howes when, à propos some proposed engagement, he said: 'As Housman once said to me when he gave me leave to print his poems, "I do it with a very bad grace".'

ing?" Mr. Orr [C. W. Orr] must be warned not to omit part of the poem, as I am told Vaughan Williams did.'

When Richards was compiling his book on Housman,[2] a friend asked Vaughan Williams if he would mind the above letter being printed. Vaughan Williams replied: 'You may print anything you like. If the biographer consents I think I ought to be allowed my say, which is that the composer has a perfect right artistically to set any portion of a poem he chooses provided he does not actually alter the sense: that makers of anthologies, headed by the late Poet Laureate [Bridges] have done the same thing—I also feel that a poet should be grateful to anyone who fails to perpetuate such lines as:

> The goal stands up, the keeper
> Stands up to keep the goal.'

The impression has sometimes been given that these remarks were addressed to Housman himself. It will be seen that this was not so.

A further incident concerning Housman and Vaughan Williams is told by Dr. Percy Withers. In the *New Statesman and Nation* of 9 May 1936, in an article 'A. E. Housman: Personal Recollections', Dr. Withers wrote:

'Since he had so often and so unaccountably allowed his verses to be set to music, and never as I knew experienced the results, it occurred to me that he might like to hear gramophone records of Vaughan Williams's setting sung by Gervase Elwes. I was oblivious of the effect until two of them had been played, and then turning in my chair I beheld a face wrought and flushed with torment, a figure tense and bolt upright as though in an extremity of controlling pain or anger, or both. . . .'

At least thirty composers have set Housman poems to music; the most popular lyric for setting is 'Loveliest of Trees', which Vaughan Williams did not set. For an interesting article on Housman's use in his poetry of musical terms and allusions see *Music and Letters*, October 1943, 'A. E. Housman and Music' by William White. It has been erroneously stated that Butterworth was the first to set Housman. In fact, his settings date from 1911, two years later than Vaughan Williams's. Somervell must have been among the first, with a song-cycle written in 1904 and first performed in February 1905.

(*a*) 3. Is My Team Ploughing? F.S. issued separately 1919. London, N.Y., etc. Boosey & Co. (© 1911 R.V.W.). (H. 9487).

2. THE WASPS. Incidental music, for tenor and baritone soloists, male chorus (TTBB), and orchestra. Words by Aristophanes, translation by H. J. Edwards, M.A. Commissioned by the Greek Play Committee,

---

[2] The following extract is from *Housman* (1897–1936) by Grant Richards (O.U.P.).

Cambridge, 1909. Complete score of incidental music comprises:
No. 1. Overture. (*Allegro vivace*).
  2. Act I. Introduction (Nocturne). *Adagio molto*.
  3.   ,,   Melodrama and Chorus. *Allegro vivace*.
  4.   ,,   The Wasps' Serenade. *Moderato*.
  5.   ,,   Chorus. *Allegro molto*.
  6.   ,,   Chorus. *Molto moderato*.
  7.   ,,   Melodrama and chorus. *Allegro*.
  8.   ,,   Melodrama and chorus. *Moderato*.
  9. Act II. Entr'acte and Introduction. *Molto moderato*.
 10.   ,,   Melodrama and chorus. *Andante con moto*.
 11.   ,,   March-Past of the Witnesses. *Moderato alla marcia*.
 12.   ,,   Parabasis. *Moderato—largamente—allegro moderato—molto vivace—allegro scherzando—andantino*.
 13. Act III. Entr'acte. *Andante con moto*.
 14.   ,,   Introduction. *Adagio*.
 14a ,,   Repeat No. 13 from letter E.
 15.   ,,   Melodrama. *Moderato alla marcia*.
 16.   ,,   Chorus. *Moderato piacevole*.
 17.   ,,   Melodrama. *Allegro*. (Asterisk at first bar indicates 'Founded on a Cambridgeshire folk song.')
 18.   ,,   Chorus and Dance. *Molto vivace—moderato—allegro vivace—allegro vivacissimo—presto—molto moderato*.

Published at Cambridge, 1909, for the Greek Play Committee as vocal score with pianoforte reduction of the orchestral part. (Gr.P.C.1). *First performance:* Cambridge, New Theatre, 26 November 1909 (with five subsequent performances on 27, 29, and 30 November and 1 December) with following cast:

PHILOCLEON..	.. ..	D. H. Robertson (*Trinity College*)
BDELYCLEON..	.. ..	J. R. M. Butler (*Trinity College*)
XANTHIAS ⎱ slaves	.. ..	⎰ E. Y. Esskildsen (*Christ's College*)
SOSIAS ⎰		⎱ W. M. Malleson (*Emmanuel College*)
DONKEY ⎱	.. ..	⎰ R. O. Bridgeman (*Trinity College*)
DOGS ⎰		⎱ R. C. Peache (*Trinity College*)
LAMP-BOYS ..	.. ..	⎰ H. S. Bodmer (*Emmanuel College*)
		⎱ A. E. Heath (*Trinity College*)
A GUEST ..	.. ..	A. Ramsay (*Gonville and Caius*)
A BAKING-GIRL	.. ..	W. F. P. Ellis (*Trinity College*)
A COMPLAINANT	.. ..	A. Rawlins (*King's College*)
THE THREE SONS ⎱		⎰ F. D. Arundel (*Emmanuel College*)
OF ⎰	..	⎨ C. A. Gordon (*King's College*)
CARCINUS ⎰		⎱ H. S. Bodmer (*Emmanuel College*)

LEADER OF THE CHORUS $\Big\{$ R. W. Pole (*King's College*)
OF WASPS

SUB-LEADERS   ..   ..   E. W. Workman (*Trinity College*)
V. S. Brown (*Jesus College*)

CHORUS: H. Dowson, A. J. W. Willink, J. S. Wilson (*King's*); G. G. Morris (*Trinity*); A. A. Guest-Williams (*St. John's*); W. C. Denis Browne, F. P. Haines (*Clare*); A. P. Bell, H. D. Statham (*Gonville and Caius*); A. G. N. Ogden (*Corpus Christi*); K. Spence, J. M. D. Stancomb, C. G. B. Stevens (*Emmanuel*); L. W. Batten (*Sidney Sussex*); F. V. Dawkins, V. C. McKiever (*Selwyn*).

SLAVES: C. M. Keddie (*King's*); N. R. Birchall, W. O. Times, R. D. Ross (*Trinity*).

KITCHEN UTENSILS: H. L. Farnell, G. L. J. Tuck (*King's*); D. S. Fraser (*St. John's*); G. H. Atkinson, G. E. H. Ferry, W. R. Lloyd (*Peterhouse*).

GUESTS, ETC.: M. T. Maxwell, F. W. Haskins (*Trinity*); F. A. Woodward (*Jesus*).

The orchestra consisted of 24 players, led by Haydn Inwards and with the pianist-composer James Friskin playing the timpani. The chorus was trained by Dr. Charles Wood. Conductor: Dr. Charles Wood.

Whereabouts of MS: Fitzwilliam Museum, Cambridge.

From the incidental music to *The Wasps*, Vaughan Williams made his:

THE WASPS, ARISTOPHANIC SUITE in FIVE MOVEMENTS.

1. Overture. *Allegro vivace*. F major.
2. Entr'acte. *Molto moderato*. E modal minor.
3. March–Past of the Kitchen Utensils. E modal minor.
4. Entr'acte. *Andante*. G major.
5. Ballet and Final Tableau.

Instrumentation: 2 flutes (2nd doubling piccolo), 2 oboes (1 opt.), 2 clarinets, 2 bassoons (1 opt.), 4 horns (2 opt.), 2 trumpets (1 opt.), 2 trombones (1 opt.), percussion (triangle, cymbal, bass drum), timpani, harp, strings. (Original Cambridge instrumentation was: 1 flute, 1 oboe, 2 clarinets, 1 bassoon, 2 horns, 1 trumpet, timpani, harp, sidedrum, cymbals, 6 violins, 2 violas, 2 violoncelli, 2 double basses.)

First performance: London, Queen's Hall, Royal College of Music Patron's Fund Concert; New Symphony Orchestra conducted by Dr. R. Vaughan Williams, 23 July 1912. (In the presence of King George V and Queen Mary.)

Duration: 25½ minutes.

Publication: Full Score, London, Schott and Company (© 1914). (A. 848). Arrangement for pianoforte duet by Constant Lambert, London, J. Curwen & Sons Ltd., Philadelphia, Curwen Inc. (©

R.V.W. 1926). Full Score, J. Curwen & Sons Ltd., U.S.A. Curwen Inc. (C.E. 90786). (© 1933). Full score and parts on hire from Faber Music. Full score of March Past, C.90858.

OVERTURE: Full score, London, J. Curwen & Sons Ltd., U.S.A. Curwen Inc. (C.E. 90785). (© 1933). Miniature score: London, New York, etc., Boosey and Hawkes Ltd. (by arrangement with Curwen) (B. & H. 8836). (© 1943). Analysis by Edwin Evans available with score or separately. Full score and parts on hire from Faber Music.

Instrumentation for overture: 2 flutes (2nd doubling piccolo), 2 oboes, 2 clarinets, 2 bassoons, 2 horns, 2 trumpets, timpani, percussion (triangle, cymbals, bass drum), harp, strings.

Duration of Overture: 10 minutes.

3. A SEA SYMPHONY for soprano, baritone, mixed chorus (SATB) and orchestra. Words by Walt Whitman as follows:

1st movement: First seven lines from 'Song of the Exposition', first published in 1871. Remainder from 'Song for All Seas, All Ships', first published in *Centennial Songs*, 1876.

2nd movement: 'On the beach at night, alone'. Poem first published 1856 under title *Clef Poem*.

3rd movement: 'The Waves'. Poem *After the Sea-Ship*, published in *Two Rivulets*, 1876.

4th movement: From 'Passage to India', first published in 1870.

Except in the third movement, the composer has omitted words and lines from the original text.

I. A Song for All Seas, All Ships. *Andante maestoso.*

II. On the beach at night, alone. *Largo sostenuto.*

III. Scherzo (The Waves). *Allegro brillante.*

IV. The Explorers. *Grave e molto adagio.*

Instrumentation: 2 flutes, 2 oboes (1 opt.), cor anglais, 3 clarinets (1 opt.), bass clarinet (opt.), 2 bassoons, 1 double bassoon (opt.), 4 horns, 3 trumpets, 3 trombones, tuba, timpani, percussion, 2 harps (1 opt.), organ (opt.), violins, violas, violoncelli, double basses.

First performance: Leeds Festival, Leeds Town Hall, 12 October 1910. Festival Chorus and orchestra, conducted by Dr. R. Vaughan Williams. Chorus Master, H. A. Fricker. Organist, Dr. Edward Bairstow. Soprano, Cicely Gleeson-White; baritone, Campbell McInnes. First London Performance: Queen's Hall, 4 February 1913. The Bach Choir and Queen's Hall Orchestra, conducted by Dr. Hugh P. Allen. Organist, Harold Darke. Soprano, Agnes Nicholls; baritone, Campbell McInnes.

Dedication: To R.L.W. [(Sir) Ralph Wedgwood, cousin of Vaughan Williams]

Duration: 67 minutes. (I, 19¼ mins.; II, 11½ mins.; III, 7 mins.; IV, 29¼ mins.)

Publication: Vocal score (© 1909) by Breitkopf and Härtel, London,[1] Leipzig, etc., pianoforte arrangement by S. O. Goldsmith and the composer (No. 26335); tonic solfa edition also published 1909; revised edition, London, Stainer and Bell (© 1918), vocal score with pianoforte arrangement as above (S. & B. 1961); full score, revised version (© 1924), Stainer and Bell (S. & B. 3036).

The vocal score of 1918 contains as a prefatory note details of the composer's revisions. These are mainly practical applications of lessons learned from performances, for example in the first movement, page 3, bars 1 and 2, the sopranos are given the words 'See where their white sails' instead of the more cumbersome 'Speckle the green and blue', and on page 28, bars 1 and 2, the tenors, instead of an optional 'token of all brave captains', sing 'from all intrepid captains'. Notation is altered in two places and bar 4, p. 45, is marked 'poco più mosso' instead of 'molto meno mosso'. In the scherzo, the chorus parts, 'A motley procession, with many a fleck of foam and many fragments' from bar 8, p. 72, to bar 6, p. 73, are optional, and the notation of the soprano part at bars 4 and 5 of p. 79 is slightly eased. The majority of revisions occur in the finale. Here again the revisions are mainly simplification of passages lying awkwardly for the voice or in order to bring the words clearly through the orchestral texture. Considerable changes in the tenor and bass parts at 'steer for the deep waters only' from last bar on p. 114 to fifth bar on p. 115 were made when the full score was published. At this time, too, an optional cut was introduced from the più lento on p. 101, bar 15, to p. 106, bar 8. It is much to be regretted that the composer provided this option, for if the cut is made the audience is deprived of one of the most moving parts of the work, the baritone solo 'Swiftly I shrivel at the thought of God'. Only an insensitive conductor, or one tightly bound by a time schedule, would willingly omit the music of this section.

A note on the 1924 full score says that the work may also be played by an orchestra of: 2 flutes (2nd changing with piccolo), 1 oboe, 1 cor anglais, 2 clarinets, 2 bassoons, 4 horns, 3 trumpets, 3 trombones, bass tuba, timpani, percussion, 1 harp, strings. In this case the conductor should direct the players to play the cues for the missing instruments which are written into their parts. In the case of the 2nd flute and cor anglais the special parts must be used. When there is no bass clarinet, the 2nd bassoon must play off the special part, except in III (Scherzo). The other instruments may be added, with corresponding advantage, in the following order of importance: organ, bass clarinet, 3rd flute, 2nd oboe, double bassoon, 2nd harp, E flat clarinet.

[1] One of R.V.W.'s favourite anecdotes was of the proofs of the first vocal score where 'cut the hawsers' appeared as 'cut the trousers'.

The various movements of this symphony may also be performed separately.

After a performance of *A Sea Symphony* in January 1945, Vaughan Williams wrote to its conductor, Sir Adrian Boult, on 1 February: 'If you ever do it again do substitute *trombones* for *horns* at the beginning – but *not both*. The other place 'O Soul thou pleasest me' is more difficult – we have tried de-muting the 4th horn – now it sticks out too much. Would you try a single cello muted *and pp added* to the 4th horn? I believe that would solve it – but it must *not* be played like a solo with lots of vibrato etc.'

Arrangement for Organ Solo. Large sostenuto (2nd movement of *A Sea Symphony*). London, Stainer and Bell Ltd. (S. & B. 2411). No. 2 of series of Organ Solos edited and arranged by Henry G. Ley.

Whereabouts of original MS.: British Library. Some early sketches 50361; vocal sketches 50362–3; printed proofs of vocal score 50364; full score 50365; printed full score with the composer's corrections, 50366. The authoritative version is the printed full score, item 50366. The MS. full score contains many marks made by various conductors.[1]

Composer's programme note: This note appeared in the programme of the Bach Choir's 1913 performance:

'The first sketches for this work (namely, parts of the Scherzo and slow movement) were made in 1903, and it was gradually worked out during the next seven years. It was first produced at the Leeds festival in 1910, and has since been performed (in a slightly revised form) at Oxford, Cambridge and Bristol.

'There are two main musical themes which run through the four movements:

1. The harmonic progression to which the opening words for the chorus are sung.
2. A melodic phrase first heard at the words "and on its limitless heaving breast, the ships".

'The plan of the work is symphonic rather than narrative or dramatic, and this may be held to justify the frequent repetition of important words and phrases which occur in the poem. The words as well as the music are thus treated symphonically. It is also noticeable that the orchestra has an equal share with the chorus and soloists in carrying out the musical ideas.

'The Symphony is written for soprano and baritone soli, chorus and orchestra. The two soloists sing in the first and last movements. The slow movement contains a solo for baritone (and also a long refrain for

---

[1] Particularly by Sir Henry J. Wood. Cf. correspondence in the *Musical Times*, April and May 1923.

orchestra alone) while the Scherzo is for chorus and orchestra only.
'The words are selected from various poems of Walt Whitman to be found in *Leaves of Grass*, namely "Sea Drift", "Song of the Exposition", and "Passage to India". R.V.W.'

Origins, etc. The sketch-books on view in the British Library are a fascinating record of the slow growth of *A Sea Symphony*, parallel with the composer's growth from his early romantic stage to his mature style. To students of the creative process, of the constant revision, development and refinement of ideas, they can be recommended as an absorbing study. To examine them in detail here would require almost a separate book, and would not necessarily be generally illuminating. A summary of major features is all that is attempted:
The work began as 'Notes for choral work *Songs of the Sea*', perhaps in emulation of Stanford. The composer has said that the Scherzo and 'On the beach at night alone' were sketched first, but sketches soon appeared marked 'Token of all brave captains', 'Beginning of the whole thing' (which was not), 'O vast rondure' and 'Today a brief recitative'. Later, under 'Walt Whitman—Sea Songs', the great opening theme exists in its final state. The closing section of the first movement underwent radical alteration. 'Token of all brave captains' was originally set, awkwardly, to the ascending phrase now associated with 'Emblem of man'. The choral fade-out had an orchestral ritornello of 13 bars as an appendage, repeating the main theme in descending octaves.
Three early versions of the slow movement exist, with the solo part given to a tenor, in the 'meno mosso' section ('A vast similitude'). The opening words are sung by tenors and basses, answered by sopranos and altos. Various alterations in the key-sequence seem to have been dictated by a desire to strengthen the dramatic value of E flat at 'Spans them' (Letter M in the vocal score). A version of this movement was completed in 1906, when the work was known to the composer as his *Ocean Symphony*. In a letter to Holst[1] from Meldreth, Cambridgeshire, thanking him for the *Two Songs without Words* (which were dedicated to Vaughan Williams) he says, 'I've just finished scoring the second movement of the Ocean'.
The third movement underwent comparatively little change.
A projected fourth movement, for baritone soloist with the sopranos and altos of the chorus, was called 'The Steersman'. The score was completed on 17 August 1906. The poem, beginning

> 'Aboard, at a ship's helm
> A young steersman, steering with care'

was first published in 1867. The steersman hears the warning bell

---

[1] *Heirs and Rebels*, p. 40.

marking a wreck and steers away from disaster so that 'the beautiful and noble ship, with all her precious wealth, speeds away gaily and safe'. But the last two lines must have been those which attracted Vaughan Williams's attention while he was planning the symphony:

'But O the ship, the immortal ship! O ship aboard
the ship!
O ship of the body—ship of the soul—voyaging,
voyaging, voyaging.'

The main theme of the first movement is quoted in this discarded movement, diminished and agitato. A derivation of this passage found its way into the finale at the 'allegro animato' section on p. 94 (nine bars after K).

Most of the revisions occur in the finale, 'The Explorers', which is the best and also the most imperfect of the four movements. Proust's remark about Flaubert's prose style—'great writers who do not know how to write'—is appropriate to Vaughan Williams in this movement. Anyone can point out its clumsiness—'floundering about like a porpoise', Cecil Gray wrote—but its moving eloquence, its power to grip heart and soul, make technicalities insignificant. The episode which gave the composer the most trouble was 'Down from the gardens of Asia descending'. This first appeared in a Sullivan-ish version for tenors, sopranos, and altos. It then became a sombre chant for male voices:

'Yet soul be sure, the first intent remains' began life sedately, in the manner of weak Parry, for the full chorus:

This was changed to:

before, in a final revision, it was related to an orchestral passage in the ultimate setting of the 'Down from the Gardens' section,

so that Adam and Eve and 'the first intent' are given thematic and symbolic unity:

'O thou transcendent' is sketched in various forms, one of them a bass entry with tremolando strings:

O thou tran-scend - ent   name - - - less

Revision of the full score also was chiefly concerned with the finale.
The major change is at p. 119 (vocal score), four bars after Z, where
sixteen bars of contrapuntal choralism on 'Sail forth, steer for the
deep waters only' are replaced by twelve which become the mighty,
imperative injunction, in unison, merely to 'sail forth'. This is so
much more effective in practice than any counterpoint, however
admirable it looked on paper.

The sketch-books contain the equivalents of pieces of a jig-saw puzzle
before they are fitted into the main picture. They show that the gesta-
tion of *A Sea Symphony* was elephantine and laborious. A fugue theme
was composed, but not used. Other parts of the text were set and discarded. A sketch-book not in the British Library includes the genesis
of 'Wandering, yearning, with restless explorations' and working-out of
'Finally, shall come the poet' and 'After the seas are all crossed'.
The sketches then merge into scraps of *On Wenlock Edge*.

Folk-song quotations: The folk song 'The Golden Vanity' is quoted by
the orchestra at 'laughing and buoyant' in the Scherzo (Vocal Score,
p. 65); and at 'surface' on p. 66 there is a snatch from 'The Bold
Princess Royal' which is repeated twice on p. 67. The quotations are
firmly woven into the texture of the music as nautical points of colour.
There is no particular virtue in being able to recognize them.

1910

1. FANTASIA ON ENGLISH FOLK SONG: STUDIES FOR AN
   ENGLISH BALLAD OPERA. For orchestra.

Unpublished: (nothing survives).

First performance: London, Queen's Hall Promenade Concert, 1 September 1910, Queen's Hall Orchestra, conducted by Henry J. Wood.

Composer's note: 'The Fantasia is divided into three sections. The
first *Allegro* is of a *risoluto* character. A short cadenza for harp and
wind instruments leads to a slow section which is the longest in the
work. Finally there is a short finale of a *scherzando* nature, towards the
end of which the themes of the first two sections reappear.'

In a letter to Harold Child, librettist of *Hugh the Drover*, telling him
of the performance of this work, Vaughan Williams wrote: 'The *slow*

middle section . . . is a sort of study for what I should like my love scene, Act II, to be like.'

Two of the tunes on which the *Fantasia* was founded were taken from the collections of Lucy Broadwood and Cecil Sharp. Otherwise little is known about this work. *The Times* critic admitted that he 'spent too much time trying to locate the beautiful fragments which flit across the score'. His indication that the work began with 'Seventeen Come Sunday' is a clue which may mean that the work was totally re-cast after the war as the suite, *English Folk Songs*, of 1923 for military band (q.v.).

2. PURCELL SOCIETY. The *Works of Henry Purcell*, Volume XVIII. 'Welcome Songs', Part 2. Full Score edited by R. Vaughan Williams.
   6. The Welcome Song performed to His Majesty in the year 1684, 'From those serene and rapturous joys'.
   7. Welcome Song, 1685, being the first song performed to King James II, 'Why, why, are all the muses mute?'
   8. Welcome Song, 1686, 'Ye tuneful muses'.
   9. Welcome Song, 1687, 'Sound the trumpet'.

   Publication: London, Novello & Co. Ltd.; New York, The H. W. Gray Co., 1910. (© The Purcell Society). Locations of the Purcell MSS. are given in the preface.

   (*a*) No. 8. WELCOME SONG, 1686, 'Ye tuneful muses raise your heads'. *Moderato.* G minor.
   Publication: Vocal Score (© 1933) London, Novello & Co. Ltd. (15911).

   (*b*) No. 9. WELCOME SONG, 1687, 'Sound the trumpet'. Orchestration by R.V.W. of the accompaniment of Moffat's edition for two voices and pianoforte.
   Instrumentation: 2 flutes, 2 oboes, 2 clarinets, 2 bassoons, 2 horns in F, 2 trumpets, 3 trombones, timpani, triangle, strings.
   Score in hire library (Edition No. 4129b) of Augener Ltd., London, since May 1934.

3. FANTASIA ON A THEME BY THOMAS TALLIS. For double stringed orchestra with solo quartet. *Largo sostenuto.*
   Instrumentation: Solo string quartet (2 violins, viola, violoncello); Orchestra I: 1st and 2nd violins, viola, violoncello (tutti), violoncello (last desk), contrabass. Orchestra II: 2 first violins, 2 second violins, 2 violas, 2 violoncelli, 1 contrabass.
   Note to conductor on full score says specifically:
   'The Second Orchestra consists of 2 First Violin players, 2 Second Violin players, 2 Viola players, 2 'Cello players and 1 C'bass player. These should be taken from the 3rd desk of each group (or in the case of the C'bass by the 1st player of the 2nd desk) and should, if

possible, be placed apart from the First Orchestra. If this is not practicable, they should play sitting in their normal places. The solo parts are to be played by the leader in each group.' Composed 1910, revised 1913, revised again 1919.

First performance: Gloucester Cathedral, 6 September 1910 (Three Choirs Festival), London Symphony Orchestra, conducted by Dr. R. Vaughan Williams. First London performance: Queen's Hall, 11 February 1913. (Balfour Gardiner Concert.) New Symphony Orchestra, conducted by Dr. R. Vaughan Williams.

Duration: 14½ minutes.

Publication: Full score, London, Goodwin & Tabb Ltd. (© U.S.A. 1921. © 1921 all countries.) Reissued by J. Curwen & Sons Ltd., London, who took over all Vaughan Williams works published by Goodwin when the latter firm ceased business in 1924. (C.E.90722). Reissued by Faber Music (C.90722).

Miniature Score: 1943, London, New York, etc. Boosey and Hawkes Ltd. (© U.S.A. 1921 Goodwin & Tabb Ltd.; © 1921 all countries). Contains loose-leaf analysis by Edwin Evans.

Arrangement for two pianofortes, by Maurice Jacobson. Two copies under one cover, both parts printed in full on Piano I and Piano II parts. London, J. Curwen & Sons Ltd.; New York, G. Schirmer Inc. © 1947 by R. Vaughan Williams and Maurice Jacobson (C.E.99106).

Note: The theme by Thomas Tallis (1505?–85) is the third ('Why fumeth in fight') of nine Psalm Tunes composed in 1567 and printed in Archbishop Parker's Psalter of that year. The book was suppressed from publication. No. 3 is a Phrygian (Third) Mode tune.

Whereabouts of MS.: Royal Academy of Music.

Revision: The closing section of the work was cut. Tallis's theme was originally repeated twice instead of once, as now.

1911

1. CHURCH SONGS. Collected by Rev. S. Baring-Gould, music arranged by Rev. H. Fleetwood Sheppard and R. Vaughan Williams. R.V.W. arranged Hymns 1–9; 11–13; 15–17; 19–21; 23–25.

Publication: London, Society for the Promotion of Christian Knowledge under the direction of the Tract Committee, 1911.

2. FIVE MYSTICAL SONGS. For baritone soloist, mixed chorus (ad. lib. SATB) and orchestra. Words by George Herbert.

1. Easter. *Maestoso.* E flat major.
2. I got me flowers. *Moderato.* E flat modal minor—G flat major.
3. Love bade me welcome. *Andante sostenuto (tempo rubato).* E modal minor.

4. The call. *Lento moderato*. E flat major. (May also be sung in D flat.)
5. Antiphon (Let all the world in every corner sing). *Allegro*. D major.
   For chorus and orchestra.
   (*a*) Appendix. Antiphon. Alternative version for voice without chorus.
   Solo voice, chorus silent, in 2 and 4 and 5 (*a*).

Instrumentation: 2 flutes, 2 oboes, 2 clarinets, 2 bassoons, 4 horns, 2 trumpets, 3 trombones, tuba, timpani, harp, strings. *Or* string quintet and pianoforte. Material available on hire.

First performance: Worcester Cathedral, 14 September 1911 (Three Choirs Festival). Campbell McInnes (baritone), Festival Chorus, London Symphony Orchestra conducted by Dr. R. Vaughan Williams. First performance in London: Aeolian Hall, 21 November 1911, Campbell McInnes (baritone), Hamilton Harty (pianoforte).

Duration: 19 minutes.

Publication: Vocal score: London, Stainer & Bell Ltd.; Leipzig, Breitkopf and Härtel; Boston, Arthur P. Schmidt (© U.S.A. 1911) (S. & B. 959). Full score, chorus parts, orchestral parts, and chorus parts for male voices also available.

Following single songs and arrangements available:

3. 'Love bade me welcome.' London, Stainer and Bell, 1911. (S. & B. 960). Orchestral material available on hire.
4. 'The Call.' Arranged for organ (2-manual). No. 1 of 'Two pieces arr. for organ by Herbert Byard'. London, Stainer & Bell Ltd. 1946. (S. & B. 5181). *Lento moderato*. E flat major.
   'The Call.' Solo song with pianoforte accompaniment. (S. & B.)
5. 'Antiphon.' London, Stainer and Bell 1911. (S. & B. 960.) (Both above in Stainer and Bell's Church Choir Library, No. 349). Antiphon. 'Let All the World.' For SATB choir and organ or orchestra. Orchestral material available on hire. (S. & B.)
   Antiphon. Arranged for organ by Henry G. Ley. London, Stainer & Bell, 1922. (© U.S.A. 1922.) (In series of organ solos edited and arranged by Henry G. Ley. No. 3. S. & B. 2402.)

Whereabouts of MS.: British Library (56064). Vocal score and a few leaves of full score (50440).

3. LONDON PAGEANT. May Day Scene.
   Unpublished.
   This score may possibly have been written for some kind of E.F.D.S. festivity associated with the Coronation of King George V. There are thirteen items, all arrangements of folk tunes and dances:

   1. 'Summer is a-coming in' and 'Henry Martin.' *Allegro molto*.
   2. May Day Songs. *Andante* for male voices. (Tunes from Cambridgeshire and Hertfordshire.)
   3. 'Nuts in May' and 'Oats and beans'.

4. Processional Morris and 'Old Heddon of Fawsley', also 'Twanky-dillo'.

5. Hobby Horse Dance.

6. 'Morris on.'

7. Processional Morris and 'Robin Hood and the Pedlar'.

8. Fanfare of trumpets.

9. Staines Morris and 'Greensleeves'.

10. 'Country Gardens', 'Princess Royal', and 'Shepherds Hey'.

11. 'Old woman tossed up in a blanket.'

12. 'Follow your lovers.'

13. 'Earl of Oxford's March' (*Maestoso*. Entry of King Henry VIII).

4. INCIDENTAL MUSIC TO GREEK PLAYS.

Unpublished, except for one item.

Almost complete scores and parts exist for settings of parts of *Iphigenia in Tauris*, *The Bacchae* and *Electra*. They were probably sung by a small group called the Palestrina Society which Vaughan Williams conducted. Isadora Duncan (1878–1927), the Californian who preached a species of revived Hellenism, asked him for music for her to dance to in *Bacchae* but she disappeared without leaving an address and nothing further was said or done. Her request was the cause of the choral work. After one chorus in *The Bacchae*, Vaughan Williams wrote the date 'October 17, 1911'. This is the only clue to the dates of these three works, but they seem to be contemporaneous, and may be roughly ascribed to 1911–14.

I. BACCHAE; translated from the Greek by Gilbert Murray (1866–1957). 34 of 38 pages of an incomplete full score in Vaughan Williams's hand, first two missing, and two blank.

Instrumentation: Flute, oboe, clarinet, bassoon, horn, harp, cymbals, violins, violas, violoncelli and double basses. Contralto solo. Mixed chorus. Chorus, 'Thou immaculate on high, hearest thou this angry King', is the most complete fragment of unpublished music. Parts for Violins I and II and III, Viola, Cellos I and II, Double bass, Flute, Oboe, Horn in F, Clarinet in B, Harp and Cymbals are all written out by the composer.

Lento solenne and *tranquillo*.

Parts, some in the composer's hand, also exist for the chorus 'Where is the Home for me?', which was published early in 1922 as a vocal duet:

WHERE IS THE HOME FOR ME? Song for soprano and mezzo-soprano. Words by Gilbert Murray, after *The Bacchae* of Euripides. *Andante moderato*. E minor and major.

Publication: London (© 1922) Edwin Ashdown Ltd. in Edwin

Ashdown's series of vocal duets for class singing. Second series, No. 91 (E.A.35192).

Note: A reference to his setting of *The Bacchae* was made by Vaughan Williams in his lectures at Cornell University in 1954, published as *The Making of Music* (1955), p. 10.[1] Discussing the two kinds of accent in poetry—'that supplied by the sense of the passage and that supplied by the nature of the metre'—he continues:

'I should like to add one personal experience. I was setting to music one of Gilbert Murray's translations of Euripides, and I came upon these lines:

> Only on them that spurn
> Joy, may his anger burn.

'I pointed out to Professor Murray that if I set the words strictly according to their meaning it would convert the verse into prose:

> Only on them that spurn joy, may his anger burn.

'If I set it strictly according to the metre it would make nonsense of the words:

> Only on them that spurn,
> Joy may his anger burn.

'He solved my difficulties by declaiming the lines to me in a manner which I can describe only by musical notation:

On - ly on them that   spurn Joy,   may his   an - ger   burn

In the MS. score of *The Bacchae*, Vaughan Williams set this particular passage thus:

On - ly on   them   that spurn   Joy,   may his   an – ger   burn

II. Incidental Music to the IPHIGENIA IN TAURIS of Euripides (translated into English rhyming verse by Gilbert Murray). MS. scores of Prelude and Four Choruses, in composer's hand, with chorus parts copied in various hands.

Note on Score: 'These choruses must be sung throughout with due regard to the true declamation of the words and the metre of the poetry. The note values of the voice parts are, for the most part, only approximate. The solos may be divided among the members of the chorus according to the compass and nature of their voices. The instrumental portion is scored for the following orchestra:

---

[1] In *National Music and Other Essays* (1963), this reference appears on pp. 210–11.

1 flute, 1 oboe, 1 clarinet, 1 bassoon (ad lib), 1 horn (ad lib), cymbals (ad lib), 1 harp, 1st violins (at least two players), 2nd violins ("), violas ("), violoncellos ("), double bass (at least one player). R.V.W.'

I. Prelude. *Andante sostenuto.*

Chorus I. (Cue: 'Evil dwelleth not in heaven') 'Dark of the sea, dark of the sea, gates of the warring water.' *Con moto.*

Chorus II. (Cue: 'A clean and joyous land doth call for thee') 'Bird of the sea rocks, of the bursting spray.' *Lento moderato.*

Chorus III. (Cue: 'Mistress thou canst read my prayer') 'Oh fair the fruits of Leto blow; a Virgin one, with joyous bow.' *Moderato.*

Chorus IV. (Cue: 'Hallowed image home') 'Go forth in bliss, ye whose lot God shieldeth, that ye perish not!' *Moderato alla marcia.*

III. INCIDENTAL MUSIC TO ELECTRA (Translated into English by Gilbert Murray).

Instrumentation: Flute, cor anglais, clarinet, bassoon, horn, cymbals, harp, violins, violas, violoncelli, double basses, chorus with soprano and alto soli, and speaker.

Practically complete full score in composer's hand and chorus and band parts in his and various hands of: Chorus: 'Child of the mighty dead, Electra.' *Moderato.* Chorus: 'O for the ships of Troy, the beat of oars.' *Moderato.* Chorus: 'Onward, O labouring tread.' *Lento.*

1912

1. DOWN AMONG THE DEAD MEN. Old English air arranged for four male voices (TTBB) unaccompanied. *Allegro.* E minor.
Publication: London, Joseph Williams Ltd. (© March 1912), (J.W.15297). Handbook of Glees, etc. No. 167). Also available with pianoforte accompaniment. Other version: Tonic solfa edition. *Allegro.* E minor. London, Joseph Williams Ltd. (© 1923) (J.W. 15297a). Written in 1906 for *Pilgrim's Progress* at Reigate.

2. THE SPANISH LADIES, traditional words and tune. Arranged for voice and pianoforte. *Allegro risoluto.* A modal minor.
Publication: London and New York, Boosey & Co. Ltd. (H.7442) (© April 1912). Also arranged for unison and mixed voices as No. 9 in Stainer and Bell's *Motherland Song Book*, Vol. IV, *Sea Songs* selected and arr. by R.V.W. and others (© 1912 Boosey & Co.).

3. ALISTER McALPINE'S LAMENT. Scottish air arr. for mixed voices (SATB) unaccompanied. Words by Robert Allan. *Largo.* D major.
Publication: London, J. Curwen & Sons Ltd. (C.E.60997) (© May 1912).

4. THE WINTER IS GONE. English folk song arranged for male voices (TTBB) unaccompanied. *Allegretto tranquillo.* C modal minor. *Publication:* London, Novello & Co. Ltd.; New York, the H. W. Gray Co. (© June 1912). In *The Orpheus*, a collection of glees and part songs for male voices, new series No. 536.

5. PHANTASY QUINTET. For 2 violins, 2 violas, 1 violoncello.

    I. Prelude. *Lento ma non troppo.*

    II. Scherzo. *Prestissimo.*

    III. Alla sarabanda.

    IV. Burlesca. *Allegro moderato.*

First performance: London, Aeolian Hall, 23 March 1914, by London String Quartet (A. E. Sammons, T. W. Petre (violins), H. Waldo Warner (viola), C. Warwick-Evans (violoncello), with James Lockyer as second viola). This was an F. B. Ellis Chamber Concert.

Dedication: To W. W. Cobbett, Esq., and the members of the London String Quartet.

Duration: 16 minutes.

Publication: London, Stainer & Bell Ltd. (© 1921) (S. & B. 2275). Full score. No. 11 of the Cobbett Series.

Composer's programme note: This note was printed in the programme of the first performance:

'This "Phantasy" was written at the request of Mr. W. W. Cobbett, as one of his series for various combinations of instruments. . . . It is in four very short movements, which succeed each other without a break. There is one principal theme (given out by the viola at the start) which runs through every movement—

    (1) Prelude (in slow 3/2 time).

    (2) Scherzo (this is a quick movement—the longest of the four).

    (3) 'Alla sarabanda.' (Here the 'cello is silent and the other instruments are muted.)

    (4) Burlesca. (This movement is, for the most part, in the form of a "basso ostinato".)

                                  R.V.W.'

Arrangement: Alla sarabanda, arr. for organ by Henry G. Ley. London, Stainer & Bell Ltd. (© 1922) (Organ solos ed. and arr. by Henry G. Ley, No. 3) (S. & B. 2402).

Note: This work is dated 1910 in some books of reference and 1914 in others. I have placed it in 1912 in view of a paragraph in the *Musical Times* for August 1912 announcing that 'Dr. Vaughan Williams has completed his Phantasy commissioned by the Musicians' Company'.

W. W. Cobbett (1847–1937) was a wealthy businessman (founder and chairman of Scandinavia Belting Ltd.) who was a distinguished amateur musician. He took a special interest in chamber music, playing first violin in his own quartet, and he spent a great deal of money on promoting chamber concerts and British chamber works. In 1905 he began a series of Cobbett Competitions and also commissioned works from British composers. In this way additions to the repertory came from York Bowen, James Friskin, Frank Bridge, Armstrong Gibbs, W. Y. Hurlstone, Herbert Howells, John Ireland, J. B. McEwen, Ivor Gurney, Stanford, Waldo Warner and Vaughan Williams. Cobbett suggested to composers that the Elizabethan form of 'Fancy' or 'Phantasy' would be a worthwhile model for works in one movement, or of four compressed into one and playing continuously. These competitions were a potent stimulant to young composers to break away from the increasingly complex structures favoured by the continental composers of the time, such as Reger.

6. FANTASIA ON CHRISTMAS CAROLS. For baritone soloist, mixed chorus (SATB) and orchestra. Words traditional. A minor. *Andante—moderato.* This Fantasia is founded on the following traditional English carols: (1) 'The truth sent from above' (words and tune) (Herefordshire); (2) 'Come all you worthy gentlemen' (words and tune) (Somerset); (3) 'On Christmas night' (words and tune) (Sussex); (4) 'There is a fountain' (tune only) (Herefordshire) together with fragments of other well-known carol tunes. The Herefordshire carols were used by permission of Mrs. E. M. Leather, that from Somerset by permission of Cecil Sharp.
Instrumentation: 2 flutes, 2 oboes, 2 clarinets, 2 bassoons, 4 horns, 3 trumpets, 3 trombones, tuba, timpani, bells (optional), organ, violins, violas, violoncelli, double basses. Orchestral material available on hire. The work may be accompanied in the following ways:
(*a*) String orchestra and organ (or pianoforte).
(*b*) Organ.
(*c*) Pianoforte and solo cello.
First performance: Hereford Cathedral, 12 September 1912 (Three Choirs Festival), Campbell McInnes (baritone), Festival Chorus, London Symphony Orchestra, conducted by Dr. R. Vaughan Williams. First London performance: Queen's Hall, 4 March 1913. Balfour Gardiner Concert. Campbell McInnes (baritone), London Choral Society, New Symphony Orchestra, conducted by Dr. R. Vaughan Williams.
Dedication: To Cecil Sharp.
Duration: 8½ minutes.
Publication: Chorus edition (SATB) London, Stainer & Bell Ltd. (© 1912 (© U.S.A. 1912) (S. & B. 1223); full score, London, Stainer & Bell Ltd. (© 1924) (S. & B. 3094). Also available: arrange-

ment for voice and pianoforte; TTBB edition, arranged for male voices by Herbert W. Pierce (© 1925) (S. & B. 3372).

Note: The 'fragments of other well-known carol tunes' are of 'The First Nowell', 'The Virgin unspotted', and 'The Wassail Bough' (Yorkshire). An 'Important Note' on the score states that the chorus are required to sing in four different ways: (*a*) Singing the words; (*b*) Singing with closed lips; (*c*) Singing 'Ah'; (*d*) Singing with 'humming tone', i.e. with open lips but with a short 'u' sound as in the word 'but'.

Whereabouts of MS: British Library. Full Score (50441).

7. FOLK SONGS FOR SCHOOLS. Arranged for unison singing with pianoforte accompaniment. Novello's School Songs, edited by W. G. McNaught. Book 232 (Nos. 1128–1138).

   1. The jolly plough boy (1128). *Allegro risoluto.* G major. Collected and arranged R.V.W.

   2. The cuckoo and the nightingale (1129). *Moderato.* D major. Collected and arranged R.V.W. The last verse (fifth) has been adapted from another ballad.

   3. Servant man and husbandman (1130). *Moderato.* F modal minor. Collected by H. E. D. Hammond, arr. R.V.W.

   4. The female highwayman (1131). *Andante.* E major. Collected and arranged R.V.W.

   5. The carter (1132). *Allegro moderato.* G modal minor. Collected and arranged R.V.W.

   6. I will give my love an apple (1133). *Andantino.* A modal minor. Collected by H. E. D. Hammond and arranged R.V.W.

   7. My boy Billy (1134). *Allegretto.* G major. Collected and arranged R.V.W.

   8. Down by the riverside (1135). *Andante con moto.* G major. Collected by H. E. D. Hammond and arranged R.V.W.

   9. The fox (1136). *Allegro.* E modal minor. Collected by H. E. D. Hammond and arranged R.V.W.

  10. Farmyard song (1137). *Allegretto.* G major. Collected by H. E. D. Hammond and arranged R.V.W.

  11. The painful plough (1138). *Allegretto grazioso.* E flat major. Collected and arranged R.V.W.

Publication: London, Novello & Co. Ltd.; New York, The H. W. Gray Co. (© 1912). Each song available separately.

Other versions of certain of the tunes are given here for convenience:

   1. The jolly plough boy.

     (*a*) Arr. for four male voices (TTBB) in *The Orpheus* new series, No. 448. *Moderato.* B flat major. Novello & Co. (© 1908).

(*b*) For voice and pianoforte as No. 18 of *Folk Songs II*. (A selection of some less known folk songs. Arr. by Cecil J. Sharp, R. Vaughan Williams and others. Compiled by Cyril Winn.) *Allegro risoluto*. G major. Novello & Co. (© 1935).

(*c*) For women's voices, with orchestral or pianoforte accompaniment; as Prologue to Cantata *Folk Songs of the Four Seasons*. (O.U.P. 1950 q.v.)

4. The female highwayman. Arranged for voice and pianoforte by R.V.W. as No. 25 in *Folk Songs I* (a selection of collected folk songs arranged by Cecil J. Sharp and R. Vaughan Williams). *Andante*. E major. *Publication:* London, Novello & Co. Ltd.; New York, The H. W. Gray Co. 1917. © 1912 for this song.

5. The carter. Arranged for voice and pianoforte by R.V.W. as No. 22 of *Folk Songs I*, as above. *Allegro moderato*. G major. © 1912.

6. I will give my love an apple. Arranged for voice and pianoforte by R.V.W. as No. 12 of *Folk Songs I*, as above. *Andantino*. A modal minor. © 1912.

7. My boy Billy. Arranged for voice and pianoforte by R.V.W. as No. 15 of *Folk Songs I*, as above. *Allegretto*. G major. © 1912.

8. Down by the riverside. Arranged for voice and pianoforte by R.V.W. as No. 8 of *Folk Songs I*, as above. *Andante con moto*. G major.

9. The fox. Arranged for voice and pianoforte by R.V.W. as No. 26 of *Folk Songs I*, as above. *Allegro*. E modal minor. © 1912.

10. Farmyard song. Arranged for voice and pianoforte by R.V.W. as No. 9 of *Folk Songs I*, as above. *Allegretto*. G major. © 1912.

11. The painful plough. Arranged for voice and pianoforte by R.V.W. as No. 31 of *Folk Songs I*, as above. *Allegretto grazioso*. E flat major. © 1912.

8. FOLK SONGS OF ENGLAND, V. Folk Songs from Sussex. Edited by Cecil J. Sharp. Collected by W. Percy Merrick. With pianoforte accompaniments by R. Vaughan Williams and Albert Robins.

1. Bold General Wolfe. *Allegro moderato*. G major.
2. Low down in the broom. *Lento tranquillo*. A modal minor.
3. The thresherman and the squire. *Moderato*. C modal minor.
4. The pretty ploughboy. *Allegretto grazioso*. D major.
5. O who is that that raps at my window? *Moderato con moto*. G modal minor.
6. How cold the wind doth blow (or The Unquiet Grave). *Andante sostenuto*. F major. With violin accompaniment ad lib. (Separate violin part.)

7. Captain Grant. *Allegro*. D major.
8. Farewell, lads. *Andante*. D modal minor.
9. Come all you worthy Christians. *Maestoso con moto*. A modal minor.
10. The Turkish lady. *Moderato con moto*. A major.
11. The seeds of love. *Andante sostenuto*. With violin accompaniment ad lib. (Separate violin part.)
12. The maid of Islington. *Andante sostenuto*. C modal minor.
13. Here's adieu to all judges and juries. *Moderato*. E modal minor.
14. Lovely Joan. *Andante con moto*. D modal minor.
15. The Isle of France. *Moderato*. E major (acc. by Albert Robins).

Publication: London, Novello & Co. Ltd. © 1912.

Other versions of certain of the above songs are given here for ease of reference:

6. The Unquiet Grave.
   (*a*) For three female voices (SSA) unaccompanied in *Folk Songs of the Four Seasons*, a cantata, 1950 (O.U.P.). It occurs in the movement 'Autumn'.
   (*b*) The above, available separately. (O.U.P.)

9. Come all you worthy Christians. In *Oxford Book of Carols* (1928, q.v.) as tune to No. 60 of Part I.

11. The seeds of love. Arranged for male voices (TBB), with pianoforte ad lib. *Andantino sostenuto*. G major. *Publication:* London, Stainer & Bell Ltd. (© 1923) in Stainer and Bell's Male Voice Choir No. 83, (S. & B. 2098). The complete words will be found in *Folk Songs from Somerset*, Vol. I, No. 1, by Cecil J. Sharp, and in Novello's School Songs, No. 954.

14. Lovely Joan.
   (*a*) Set for contralto and orchestra in Act II of *Sir John in Love*, when Mrs. Quickly sings one verse. 'An obscene ballad such as Mrs. Quickly might very well have on her lips,' Frank Howes says.[1]
   (*b*) For voice with accompaniment for any instrument suitable, in *The Penguin Book of English Folk Songs*, edited by R. Vaughan Williams and A. L. Lloyd (London 1959), p. 64.

9. EVENING HYMN (Purcell, arranged for voice and string orchestra by R. Vaughan Williams).
This was sung by Campbell McInnes at a Hallé Concert in Manchester on 22 February 1912. Percy Pitt conducted. Dorothy Silk sang it at the Three Choirs Festival in 1932, and it was performed at the Leith Hill Festival. The full score is lost, but the parts for strings

---

[1] *The Music of Ralph Vaughan Williams* (London, 1954), p. 282.

in two keys, G major and F major, are in the care of the Oxford
University Press.

10. WARD THE PIRATE. English Folk Song arranged for mixed
chorus (SATB) and small orchestra.
Instrumentation: 2 flutes, 2 oboes, 2 clarinets, 2 bassoons, timpani,
cymbals, triangle, strings. *Moderato alla marcia.*
Unpublished. MS. full score and band parts in various hands. I date
this arrangement 1912 in view of the amount of folk-song settings
which the composer made at this time. Some of the copying is in the
same distinctive hand as much of the Greek Plays music.

11. TARRY TROWSERS. *Allegretto.* English Folk Song, arranged as
in 10.
Unpublished.

12. AND ALL IN THE MORNING (On Christmas Day). *Maestoso.*
Derbyshire carol, arranged as in 10.
Unpublished.

13. The CARTER. *Allegro moderato.* English Folk Song.
Instrumentation: 2 flutes, 2 oboes, 2 clarinets, 2 bassoons, 2 horns,
2 trumpets, 2 trombones, timpani, percussion, harp and strings.
Unpublished.

14. MINEHEAD HOBBY-HORSE. English Folk Dance. *Moderato.*
Unpublished.
Instrumentation: flute, piccolo, oboe, bassoons, clarinets, horn,
trumpet, triangle, bass drum, pianoforte, strings.

15. PHIL THE FLUTER'S DANCING. English Folk Dance. 'Quick
and lively.' Arranged for flute and strings.
Unpublished.

16. THE OLD HUNDREDTH. Organ accompaniment for verse 3 and
last verse of the hymn-tune 'The Old Hundredth', contributed to a
volume of varied organ accompaniments (plus unison voices) for
certain tunes in *Hymns Ancient and Modern* published in 1912 by the
proprietors of *Hymns Ancient and Modern.*

1913

1. MANNIN VEEN (Dear Mona). Manx traditional melody arranged
for mixed chorus (SATB), unaccompanied. *Andante sostenuto.* Melody
and words from Dr. Clague's MS. collection.
Publication: London, J. Curwen & Sons Ltd. (© 1913). C.E.61002.
(*The Choral Handbook.*)
Other version: Arrangement for male chorus (TTBB) by Herbert Pierce
also available. (C.E.50759.)
This song was probably arranged in 1912 or earlier, as the last page
of the score bears an imprint 336/5.12. It was not released until 1913.

2. LOVE IS A SICKNESS. Ballet for four voices (SATB) unaccom-

panied. Words by Samuel Daniel (1562–1619). *Allegretto.* G minor.
Publication: London, Stainer & Bell Ltd. (Stainer & Bell's choral library for mixed voices, No. 97); Leipzig, Breitkopf and Härtel; Boston, A. P. Schmidt (© U.S.A. 1913).

3. O PRAISE THE LORD OF HEAVEN. Anthem for two full choirs and semi-chorus, unaccompanied. Text: Psalm 148 (Prayer Book version). *Con moto.*
First performance: London, St. Paul's Cathedral, 13 November 1913, London Church Choir Association (40th Annual Festival). Conducted by Dr. H. Walford Davies.
Publication: London, Stainer & Bell Ltd. (© 1914) (new and revised edition). S. & B. 1713. Stainer and Bell's Church Choir Library, No. 194.
Note: This anthem is intended for a large building and a chorus of some hundreds of voices. The semi-chorus should be about one-sixth of either of the two full choruses.

4. FIVE ENGLISH FOLK SONGS. Freely arranged for unaccompanied mixed chorus (SATB)
   1. The dark-eyed sailor. *Andante quasi allegretto.* G major.
   2. The springtime of the year. *Adagio.* E modal minor. The text is taken from a long ballad also known as 'Lovely on the water'. First two verses only.
   3. Just as the tide was flowing. *Allegro vivace.* A major. Words slightly revised.
   4. The lover's ghost (or Well met, my own true love). *Lento ma non troppo.* C sharp minor. Words amplified from two broadside versions.
   5. Wassail Song. (Gloucestershire). *Vivace.* A major.
   First performance: Probably at some competitive festival. First London performance of three of the songs, Nos. 1, 3 and 5, was in the Physiological Theatre of Guy's Hospital by the Guy's Hospital Musical Society at a choral and orchestral concert on 1 May 1914, conducted by W. Denis Browne.
   Publication: London, Stainer & Bell Ltd. (© 1913). (S. & B. 1559–63).
   Other versions:
   1. The dark-eyed sailor.
      (*a*) Unison song accompanied, in S. & B.'s Unison Songs (No. 141). *Andante quasi allegretto.* G major. *Publication:* London, Stainer & Bell, 1935.
      (*b*) Mixed chorus (unaccompanied) SATB (with divisi). Stainer and Bell, 1920. S. & B. Choral Library, No. 128.
   2. The springtime of the year.
      (*a*) Mixed chorus unaccompanied (SATB) (with divisi) Stainer and

Bell, 1920. S. & B. Choral Library No. 129.

3. Just as the tide was flowing.

    (*a*) Unison song, with pianoforte accompaniment, and for mixed voices. *Allegretto.* G major. *Publication:* London, Stainer & Bell Ltd., 1919. (S & B. 2121) as No. 3 in *Motherland Song Book* Vol. IV, *Sea Songs* for unison and mixed voices selected and arranged by R. Vaughan Williams and others. Available separately.

    (b) Mixed chorus unaccompanied (SATB) with divisi. Stainer and Bell, 1920. S. & B. Choral Library No. 130.

4. The lover's ghost.

    (*a*) Mixed chorus unaccompanied (SATB) with divisi. Stainer and Bell, 1920. S. & B. Choral Library No. 131.

    (*b*) Arranged by R.V.W. for voice and pianoforte in *Folk Songs from Newfoundland*, Vol. II, Ballads, No. 7. *Andante moderato.* C major. O.U.P. 1934.

5. Wassail Song.

    (*a*) For mixed chorus unaccompanied (SATB) with divisi. Stainer and Bell, 1920. S. & B. Choral Library No. 132.

    (*b*) Arranged for unison voices with descant, and orchestral accompaniment in cantata *Folk Songs of the Four Seasons*, O.U.P., 1950 (q.v.). Available separately.

    (*c*) Arranged for unaccompanied male chorus (TTBB) with divisi, by Herbert Pierce. Stainer and Bell.

5. A LONDON SYMPHONY. For Orchestra, in G major, in four movements.

    I. *Lento—allegro risoluto.*

    II. *Lento.*

    III. Scherzo (Nocturne). *Allegro vivace.*

    IV. Finale. *Andante con moto—maestoso alla marcia (quasi lento)— allegro—maestoso alla marcia—*Epilogue, *andante sostenuto.* *Instrumentation:* 3 flutes, 2 oboes, cor anglais, 2 clarinets, bass clarinet, 2 bassoons, double bassoon, 4 horns, 2 trumpets, 2 cornets, 3 trombones, tuba, timpani, percussion (side drum, triangle, bass drum, cymbals, glockenspiel, jingles), harp, violins, violas, violoncelli, double basses.

Note on score states:

'In the absence of certain instruments the parts of other instruments have been "cued" so that their more important passages shall not be omitted.

'The following are the reductions in instrumentation which are possible; but they should not be used except in case of absolute necessity.

'(1) The 3rd flute can be omitted. (In this case the 2nd flute player must play off the special copy marked "2nd flute and piccolo".).

'(2) The 2nd oboe and cor anglais parts can be performed by the same player, one or the other being omitted as directed in the part.

'(3) The two trumpet and two cornet parts can be condensed into two cornet (or trumpet) parts by using the special copy marked "For reduced orchestra". (*N.B.* In the case of there being 3 (but not 4) trumpets or cornets, the first trumpet and first and second cornet parts should be played.)

'(4) The bass clarinet and double bassoon can be omitted.

'In all cases the various instruments which have parts for the absent instruments "cued" should play the cues.

'The (') is to be interpreted as a slight "breath-mark", not as a pause. R.V.W.'

This symphony was completed by the end of 1913.

First performance: Original version, London, Queen's Hall, 27 March 1914, at an F. B. Ellis concert of Modern Orchestral Music. Queen's Hall Orchestra, conducted by Geoffrey Toye. First performance of reconstructed score (original having been mislaid): Bournemouth, Winter Gardens, Bournemouth Municipal Orchestra, conducted by Dan Godfrey, 11 February 1915. *First revision*, first performance: London, Queen's Hall, 18 March 1918, New Queen's Hall Orchestra, conducted by Adrian Boult. *Second revision*, first performance: London, Queen's Hall, Concert of first annual congress of British Music Society, 4 May 1920. London Symphony Orchestra, conductor Albert Coates. *Third revision*, first performance: London, Queen's Hall, Royal Philharmonic Society concert, 22 February 1934, London Philharmonic Orchestra, conducted by Sir Thomas Beecham.

Duration: 44 minutes. Original version took between 55 and 60 minutes.

Dedication (from second revision onwards)*:* To the memory of George Butterworth.

Publication: London (© 1920), Stainer & Bell Ltd. (© 1920 in U.S.A. by R.V.W.). Full score, 199 pages (Carnegie Collection of British Music). (S. & B. 2230). The original (1914) version was never published. The second (1920) revision was the first published edition, but it did not bear the superscription 'Revised edition'. The score marked 'Revised edition' refers to the 1933 third revision, which was first played in 1934. Therefore: Revised edition of 193 pages (Carnegie Collection of British Music), Full Score and Miniature Score, London, Stainer & Bell Ltd. © 1920 in U.S.A. by R.V.W. (S. & B. 2230), is the current and final edition and bears the notice: 'This revised edition supersedes the original version which should no longer be used.' Stainer and Bell have no record of the date of publication of the revised edition, but 1936 is highly probable. Orchestral parts available on hire. Centenary edition of full score, with introduction by Michael Kennedy, London, Stainer and Bell Ltd. © 1972.

Other versions:

(*a*) Arranged for pianoforte solo by Vally Lasker, in, it is believed, 1920. London, Stainer and Bell (© U.S.A. 1922). (S. & B. 2339.)

(*b*) Slow movement, Lento, arranged for the organ by Henry G. Ley, London, Stainer & Bell Ltd. (© U.S.A. 1922) as No. 1 of Organ Solos, edited and arranged by Henry G. Ley. (See *A Sea Symphony* for No. 2.)

(*c*) Arranged for pianoforte duet by Archibald Jacob. London, Stainer & Bell Ltd. (© 1924) (S. & B. 2955.)

Revisions: The original MS. full score, sent to Fritz Busch in Germany in July 1914, was lost.[1] What it contained can be seen from the first piano score now in the British Museum. It was reconstructed from the band parts by the composer and his friends, Butterworth, E. J. Dent and Geoffrey Toye, and played at Bournemouth in 1915 and at Queen's Hall by the New Queen's Hall Orchestra conducted by Adrian Boult, on 18 February 1918. This score is now in the British Library. For a third performance a month later the composer made some cuts. Boult wrote in the *Musical Times* of October 1958: 'He came to my room in a distant outcrop of the War Office and sat among the samples of boots, which then occupied most of my time, and made some cuts in the score of the London Symphony, ready for its third [fifth, in fact] performance in 1918.'

In the period between this performance and that on 4 May 1920, the composer made alterations in all but the first movement, which he never revised:

2nd movement: (1) Slight reduction of exposition after eighth bar. (2) Considerable variation of the section from the end of the development (10 bars after G in revised full score) to the recapitulation (at K). The present version replaces 43 bars in which the viola solo at letter D was recalled and reduces the section to 25 bars. (3) In the eight bars from K to L the bass in D flat was altered to a cadence, A flat—D flat, which formed the ground for a passage of vibrating string chords in descending semitones.

3rd movement: The present 72-bar coda (letter V) took the place of a new episode in B major and a second trio, an episode in 3/4 time, poco animato, which had folk-song-like snatches of tune and remini-

---

[1] Letter from R.V.W. to the author: 'I think it was Tovey who suggested I should send it to Busch.'

scences of the movement's first and second themes.

4th movement: (1) In the Allegro section (beginning at E) the present 15 bars between H and K which lead to the recapitulation of the 'con fuoco' section replaced 34 bars of a development of the opening Andante con moto and of the fragments of themes at seven bars after E and one bar after F. This condensation meant that the second 'con fuoco' entry was brought nearer to its first, so its key was raised a tone higher. (2) The return of the march-tune at M, with the three preceding bars of introductory matter for horns and lower strings was a substitution for 39 bars of a new andantino episode in 4/4 time:

with a quite different return to the march. The andantino theme was later used on muted horns to introduce the Westminster three-quarter chime but this, too, was scrapped. (3) The epilogue has undergone a continual process of reduction. From S to T has been almost untouched, but in the 1914 score the section T to W consisted of 55 bars of pianissimo writing for strings, woodwind and brass in which the four-note theme which opens the symphony was recalled (eight bars), expanded (17 bars) and played in canon (30 bars). This was reduced in the 1920 published score by cutting the canon to seven bars, making 32 in all. (4) The concluding half-cadence (X) was originally a switch from G major to E flat minor, repeated. The triads were expanded to augmented fifths.

After 1920 and before publication of the final revised score, further alterations were made. Writing to Maud Karpeles on 5 April 1933, Vaughan Williams said: '*London Symphony* (Phil.) Feb. 22 [1934]—special revised version with some of the bad bits cut out.' For a performance by students of the Royal College of Music under Constant Lambert on 12 June 1936, there were 'two new cuts . . . one in the slow movement and one in the epilogue, both suggested by the composer', according to the *Monthly Musical Record*. The alterations since 1920 are:

2nd movement: (1) One bar deleted at 18 after F. (2) The 25 bars from 10 after G to K again reduced to 16 by omitting nine bars of the Tempo I section. The cor anglais solo was revised, and solos for oboe, viola and horn omitted together with a six-bar passage for strings. (3) The section from K to the end, 21 bars in the 1920 score, was reduced to 19 by omission of two bars in the K—L section and the replacement of the passage of sul ponticello chords by plain chords of major sevenths. An interesting comment on this revision was made in a letter to the *Musical Times* of January 1959, p. 24, by the distinguished American composer and conductor, Bernard Herrmann. He wrote:

'When I first began to perform the work, the only set of parts and score available in New York was that of the first [actually second, 1920] version. The slow movement at that time possessed six remarkable bars at the letter K which later the composer omitted. . . . It has always been my intense reaction, and of course a subjective one, that these bars were one of the most original poetic moments in the entire symphony. It is at this moment as though, when the hush and quietness have settled over Bloomsbury of a November twilight, that a damp drizzle of rain slowly falls, and it is this descending chromatic ponticello of the violins that so graphically depicts it.

'Years later this set of parts was withdrawn by the New York agents and a new set of the revised version of the symphony was sent out with, alas, these magical six bars omitted. On one occasion I spoke to Vaughan Williams about these bars and expressed my deep regret about their deletion. He replied that he had revised this work three times—"Oh, it's much too long, much too long, and there was some horrid modern music in the middle—awful stuff. I cut that out— couldn't stand it." And that was as far as I could ever get with him to discuss the possibility of restoring those bars.

'I for one shall always regret this deletion, for it remains in my memory as one of the miraculous moments in music, and its absence in the present version is felt like the absence of a dear, departed friend. It will always be an enigma to me why these bars were removed, for in their magic and beauty they had caught something of London which Whistler captured in his Nocturnes.'

The bars to which Mr. Herrmann referred are these:

4th movement: (1) The bar before T was deleted. (2) The T—W section of epilogue was cut again from 32 bars to eight by a total jettisoning of all the augmentation and canon of the motto-theme, leaving only the Lento (molto largamente) theme to be followed rather abruptly by the final tranquillo section.

On the whole, the effect of the cuts, often ruthless, has been to tauten the work's structure. Sir Adrian Boult has said: 'Many of us regretted the cuts at that time, but we now see that he was right.'[1] Sir Arnold Bax, however, regretted the deletion of what he described as 'a mysterious passage of strange and fascinating cacophony'[2] at the end of the scherzo.[3]

Composer's Programme notes: The composer wrote the following note in 1920:

'The title *A London Symphony* may suggest to some hearers a descriptive piece, but this is not the intention of the composer. A better title would perhaps be "Symphony by a Londoner", that is to say, the life of London (including, possibly, its various sights and sounds) has suggested to the composer an attempt at musical expression; but it would be no help to the hearer to describe these in words. The music is intended to be self-expressive, and must stand or fall as "absolute" music. Therefore, if listeners recognize suggestions of such things as the "Westminster Chimes" or the "Lavender Cry" they are asked to consider these as accidents, not essentials of the music. The work consists of the usual four symphonic movements, namely:

1. *Lento*, leading to *allegro risoluto*.
2. *Lento*.
3. *Scherzo* (Nocturne).
4. *Maestoso alla marcia*, leading to Epilogue in which the theme of the opening Lento recurs.

'*A London Symphony* was first performed in the Spring of 1914, at one of the late Mr. F. B. Ellis's concerts (conductor, Mr. Geoffrey

---

[1] *Musical Times*, October 1958.

[2] *Farewell My Youth*, by Arnold Bax (London), p. 93.

[3] The earliest recording of the symphony was made for Columbia in 1926 by Sir Dan Godfrey with the London Symphony Orchestra (L 1717–22). It includes Mr. Herrmann's favourite passage.

Toye); since then it has been revised, and the first performance of the revised version took place under Mr. Albert Coates in May 1920.'

The composer expanded this note in several important details for a concert of the Liverpool Philharmonic Society on 1 December 1925: 'It has been suggested that this symphony has been misnamed, it should rather be called "Symphony by a Londoner". That is to say it is in no sense descriptive, and though the introduction of the "Westminster Chimes" in the first movement, the slight reminiscence of the "Lavender Cry" in the slow movement, and the very faint suggestion of mouth organs and mechanical pianos in the Scherzo give it a tinge of "local colour", yet it is intended to be listened to as "absolute" music. Hearers may, if they like, localize the various themes and movements, but it is hoped that this is not a necessary part of the music. There are four movements: The first begins with a slow prelude; this leads to a vigorous allegro—which may perhaps suggest the noise and hurry of London, with its always underlying calm. The second (slow) movement has been called "Bloomsbury Square on a November afternoon". This may serve as a clue to the music, but it is not a necessary "explanation" of it. The third movement is a nocturne in form of a Scherzo. If the hearer will imagine himself standing on Westminster Embankment at night, surrounded by the distant sounds of the Strand, with its great hotels on one side, and the "New Cut" on the other, with its crowded streets and flaring lights, it may serve as a mood in which to listen to this movement. The last movement consists of an agitated theme in three-time, alternating with a march movement, at first solemn and later on energetic.[1] At the end of the finale comes a suggestion of the noise and fever of the first movement—this time much subdued—then the "Westminster Chimes" are heard once more: on this follows an "Epilogue" in which the slow prelude is developed into a movement of some length. The Symphony was finished in 1913, and first performed on March 27, 1914, under the direction of Mr. Geoffrey Toye.'

Whereabouts of MS.: Reconstructed 1913 full score, in four handwritings, British Library (Add. MSS. 51317A–D). B.L. also has sketches (50367) and pianoforte scores (50368). 2-piano arrangement of Scherzo, part for piano II, copy (57287).

6. INCIDENTAL MUSIC TO MAETERLINCK'S 'THE DEATH OF TINTAGILES'. Unpublished. MS., not in composer's writing, in

---

[1] A descriptive programme of the Symphony by Albert Coates, written in 1920, speaks of 'the hunger-march' at this point. The note was said to have been written with the composer's agreement, and geographically it certainly agrees with R.V.W.'s amplified note.

possession of Basil Ashmore, Esq. Performed in June 1913. The music was used for a B.B.C. broadcast of the play on 30 August 1975 (B.B.C. Welsh Symphony Orchestra, conducted by Rae Jenkins).

There also exists an MS. short score of incidental music to *The Blue Bird* to illustrate the following episodes:

Moderato, 49 bars: Tytyl turns the diamond. *2 bars:* The clock prepares to strike. *26 bars:* The clock strikes *12*; at each stroke a girl comes out of the clock. *16 bars:* Dance of the hours (each girl has a bell. 4 girls stand and strike 4 bells while the rest dance). *8 bars:* 4 other girls strike their bells while the rest dance. *8 bars:* 4 more girls strike their bells while the rest dance. *24 bars:* The 12 hours dance together, striking their bells every 4 bars. *7 bars:* The loaves come out of the bread pan. *21 bars:* Loaves dance. *33 bars:* The loaves and hours dance together. *8 bars:* Fire springs out of the chimney. *55 bars:* Fire dance (waltz). *8 bars:* The sink begins to glow (violin solo). *15 bars:* The water tap begins to sing. *47 bars:* Water begins to dance. *102 bars:* Fight between Fire and Water. *28 bars:* General dance. *2 bars:* 'They rush to their "homes".' *21 bars:* The three knocks. *4 bars:* 'Very long pauses between dialogue.' *26 bars:* The window opens and they go out.

7. INCIDENTAL MUSIC TO 'THE MERRY WIVES OF WINDSOR'. Written in 1913 for F. R. Benson's Shakespearean season at Stratford-upon-Avon. A page of MS score, *molto moderato*, for flute, oboe, clarinet, horn, cornet, timpani and strings is all that survives of this music. It is identifiable by V.W.'s notes in blue pencil on the bottom of the page:

'*Pp* to commence at cue "no man their works must eye". [*Merry Wives*, Act V, Sc. V, Falstaff: "They are fairies; he that speaks to them shall die. I'll wink and couch: no man their works must eye."] *f* and *allegro* at cue " 'tis one o'clock". STOP [Mrs. Quickly: "Away, disperse: but till 'tis one o'clock our dance of custom round about the oak of Herne the hunter, let us not forget."] No. 6 cue "pinch him to your time". See book.' [Mrs. Quickly: 'About him, fairies; sing a scornful rhyme; and, as you trip, still pinch him to your time.'] It is known that he used the folk song 'Greensleeves' in this music.

Whereabouts of MS.: Fragment mentioned above in private possession.

8. INCIDENTAL MUSIC TO 'KING RICHARD II'. Written in 1913 for F. R. Benson's Shakespearean season at Stratford-upon-Avon.

Instrumentation: 1 piccolo, 1 flute, 1 oboe, 1 clarinet, 1 horn, 1 cornet, 1 trombone, percussion, strings.

Contains 32 numbers, most of which are fanfares or entrance-music. Of the 10 more substantial items, three are 'composed': (1) A march for Richard's entrance; (2) *Agnus Dei*, for soprano and organ, in the style of a Rouen church melody; (3) Prelude to Act V. The remaining seven are arrangements of traditional tunes; these include: (*a*) *Greensleeves* (for the Queen and her suite); (*b*) *Princess Royal* (for Bolingbroke's entry); (*c*) *The Springtime of the Year*, with *Bonny Sweet Robin*; (*d*) *I'll go and 'list*, as a march for Bolingbroke before his coronation ('Lords, prepare yourselves'); (*e*) *Jamaica*, for voice (wordless) and violin, for use in Act V; (*f*) *Exultet caelum laudibus* (*English Hymnal*, 176) for Bolingbroke's triumph; (*g*) Requiem plainsong for Richard's death.

Whereabouts of MS.: Stratford-upon-Avon, Shakespeare Memorial Theatre Library.

9. INCIDENTAL MUSIC TO KING HENRY IV, PART 2. Written in 1913 for F. R. Benson's Shakespearean season at Stratford-upon-Avon. Music composed for following situations:
At the Boar's Head: (*a*) Anonymous *Alman* from Fitzwilliam Virginal Book (14) for the 'Music' (Act II, Scene 4); (*b*) *Half Hannikin*, for the 'merry song'; (*c*) *Princess Royal*, for Prince Hal; (*d*) *Lady in the Dark*, for Doll Tearsheet.
Henry IV's death-bed: Dowland's *Lacrimae* pavan, arranged for strings.
Finale: Arrangement of carol, *Angelus ad Virginem*.
Whereabouts of MS.: Stratford-upon-Avon, Shakespeare Memorial Theatre Library.

10. INCIDENTAL MUSIC TO KING RICHARD III. Written in 1913 for F. R. Benson's Shakespearean season at Stratford-upon-Avon. Surviving music includes Hampshire *Dargason*; the *Requiem* used in *King Richard II*, this time for voices only; a march for Richard's entrance in Act IV, Scene 4; a fanfare—repeat ad lib.— for Richard's defeat at Bosworth, with a B flat—A minor harmonic progression which anticipates later and greater works.
Whereabouts of MS.: Stratford-upon-Avon, Shakespeare Memorial Theatre Library.

11. INCIDENTAL MUSIC TO KING HENRY V. Written in 1913 for F. R. Benson's Shakespearean season at Stratford-upon-Avon. Only two items, numbered 20 and 21, survive. They are the Agincourt Song and a song 'J'aimons les filles' for Act III, Scene 7.
Whereabouts of MS.: Stratford-upon-Avon, Shakespeare Memorial Theatre Library. See 1934 for overture 'Henry V'.

12. INCIDENTAL MUSIC TO 'THE DEVIL'S DISCIPLE' (by George Bernard Shaw). Written in 1913 for F. R. Benson at Stratford-upon-Avon. Music was simply three arrangements: 'The British Grenadiers', the march from *Judas Maccabaeus*, and a verse of 'Yankee Doodle'.

Whereabouts of MS.: Stratford-upon-Avon, Shakespeare Memorial Theatre Library.

1914

1. BOY JOHNNY AND IF I WERE A QUEEN. Songs for voice and pianoforte. Words by Christina Rossetti.
    I. Boy Johnny. *Andante con moto.* E modal minor.
    II. If I were a Queen. *Allegretto grazioso.* E major.
    Publication: London and New York, Boosey & Co. Ltd. (H.8416.) Reissue of songs composed in 1902 (q.v.).

Several works were written or partially written in 1914 which did not attain performance until after the Great War, among them *Hugh the Drover, The Lark Ascending* and the Four Hymns. Only the Four Hymns can be included accurately within 1914: they were in proof in July 1914, and were to have been sung at that year's Worcester meeting of the Three Choirs. The other works were probably revised and are therefore included as post-war works.

2. FOUR HYMNS. For tenor voice, with accompaniment of pianoforte and viola obbligato, or string orchestra and viola obbligato.
    I. Lord! Come Away. *Maestoso.* D minor. Text: Bishop Jeremy Taylor (1613–67). In 'The second hymn for Advent', or 'Christ's coming to Jerusalem in triumph' from the Festival hymns in *The Golden Grove* (Oxford, 1839), p. 207.
    II. Who is this fair one? *Andante moderato.* F minor. Text: Isaac Watts (1674–1748). From *Hymns and Spiritual Songs*, 1707–9; Hymns 449 and 450 in *Praise to the Triune God* (London, 1852).
    III. Come love, come Lord. *Lento.* G minor. Text: Richard Crashaw (1612?–49). From 'The hymn of St. Thomas, in adoration of the Blessed Sacrament, adoro te'. Last verse, p. 81, 1.51 in *The Religious Poems of Richard Crashaw.* (London, 1914.)
    IV. Evening hymn. *Andante con moto.* E major. Text: 'O gladsome light', translated from the Greek by Robert Bridges (1844–1930).
    First performance: Cardiff, 26 May 1920. Steuart Wilson (tenor), Alfred Hobday (viola), London Symphony Orchestra, conducted by Julius Harrison. First performance in London: Aeolian Hall, 19 October 1920. Steuart Wilson (tenor), A. Hobday (viola), Chamber Orchestra (leader W. H. Reed), conducted by Dr. R. Vaughan Williams.
    Publication: London, New York, etc. (© 1920) Boosey & Co. F.S. Viola part separate. Parts for string orchestra available on hire.
    Dedication: To J.S.W. [Sir Steuart Wilson.]
    Duration: 15 minutes.

Note: A version of the accompaniment for pianoforte quintet was played at the Aeolian Hall, London, on 27 March 1925, by the Snow Quartet with Anthony Bernard (piano).

SKETCH-BOOKS AND FRAGMENTS OF MS. Vaughan Williams did not date his sketch-books, and some obviously cover a wide span of years. He used them to work out a particular passage and would mark his often illegible notation 'better version of . . .' or 'Last line of . . .' Here is a list of his sketches up to 1914. It does not include the many books of *A Sea Symphony*:

(*A*) 1. Last verse and verse 1, with notes for 2nd verse and 3rd verse of setting of Charles Wesley's 'Come O thou traveller unknown': This never materialized.

    2. 'The Call—G. Herbert.' 3 verses.

    3. 'Analysis of fugue at end of Glazunov.' This is the fugue from the Sixth Symphony, which was first played in England at a Philharmonic Society concert conducted by Frederic Cowen on 19 May 1904.

    4. Clun song—last verse.

    5. Chorus parts of 'Rise heart'. This sketch-book is in British Library (57294C).

(*B*) MS. of 'Saraband—Helen'. Setting of Christopher Marlowe's 'Was this the face that launched a thousand ships?' for tenor solo, SATB chorus, and orchestra. British Library has sketches of this work (50455). Full MS. in private possession.

1915

1. 'SONGTIME', a book of rhymes, songs, games, hymns, and other music for all occasions in a child's life, edited by Percy Dearmer and Martin Shaw, London, J. Curwen & Sons, 1915.
Included were:

    (*a*) *An Acre of Land*, 'noted by R. Vaughan Williams from Mr Frank Bailey of Coombe Bisset, 1904', set for unison voices and piano by M. Shaw.

    (*b*) *Quem pastores*, melody from a 15th-century German MS., arranged by R. Vaughan Williams, to words by P. Dearmer, 'Jesu, good above all others'. See 1928, *The Oxford Book of Carols*, carol no.79.

    (*c*) Hymns, 595 (East Horndon), 599 (Shipston) and 606 (St Hugh) from *The English Hymnal*.

1917

1. SELECTION OF COLLECTED FOLK SONGS, Vol. 1 (36 songs). Arranged for voice and pianoforte by Cecil J. Sharp and R. Vaughan

Williams. Songs arranged by R. Vaughan Williams (copyright date in parentheses):

8. Down by the riverside. (© 1912.) *Andante con moto.* G major. (Collected by H. E. D. Hammond.)
9. Farmyard Song. (© 1912.) *Allegretto.* G major. (Ditto.)
12. I will give my love an apple. (© 1912.) *Andantino.* A modal minor. (Ditto.)
15. My boy Billy. (© 1912.) *Allegretto.* G major. (Collected by R.V.W.)
22. The Carter. (© 1912.) *Allegro moderato.* G modal minor. (Ditto.)
25. The female Highwayman. (© 1912.) *Andante.* E major. (Ditto.)
26. The fox. (© 1912.) *Allegro.* E modal minor. (Collected by H.E.D.H.)
31. The painful plough. (© 1912.) *Allegretto grazioso.* E flat major. (Collected by R.V.W.)

(This collection is undated, copyrights ranging from 1908–13. It may have appeared in 1914 or its preparation may have been delayed by the war. Its date of receipt at the British Museum is 9 August 1917, and therefore this date has been accepted.)

Publication: London, Novello & Co. Ltd.; N.Y., The H. W. Gray Co.

1919

1. MOTHERLAND SONG BOOK, I. Official publication of the League of Arts for National and Civic Ceremony. Songs for unison and mixed voices. Harmonization by R.V.W.:
   13. O God of earth and altar. D minor. English traditional melody. Words by G. K. Chesterton. (*English Hymnal*, No. 562.)
   Publication: London, Stainer & Bell Ltd. (S. & B. 1971.)
2. MOTHERLAND SONG BOOK, II, Part 1. Sea songs for unison and mixed voices arranged by Martin and Geoffrey Shaw. Edited by R. Vaughan Williams. All published separately.
   Publication: London, Stainer & Bell Ltd. (© 1919.) (S. & B. 1987.)
3. MOTHERLAND SONG BOOK, III. Sea songs for unison and mixed voices, selected and arranged by R. Vaughan Williams and others. All published separately. Arrangements by R.V.W.:
   1. The Arethusa. *Allegro risoluto.* D minor. Words by Prince Hoare (1755–1834). Adapted from a traditional melody by W. Shield. (© U.S.A. 1919.) (S. & B. 2116.)
   5. Full fathom five. *Andante.* C major. Words by William Shakespeare (1564–1616) from *The Tempest*, Act I, Sc. ii. Music by Henry Purcell. (© U.S.A. 1919.) (S. & B. 2117.)
   6. Jack the sailor. *Allegretto.* D major. Folk song for male voices (TTBB) with or without accompaniment. (© R.V.W. 1919; © U.S.A.

1919 S. & B.) (S. & B. 2120.)

8. We be three poor mariners. *Allegro moderato.* E flat major. Old English song arranged for mixed voices and for three male voices (TTB) unaccompanied. (© U.S.A. 1919.) (S. & B. 2123.)
Publication: London, Stainer & Bell Ltd.

4. MOTHERLAND SONG BOOK, IV. Sea songs for unison and mixed voices. Selected and arranged by R. Vaughan Williams and others. All published separately. Arrangements by R.V.W.:
1. The Golden Vanity. *Allegro moderato.* C major. Folk song. (© U.S.A. 1919.) (S. & B. 2118.)
3. Just as the tide was flowing. *Allegretto.* G major. Folk song. (© U.S.A. 1919.) (S. & B. 2121.)
9. The Spanish Ladies. *Allegro risoluto.* A modal minor. Folk song. (© 1912 Boosey & Co.)
Publication: London, Stainer & Bell Ltd.

5. EIGHT TRADITIONAL ENGLISH CAROLS. Arranged for voice and pianoforte. An unaccompanied version of each carol is included for mixed choir (SATB).
1. And all in the morning. (On Christmas Day.) (Derbyshire.) *Maestoso.* A modal minor. Collected by R.V.W. Castleton, 1908.
2. On Christmas Night. (Sussex.) *Allegretto grazioso.* G major. Collected by R.V.W. Monk's Gate, 1904.
3. The Twelve Apostles. (Staffordshire.) *Andante.* G modal minor.
4. Down in yon forest. (Derbyshire.) *Andantino.* A modal minor. Collected by R.V.W. Castleton, 1908.
5. May-day Carol. (Cambridgeshire.) *Larghetto.* E modal minor. Collected by R.V.W. Fowlmere, 1907.
6. The truth sent from above. (Herefordshire.) *Andante sostenuto.* G modal minor. Collected by R.V.W. King's Pyon, 1909.
7. The birth of the Saviour. (Derbyshire.) *Largo.* G modal minor.
8. The Wassail Song. (Yorkshire.) *Allegro.* E modal minor. Unison only.
Publication: London, Stainer & Bell Ltd.
Other versions of these carols are listed here for convenience:
2. On Christmas Night.
 (*a*) Voices in unison as No. 24 in *Oxford Book of Carols* (1928). Another tune is O.B.C. Appendix (No. 2).
 (*b*) Arranged for women's voices (SSAA) in A major, unaccompanied, by E. Harold Geer. Stainer and Bell Church Choir Library, No. 337. (©. 1928.) (S. & B. 3900.)
 (*c*) Tune included in *Fantasia on Christmas Carols* (1912)
4. Down in yon forest.
 (*a*) For soloist and choir in *Oxford Book of Carols*, No. 61.

(*b*) Rearranged for women's voices (solo S, SSAA) with pianoforte accompaniment and unaccompanied, by E. Harold Geer. Stainer and Bell Church Choir Library, No. 338. (© 1928.) (S. & B. 3901.)

5. May-day Carol.

(*a*) Unison setting, with version for unaccompanied singing, in *Oxford Book of Carols*, as No. 47.

6. The truth sent from above.

(*a*) Unison setting, with version for unaccompanied singing, in *Oxford Book of Carols*, as No. 68.

(*b*) Tune included in *Fantasia on Christmas Carols* (1912).

6. THE TURTLE DOVE. Folk song collected and arranged for male voices, with pianoforte accompaniment ad libitum. Solo part for tenors and baritones. Chorus TBB. *Andante sostenuto.* B flat modal minor.

Publication: J. Curwen & Sons Ltd. (© 1919.) (C.E.50570.)

Other versions:

(*a*) Mixed voices (SSATB) with baritone solo. Unaccompanied. *Andante sostenuto.* B flat modal minor. J. Curwen & Sons Ltd. (© 1924.) (C.E.61175.) Also available in tonic solfa.

(*b*) Unison with pianoforte accompaniment. *Andante moderato.* B flat modal minor. J. Curwen & Sons Ltd. (© U.S.A. 1934 R.V.W.) (C.E.71872.) This 1934 version also available with orchestra (material available on hire). *Instrumentation:* 1 flute, 1 clarinet, 2 horns, harp, strings.

1920

1. THREE PRELUDES, founded on Welsh hymn tunes. For organ.

    1. BRYN CALFARIA (Melody by W. Owen, 1814–93). *Maestoso.* G modal minor.

    2. RHOSYMEDRE (or 'Lovely') (Melody by J. D. Edwards, 1805–85). *Andantino.* G major.

    3. HYFRYDOL (Melody by R. H. Prichard, 1811–87). *Moderato maestoso.* C major.

Dedication: To Alan Gray.

Duration: 8½ minutes.

Publication: London, Stainer & Bell Ltd. (© U.S.A. 1920.) (S. & B. 2155.)

Other versions:

(*a*) Orchestral version of (2) and (3) by Arnold Foster.

    (2) *Andantino.* G major.

        Instrumentation: 2 flutes, 1 oboe, 2 clarinets, 2 bassoons, 2 horns, 1 trumpet, strings; or strings only, or by flute, strings and any of above wind instruments.

Duration: 4 minutes.
Publication: London, Stainer & Bell Ltd. (© 1938.) (S. & B. 4850.)

(3) *Moderato maestoso.* C major.
Instrumentation: 2 flutes, 2 oboes, 2 clarinets, 2 bassoons, 2 horns, 2 trumpets, timpani, strings; or strings only.
Duration: 3 minutes.
Publication: London, Stainer & Bell Ltd. (© 1951.) (S. & B. 5292.)

(*b*) Arrangement of (1), (2) and (3) for two pianofortes, by Leslie Russell, 1939.
Publication: London, Stainer & Bell Ltd. (© 1939.) (S. & B. 4938.)

2. O CLAP YOUR HANDS. Motet for mixed chorus (SATB) and organ. Text from Psalm 47, with marginal version of v.7. *Allegro.* B flat major.
Publication: London, Stainer & Bell Ltd. (© U.S.A. 1920.) Stainer and Bell's Church Choir Library, No. 222. (S. & B. 2222.)
Other version: With orchestral accompaniment (parts available on hire).
Instrumentation: 3 trumpets, 3 trombones, tuba (ad lib.), timpani, cymbals (ad lib.), and organ.
Whereabouts of MS.: Full score. British Library (52601 & 50442).

3. OUR LOVE GOES OUT TO ENGLISH SKIES. Patriotic Song, adapted from a march in *The Indian Queen* by Henry Purcell, for unison or mixed choir (SATB) with accompaniment; and for mixed chorus or male chorus unaccompanied. Words by Harold Child.
Moderato, alla marcia. G major (accompanied); A major (SATB); B flat major (TTBB).
Publication: London, Stainer & Bell Ltd. (© U.S.A. 1920.) Stainer and Bell's Choral Library, No. 163. (S. & B. 2029.)
Other version: Unison voices, with accompaniment for strings, 1924. *Moderato alla marcia.* G major.
Publication: London, Stainer & Bell Ltd. (© 1924.) (S. & B. 2898.)

4. TWELVE TRADITIONAL CAROLS FROM HEREFORD-SHIRE. Collected, edited and arranged for voice and pianoforte, or to be sung unaccompanied (SATB) by Mrs. E. M. Leather and R. Vaughan Williams.

1. The Holy Well (1st version). *Allegretto.* F major (unaccompanied, G major).
2. The Holy Well (2nd version). *Moderato.* A modal minor.
3. Christmas now is drawing near at hand. *Lento moderato.* E major. (unaccompanied, F major).
4. Joseph and Mary (to the tune 'There is a fountain'). *Andante.* A modal minor (unaccompanied, B flat modal minor).

5. The Angel Gabriel. *Allegretto*. G major (unaccompanied, A major).
6. God rest you merry, gentlemen. *Andante*. E flat major (unaccompanied, F major).
7. New Year's Carol. *Andante con moto*. G major.
8. On Christmas Day (All in the morning). *Lento*. G modal minor (unaccompanied, A modal minor).
9. Dives and Lazarus. *Andante moderato*. F major (unaccompanied, G major). MS. in British Library (58372K).
10. The miraculous harvest (or The carnal and the crane). *Andante moderato*. A modal minor.
11. The Saviour's Love. *Andante non troppo*. G major.
12. The Seven Virgins (or Under the leaves). *Andantino*. G modal minor.

Publication: London, Stainer & Bell Ltd. (© U.S.A. 1920.) (S. & B. 2042.)

Note on score: 'These carols were collected in the neighbourhood of Weobley in Herefordshire and appeared in their original form in the *Journal of the Folk Song Society*, Vols. II and IV. Corruptions of texts have been emended, and missing lines and verses supplied from other sources.' Most of the carols were collected in September 1912, and September 1913.

Other versions:

(*a*) All 12 are available for unison singing with accompaniment, and as separate leaflets.
(*b*) 1. and 2. The Holy Well. Harmonization in the *Oxford Book of Carols* by R.V.W. as Appendix No. 4 and by Elizabeth Maconchy as No. 56.

    4. Joseph and Mary. Setting for tenors only, other voices to vocalize, in *Oxford Book of Carols* as No. 115. The words 'There is a fountain', to which Mrs. Esther Smith sang this tune at Weobley were discarded as probably untraditional. See *Journal of the Folk Song Society*, ii, 133, and iv, 21.

    6. God rest you merry. Arranged for tenor, baritone or bass, unaccompanied, and male voices (TTBB), unaccompanied, as one of Nine Carols for Male Voices (O.U.P., Oxford Choral Song, No. 665). *Allegro*. F minor.
    Publication: London, Oxford University Press (© 1942).

    9. Dives and Lazarus.
        (*a*) Unison setting in *Oxford Book of Carols* as No. 57. Variant of tune, with harmonies from No. 601 of *English Hymnal*, in *O.B.C.* Appendix No. 5.
        (*b*) Arranged for tenor, baritone or bass, unaccompanied, and male voices (TTBB) unaccompanied, as one of a set of Nine

Carols for Male Voices (O.U.P.Oxford Choral Song, No. 673).

Publication: London, Oxford University Press (© 1942).

10. The miraculous harvest.
   (*a*) Unison setting in *Oxford Book of Carols* as No. 53.
   (*b*) Separate publication (1928) of (*a*).
12. The Seven Virgins. Unison setting in *Oxford Book of Carols* as No. 43.

5. THE LARK ASCENDING. Romance for violin and orchestra.
Andante sostenuto—Allegretto tranquillo (quasi andante).
Instrumentation: Solo violin, 2 flutes, 1 oboe, 2 clarinets, 2 bassoons, 2 horns, triangle, strings. Also scored for Chamber Orchestra thus: Solo violin, 1 flute, 1 oboe, 1 clarinet, 1 bassoon, 1 horn, 1 triangle, 3 (or 4) first violins, 3 (or 4) 2nd violins, 2 violas, 2 celli, 1 double bass. When performed in this way, players must 'play in' all cues in small notes and those enclosed in brackets marked Ch.O.
First performance: Shirehampton, Public Hall, at a concert of the Avonmouth and Shirehampton Choral Society, 15 December 1920, in special arrangement for violin and pianoforte made by the composer for the occasion, by Marie Hall (violin) and Geoffrey Mendham (pianoforte). First performance in London, in orchestral version: Queen's Hall, Concert of second Congress of British Music Society, 14 June 1921. British Symphony Orchestra, conducted by Adrian Boult; Soloist, Marie Hall.
Dedication: To Marie Hall.
Duration: 13 minutes.
Publication: Full score, London, Oxford University Press, 1926 (© 1925); miniature score © 1925, published 1927. Material on hire.
Other version: Arrangement for violin and pianoforte, London, O.U.P. 1926 (© 1926).
Note: Although this work was written in 1914, it was revised in 1920 and has therefore been included as a post-war work. It was again revised before publication of the full score. The music is prefaced by an extract from 'The Lark Ascending' by George Meredith (1828–1909):

He rises and begins to round,
He drops the silver chain of sound,
Of many links without a break,
In chirrup, whistle, slur and shake

. . . . . .

For singing till his heaven fills,
'Tis love of earth that he instils,
And ever winging up and up,

Our valley is his golden cup,
And he the wine which overflows
To lift us with him as he goes.

. . . . . .

Till lost on his aerial rings
In light, and then the fancy sings.

Revisions: On the manuscript of the violin and pianoforte score the composer originally quoted four extra lines of Meredith's poem as a third stanza. They were:

He is the dance of children, thanks
Of sowers, shout of primrose banks
And eyes of violets while they breathe;
All these the circling song will wreathe. . . .

This score, all of it in the composer's hand, shows that at one point he altered the initial tempo to Lento, but reverted to Andante sostenuto when the work was published. The violin part was elaborated from six bars after H to K. Two bars before L were deleted, and there was extensive re-writing from two before N until two after U with 11 bars before T deleted before publication. Seven bars after what is now five before W were deleted and the violin's final cadenza was considerably rewritten, mainly to make it simpler for the soloist. None of the cuts is important; all were directed, as was invariably the case, towards tautening the structure.

Whereabouts of MS.: Original MS. of violin and pianoforte arrangement in British Library (52385). Original full score must be presumed to be lost.

6. SUITE OF SIX SHORT PIECES FOR PIANOFORTE.

1. Prelude. *Molto moderato (quasi lento).* G major.
2. Slow dance. *Andante grazioso.* E modal minor.
3. Quick dance. *Allegro molto.* E modal minor.
4. Slow Air. *Lento.* G modal minor.
5. Rondo. *Andante con moto.* D modal minor.
6. Pezzo ostinato. *Allegretto.* G major.

Duration: 12 minutes.

Publication: London, Stainer & Bell Ltd. (© U.S.A. 1921.) (S. & B. 2031.) This work was published in January 1921, and must therefore have been composed in 1920 or earlier.

Other version: Arranged for string orchestra as THE CHARTER-HOUSE SUITE and scored (in collaboration with the composer), edited, fingered and bowed by James Brown, Editor of the Polychordia String Library. Movement titles and keys unchanged.

Publication: London, Stainer & Bell Ltd., 1923. (© U.S.A. 1923). Score includes a pianoforte part which is not meant to be played at a performance by full orchestra. (S. & B. 2599.) (Polychordia String Library, No. 204.)

7. SUITE DE BALLET. For flute and pianoforte.

 I. Improvisation.

 II. Humoresque—*presto.*

 III. Gavotte—*quasi lento.*

 IV. Passepied—*allegro vivacissimo.*

First performance: London, home of Mrs. Hammersley at 62 Cadogan Place, 20 March 1920. Louis Fleury (flute), First public performance: B.B.C. Home Service, 9 April 1962. Geoffrey Gilbert (flute), Frederick Stone (pianoforte).

Duration: 7 minutes.

Publication: London, Oxford University Press, 1961, in edition by Roy Douglas.

Note: This work was found among the composer's manuscripts after his death. It was complete except for some tempo and expression marks, which have been supplied by Mr. Douglas. I think that it was one of the works, like *The Lark Ascending,* held over from 1914 to 1919. It was almost certainly sketched in 1913 for the great French flautist Louis Fleury, whom Vaughan Williams had met at Stratford and in Paris in that year. A work for a solo instrument was usually written with a particular performer in mind. The manuscript book in which sketches for the suite occur is marked 'Herefordshire Folk Songs'. This again indicates 1913; although sketch-books are an unsure guide (Vaughan Williams would return to one after many years) this clue, combined with Fleury, seems convincing. The content of the music shows that Vaughan Williams was developing towards the bi-tonality of *The Shepherds of the Delectable Mountains,* a development plainly to be traced in the early Nocturnes and the Four Hymns, all pre-1914 works.

1921

1. LEAGUE OF NATIONS SONG BOOK. Official publication of the League of Arts, Vol. V. Words edited by the Rev. Percy Dearmer, music edited by Martin Shaw. Contains 2 hymns arranged by Vaughan Williams:

 No. 5. Pilgrim Song (Monk's Gate). E flat major. (Adapted from an English traditional melody, *English Hymnal* No. 402.)

 No. 8. Chesterton's Hymn (King's Lynn). D modal minor. (English traditional melody, E.H. No. 562.)

 Publication: London, Stainer & Bell Ltd. (S. & B. 2297.)

2. LORD, THOU HAST BEEN OUR REFUGE. Motet for chorus (SATB), semi-chorus (SATB) and orchestra (or organ). *Lento moderato.* D minor—major.

Instrumentation: 2 flutes, 2 oboes, 2 clarinets, 2 bassoons, 4 horns, 2 trumpets, 3 trombones, tuba, timpani, organ, strings. *Or* strings and organ.

Duration: 7 minutes.

Publication: London, J. Curwen & Sons Ltd. (© 1921.) Vocal score (C.E.80592). Orchestral parts available on hire.

Note: Text is taken from Psalm 90. The motet has as a kind of descant the hymn-tune 'O God our help in ages past' (St. Anne).

Whereabouts of MS.: British Library (52620).

3. HYMNS. Selected from the *English Hymnal* as suitable for occasional use, and in congregational practices in singing. Contains 24 hymns with accompaniments including two by Vaughan Williams:

No. 402. Monk's Gate. (He who would valiant be). Arranged R.V.W.

No. 641. Sine Nomine. (For all the Saints.) Set by R.V.W.

Publication: London, Oxford University Press, 1921.

4. FOR ALL THE SAINTS. Processional hymn ('Sine Nomine'). Words and staff notation from *English Hymnal* No. 641, arranged for unison singing and for SATB. Text by Bishop W. W. How (1823–97), 'Funeral Hymn'.

Publication: London, Oxford University Press, for the Church Music Society, 1921.

Other versions of this hymn:

(*a*) For unison congregational use in the *English Hymnal* (1906 and 1933) as No. 641.

(*b*) For unison congregational use in *Songs of Praise* as No. 110 in 1925 edition and No. 202 in Enlarged Edition of 1931.

(*c*) As No. 79 in *Hymns for To-day, Missionary and Devotional.* Published, 1930, by The Psalms and Hymns Trust.

(*d*) For unison congregational use in *Hymns Selected from the English Hymnal.* London, O.U.P. 1921, enlarged edition 1932.

(*e*) For unison congregational use in *Songs of Praise for Children* (edited Percy Dearmer, Martin Shaw, R. Vaughan Williams, G. W. Briggs), as No. 87. *Published*, 1933, by Oxford University Press, full music edition.

(*f*) For unison congregational use in *The Daily Service, Prayers and Hymns for Schools* (editors: Prayers, G. W. Briggs; Hymns, Percy Dearmer, R. Vaughan Williams, Martin Shaw, G. W. Briggs) as No. 97. *Published*, 1936, by Oxford University Press (two later editions 1938, with supp. 1939).

(*g*) As in (*e*) in *Songs of Praise: The Children's Church*, O.U.P. 1936. Editors as in (*f*).

(*h*) For unison congregational singing in *Tunes Selected from Songs of Praise* (edited by R. Vaughan Williams and Martin Shaw) as

No. 27. *Published*, London, Oxford University Press, 1943.

(*j*) Arranged by Dr. Henry G. Ley as an anthem for saints' days, for congregation, SATB choir and organ or orchestra. *Instrumentation* (arr. W. V. Todd): 2 flutes, 2 oboes, 2 clarinets, 2 bassoons, 4 horns, 2 trumpets, 3 trombones, tuba, percussion, organ, strings. *Publication:* London, Oxford University Press (© 1948). Material available on hire. The congregational part to this setting was published in 1949 (© 1949).

(*k*) Freely arranged for voices (SAB) and organ by Sir Ernest Bullock, Oxford Easy Anthems, E.79. O.U.P. © 1957.

5. THE LASS THAT LOVES A SAILOR. Words and music by Charles Dibdin (1745–1814). Edited and arranged for unison or SATB (with soprano solo) with pianoforte accompaniment. Text from *The Round Robin. Moderato.* F major.
Publication: London, Stainer & Bell Ltd. (© U.S.A. 1921.) Stainer and Bell's Choral Library, No. 167 (S. & B. 2075).

6. THE MERMAID. Old Song, arranged for SATB (with soprano solo), unaccompanied, or unison with pianoforte accompaniment. *Poco allegro.* E flat major.
Publication: London, Stainer & Bell Ltd. (© U.S.A. 1921.) Stainer and Bell's Choral Library, No. 168. (S. & B. 2076.)

7. HEART OF OAK. Tune by William Boyce (1710–79) from *Harlequin's Invasion*, 1759, arranged for unison singing with pianoforte accompaniment, for male voices (TTB) unaccompanied, and for SATB (with soprano solo) and pianoforte accompaniment. *Moderato maestoso.* B flat major (unison); C major (TTB).
Publication: London, Stainer & Bell Ltd. (© U.S.A. 1921.) Stainer and Bell's Choral Library, No. 169 (S. & B. 2077).

8. THE FARMER'S BOY. Old English air, arranged for male voices (TTBB), unaccompanied. *Moderato risoluto.* B flat major.
Publication: London, Stainer & Bell Ltd. (© U.S.A. 1921.) Stainer and Bell's Male Voice Choir Library, No. 78 (S. & B. 2078).
Other versions:

(*a*) Tonic solfa edition for male voices (TBB) with Welsh words only. Yr Hogyn Gyrru'r Wedd. (Translated by C. Davies.) Stainer and Bell's Male Voice Choir Library, No. 78a. (© 1938.) (S. & B. 4849.)

(*b*) Original version reprinted 1942 in *News Chronicle* Music Competition for H.M. Forces. Words and music of the prescribed part-songs in the choral classes—Class II. Male Voice Choirs. London: The News Chronicle Publications Department.

9. LOCH LOMOND. Scottish air, arranged for male voices (TTBB) with baritone solo, unaccompanied. *Slow.* G major.

Publication: London, Stainer & Bell Ltd. (© U.S.A. 1921.) Stainer and Bell's Male Voice Choir Library, No. 79 (S. & B. 2079). *Other version:* Arranged for mixed voices (SSATB) unaccompanied. *Slow.* G major. *Publication:* London, Stainer & Bell Ltd. (© 1931.) Stainer and Bell's Choral Library, No. 262 (S. & B. 4198). Tonic solfa transcription by H. J. Timothy also available.

10. OLD FOLKS AT HOME. Melody by Stephen Foster (1826–64). Arranged for male voices (TTBB) with baritone solo. (A collection of the harmonies often improvised by members of the British Expeditionary Force.) *Slow.* D major.
    Publication: London, Stainer & Bell Ltd. (© U.S.A. 1921.) Stainer and Bell's Male Voice Choir Library, No. 80. (S. & B. 2080.)

11. MERCILESS BEAUTY. Three rondels for high voice, with accompaniment for string trio (2 violins, 1 violoncello) or pianoforte. Words attributed to Geoffrey Chaucer (1340?–1400); but in the O.U.P. edition of *The Complete Works of Geoffrey Chaucer*, edited by F. N. Robinson, they are in the section 'Poems of doubtful authorship'.
    1. Your eyën two. *Andante con moto.* G minor.
    2. So hath your beauty. *Lento moderato.* D minor.
    3. Since I from love. *Allegro.* A major.
    First performance: London, Aeolian Hall, 4 October 1921. Steuart Wilson (tenor), Dorothy Longman and Kitty Farrer (violins), Valentine Orde (cello).
    Duration: 7 minutes.
    Publication: London, J. Curwen & Sons Ltd. (© 1922.) (C.E. 2953.) Faber Music, piano score with parts (C.02953).

12. FANFARE (18 bars). 'So he passed over, and all the trumpets sounded for him on the other side.' For double chorus of women's voices (SA), trumpets, cello, double bass, and bells.
    Publication: London, Goodwin & Tabb Ltd. in *Fanfare*, a musical causerie issued on the 1st and 15th of every month. Vol. I, No 4, p. 70. 15 November 1921.

Note: This fanfare appears almost unaltered in *The Shepherds of the Delectable Mountains*, full score, p. 31–3 at (27).

13. A PASTORAL SYMPHONY. For full orchestra, with soprano (or tenor) voice, in four movements:
    I. *Molto moderato.*
    II. *Lento moderato.* (Originally *Andantino.*)
    III. *Moderato pesante.*
    IV. *Lento.*
    Instrumentation: 3 flutes (3rd to play piccolo), 2 oboes, cor anglais, 3 clarinets (3rd to play bass clarinet), 2 bassoons, 4 horns, 3 trumpets,

3 trombones, bass tuba, timpani, percussion (side drum, triangle, bass drum, cymbals, glockenspiel), harp, celesta, strings, soprano or tenor voice. By playing the cues in the parts of other instruments the following may be dispensed with: 3rd flute (2nd to play piccolo in Scherzo), 2nd oboe (cor anglais is essential), 3rd clarinet and bass clarinet, 3rd trumpet, celesta, solo voice (clarinet may be substituted). *First performance:* London, Queen's Hall, 26 January 1922, Royal Philharmonic Society concert. Orchestra of the R.P.S. conducted by Adrian Boult. Soprano soloist: Flora Mann. The work had previously been played privately at Friday rehearsals by the Students' orchestra of the Royal College of Music, with Boult conducting and Frederick Thurston playing the clarinet substitution for the solo soprano part. It is worth recording, therefore, that the work's *second* performance was at the R.C.M. on 17 February 1922, conducted by Boult, with Thurston as soloist, and members of the New Queen's Hall Orchestra. *Duration:* 35 minutes.
Publication: London, J. Curwen & Sons Ltd., 1924 (© U.S.A. 1924. R.V.W.). Miniature score, Boosey and Hawkes (16696). Full score and parts on hire from Faber Music.
Composer's programme note (written for the first performance):
The mood of this Symphony is, as its title suggests, almost entirely quiet and contemplative—there are few *fortissimos* and few *allegros*. The only really quick passage is the *Coda* to the third movement, and that is all *pianissimo*.
In form it follows fairly closely the classical pattern, and is in four movements.
I. *Moderato.*—The opening subject is as follows:

This leads to a cadence which is frequently referred to later on—

and is followed by a new figure—

first played by the cor-anglais and taken up by the other instruments, which leads in its turn to a new subject in A minor:

Other tributary figures are:

_and—

After a cadence in A major a solo violin takes up the principal subject and develops it thus:

There is no full re-statement of the principal subject, but Nos. 3 and 4 are recapitulated with slight variations, and the movement ends with a *Coda* founded on No. 1.

II. *Andantino.*—This movement commences with the following theme on the horn:

followed by this passage on the strings—

which leads to a long melodic passage suggested by the opening subject:

There is no definite second subject, but its place is taken by a fanfare-like passage on the trumpet (note the use of the true harmonic 7th, only possible when played on the natural trumpet):

This leads to a resumption of Nos. 8 and 9, and at the end of the movement the two principal subjects are heard in combination (clarinet and horn).

III. *Moderato pesante.* —This movement is of the nature of a slow dance, and is chiefly founded on the following rhythmic figure:

Other subjects in this movement are—

and—

The following is the theme of a kind of *Trio* in quicker time:

After this the opening recurs, followed again by the *Trio*; and the movement ends with a *Coda* (*presto* and *pianissimo*) founded on this subject:

and—

IV. *Lento—Moderato Maestoso.*—This movement starts with this introductory passage, unharmonized except for a drum-roll:

The principal subject is as follows:

given first to the wind, and then taken up by the strings.

The middle section of the movement is founded on the introductory passage (No. 16), after which the principal subject returns in shortened form, and the movement ends as it began, except that the introductory passage (No. 16) is accompanied, not by the drum, but by a high note held by the strings.   R.V.W.

Whereabouts of MS: Full score dated 28 June 1921, and a few sketches in British Library, (50369). Version for 2 pianos (57981).

The composer first began to think about this symphony on active service in France, 1916. The principal subject of the finale was fully sketched in 1920. The famous trumpet passage, now in E flat, was sketched as in C. An early two-piano version of the work is 10 bars shorter at the end of the scherzo. On the full score Vaughan Williams wrote this note at the trumpet cadenza of the slow movement:

'It is important that this passage should be played on a true E flat trumpet (preferably a cavalry trumpet) so that only *natural* notes may be played and that the B flat (7th partial) and D (9th partial) should have their true intonation. This can, of course, be also achieved by playing the passage on an F trumpet with the 1st piston depressed. If neither of these courses is possible the passage must of course be played on a B flat or C trumpet and the pistons used in the ordinary way—but this must only be done in case of necessity.'

The orchestral trumpeter, Ernest Hall, contributed some interesting facts about this trumpet passage to the Vaughan Williams memorial issue of the *R.C.M. Magazine*:[1] 'He [R.V.W.] was anxious to purchase such an instrument [an open E flat trumpet] so that it might always

[1] Vol. LV, No. 1, Easter Term 1959, pp. 34–5.

be available for use when a player was unable to procure one. He eventually acquired one from the late Mr. Frank James. Herbert Barr played it at the first performance. . . . At a later performance (about 1927, at the Leeds Festival)[2] in which I was to play the cadenza, I approached V.W. to ask if I might use the instrument. He very kindly lent it to me. . . . At the Leeds performance, at Sir Thomas Beecham's request, I played off stage away from the orchestra; but the composer did not like it played that way.'

Revision in 1950–1, incorporated in printed score, 1954. First movement: first 3 bars of flute re-written; 4 bars of the 2nd violin, with rests deleted and the part doubling first violin. Fourth movement: a few dynamics added and a slight rearrangement of rests between flute and oboe. The most important change in the scoring was in the third movement, where the first trumpet was added to the first oboe on the latter's first entry and in a similar passage later.

14. A FARMER'S SON SO SWEET. Folk Song arranged for male voices (TBar.B.) with pianoforte accompaniment ad lib. Words and melody from Cecil J. Sharp's *Folk Songs from Somerset.*
Dedication: To the English Singers.
Publication: London, Stainer & Bell Ltd., 1923. (© 1921). Stainer and Bell's Male Voice Choir No. 84. (S. & B. 2099.)
Other version: arranged for mixed voices (SSATBar.B) Stainer and Bell's Choral Library No. 215 (S. & B. 3554).

1922

1. DIRGE FOR FIDELE. Song for two mezzo-sopranos, with pianoforte accompaniment. Words by William Shakespeare. *Cymbeline,* Act IV, Sc. ii. Andante tranquillo. E major. Probably composed 1895.
Publication: London, Edwin Ashdown Ltd. (© 1922) in Edwin Ashdown's series of vocal duets for class singing, 2nd series, No. 90. (E.A.35191.) Arranged for organ in 1928 by Alec Rowley for organ album (Ashdown © 1928) and now published separately.

2. O VOS OMNES ('IS IT NOTHING TO YOU ?') Motet for mixed voices (SSAATTBB) with alto solo, unaccompanied. Words from the Office of Tenebrae for Maundy Thursday. *Andantino* (in free rhythm) C major, minor, A major.
First performance: London, Westminster Cathedral Choir, conducted by Dr. R. R. Terry, 13 April, 1922.
Dedication: To Dr. R. R. Terry.
Publication: London, J. Curwen & Sons Ltd. (© 1922). (C.E.80594.)
English version: 'Is It Nothing to You ?' adapted by Maurice Jacobson (C.E.80787) and published in 1950.

[2] Actually 1928.

Whereabouts of MS.: British Museum, Autograph (52620).

3. IT WAS A LOVER AND HIS LASS. Part Song for two voices, with pianoforte accompaniment. Words by William Shakespeare, *As You Like It*, Act V, Sc. ii. *Allegro piacevole.* E modal minor.
Publication: London, J. Curwen & Sons Ltd. (© 1922) (C.E.71571).
Whereabouts of MS.: British Library (52620).

4. CA' THE YOWES. Scottish folk song arranged for tenor solo and mixed chorus (SATB) unaccompanied. Words by Robert Burns (1759–96) from 'Hark! the Mavis'. *Lento.* B modal minor.
Publication: London, J. Curwen & Sons Ltd. (© 1922) (C.E. 61128).
Other versions:
(*a*) Tonic solfa edition.
(*b*) Transcription for baritone solo and male chorus (TTBB), unaccompanied, by Herbert Pierce. (© 1925 by H. Pierce.)
Lento. A modal minor.
Publication: J. Curwen & Sons Ltd., 1925 (C.E.50626).
Whereabouts of M.S.: British Library (52620).

5. MASS IN G MINOR, for soloists (SATB) and double chorus, unaccompanied (with organ part ad lib.). Probably composed 1920–1.
  I. Kyrie—*slow.*
  II. Gloria in excelsis—*lento—allegro—andante con moto.*
  III. Credo—*allegro con moto—poco tranquillo.*
  IV. Sanctus—*andante con moto.*
        Osanna I—*moderato maestoso.*
        Benedictus—*moderato tranquillo.*
        Osanna II—*moderato maestoso.*
  V. Agnus Dei—*moderato.*
First performance: Birmingham, Town Hall, 6 December 1922, City of Birmingham Choir, conducted by Joseph Lewis. First liturgical performance: London, Westminster Cathedral, 12 March 1923, Choir of Westminster Cathedral conducted by Dr. R. R. Terry. First London concert performance: Queen's Hall, 7 April 1923. Wolverhampton Music Society, conducted by Joseph Lewis.
Dedication: To Gustav Holst and his Whitsuntide Singers.
Duration: 25 minutes.
Publication: London, J. Curwen & Sons Ltd., May 1922. © 1922. (C.E.3642). Copyright in U.S.A., renewed 1950, R. Vaughan Williams. Faber Music (C.03642).
Composer's note on score: 'This Mass is, of course, intended to be sung unaccompanied; the "organ introductions" are only to be used in case of necessity to give the pitch at the start and to restore it if lost during the course of a movement. Organists are particularly asked *not* to modulate from the key to which the chorus may have fallen, during the

course of the movement, back to the true key. An *ad libitum* organ part has been added, which may be used if it is not found practicable to sing the Mass entirely *a capella*. R.V.W.'

Whereabouts of MS: British Library, Vocal Score (50444); organ part sketches (50443).

English Version:

COMMUNION SERVICE IN G MINOR. Adapted by Maurice Jacobson from the Mass in G minor and revised by the composer, with organ part ad lib. as above.

    I. Responses to Commandments (after I to IX and after X).—*Slow*.

    II. Kyrie—*slow*.

    III. Creed—*allegro con moto*.

    IV. Sanctus—*andante con moto*.

    V. Benedictus—*moderato tranquillo*.

    VI. Agnus Dei—*moderato*.

    VII. Gloria in excelsis—*lento*.

Appendix: Hosanna—*moderato maestoso*.

Publication: London, J. Curwen & Sons Ltd. © 1923, renewed 1951. (C.E.3647.)

6. THE SHEPHERDS OF THE DELECTABLE MOUNTAINS. A pastoral episode founded upon *The Pilgrim's Progress* by John Bunyan (1628–88). Set in one act, for six soloists, women's chorus (off stage) and small orchestra.

Instrumentation: 2 flutes, 1 oboe, 1 cor anglais, violins, violas, violoncellos, double basses; (off stage): 2 trumpets, harp, 3 bells. Number of strings not to exceed six first violins, six seconds, four violas, four cellos, and two double basses. Minimum orchestra to be 2 each of 1st and 2nd violins, violas and cellos, 1 double bass, and woodwind.

First performance: London, Royal College of Music, 11 July 1922, with the following cast:

KNOWLEDGE, 1st Shepherd (baritone)   ..   ..   Archibald Winter

WATCHFUL, 2nd Shepherd (tenor)   ..   Leonard A. Willmore

SINCERE, 3rd Shepherd (baritone)   ..   ..   Keith Falkner

PILGRIM (baritone)   ..   ..   Richard B. Kyle

CELESTIAL MESSENGER (tenor)   ..   ..   ..   John K. McKenna

THE VOICE OF A BIRD (soprano) ..   ..   .. Dorcas M. Tomkins

CELESTIAL VOICES: M. Benson, B. M. Carr, K. Davis, O. de Foras, U. Gale, K. Hamilton, M. Haworth, E. Lewis, P. Norton, M. Russell, R. Shepherd, C. Taylor, L. K. Young.

Producer: Humphrey Procter-Gregg, who mounted the opera with Michael H. Wilson. Conductor: Arthur Bliss. The orchestra at the first performance was two each of 1st and 2nd violins, violas and cellos, 1 double bass, 2 flutes, oboe and cor anglais. Off stage were 2 trumpets, tambourine, cymbals, bells and harp. Conductor of the off-stage orchestra was Gordon Jacob.

Duration: 23 minutes.

Publication: Full Score, London, Oxford University Press, © 1925. Vocal Score, with German translation of the text, © 1925. Chorus Score, published 1927. Orchestral parts available on hire.

Note: Although an independent work, this episode is now also incorporated, with the final section omitted, into the morality *The Pilgrim's Progress* (1951) as Act IV, Sc. ii.

1923

1. HIGH GERMANY. Folk Song arranged for male voices, with pianoforte accompaniment ad lib. Solos for tenor and bass. Words and melody from Cecil Sharp's *Folk Songs of England*, Vol. I (Novello & Co.).
   Alla marcia. D modal minor.
   Publication: London, Stainer & Bell Ltd. (© 1923). Stainer and Bell's Male Voice Choir No. 82 (S. & B. 2097).

2. OLD KING COLE. A ballet for orchestra and chorus (ad lib).
   Characters: Old King Cole,* Queen Helena* (his daughter), Lord Chamberlain, Grotesque, Head Cook,* Head Pipe Attendant,* six small cooks, six pipe dancers, 1st fiddler (wild man),* 2nd fiddler (romantic boy),* 3rd fiddler (folk clown),* six wild men, trumpeter,* court singers,* King's attendants, Court Ladies.

   * Do not dance.

   Instrumentation: 3 flutes (3rd ad lib.), 2 oboes (2nd ad lib.), 2 clarinets, 2 bassoons, 4 horns (3rd and 4th ad lib.), 2 trumpets, 2 tenor trombones, 1 bass trombone (ad lib. if tuba is used), tuba, timpani, glockenspiel (ad lib.), triangle, side drum, bass drum, cymbals, celesta (ad lib.), harp, chorus (ad lib.), strings.

   First performance: Cambridge (Festival of British Music inaugurated by the University Musical Society), 5 June 1923, in Nevile's Court, Trinity College. Arranged, produced and danced by members of the Cambridge Branch of the English Folk Dance Society and conducted by Bernhard Ord. Among those who played leading parts were:

KING COLE	Professor Sir Melvill Jones
QUEEN HELENA	Mrs. Edward Vulliamy
HEAD COOK ..	Rev. H. Burnaby, Dean of Emmanuel College
1ST FIDDLER	T. H. Marshall, Fellow of Trinity
(afterwards a professor at London School of Economics)	
2ND FIDDLER	Elsie Avril
3RD FIDDLER	Arthur Morris

PRODUCER .. John Burnaby (later Regius Professor of Divinity)
Scenario: Devised by Mrs. Vulliamy, in association with Dr. Vaughan Williams.

King Cole, of Colchester, defended his independence against the Romans. He was a patron of the arts and his daughter Helena was the most accomplished musician of her age. She married Constantius, the Roman General, became Empress and was the mother of Constantine the Great. At the time of the ballet she is visiting her father, who provides an evening's entertainment for her. She has brought him a present from his son-in-law, her husband, a wonderful new oriental pipe. It is brought on, the pipe is lit and the tube is uncoiled. The King likes it, but something goes wrong and he casts it aside, calling for his bowl. When he has drunk from it he summons three musicians to the best of whom Helena has agreed to award a prize. The first is a gipsy who, has brought some primitive companions from his wild part of England to dance to his playing of a Morris jig ('Go and 'list for a sailor', from Sherborne, Glos.); the second is a more romantic fellow, a dreamer, who plays an emotional tune ('A bold young farmer', from Vaughan Williams's MS collection) which enraptures everyone except the King, who begins to drop off to sleep. The third fiddler restores gaiety by playing 'The Jolly Thresherman', to which the Sword Dance from Escrick, Northumberland, is danced, with snatches of 'The Fisher Laddie' and 'The Oyster Girl'. King Cole has enjoyed this best and gives the third fiddler the prize without consulting Helena. She would have preferred to give it to No. 2 whose playing has sent her imagination into a world of romance. But the King's choice is the popular one, and after the prize has been given, there is a general dance (to a quick 'Running Set' step), during which cooks are seen carrying dishes into the hall. Supper is announced and King Cole leads the way with alacrity. The court is deserted now, except for the second fiddler who is still absorbed in his visions. He walks off playing, and Helena comes to the door to listen. She throws him a rose but he does not notice it and goes off, lost to everything except his music.

Duration: 22 minutes.

Publication: London, J. Curwen & Sons Ltd. (© 1924 R.V.W.). Chorus Edition (C.E.3657); full score, London and Philadelphia, J. Curwen & Sons Ltd. (© 1925, R.V.W.) (C.E.90746). Full score and parts on hire from Faber Music.

Other version: Piano arrangement by Maurice Jacobson with violin obbligato, ad lib., by R.V.W. J. Curwen & Sons Ltd. (© 1924 R.V.W.) (C.E.3657).

Origins: The most authoritative account of the origins of this ballet is given in a private letter from Mrs. John Burnaby from which the following quotations are taken:

'I was very keen to arrange and produce a ballet [for the Cambridge branch of the E.F.D.S.]. . . . I suggested that we should ask V.W. if he would write music for us. He at once assented but said we must suggest a subject. We all made suggestions and Mrs. Vulliamy's idea of 'Old King Cole' pleased him most.[1] She visited him several times and together they worked out the scenario. He sent us piano parts to rehearse with. I composed most of the dances with the help of the dancers and taught all the dancers. We rehearsed on my mother's tennis court marked out to the size of [the acting area of] Nevile's Court. . . . We had to get the full score copied . . . the final instalment came only two weeks before the performance! . . . He [R.V.W.] came to the dress rehearsal and tore out his hair at all the wrong notes being played. He and Dr. Rootham and Boris Ord sat up all night correcting the parts. He told me afterwards that he had no idea how difficult it was until he rehearsed it with a professional orchestra. We only had the C.U.M.S. amateurs with very little rehearsal. . . . The Pipe Dance was composed of Morris steps as they unwound an enormously long hookah. The Bowl Dance was danced by boys with wooden spoons which they hit together as in a Morris Stick Dance and used to stir the concoction in the bowl. . . . The ballet was composed and invented especially for Nevile's Court and could never be the same again. . . . The two processions entered on each side along the cloisters and Old King Cole came on through the Hall door on to the Tribune—Exeunt at the end through that door into the Hall for the banquet! The 2nd fiddler going off alone to the right down the cloister. The orchestra was in the right cloister. Our second performance in 1923 was at 8.30 p.m. and the sunset glowing over the Wren Library on to the stage made a beautiful effect.'

One letter to Mrs. Vulliamy from the composer, undated from Cheyne Walk, survives. It refers to the end of the ballet:

Dear Mrs. Vulliamy,

Certainly have a dance of some kind—but I think not too *formal* a dance. The idea is that after all the bustle of the earlier scenes there is a sudden *hush* when the slow tune is heard and silence—it might gradually grow into a dance or a series of slow movements expressive of the fascination of the tune—Is this possible?

Yours sincerely, R. Vaughan Williams.

P.S. You have an unaccompanied *folk dance* for the 3rd fiddler.

The ballet was revived in Nevile's Court on 7 and 8 June 1926 in aid of the Cecil Sharp Memorial Fund.

Note: The pianoforte score is headed by a note by the composer point-

---

[1] She took the idea from Spenser's *Faerie Queene*.

ing out that details of dances given in the score are 'only suggestions. But it is important that the dance at the entry of the First Fiddler should be a real Morris, and that the ad lib. dance of the Third Fiddler should be a true folk dance. The dresses need not be historical or "period", but may be purely fantastic. The parts of the three fiddlers should, if possible, be played by three performers on the stage: failing this, they must be played by the leader of the orchestra.'

3. ENGLISH FOLK SONGS. Suite for military band, transcribed in 1924 by Gordon Jacob for full orchestra and for brass band.

    I. March: 'Seventeen come Sunday'. *Allegro*. F minor.

    II. Intermezzo: 'My Bonny Boy'. *Andantino—allegretto scherzando*. F minor.

    III. March: 'Folk Songs from Somerset'. *Allegro*. B flat.

Instrumentation:

Military band: 1 D flat flute, 1 concert flute, 1 E flat clarinet, 1 oboe, 2 solo B flat clarinets, 3 B flat clarinets, 2 bassoons, 1 E flat alto saxophone, 1 B flat tenor saxophone, 1 E flat baritone saxophone, 2 cornets (1 solo), 1 B flat trumpet, 4 horns, 2 trombones, 1 bass trombone, 2 euphoniums (bass and treble), 2 basses, 1 drum, timpani.

Brass band: 1 E flat soprano cornet, 3 solo B flat cornets, 2 B flat repiano cornet and flügel horn, 2 2nd B flat cornets, 2 3rd B flat cornets, 3 E flat horns, 2 E flat baritones, 2 trombones, 1 bass trombone, 2 euphoniums (treble), 2 E flat basses, 2 B flat basses, 1 drum.

Full Orchestra: 2 flutes (1 piccolo), 1 oboe, 2 clarinets, 1 bassoon, 2 horns, 2 trumpets, 2 trombones, timpani, cymbals, bass drum, side drum, triangle, strings.

Or: 2 flutes (1 piccolo), clarinet, trumpet, 2 trombones, timpani, percussion, strings.

First performance: Kneller Hall, 4 July 1923. Band of Royal Military School of Music, conducted by Lieutenant Hector E. Adkins (Director of Music, Kneller Hall, 1921–43).

Duration: 11 minutes.

Publication: London,. Boosey and Hawkes. Military Band version © 1924; brass band version, 1956; orchestral full score, 1942.

Other version: Arranged for pianoforte solo by Michael Mullinar, 1949.

Note: The English folk songs quoted in this suite are: In I: *Dives and Lazarus* (in the bass), *Seventeen Come Sunday*, and *Pretty Caroline*; in II, *My Bonny Boy*, and *Green Bushes*; in III, *Blow away the morning dew*, *High Germany*, *The trees so high* and *John Barleycorn*.

4. SEA SONGS. Quick March for military and brass bands, transcribed in 1942 for full orchestra by the composer.

Instrumentation: Brass and military as for *English Folk Songs*. Full orchestra: 2 flutes, 2 oboes, 2 clarinets, 2 bassoons, 2 horns, 2 trumpets,

2 trombones, timpani, percussion, strings. *Or* 2 flutes, 1 clarinet, 1 trumpet, 2 trombones, timpani, percussion, strings.

First performance: Almost certainly during British Empire Exhibition, Wembley, April 1924.

Duration: 4 minutes.

Note: this work is based on *Princess Royal, Admiral Benbow,* and *Portsmouth.*

Publication: London, Boosey and Hawkes, brass and military versions, 1924; full orchestra 1943.

5. LET US NOW PRAISE FAMOUS MEN. Unison song, with accompaniment for pianoforte, organ or small orchestra. Text selected from *Ecclesiasticus,* Ch. 44. *Andante con moto.* C major.

Instrumentation (by Arnold Foster)*:* 2 flutes, 2 oboes, 2 clarinets, 2 bassoons, 4 horns, 3 trumpets, 3 trombones, timpani, organ (opt.), strings.

Publication: London, J. Curwen & Sons Ltd. (© 1923) (C.E.71619). Orchestral parts on hire.

Other versions:

(*a*) As solo song with orchestral or pianoforte accompaniment (C.E.2446).

(*b*) As hymn tune 'Famous Men', No. 432 in *Songs of Praise* (enlarged edition), London, Oxford University Press, 1931.

(*c*) Arrangement for unaccompanied mixed choir (SATB) by Maurice Jacobson. J. Curwen & Sons Ltd. 1959. (C.E.61498.)

6. TWO PIECES FOR VIOLIN AND PIANOFORTE.

   I. Romance—*Andantino.* F sharp minor—A major.

   II. Pastorale—*Andante con moto.* E modal minor.

Dedication: To D.M.L. [Dorothy Longman, first wife of R. J. Longman, the publisher. She was a talented violinist and for many years played in the orchestra at the Leith Hill Festival.]

Publication: London, F. & B. Goodwin Ltd. (© U.S.A. 1923.) Reissued by J. Curwen & Sons Ltd. (C.E.94016 and 94017.)

Note: It is more than likely that these pieces were written before the First World War.

1924

1. TOCCATA MARZIALE. For military band. *Allegro maestoso.* B flat major. Originally intended as movement of a Concerto Grosso.

Instrumentation: D flat flute and piccolo, concert flute and piccolo, 2 E flat clarinets, 4 B flat clarinets (one solo), 2 oboes, bassoon, B flat soprano, E flat alto, tenor and baritone saxophones, 2 B flat cornets, 4 horns in F, 2 B flat trumpets, 2 trombones, bass trombone, euphonium, basses, drums, timpani in F and B flat. (The trumpet part is essential and must be played on cornets if trumpets are not available.)

First performance: Wembley, British Empire Exhibition, 1924. Band of Royal Military School of Music, conducted by Lieut. H. E. Adkins.
Duration: 4 minutes.
Publication: London, Paris, etc., Hawkes & Son (© 1924). (The Hawkes Souvenir Edition of music for military band. Issued in commemoration of the British Empire Exhibition, 1924, No. 473.) (H. & S. 6239.) 3-stave conductor and parts now available from Boosey and Hawkes.
Whereabouts of MS.: British Library has copy of 2-piano arrangement (57287), and copy of full score (59796).

2. HUGH THE DROVER, or 'Love in the Stocks'. A romantic ballad opera in two acts, for nine soloists, mixed chorus and orchestra. Words by Harold Child (1869–1945).
Instrumentation: 2 flutes, 2 oboes, 2 clarinets, 2 bassoons, 4 horns, 2 trumpets, 3 trombones, tuba, timpani, percussion (4 players), harp, strings, stage band.
Characters (in order of entrance):

A Cheap Jack (baritone)
A Shell-fish Seller (bass)   } Members of the chorus.
A Primrose Seller (contralto)
A Showman (high baritone)
A Ballad Seller (tenor)
Susan (soprano)
Nancy (contralto)   } Members of the chorus.
William (tenor)
Robert (bass)
Mary (the Constable's Daughter) (soprano)
Aunt Jane (the Constable's Sister) (contralto)
The Turnkey (tenor)
The Constable (bass)
John the Butcher (bass baritone)
A Fool (baritone from the chorus)
Hugh the Drover (tenor)
An Innkeeper (bass from the chorus)
A Sergeant (high baritone)
Inhabitants of the town
Toy-lamb Sellers
Primrose Sellers   } Chorus SCTB
Village Boys
Soldiers
Stall-keepers
Showman's troupe   } Non-singing
Bugler
Drummer

Place: a small town in the Cotswolds (Northleach was intended).
Scene: Act I. A fair in an open field near the town, about 11 a.m. on
Monday, 30 April, in the early years of the 19th century (about 1812).
Act II. A street in the town. Scene I, The same afternoon; Scene II,
4 a.m. on Tuesday, 1 May.

First performances: London, Parry Opera Theatre of the Royal College
of Music, five 'private dress rehearsals' on 4, 7 (two), 9 and 11 July
1924. Certain changes of cast are indicated below:

	Original Cast	
	4, 7 (evening) and 11 July	7 (matinée) and 9 July
HUGH THE DROVER ..	John Dean	Trefor Jones
JOHN THE BUTCHER ..	Gavin Gordon-Brown	H. Leyland White
THE CONSTABLE ..	Arthur G. Rees	Keith Falkner
THE TURNKEY ..	William Wait	
A CHEAP JACK ..	Dunstan Hart	
A SHELL-FISH SELLER	Philip B. Warde	
A SHOWMAN	Robert Griffin	
A BALLAD SELLER ..	William Herbert	
WILLIAM	William Weber	
ROBERT	Keith Falkner	Arthur G. Rees
INNKEEPER	Robert Griffin	
SERGEANT	J. M. Sinnett Jones	Philip B. Warde
FOOL	Richard Austin	
MARY	Muriel Nixon	Odette de Foras
AUNT JANE	Mona Benson	
SUSAN	Sybil Evers	
NANCY	Stephanie Tarrant	Mary J. Scott
PRIMROSE SELLER ..	Janet I. Powell	
TOY-LAMB SELLERS ..	Elizabeth Johnson Dorothy Saunders Bertha Steventon	
DANCING GIRL ..	Florence McHugh	
TRUMPETER	Henry Dancy	
DRUMMER AND CHORUS	Harold Davidson	

Conductor: S. P. Waddington. Producer: Cairns James. Stage
Manager: H. Procter-Gregg (who also modelled the scenery).

First public performance: London, His Majesty's Theatre, 14 July 1924,
by British National Opera Company, with following cast:

A CHEAP JACK ..	..	Raymond Ellis
A SHELL-FISH SELLER	..	Eric Fort
A PRIMROSE SELLER	..	Molly Street
A SHOWMAN ..	..	William Michael

A BALLAD SELLER	..	..	Browning Mummery
SUSAN	..	..	..	Gladys Leathwood
NANCY	..	..	..	Hilda Fox
WILLIAM	..	..	..	Archibald Cooper
ROBERT	..	..	..	Philip Bertram
MARY	..	..	..	Mary Lewis
AUNT JANE	..	..	Constance Willis
TURNKEY	..	..	..	Frederick Davies
CONSTABLE	..	..	William Anderson
JOHN THE BUTCHER	..	Frederic Collier
FOOL	..	..	..	Leon Russell
HUGH THE DROVER	..	Tudor Davies
INNKEEPER	..	..	Harold Wilton
SERGEANT	..	..	Franklyn Kelsey

Conductor: Malcolm Sargent. Producer: Cairns James.

Dedication: To Sir Hugh Allen from Author and Composer.

Duration: About 2 hours. (Without Act II, Scene 1, about 96 mins.)

Publication: London, J. Curwen & Sons Ltd. (© R.V.W. 1924.) Vocal Score, © renewed 1952. (C.E.3661.) Material available on hire. The Vocal Score (1959 revision) contains a synopsis of the plot, written by the composer, fuller and rather better than his earlier version quoted by Frank Howes in *The Music of Ralph Vaughan Williams* (1954), pp. 255–6. This was reissued in 1977 by Faber Music as Curwen Edition C.03661, with introduction by Michael Kennedy © 1977.

Note: The following traditional tunes are used in the opera: 'Primroses', 'May Day Carol' (versions collected by R.V.W. at Fowlmere, Cambs., 1907, and by Lucy Broadwood at King's Langley, Herts.), 'Toy Lambs', 'Cockles' (version collected by F. Kidson), 'Tuesday Morning', and 'Morris Dance' (from Cecil Sharp's collection), 'Maria Martin',[1] 'Maying Song'. The tune on the bells in Act II is the psalm-tune 'York'. The drinking song is suggested by a traditional melody.

Revisions: This opera was written between 1910 and 1914 and was several times revised.

One of the first deletions was a harangue by Hugh on the virtues of living the open-air life which occurred after the soldiers had marched John the Butcher away. There was a complex ensemble in which everyone urged Hugh and Mary to settle in the town and to which Hugh replied, 'I do not love your towns, the smooth sleek life which knows no ups and downs'. Only the recitative of this song survives ('Now you are mine') and is followed by a love duet ('Lord of my life')

[1] There is an anachronism when the ballad-seller offers 'Maria Martin', as her murder in the Red Barn did not take place until 1824.

which was originally part of the scene in the stocks. In extensive revisions in 1956 the composer inserted an aria for Aunt Jane in which she pleads with Mary to 'stay with those who love you' and to comfort her in her old age. Mary declares that her place is at Hugh's side.

The present Act II, Scene 1, marked optional in the score, was inserted in 1933 when the opera was revived for the jubilee of the Royal College of Music on 15 June 1933, with Sir Thomas Beecham conducting and Trefor Jones as Hugh, Mabel (Margaret) Ritchie as Mary, Mona Benson as Aunt Jane and Leyland White as John.

The definitive version of the score is that published in 1959, incorporating the extensive 1956 revisions of dialogue, action and music of which a list was issued by Curwen in 1956. These were directed towards removing some of the more stilted dialogue, tightening the action and strengthening the ending of the opera with which the composer had never been wholly satisfied. The first performance of the finally revised score was at Sadler's Wells Theatre on 29 February 1956.

Whereabouts of MS.: British Library, vocal score (50843); printed (1924) vocal score with MS. additions by R.V.W.; fragments and discards, mostly in full score (50406).

Songs from the opera. The following songs from *Hugh the Drover* are available separately:

(*a*) Here, Queen uncrown'd. Mary's song from Act II, Sc. 2, arranged for women's voices (SSC) by Maurice Jacobson, with orchestral accompaniment or pianoforte.
   Instrumentation: As for *A Cotswold Romance* (See below).
   Publication: London, J. Curwen & Sons Ltd. (© 1951) (C.E. 72255).

(*b*) Hugh's Song of the Road (Act I). Arranged for mixed voices (SATB) with orchestral accompaniment or pianoforte by Maurice Jacobson.
   Publication: London, J. Curwen & Sons Ltd. (© 1952) (C.E. 61450).

(*c*) Sweet little linnet (Hugh's Song, Act I). Arranged for mixed voices (SATB) unaccompanied, by Michael Mullinar.
   Publication: London, J. Curwen & Sons Ltd. (© 1951) (C.E. 61441).

The remainder were arranged for solo voice and accompaniment by the composer and published in 1924 by J. Curwen & Sons Ltd.:

(*d*) Alone and Friendless (Hugh's Song, Act I). For voice and pianoforte, or for orchestra as in the opera. (C.E.2349.)

(*e*) Gaily I go to die (Hugh's song, Act II, Sc. 2). For voice and pianoforte. (C.E.2347.)

(*f*) Here on my throne (Mary's song, Act II, Sc. 2). For voice and pianoforte. (C.E.2350.)

(*g*) Life must be full of care (Aunt Jane's song, Act I). For voice and pianoforte. (C.E.2344.)

(*h*) The Showman's Songs (Act I). With choruses. (1) Cold blows the wind on Cotsall. (2) The Devil and Bonyparty. (C.E.2961.)

(*j*) Song of the Road (Act I). For voice and pianoforte, or orchestra as in the opera. (C.E.2346.)

(*k*) Sweet Little Linnet (Act I) (C.E.2345). For voice and pianoforte.

(*l*) Two duets (tenor and soprano). (1) Ah, Love, I've found you (Act I). (2) Hugh my Lover (Act II, Sc. 2). (C.E.2962.)

For convenience of reference, details are here given of:

A COTSWOLD ROMANCE. Cantata, for tenor and soprano soloists, mixed chorus (SATB) and orchestra, by Maurice Jacobson, adapted from the opera *Hugh the Drover*. Words by Harold Child.

Instrumentation: 2 flutes, 2 oboes, 2 clarinets, 2 bassoons, 4 horns, 2 trumpets, 3 trombones, tuba, timpani, harp, percussion (cymbals, bass drum, side drum, triangle), strings. *Or:* strings and pianoforte, which can be augmented at the conductor's discretion by woodwind, brass, etc., taken from the orchestral version.

1. Mixed voice chorus, 'The Men of Cotsall'.
2. SATB unaccompanied, 'Sweet Little Linnet'.
3. Tenor and SATB, 'Song of the Road'.
4. Tenor, soprano and SATB, 'Love at first sight'.
5. SATB with baritone solo (from chorus), 'The Best Man in England'.
6. Tenor solo, 'Alone and friendless'.
7. Tenor, soprano and SATB, 'The Fight and its Sequel'.
8. Tenor solo, 'Hugh in the Stocks (Gaily I go to die)'.
9. Soprano and SATB, 'Mary escapes'. (*a*) Alternative version for women's voices, 'Here, Queen Uncrown'd'.
10. Tenor, soprano and SATB, 'Freedom at last'.

First performance: London, Central Hall, Tooting Broadway, 10 May 1951, South-West London Choral Society, South-West Professional Orchestra, Olive Groves (soprano), James Johnston (tenor), Arnold Matters (baritone), conducted by Frank Odell.

Duration: 50 minutes.

Publication: London, J. Curwen & Sons Ltd. (© U.S.A. 1951 by R.V.W. and Maurice Jacobson) (C.E.3726). Vocal score, chorus score, full score, and parts on hire, Faber Music.

Note: The score has a synopsis written by Vaughan Williams. It is this synopsis, slightly altered, which is now also in the score of the opera. A note on the score states that the names of both composer and adapter must be shown on all posters, leaflets, programmes and other publicity matter. The cantata was arranged because Curwen's had for many years received inquiries for a concert version of the opera. Performances of the opera in the concert hall never 'worked', because the choral work is so closely interwoven with the opera. The composer suggested that Maurice Jacobson should make a cantata from it, 'more or less in collaboration with him'.[1] At the same time a good deal of the scoring of the opera itself was revised.

It will perhaps be helpful to recall here that in 1939, when Mrs. E. Priestley (then Miss Price) was competing in the Cheltenham Musical Festival for which the test piece for dramatic soprano was 'Here on my throne', neither she nor her teacher could decide on the correct tempo. Miss Price therefore wrote to the composer, who replied, on 27 February 1939:

'The tempo of my "Here on my throne" should be about ♩ = 72 or a little slower. Please DO NOT use this opinion as an authority if the judge disagrees with your rendering—these things are a matter of opinion.'

One is happy to record that Stuart Robertson, the adjudicator, placed Miss Price first in her class.[2]

3. TWENTY-FIVE VOCAL EXERCISES. Founded on Bach's Mass in B minor. By Gertrude Sichel and R. Vaughan Williams.

These exercises are not passages from the Mass itself, but are suggested by such passages. They may be sung at any pitch suitable to the voice of the singer using them.

Publication: London, Stainer & Bell Ltd. (© 1924) (S. & B. 2936).

4. 'MR. ISAACS MAGGOT'. English traditional country dance tune. Arranged by R.V.W. for clarinet, pianoforte, triangle and strings. *Unpublished.*

First performance: Abinger, Surrey, opening of Village Hall, January 1925. Edward Bridges (clarinet), Mrs. Tatham (pianoforte), Frances Farrer (triangle), Kitty Farrer (1st violin), Miss C. Kirkland (2nd violin), Anne Farrer (violoncello), conducted by Dr. R. Vaughan Williams.

Whereabouts of MS.: Formerly in possession of the late Dame Frances Farrer.

1925

1. TWO POEMS BY SEUMAS O'SULLIVAN. Set for voice and pianoforte accompaniment, but may be sung unaccompanied. Text

---

[1] Maurice Jacobson, in a letter to the author 22 August 1962, from which these facts are taken.

[2] Information from Mrs. E. Priestley of Hamsterley Hill, Co. Durham. Letter dated 6 June 1959.

by 'Seumas O'Sullivan', pseudonym of James Starkey (1879–1958).
1. The Twilight People. *Andante con moto*. C minor.
2. A Piper. *Allegro molto*. D modal minor.
First performance: London, Aeolian Hall, 27 March 1925. Steuart
Wilson (tenor), Anthony Bernard (pianoforte).
Publication: London, Oxford University Press (© 1925).
Other version: The Twilight People, published separately in 1932,
in B flat minor.

2. THREE SONGS FROM SHAKESPEARE. Set for voice and
pianoforte.
1. Take, O take, those lips away.(*Measure for Measure,*Act IV, Sc. 1.)
Lento. E minor.
2. When icicles hang by the wall. (*Love's Labour's Lost*, Act V, Sc. 2.)
Allegro. F minor.
3. Orpheus with his lute. (*King Henry VIII*, Act III, Sc. 1.) *Andante
tranquillo*. G major.
First performance: London, Aeolian Hall, 27 March 1925. Steuart
Wilson (tenor), Anthony Bernard (pianoforte).
Publication: London, O.U.P. (© 1925).
Other versions:
1. Take, O take. Unison song. *Lento*. F sharp minor.
Publication: London, O.U.P. 1926 (© 1925) in Oxford Choral Songs
(General Editor, W. G. Whittaker), No. 50.
2. When Icicles Hang. Unison song. *Allegro*. F minor.
Publication: London, O.U.P. 1926 (© 1925) as O.C.S., No. 51.
3. Orpheus with his lute.
(*a*) Unison song, with accompaniment for strings. *Andante tran-
quillo*. F major.
Publication: London, O.U.P. 1926 (© 1925) as O.C.S., No. 52.
Parts available on hire.
(*b*) Also for mixed chorus (SATB).

3. FOUR POEMS BY FREDEGOND SHOVE. Set for voice and
pianoforte. Words by Fredegond Shove (1889–1949).
1. Motion and Stillness. Composed in 1922 (dated MS.). *Lento*.
2. Four Nights. *Andante*.
3. The New Ghost. *Tempo rubato (senza mizura)*.
4. The Water Mill. *Allegretto tranquillo*.
First performance: London, Aeolian Hall, 27 March 1925. Steuart
Wilson (tenor), Anthony Bernard (pianoforte).
Publication: London, O.U.P. (© 1925).
Other versions: All four published separately. Nos. 1 and 2 also available together. No. 4 arranged for low voices (1925–6).
Original MS. of *Motion and Stillness* in British Library (50480).

4. THREE POEMS BY WALT WHITMAN. Set for voice and pianoforte. Words by Walt Whitman.
   1. Nocturne, from *Whispers of Heavenly Death*. *Andante con moto*. D minor.
   2. A Clear Midnight, from *From Noon to Starry Night*. *Lento*. G major.
   3. Joy, Shipmate, Joy! from *Songs of Parting*. *Allegro pesante*. G major.
   Publication: London, O.U.P. (© 1925).

5. FLOS CAMPI. Suite for solo viola, small wordless mixed chorus (SATB) and small orchestra. Each movement is headed by a Latin quotation, with English translation, from *The Song of Solomon*.
   Instrumentation: Flute (also taking piccolo), oboe, clarinet, bassoon, horn, trumpet, percussion (bass drum, cymbals, triangle, tabor or tambourine without jingles played with a hard stick. Two players required), harp, celesta, 1st violins (not more than six), 2nd violins (not more than six), violas (not more than four), cellos (not more than four), double basses, (not more than two), solo viola. Chorus to number 20 (three 1st sopranos, three 2nd sopranos, three 1st altos, three 2nd altos, two 1st tenors, two 2nd tenors, two 1st basses, two 2nd basses) or 26 (four 1st sopranos, four 2nd sopranos, four 1st altos, four 2nd altos, two 1st tenors, three 2nd tenors, two 1st basses, three 2nd basses).
   I. Sicut lilium inter spinas, sic amica mea inter filias. . . . Fulcite me floribus, stipate me malis, quia amore langueo. 'As the lily among thorns, so is my love among the daughters. . . . Stay me with flagons, comfort me with apples; for I am sick of love.'[1] (Ch. II, v. 2 and 5.) *Lento*. A minor.
   II. Iam enim hiems transiit; imber abiit, et recessit; flores apparuerunt in terra nostra, tempus putationis advenit; vox turturis audita est in terra nostra. 'For, lo, the winter is past, the rain is over and gone, the flowers appear on the earth, the time of the singing of birds is come, and the voice of the turtle is heard in our land.' (Ch. II, v. 11 and 12.) *Andante con moto*. G major.
   III. Quaesivi quem diligit anima mea; quaesivi illum et non inveni. . . . 'Adjuro vos, filiae Jerusalem, si inveneritis dilectum meum, ut nuntietis ei quia amore langueo' . . . quo abiit dilectus tuus, O pulcherrima mulierum? Quo declinavit dilectus tuus? ut quaeremus eum tecum. 'I sought him whom my soul loveth, but I found him not. . . . "I charge you, O daughters of Jerusalem, if ye find my beloved, tell him that I am sick of love". . . . Whither is thy beloved gone, O thou fairest among women? Whither is thy beloved turned aside? that we may seek him with thee.'

---

[1] This phrase is corrupted by modern usage. It means here, literally, 'I languish for love' or 'I faint from longing'.

(Ch. III, v. 1, Ch. V, v. 8, Ch. VI, v. 1.) *Lento (senza misura).* B minor.

IV. En lectulum Salomonis sexaginta fortes ambiunt . . . omnes tenentes gladios, et ad bella doctissimi. 'Behold his bed (palanquin), which is Solomon's, three score valiant men are about it. . . . They all hold swords, being expert in war.' (Ch. III, v. 7 and 8.) *Moderato alla marcia.* C minor.

V. Revertere, revertere Sulamitis! Revertere, revertere ut intueamur te. . . . Quam pulchri sunt gressus tui in calceamentis, filia principis. 'Return, return, O Shulamite! Return, return that we may look upon thee. . . . How beautiful are thy feet with shoes, O Prince's daughter.' (Ch. VI, v. 13 and Ch. VII, v. 1.) *Andante quasi lento (largamente).* E modal minor.

VI. Pone me ut signaculum super cor tuum. 'Set me as a seal upon thine heart.' (Ch. VIII, v. 6.) *Moderato tranquillo.* B minor.

First performance: London, Queen's Hall, 10 October 1925. Queen's Hall Orchestra, conducted by Sir Henry Wood, Lionel Tertis (viola), select choir of 35 voices from Royal College of Music.

Dedication: To Lionel Tertis.

Duration: 20 minutes.

Publication: London, O.U.P. (© 1928), full score; vocal score with pianoforte accompaniment arranged by Gordon Jacob (© 1928); solo viola score; miniature score. Orchestral material on hire. Slight revisions were made before publication, notably the designation of exact numbers of voices required.

Composer's programme note (written for a performance in 1927): When this work was first produced two years ago, the composer discovered that most people were not well enough acquainted with the Vulgate (or perhaps even its English equivalent) to enable them to complete for themselves the quotations from the 'Canticum Canticorum', indications of which are the mottoes at the head of each movement of the Suite.

Even the title and the source of the quotations gave rise to misunderstanding.

The title 'Flos Campi' was taken by some to connote an atmosphere of 'buttercups and daisies', whereas in reality 'Flos Campi' is the Vulgate equivalent of 'Rose of Sharon' (*Ego Flos Campi, et Lilium Convallium,* 'I am the Rose of Sharon, and the Lily of the valleys').

The Biblical source of the quotations also gave rise to the idea that the music had an ecclesiastical basis. This was not the intention of the composer.

[The quotations above the movements were given in Latin and English but are here omitted.]

1. The opening theme:

is played by the oboe, and is answered by the following:

on the solo viola. Next comes the following theme (flute and viola):

which is also used in later movements.

2. Over a murmuring accompaniment of voices and muted strings the viola plays the following melody:

This is taken up by oboe and other wind instruments, and towards the end of the movement is sung by the chorus.

3. In this movement recitative-like passages on the viola alternate with answering passages for the trebles and altos of the chorus.

4. A march, of which the following are the principal subjects:

played by clarinet and bassoon, and:

played by the viola.

Later on Exs. 5 and 6, with their counterpoints, are heard in combination. The chorus does not enter till the end of this movement.

5. A slow dance with these themes:

(orchestra and chorus):

(viola solo) accompanied by a persistent rhythm in the percussion. Towards the end of the movement themes (Ex. 1) and (Ex. 3) reappear. 6. This movement is developed entirely out of the following theme:

first by the orchestra, then by the chorus. This is interrupted towards the end by a reminiscence of Exs. 1 and 2. The theme of the movement is then taken up again softly by the chorus, flute and solo viola. R.V.W. *Whereabouts of MS:* Unknown.

6. SANCTA CIVITAS (The Holy City). Composed 1923–5. An Oratorio for tenor and baritone soloists, mixed chorus (SATB), semichorus, distant chorus, and orchestra. Text from the Authorized Version of the Bible. (*Revelation*, from Ch. XVIII, XIX, XXI and XXII) with additions from Taverner's Bible (1539) and other sources.

Instrumentation: 3 flutes, 2 oboes, 1 cor anglais, 2 clarinets, 2 bassoons, 1 double bassoon, 4 horns, 3 trumpets, 3 trombones, tuba, percussion (side drum, bass drum, cymbals, pianoforte), harp, organ, violins, violas, violoncellos, double basses. The semichorus should sit behind the full chorus and consist of about 20 singers (6, 6, 4, 4). The distant choir should if possible be out of sight and must have a special conductor. It should consist of boys' voices if possible. The distant trumpet must be placed with the distant choir. The tempo marks are approximate. The pace must be free and elastic throughout.

The score is headed by the following quotation, in Greek with no English translation (for translation see Chapter Seven), from the *Phaedo* of Plato, 114D:

Τὸ μὲν οὖν ταῦτα διισχυρίσασθαι οὕτως ἔχειν, ὡς ἐγὼ διελήλυθα, οὐ πρέπει νοῦν ἔχοντι ἀνδρί · ὅτι μέντοι ἢ ταῦτ' ἐστὶν ἢ τοιαῦτ' ἄττα περὶ τὰς ψυχὰς ἡμῶν καὶ τὰς οἰκήσεις, ἐπείπερ ἀθάνατόν γε ἡ ψυχὴ φαίνεται οὖσα, τοῦτο καὶ πρέπειν μοι δοκεῖ καὶ ἄξιον κινδυνεῦσαι οἰομένῳ οὕτως ἔχειν—καλὸς γὰρ ὁ κίνδυνος—καὶ χρὴ τὰ τοιαῦτα ὥσπερ ἐπάδειν ἑαυτῷ.

First performance: Oxford, Sheldonian Theatre, 7 May 1926. Arthur Cranmer (baritone), Trefor Jones (tenor), Oxford Bach Choir,

Oxford Orchestral Society, conducted by H. P. Allen. First perform-
ance in London: Central Hall, Westminster, 9 June 1926. Roy
Henderson (baritone), Steuart Wilson (tenor), The Bach Choir, The
Temple Choristers, G. Thalben-Ball (organ). London Symphony
Orchestra, conducted by Dr. R. Vaughan Williams.
Duration: 31 minutes.
Publication: London, J. Curwen & Sons Ltd. (© 1925 R.V.W.)
Vocal score (with pianoforte accompaniment arranged by Havergal
Brian). Faber Music (C.03663). Full score and parts on hire.
Whereabouts of MS.: Full score with English words, British Library
(50445), voice parts with Latin words (50446). Early vocal score in
Bodleian Library, Oxford. This shows that the composer had set and
discarded an episode of fewer than 20 bars which had its place at the
ninth bar after Fig. 40 in the vocal score. The words were from
Rev. XXII, v. 1 and 2. 'And he shewed me a pure river of water of
life . . .', set for three to four altos, in the pentatonic manner of the
violin solo, with a high descant. The episode, rewritten and shortened,
now occurs seven bars after Fig. 45.

7. CONCERTO IN D MINOR (CONCERTO ACCADEMICO).
    For violin and string orchestra. Composed 1924–5.
    Instrumentation: Solo violin, violins, violas, violoncellos, double
    basses.
    I.   *Allegro pesante.*
    II. *Adagio—tranquillo.*
    III. *Presto.*
    First performance: London, Aeolian Hall (Gerald Cooper Concert),
    6 November 1925. Jelly d'Aranyi (violin), London Chamber
    Orchestra, conducted by Anthony Bernard.
    Dedication: To Jelly d'Aranyi.
    Duration: 14 minutes.
    Publication: London, O.U.P. (© 1927), full score and miniature
    score. Arrangement for violin and pianoforte by Constant Lambert
    (© 1927).
Note: The composer notes in the score that the principal theme of the
finale is taken 'in part' from *Hugh the Drover*, where it occurs in Act II,
Scene II at letter |A|, just after 'belly with beer' and accompanies a roar
of laughter from inside the inn. The top notes of bars 3, 4 and 5 of |A|
are identical with the first bars of the concerto theme, except that they
are a fifth lower. The title 'Concerto Accademico' was 'dropped' by the
composer in about 1951, when he slightly revised the solo part for a
Menuhin performance in London on 25 September 1952.
Whereabouts of MS.: British Library, Egerton MS. 3251. Copy of 2nd
movement arranged for 2 pianos (57287).

8. DAREST THOU NOW, O SOUL. Unison song for voice and piano-forte, or strings. Words by Walt Whitman, from *Whispers of Heavenly Death*. *Andante con moto*. G major.
Publication: London and Philadelphia, J. Curwen & Sons Ltd. (© 1925 R.V.W.). (C.E. 71669).
Whereabouts of MS.: British Library (52620).

9. 'THE GIANT' FUGUE. Transcription for strings of Fugue by J. S. Bach, by R. Vaughan Williams and Arnold Foster. *Allegro*. D minor.
Publication: London, O.U.P. (© 1925). Oxford Orchestral Series (General Editor W. G. Whittaker) No. O6.

10. MAGNIFICAT and NUNC DIMITTIS (THE VILLAGE SER-VICE). Set to music for the use of village choirs for mixed chorus (SATB) and organ.
I. Magnificat. *Moderato* (not too slow). C major.
II. Nunc Dimittis. *Andante moderato*. E flat major.
Publication: London, J. Curwen & Sons Ltd. (© 1925 R.V.W.). (C.E. 80640).
Whereabouts of M.S.: British Library (52620).

11. SONGS OF PRAISE. Words Editor, The Rev. Percy Dearmer; Music Editors, R. Vaughan Williams and Martin Shaw. London, Oxford University Press, 1925.
This first edition contains the following original tunes by Vaughan Williams (asterisk indicates that the tune first appeared in the *English Hymnal*):
  37. Magda ('Saviour, again to Thy dear name')
  41. (i) Oakley ('The night is come like to the day')
*110. Sine Nomine ('For all the saints')
 123. (i) Cumnor ('Servants of God, or sons')
 185. Guildford ('England, arise! the long, long night is over')
*217. Down Ampney ('Come down, O love divine')
*406. Randolph ('God be with you till we meet again')
 443. King's Weston ('At the name of Jesus')
*445. (i) Salve Festa Dies ('Hail Thee, Festival Day')
        All the new tunes are © 1925 R.V.W.
The following tunes were arranged by Vaughan Williams. Unless otherwise stated, the sources of the tunes are English traditional melodies. Only arrangements which did *NOT* appear in the *English Hymnal* are included:
  12. Danby (' 'Tis winter now; the fallen snow')
     (This is a different arrangement from that which appears in the *English Hymnal*.)
  51. Macht Hoch die Thür ('It was the calm and silent night!')
     Adaptation of melody by J. A. Freylinghausen (1670–1739)

163. (ii) Valor ('O valiant hearts')

182. Ach! Wan Doch Jesu, Liebster mein ('Through all the long dark night of years'). Adaptation of melody from *Trutz-Nachtigall*, 1649.

200 (ii) Eventide ('Abide with me') *Descant*

226. Regina ('Dear Lord and Father of mankind')

246. (ii) Crüger ('Hail to the Lord's Anointed') *Descant* for verse 3

249. Freuen wir uns ('Hark my soul! it is the Lord'). Adaptation of melody from *Ein Neues Gesangbüchlein* (M. Weisse, 1531).

293. Wächterlied ('Lord Christ, when first Thou cam'st to men'). Adaptation of 16th century German melody.

296. Il Buon Pastor ('Lord of health, Thou life within us'). Adaptation from a melody in *Canzuns Spirituaelas* (Upper Engadine, 1765)

327. Engadine ('O most mighty, O most holy'). Adaptation from a melody in *Canzuns Spirituaelas* (Upper Engadine, 1765).

330. Londonderry ('O son of man, our hero strong and tender'). Irish traditional melody.

352. (ii) Essex ('Say not the struggle nought availeth')

353. Milites ('Soldiers of Christ, arise'). Adaptation of melody set to these words in Harmonia Sacra, compiled by John Page (1760(?)–1812).

372. St. Gabriel ('Then welcome each rebuff'). Adaptation of 17th century German hymn tune.

408. Mariners ('Lord, in the hollow of Thy hand')

415. O mentes perfidas ('Thy Kingdom come, O God'). Melody from *Piae Cantiones* (1582).

438. Hardwick ('So here hath been dawning')

440. Bamberg ('The year's at the spring'). Adaptation of 17th-century German melody.

442. Resonet in laudibus ('Who within that stable cries'). Adaptation of 14th-century German carol.

All arrangements not in *English Hymnal* are © 1925 R.V.W.

Separate publications from *Songs of Praise*. All published in London by O.U.P. (© 1925 R.V.W.):

(*a*)   12. Danby (' 'Tis winter now, the fallen snow'). Words by Samuel Longfellow (1819–92). Unison. In moderate time.

(*b*)   37. Magda ('Saviour, again to Thy dear name'). Words by John Ellerton (1826–93). SATB. In moderate time, not too slow. D major.

(*c*)   41 (i) Oakley ('The night is come'). Words by Sir Thomas Browne (1605–82). SATB. In moderate time. E modal minor.

(*d*)   123 (i) Cumnor ('Servants of God, or sons'). Words by Matthew

Arnold (1822–88). SATB. In moderate time. C minor–E flat major.

(e) 185. Guildford ('England arise!'). Words by Edward Carpenter (1844–1929). Unison. Not too slow. A modal minor.

(f) 200. Eventide ('Abide with me'). Words by H. F. Lyte (1793–1847). Music by W. H. Monk (composed 1861). Descant by R.V.W. Slow. E flat major.

(g) 246. Crüger ('Hail to the Lord's anointed'). Words by J. Montgomery (1771–1854). Music adapted by W. H. Monk (1861) from chorale by J. Crüger (1640). Descant by R.V.W. Slow and dignified. F major.

(h) 438. Hardwick ('So here hath been dawning'). Words by Thomas Carlyle (1795–1881). SATB. In moderate time. F major.

(j) 443. King's Weston ('At the name of Jesus'). Words by Caroline M. Noel (1817–77). Unison. With vigour. E modal minor. Also SATB with organ accompaniment. E minor (© 1927) (Oxford Anthem A. 158).

1926

1. SIX STUDIES IN ENGLISH FOLK SONG for violoncello and pianoforte.

    I. *Adagio.* E modal minor.

    II. *Andante sostenuto.* E flat.

    III. *Larghetto.* D modal minor.

    IV. *Lento.*

    V. *Andante tranquillo.* C major.

    VI. *Allegro vivace.*

First performance: London, Scala Theatre, English Folk Dance Society Festival, 4 June 1926. May Mukle (violoncello), Anne Mukle (pianoforte).

Dedication: To May Mukle.

Duration: 10 minutes.

Publication: London, Stainer & Bell Ltd. (© 1927). (S. & B. 3667–1).

Other versions:

(1) Alternative versions of solo part for violin (S. & B. 3667–2); viola (S. & B. 3667–3) and clarinet (S. & B. 3667–4).

(2) Arranged by Arnold Foster in 1957 for cello and small orchestra. Instrumentation: 2 flutes, 1 oboe, 2 clarinets, 2 bassoons, harp (or pianoforte), solo cello, strings. (S. & B. 5399).

These studies are not exact transcriptions of identifiable folk songs, but each is founded on a strophic melody with a likeness to a type of folk song. Nevertheless, the origins of the studies are identifiable thus:

1. 'Lovely on the Water' (The Springtime of the Year); 2. 'Spurn Point'; 3. 'Van Dieman's Land'; 4. 'She Borrowed Some of her Mother's Gold'; 5. 'The Lady and the Dragoon'; 6. 'As I walked over London Bridge'.

2. ON CHRISTMAS NIGHT. A Masque with dancing, singing and miming, freely adapted from Dickens's *A Christmas Carol* by Adolf Bolm and R. Vaughan Williams, with music devised as a quodlibet of folk tunes and country dances by the latter.

Characters: Scrooge; Marley's Ghost; Spirit of Christmas; Three Miss Fezziwigs; Their Six Admirers; The Milkman; The Baker; The Boy-from-over-the-way; his friend; The Girl-from-next-door-but-one; Mr. and Mrs. Fezziwig; Scrooge as a young man; The Fiddler; Watchman; Shepherds; The Three Kings and other characters of the Nativity; Father, Mother and Daughter; Mr. and Mrs. Cratchit; Tiny Tim; Madonna and Child and attendant angels.

Singing parts (both solos (off-stage)): Watchman (baritone); mezzo-soprano; unison voices; wordless SATB chorus.

Instrumentation: 1 flute (doubling piccolo), 1 oboe, 1 clarinet, 1 bassoon, 1 horn, 1 trumpet, 1 tenor trombone, timpani, percussion (2 players), harp, celesta (optional), pianoforte, strings.

First performance: Chicago, Illinois, Eighth Street Theatre, 26 December 1926, by Bolm Ballet, with the Delamarter Orchestra, conducted by Eric Delamarter, and scenery by Nicolas Remisoff. First concert performance (music only) in London as *A Christmas Carol Suite*, New English Music Society Concert, Park Lane Hotel, 17 December 1929, conducted by Anthony Bernard; first English performance as ballet, Cecil Sharp House, 29 December 1935, produced by Frederic Wilkinson with Douglas Kennedy as the Watchman, Anna Walker as the Virgin Mary and orchestra conducted by Imogen Holst.

Dedication: To Douglas Kennedy, with thanks for his splendid 'Watchman'.

Duration: About 30 minutes.

Publication: London, O.U.P. (© 1957) vocal score, with pianoforte arrangement by Roy Douglas. Orchestral material available on hire.

Note on score: The following carols may be sung at certain points at the discretion of producer and conductor:

Page 8 one bar before 2—*A Virgin Most Pure* (*Oxford Book of Carols* No. 4, first tune). Trebles only, unaccompanied, in F.

Page 25 at 63—*On Christmas Night* (O.B.C. No. 24). Unison, unaccompanied, in F.

Page 26 at 68—*As Joseph Was a-Walking* (O.B.C. No. 66, words of part II, tune of part III). Unison, unaccompanied, in A flat.

Scenario: A short prelude (based on 'The First Nowell') is followed by off-stage voices singing 'God rest you merry'. Scrooge is seen, as in the famous illustration, night-cap on head, supping his gruel. The singing disturbs him and he goes to the window and shakes his fist at the carol-singers. He hobbles back to his chair, leaving the window open. Marley's Ghost enters through the door and dances a grotesque dance. Scrooge falls on his knees, Marley drags him to the window and disappears. Mysterious wailings are heard and Scrooge faints. The Spirit of Christmas appears (a young boy), raises Scrooge up and leads him to the door. The stage blacks out and re-lights outside Fezziwig's house in a London street. Characters such as the Milkman cross the stage and go into Fezziwig's, to the tune of a country dance. Scrooge and the Spirit enter and watch. The third scene is in Fezziwig's parlour where a large company is dancing 'Haste to the Wedding'. Scrooge enters and watches, but none sees him. The Fezziwigs enter, with their three daughters and Scrooge as a young man, and greet their guests, to the tune 'Jamaica'. The Three Miss Fezziwigs and their six admirers dance 'Putney Ferry', followed by the boy-from-over-the-way who dances a solo Morris jig, 'Bacca Pipes' (variants of 'Greensleeves'), to a piccolo accompaniment. All join in until interrupted by the Fiddler, who starts tuning 'like fifty stomach aches', and strikes up 'The Triumph'. Fezziwig calls for 'Sir Roger de Coverley' and he and his wife lead off. At the height of the dance, midnight strikes, the party breaks up and the stage darkens; the prelude theme returns, lento, and off-stage the Watchman sings 'Past twelve o'clock'. The stage gradually lightens to the music of 'The First Nowell' and 'God rest you merry' in the orchestra. Moonlight and snow illuminate the scene. Watchman, now on-stage, is looking at an approaching procession, headed by the Spirit, followed by Shepherds, the Three Kings and others. It passes across the stage, while the tunes 'On Christmas Night' and 'The First Nowell' are interwoven in the orchestra. Black-out, and then an early Victorian drawing-room with parents sitting by the fire and a young girl playing on the pianoforte a version of 'The Seeds of Love'. A young man, Scrooge's former self, sits beside her. The scene again changes to Bob Cratchit's parlour, with supper half-finished and Tiny Tim in his chair. The children march round carrying out the remains of the goose. The pudding is brought in to the dance 'Hunsdon House'. Cratchit raises his glass to drink Scrooge's health, Scrooge being invisible, though present. Tiny Tim refuses to drink, to Scrooge's visible agitation. The children then dance the 'Black Nag' and afterwards, at Tim's instigation, kneel for evening prayer ('The White Paternoster'). Off-stage a voice sings 'The First Nowell', and a vision of the Nativity, as in an Italian picture, appears. The procession enters, followed by all the characters in the masque. All kneel except Scrooge, but Tim goes to him and leads him into the company, where he too kneels. Orchestra, voices and bells thunder out 'The First Nowell', which dies away into the music of the prelude and ends *niente*.

This revised scenario differs from the original version. Marley's Ghost did not appear; instead Scrooge in a dream saw the Three Kings and other characters pass across the stage to the music of the country dance 'Tink a Tink' (from Cecil Sharp's collection). This led into the Fezziwig ball. 'Tink a Tink' now accompanies the scene in the street outside the Fezziwigs' home. The Cratchits and Tiny Tim were not included in the original scenario. After the Victorian drawing-room scene, Dickens was followed more closely, because his vision of Scrooge's first love as the mother of a happy family at a children's party was enacted to the music which now accompanies the Cratchits' Christmas. Some of these changes arose from suggestions made to the composer by Mr. Frederic Wilkinson, headmaster of the Polytechnic Secondary School (now the Quintin School) who produced the 1935 version at Cecil Sharp House to Douglas Kennedy's choreography.[1]

To his detailed criticisms sent on 15 January 1936, Vaughan Williams replied on 11 August 1937:

Dear Mr. Wilkinson,

I find I have been a year and a half answering your letter! Now at last I am reconsidering the ballet.

My suggestion is to *cut out Scrooge altogether*—call the Ballet 'Xmas Eve' or some such title—keep all the first part up to the end of the procession of the 3 Kings (cutting the few bars which apply to Scrooge), then devise a new scene to incorporate as much of the present music as we can.

As regards your detailed criticism

(1) Entrance of characters—I don't feel we want more here—we don't want their identity grasped too much—they simply flit across the stage—after all, they all appear again in the ball scene and we can 'identify' them then.

(2) Personally I like the idea of the children dancing Hunsdon House—something prim to 'show how nicely the children can dance' (of course it did not get a chance with those lumpy children)—I don't believe we need always represent children as being rowdy—and they have a chance of being rowdy immediately before and after. Perhaps H. House is too long—it cd. easily be shortened and/or a quick dance added (they introduced 'Black Nag' in America)—but I am liable to persuasion on this point.

(3) The prayer scene I still like—I know it is sentimental—but *very* Dickensy and after all the whole thing is sentimental—again I am open to persuasion.

(4) I *like* all the characters appearing in the Apotheosis like the 'donore' in an Italian 'Sancta Famiglia'.

---

[1] Mr. Wilkinson was a friend of Holst, whom he met when he produced a programme of Holst's works in Liverpool.

(5) I think the 'Bacca Pipes' jig in the Ball Scene is too long—but this can easily be put right by optional cuts.

(6) If we keep Scrooge we must certainly introduce Cratchit and I don't think I feel up to that—besides a scene like that wd. become drama and cease to be ballet (also I don't think I cd. stomach Tiny Tim).

I suggest for title 'Xmas Eve' (*suggested by scenes from Dickens'* 'Xmas Carol'). . . .

Yours sincerely, R. Vaughan Williams

In the end a compromise was reached. Scrooge is kept, Cratchit and Tiny Tim are introduced, 'Black Nag' is added, the score is liberally strewn with optional cuts and the Three Kings are brought into the Snow Scene. The latest version is consequently rather disjointed, for the composer obviously wished to keep the work short and within the range of amateurs. It is a pity that he did not write an opera on the subject, into which his favourite Christmas music could have been incorporated much as the folk songs are incorporated in *Sir John in Love*. Even so, *On Christmas Night* is a charming seasonal work, at its most poetic when the Watchman sings off-stage. This was an effect Vaughan Williams enjoyed. A similar episode in *The Pilgrim's Progress* is one of the most beautiful parts of the score, and the Ballad Seller's song on May morning in Act II, Scene II of *Hugh the Drover* is another fine moment. They probably owe their existence to the profound impression made upon Vaughan Williams both by the Nightwatchman's Aria in *Die Meistersinger* and certainly by the recounted experience of a folk singer who heard the May Song sung at night by a friend.

Whereabouts of MS: British Library. Two full scores. (50407-8).

1927

1. ALONG THE FIELD. Eight Housman Songs for voice and violin. Words by A. E. Housman (1859-1936).

1. We'll to the woods no more (Last Poems, Prologue). *Moderato.*
2. Along the field (*A Shropshire Lad*, XXVI). *Allegretto.*
3. The half-moon westers low (*Last Poems*, XXVI). *Andante sostenuto.*
4. In the morning (*Last Poems*, XXIII). *Allegro moderato.*
5. The sigh that heaves the grasses. (*Last Poems*, XXVII). *Andante sostenuto.*
6. Goodbye. (*A Shropshire Lad*, V). *Allegretto grazioso e molto moderato.*
7. Fancy's Knell. (*Last Poems*, XLI). *Allegro moderato.*
8. With rue my heart is laden. (*A Shropshire Lad*, LIV). *Lento ma non troppo.*

First performance: London, Grotrian Hall, 24 October 1927. Joan

Elwes (soprano), Marie Wilson (violin); revised version: recording (not issued) for Argo, 17 February 1954, Nancy Evans (mezzo-soprano), Leonard Hirsch (violin); in public, London, Wigmore Hall, 26 May 1955, by same artists.

Publication: London, O.U.P. (© 1954).

Note: At the first performance only seven of the songs were sung. It has been impossible to discover which were sung. Nos. 5 and 8 of the above are the only ones mentioned by name in press notices of the concert.

When the composer revised them for publication he destroyed one of his original nine settings, that of 'The Soldier'.

Whereabouts of MS: British Library, six songs. (50481). The six (with their *original* numbering in brackets) are: 'We'll to the woods' (1); 'Along the Field' (2); 'The half-moon' (3); 'In the Morning' (6); 'Fancy's Knell' (8) 'With rue' (9).

1928

1. TE DEUM IN G. To be sung Decani and Cantoris (SATB men's and boys' voices) with organ or orchestra. Text from Book of Common Prayer. *Con Moto.* G major.

   Instrumentation: (arr. Arnold Foster) 2 flutes, 2 oboes, 2 clarinets, 2 bassoons, 4 horns (2 opt.), 2 trumpets, 3 trombones, tuba (opt.), timpani, cymbals, pianoforte, strings. *Or* strings and pianoforte (or organ).

   First performance: Canterbury Cathedral, 4 December 1928, at enthronement of Dr. Cosmo Gordon Lang as Archbishop of Canterbury, for which occasion it was written. Choirs of Canterbury Cathedral and the Chapel Royal, conducted by Walford Davies; Charlton Palmer (organ).

   Publication: London, O.U.P. (© 1928). Material available on hire.

2. THE OXFORD BOOK OF CAROLS. Edited by The Rev. Percy Dearmer (words); R. Vaughan Williams and Martin Shaw (music). The following original tunes were written by Vaughan Williams for this book:

   173. The Golden Carol.[1] *Allegro vivace.* Traditional words, 15th century. 'Now is Christèmas y-come'. Version used by F. Sidgwick in *Ancient Carols*, 1908.

   185. Wither's Rocking Hymn. *Lento con moto.* Words by George Wither (1588–1667), from *Halelujah*, 1641. 'Sweet baby, sleep! What ails my dear?'

---

[1] An arrangement of 'The Golden Carol' for unison SATB with organ or pianoforte accompaniment by Erik Routley is published as Oxford Choral Song U102 (© O.U.P. 1963).

186. Snow in the Street. *Andante con moto*. Words by William Morris (1834–96), from 'The Land East of the Sun and West of the Moon' in *The Earthly Paradise* (1868–70). 'From far away we come to you.'

196. Blake's Cradle Song. *Andantino*. Words by William Blake (1757–1827), from *Songs of Innocence* (1789). 'Sweet dreams, form a shade o'er my lovely infant's head.'

The following Carols were arranged by Vaughan Williams:

7. Hereford Carol ('Come all you faithful Christians').

17. All in the morning ('It was on Christmas Day').

24. Sussex Carol ('On Christmas night').

31. Gloucestershire Wassail ('Wassail, wassail, all over the town!').

36. The Salutation Carol ('Nowell, This is the salutation').

39. This endris night ('This endris night I saw a sight').

43. The Seven Virgins ('All under the leaves, the leaves of life').

45. Sussex Mummers' Carol ('O mortal man, remember well'). Alternative harmonisation to Lucy Broadwood's arrangement.

47. May Carol ('Awake, awake, good people all').

51. The Sinners' Redemption ('All you that are to mirth inclined').

53. The Carnal and the Crane ('As I passed by a riverside').

55. The Miraculous Harvest (' "Rise up, rise up, you merry men all" ').

57. Dives and Lazarus ('As it fell out upon one day').

61. Down in yon forest ('Down in yon forest there stands a hall').

68. The truth from above ('This is the truth sent from above').

77. Song of the Crib ('Joseph dearest, Joseph mine').

79. Quem pastores laudavere ('Quem pastores laudavere').

115. Joseph and Mary ('O Joseph being an old man truly').

131. Coverdale's Carol ('Now blessed be thou, Christ Jesu').

132. Psalm of Sion ('O mother dear, Jerusalem').

134. (with Martin Shaw) If ye would hear ('If ye would hear the angels sing').

138. O little town ('O little town of Bethlehem').

142. Children's Song of the Nativity ('How far is it to Bethlehem?').

An appendix gives folk tunes proper to certain carols in Part I of the *O.B.C.* All but one are arranged R.V.W.:

1. A Virgin most pure (No. 4).[1] Tune noted by Cecil Sharp in Shropshire, 1911. *Journal of the Folk Song Society*, Vol. V, p. 24.

2. On Christmas Night (Sussex carol, No. 24). Tune noted by Dr.

---

[1] Vaughan Williams in about 1956 made an arrangement of this carol for soprano solo and SATB chorus, unaccompanied, dedicated 'to Margaret Field-Hyde and her Golden Age Singers' (O.C.S.X107. © O.U.P. 1963). MS. in British Library (50379–80).

Culwick in Dublin, 1904. *J.F.S.S.*, Vol. II, p. 126.
3. The Moon shines bright (Bellman's Song, Part I, No. 46).
   (*a*) Tune noted by Lucy Broadwood, Surrey, 1894. *J.F.S.S.*, Vol. I, p. 176.
   (*b*) Tune noted by Godfrey Arkwright at Kingsclere, Hants, 1897. *J.F.S.S.*, Vol. I, p. 178.
4. The Holy Well (No. 56). Tune noted by Sharp at Camborne, 1913. *J.F.S.S.*, Vol. V, p. 4.
5. Dives and Lazarus (No. 57). Tune noted by Miss Andrews and Dr. Darling at Eardisley, Herefordshire, 1905.
6. Come all ye worthy Christian men (Job) (No. 60).
   (*a*) Tune noted by Percy Merrick. (By permission of Novello & Co.) *J.F.S.S.*, Vol. I, p. 74e.
   (*b*) Tune noted by R.V.W. near Horsham, 1904. *J.F.S.S.*, Vol. II, p. 118.

Except where otherwise stated, tunes and arrangements above are © 1928 R.V.W.

Publication: London, O.U.P. © 1928. Carols Nos. 31, 36, 39, 55, 77, 79, 132, 134, 138, 142, 173, 185, 196 all available separately, published 1928.

Also available:
1. *The Oxford Book of Carols for Schools.* Contains 50 carols from the O.B.C. arranged for unison singing. © O.U.P. 1956.
2. *English Traditional Carols.* Edited by R. Vaughan Williams and Martin Shaw. Contains 21 carols from the O.B.C. arranged for soprano (or trebles) and alto voices in two, three and four parts. Some with descant. © O.U.P. 1954.

3. SIR JOHN IN LOVE. An Opera in Four Acts, the libretto based on Shakespeare's *The Merry Wives of Windsor* (with German translation by Anton Mayer), for 20 soloists, mixed chorus and orchestra.

Instrumentation: 2 flutes, 2 oboes, 1 cor anglais, 2 clarinets, 2 bassoons, 2 horns, 2 trumpets, trombone, timpani, percussion, rattle, bells, harp, strings.

Characters (in order of appearance):
*Shallow, a country Justice (tenor or baritone)
 Sir Hugh Evans, a Welsh parson (high baritone)
 Slender, a foolish young gentleman (tenor)
*Peter Simple, his servant (tenor or baritone)
 Page, a citizen of Windsor (baritone)
 Sir John Falstaff (baritone)
*Bardolph ⎫
 Nym   ⎬ Sharpers attending Falstaff ⎰ (tenor)
 Pistol   ⎭   ⎨ (baritone)
                                            ⎱ (bass)

Anne Page, Page's daughter ⎧ (soprano)
Mrs. Page, Page's wife ⎨ (soprano)
Mrs. Ford, Ford's wife ⎩ (mezzo-soprano)
Fenton, a young gentleman of the Court at Windsor (tenor)
Dr. Caius, a French physician (high baritone)
*Rugby, his servant (bass)
Mrs. Quickly, his housekeeper (mezzo-soprano or contralto)
The Host of the Garter Inn (baritone)
Robin, Falstaff's page (non-singing)
Ford, a citizen of Windsor (bass)
*John ⎫ (baritone)
*Robert ⎬ Ford's servants (baritone)
William, Mrs. Page's son (non-singing)
Alice Shortcake, Bardolph's sweetheart (non-singing)
Jenny Pluckpears, Nym's sweetheart (non-singing)
Girl friends of Anne Page ⎫
Women servants of Ford ⎬ S. and A (chorus)
Citizens of Windsor ⎫
Servants of Ford and Page ⎬ T. and B. (chorus)
Boy friends of William Page (non-singing)
Dancers and Flute Player in Act IV.

* Denotes that these parts may be taken by members of the chorus. Also in case of necessity Shallow and Caius can be doubled by one singer. In this case (1) at the end of Act II Bardolph must come on instead of Shallow; (2) in Act III, Scene I, the small notes for Page, Host and Rugby to be sung; (3) in Act III, Scene II, and Act IV, the part of Shallow to be omitted. It is also physically possible to double the parts of Fenton and Bardolph but this is not desirable.

Act I. A Street in Windsor.
Act II, Scene I. A Room in Page's House.
  Scene II. A Room in the Garter Inn.
Act III, Scene I. A Field near Windsor.
  Scene II. A Room in Ford's House.
Act IV, Scene I. A Room in Ford's House.
  Scene II. Windsor Forest.

Note: Act II, Scene I, Act III, Scene I, and Act IV, Scene I, can be played in front of curtains if preferred.

First performance: London, Parry Opera Theatre of the Royal College of Music, 21 March 1929 (Four private performances sponsored by the Ernest Palmer Fund for Opera Study). The cast was altered in some performances; both original casts are therefore given below:

	21 and 22 March	25 and 26 March
SHALLOW ..	Alfred Walmsley	..
SIR HUGH EVANS ..	Albert Kennedy	..
SLENDER	Philip Warde	..

PETER SIMPLE	..	William Herbert	..
PAGE	.. ..	Thomas Dance	..
SIR JOHN FALSTAFF		Leyland White	Richard Watson
BARDOLPH	..	Howard Hemming	..
NYM	.. ..	Charles Holmes	..
PISTOL	.. ..	George Hancock	{ George Hancock (25) / Alex Henderson (26)
MRS. PAGE	..	May Moore	Elizabeth Ryan
ANNE PAGE	..	Olive Evers	Marjorie Woodville
MRS. FORD	..	Veronica Mansfield	Meriel St. C. Green
MRS. QUICKLY	..	Hilda Rickard	Marjorie Haviland
FENTON	.. ..	A. Bamfield Cooper	..
DR. CAIUS	..	Douglas Tichener	{ Walter Saull (25) / Douglas Tichener (26)
RUGBY	.. ..	Frederick Lloyd	..
FORD	.. ..	Clifford White	..
HOST	.. ..	John Greenwood	..
ROBIN	.. ..	James Flack	..
JOHN	.. ..	John Huson	..
ROBERT	.. ..	John Gibson	..

CHORUS of 27 among whom the names Marjorie Westbury and Muir Mathieson may be noted. Nine fairies and imps, one of them being Imogen Holst.

Conductor: Dr. Malcolm Sargent; producer: Cairns James; stage manager: H. Procter-Gregg; Scenery designed and arranged by H. Procter-Gregg and Simpson Robinson; dances arranged by Penelope Spencer; S. P. Waddington and Hermann Grunebaum assisted in the preparation of the music.

Dedication: To S. P. Waddington.

My dear Waddington,

I venture to dedicate this Opera to you firstly as a token of my admiration for you as a man and a musician and secondly to show my gratitude to you for all your help and encouragement in this and all my work.

I sometimes feel that you ought, with all your skill and knowledge, to despise my comparatively amateurish efforts. It really seems ridiculous that I should spend my time writing operas while you spend yours teaching elementary harmony to unwilling flappers. However, everyone knows that whilst you could, if you would, write a first-rate opera, I, on the other hand, should be entirely incompetent to teach elementary harmony. So I suppose things must remain as they are.

Yours ever gratefully,
R. Vaughan Williams.

Duration: About 2 hours without the added (optional) Prologue, Episode and Interlude.

Publication: London, O.U.P. (© 1930) Vocal Score. Chorus parts and orchestral material on hire. The opera was written between 1924 and 1928.

Note: The vocal score contains a Preface and suggestions for the final dance. The following folk songs are incorporated into the opera (page No. refers to vocal score):

'A sailor loved a farmer's daughter', p. 7. 'A sailor from the sea', p. 15. 'Robin Hood and the Bishop', p. 42. 'Vrai dieu d'amours, comfortez moy' (old French chanson), p. 51. 'John, come kiss me now', p. 71. 'Lovely Joan', p. 106. 'To Shallow Rivers' (tune of *Black-eyed Susan*), p. 158. 'Peg-a-Ramsey', p. 178. 'Greensleeves', p. 195. 'T'old wife o' Dallowgill', p. 212. And also Psalm Tune 'St. Mary' (Prys's *Welsh Psalter*, 1621), p. 159. Folk dance, 'Speed the plough', p. 187. Folk dance 'Half Hannikin', p. 305.

———

Various interpolations from other authors and other plays by Shakespeare were made by Vaughan Williams in his libretto. Here is a list of them:

Act I, p. 26: 'Weep eyes, break heart' from *A Chaste Maid in Cheapside* by Thomas Middleton (1570?–1627), Act I, p. 27. 'Do but look on her eyes' from *The Devil is an Ass* by Ben Jonson (1572?–1637), known as *The Triumph.*

Act I, p. 30: 'Have you seen but a bright[1] lily grow?' (Ben Jonson, as above). 'Come, O come, my life's delight' (Thomas Campion, 1567–1619).

Act I, p. 59: 'Back and side go bare', from *Gammer Gurton's Needle*, (Act II). R.V.W. attributes the words to John Still, Bishop of Bath and Wells (1543–1607). In the *Oxford Dictionary of Quotations* and the *Concise Cambridge History of English Literature*, authorship is attributed to William Stevenson (1530?–75). One prefers to side with R.V.W. and imagine that the people of Bath and Wells had a bishop who could write a drinking song with the line 'But belly, God send thee good ale enough, whether it be new or old'. Bishop of Bass and Worthington, perhaps?

Act I, p. 90: 'When daisies pied', from *Love's Labour's Lost*, Act V, Scene II.

Act II, p. 107: 'Sigh no more, ladies', from *Much Ado About Nothing*, Act II, Scene III.

Act II, p. 131: 'O that joy so soon should waste', from *Cynthia's Revels* by Ben Jonson.

———

[1] Not, in this case, 'whyte'.

Act II, pp. 158–9: Psalm 137 and stanza from *The Passionate Shepherd* by Christopher Marlowe (1564–93).

Act III, p. 195: 'Greensleeves'. Words of this version taken from the miscellany *A Handefull of Pleasant Delites* (1584). Spelling modernized.

Act III, p. 196: 'Have I caught my heavenly jewel?' by Sir Philip Sidney (1554–86).

Act IV, p. 226: 'The falling out of faithful friends renewal is of love'. Madrigal 'In going to my naked bed' by Richard Edwards (1523?–66) in *The Paradise of Dainty Devices* (1576).

Act IV, p. 284: 'See the chariot at hand here of love wherein my lady rideth'. (Ben Jonson, from *The Triumph*.)

Act IV, p. 294: 'Whether men do laugh or weep', from *A Book of Airs* (1601) by Philip Rosseter (1568?–1623) and Thomas Campion, attributed Campion.

Whereabouts of MS: British Library, Full Score Acts I–IV (50410A–D). Also typed libretto with MS. additions by composer. Copy of piano part II of 2-piano arrangement of seven episodes from 'Fat Knight' (57284).

3A. PROLOGUE, EPISODE AND INTERLUDE. From the Opera *Sir John in Love.*

Instrumentation as for *Sir John in Love.*

Characters: Prologue (to be played before Act I).

   Moderato. B flat major.

   Queen Elizabeth (silent).

   *Lord Hunsdon, the Lord Chamberlain (baritone).

   *Master of the Revels (baritone).

   Hemynge (dressed for part of Falstaff) (baritone).

   The Lord Chamberlain's Players (dressed for their parts in the *Merry Wives of Windsor*).

   Musicians, tumblers and dancers attached to the players.

   Courtiers and Court ladies.

   Servants and followers of the Court.

The *Prologue* makes no pretence to historical accuracy.

Scene: The Great Hall of Windsor Castle (or, if more convenient, the interior of a Pavilion).

Episode (To be played in Act I between the exit of Mrs. Quickly and the Tavern Scene: vocal score p. 58 immediately before 34.)

   Allegretto. F major.

   Bardolph (tenor).

   Nym (baritone).

   Pistol (bass).

---

* As Rugby, Simple, John and Robert do not appear in the procession of players, two of them can, if necessary, double these parts.

Chorus of ladies and gentlemen of the Court.

Interlude (To be played between Scenes I and II of Act II at 14a in vocal score, p. 115, or between Acts I and II.) *Andante moderato*. F minor.

Anne Page (soprano).

Fenton (tenor).

Host (baritone).

Dr. Caius (high baritone).

Slender (tenor).

Young men and women (Anne Page's companions).

A piper, a drummer.

Scene: A footpath near Windsor.

First performance: Bristol Opera School, Victoria Rooms, Clifton, 30 October 1933, produced and conducted by Robert Percival with Dorothy Hill as the Queen, and Percival Goodway as Falstaff. Six performances were given.

Publication: London, O.U.P. (© 1936). Vocal score and orchestral parts on hire only. Prologue now withdrawn.

Note: The Prologue was based on the tradition that Queen Elizabeth suggested that Falstaff should be shown in love. The episode deals with the pickpocket activities of Nym, Bardolph and Pistol and includes the line 'The good humour is to steal at a minim's rest'.[1] The Interlude develops the wooing of Anne Page by Fenton. The following are the sources of the libretto, besides Shakespeare:

Prologue, p. 4: 'O beauteous queen of second Troy'. Pastiche by R.V.W. based on madrigal by Byrd 'This sweet and merry month'.

Episode, p. 18: 'Say dainty dames shall we go play?' from madrigal by Thomas Weelkes (1575?–1623).

Interlude, p. 34: 'Beauty clear and fair', from *The Elder Brother* by John Fletcher (1579–1625).

Interlude, p. 38: 'Fair and fair and twice so fair', from *The Arraignment of Paris* (1583) by George Peele (1558–97).

Interlude, p. 51: 'I mun be married a-Sunday', from *Ralph Roister Doister* (*c.* 1553) by Nicholas Udall (1505–56).

Whereabouts of MS.: British Library. Full score (50409).

3B. IN WINDSOR FOREST. Cantata for mixed chorus (SATB) and orchestra, music adapted from the opera *Sir John in Love*.

Instrumentation: 2 flutes, 2 oboes, 2 clarinets, 2 bassoons, 2 horns, 2 trumpets, 1 trombone, timpani, percussion, harp (or pianoforte), strings. *Or* strings and pianoforte.

---

[1] Cf. article by R.V.W. on this text reprinted in *National Music and Other Essays* (1963).

    I. The Conspiracy ('Sigh no more, ladies') for women's voices. *Allegro.* E minor.

    II. Drinking Song ('Back and side go bare') for men's voices. *Allegro pesante.* A minor.

    III. Falstaff and the Fairies ('Round about in a fair ring-a'). *Allegretto.* E flat.

    IV. Wedding Chorus ('See the chariot at hand'). *Andante moderato.* E flat.

    V. Epilogue ('Whether men do laugh or weep'). *Moderato maestoso.* B flat major.

Texts for above are as in *Sir John in Love* except for III which is expanded from the opera and is based on an amalgam of Shakespeare, Thomas Ravenscroft (*c.* 1592–1635) and John Lyly (1554?–1606).

First performance: London, Queen's Hall, 14 April 1931. National Provincial Bank Musical Society, conducted by Herbert J. Baggs. (Described as 'first complete performance with orchestra'.)

Duration: 16 minutes.

Publication: London, O.U.P. (© 1931) Vocal score. Orchestral parts on hire.

Whereabouts of MS.: British Library. Full score (50450).

Other versions: (*a*) arranged for women's voices (SSA.) by Guthrie Foote. O.U.P. (vocal score) (© 1954). (*b*) The following songs from *In Windsor Forest* are available separately:

    I. Sigh no more, ladies. For women's voices (SSAA) with orchestra, or strings and pianoforte. *Allegro.* E minor.

    Instrumentation: flute, piccolo, 2 oboes, 2 clarinets, 2 bassoons, 2 horns, 2 trumpets, 1 trombone, timpani, percussion, strings.

    Publication: London, O.U.P. (© 1931) Vocal score. Parts on hire.

    II. Drinking Song. ('Back and side go bare'). For male voices (TTBB) with orchestra, or strings and pianoforte.

    Instrumentation: As in opera.

    Publication: London, O.U.P. (© 1931) Vocal score. Parts on hire.

    IV. Wedding Chorus ('See the chariot at hand').

        (*a*) For mixed chorus, with orchestra, or strings and pianoforte. *Instrumentation:* As in opera.

        Publication: London, O.U.P. (O.C.S.X.60) (© 1930).

        (*b*) For women's voices (SSA), arranged by Guthrie Foote, with instrumentation as for 'Sigh no more, ladies'. O.U.P. (© 1954).

        (*c*) Solo song for baritone or mezzo voice with pianoforte accompaniment. *Andante moderato.* C major.

    Publication: London, O.U.P. (© 1934).

(*d*) Solo song for tenor and pianoforte. *Andante moderato.* E flat major.

Publication: London, O.U.P. (© 1934).

The several arrangements of *Greensleeves* will be found under 1934, the date of its first separate publication.

1929

1. BENEDICITE. For soprano solo, mixed chorus (SATB) and orchestra. Words from 'The Song of the Three Holy Children' (Apocrypha) and 'Hark, my soul, how everything', by John Austin (1613–69).

   Instrumentation: 2 flutes (2nd doubling piccolo), 2 oboes, 2 clarinets, 2 bassoons, 4 horns, 2 trumpets, 3 trombones, timpani, percussion, celesta (ad lib.), pianoforte, strings. *Or* 2 flutes, 1 oboe, 2 clarinets, 1 bassoon, 2 horns, 1 trumpet, 1 trombone, pianoforte, strings. *Or* strings and pianoforte only.

   First performance: Dorking, The Drill Hall, Leith Hill Musical Festival, 2 May 1930. Margaret Rees (soprano), Leith Hill Festival Chorus (Towns) and Orchestra, conducted by Dr. R. Vaughan Williams. First performance in London: Southwark Cathedral, 21 February 1931, Special Choir, members of London Symphony Orchestra, conducted by Edgar T. Cook. Joan Elwes (soprano), C. Thornton Lofthouse (pianoforte).

   Dedication: To L.H.M.C. [Leith Hill Musical Competition] Towns Division.

   Duration: 15 minutes.

   Publication: London, O.U.P. (© 1929) Vocal score. Orchestral parts on hire. Full score O.U.P. © 1970.

   Whereabouts of MS.: British Library, full score (50447). 2-piano arrangement (57285).

   Other version: Arranged by Jean Storry for soprano solo, women's chorus (SSAA), and orchestra.

   Publication: London, O.U.P (© 1964). Orchestral parts on hire (the orchestration is unchanged from the original version).

2. THE HUNDREDTH PSALM. For mixed chorus (SATB) and orchestra. Words from Psalm C and Doxology from *Daye's Psalter* of 1561. *Andante maestoso.* E minor.

   Instrumentation: 2 flutes, 2 oboes (1 optional), 2 clarinets, 2 bassoons, 1 double bassoon (opt.), 4 horns (2 opt.), 2 trumpets, 1 trombone (opt.), tuba, timpani (opt.), cymbals (opt.), organ (opt.), strings. *Or* strings and organ or pianoforte.

   First performance: Dorking, The Drill Hall, 29 April 1930. Leith Hill Festival Chorus (Division II) and Orchestra, conducted by Dr. R. Vaughan Williams. First London performance: Morley College Choir

and Orchestra, conductor Arnold Foster, on 24 May 1930.
Dedication: To L.H.M.C. Div. II.
Duration: 8 minutes.
Publication: London, Stainer & Bell Ltd. (© 1929). Vocal Score
(S. & B. 4011). Orchestral parts on hire.
Whereabouts of MS.: British Library. Full score (50449).

3. THREE CHORAL HYMNS. For baritone (or tenor) solo, mixed
chorus (SATB) and orchestra. Words by Miles Coverdale, Bishop of
Exeter (1488–1569), translated from the German. The texts of Nos.
2 and 3 are after Martin Luther (1483–1546). Spelling is modernized,
but original is printed before each hymn.
1. Easter Hymn. *Moderato.* D minor.
2. Christmas Hymn. *Allegretto tranquillo.* F major.
3. Whitsunday Hymn. *Andantino.* C major.
Instrumentation: 2 flutes, 2 oboes (1 opt), 2 clarinets, 2 bassoons,
4 horns, 2 trumpets, 3 trombones (opt.), tuba (opt), timpani, cymbals
(opt.), organ (opt.), strings. *Or* strings and pianoforte, or pianoforte
and organ.
First performance: Dorking, The Drill Hall, 30 April 1930. Ian Glennie
(tenor), Leith Hill Festival Chorus (Div. I) and Orchestra, conducted
by Dr. R. Vaughan Williams. First performance in London: South-
wark Cathedral, 21 February 1931, William Groves (tenor), Special
Choir and members of L.S.O., conducted by Edgar T. Cook.
Dedication: To L.H.M.C. Division I.
Duration: 11 minutes.
Publication: London, J. Curwen & Sons Ltd. (© U.S.A. 1930,
R.V.W.). Faber Music, vocal score (C.03685); full score and parts on
hire.
Other Versions: Each hymn was published separately by Curwen's
(C.E. 80679–81) in vocal score (© U.S.A. 1930, R.V.W.). The title of
III is given as 'Whitsuntide Hymn' in the separate edition.
Whereabouts of MS.: British Library. Full score (57723), II and III
vocal score (50448). Copy of I (59796).

4. THREE CHILDREN'S SONGS FOR A SPRING FESTIVAL.
For voices in unison with strings accompaniment. Words by Frances
M. Farrer (1895–1977).
1. Spring. *Allegretto.* F major.
2. The Singers. *Allegro.* D minor-major.
3. An Invitation. *Allegro moderato.* G minor.
First performance: Dorking, The Drill Hall, 1 May 1930, Leith Hill
Festival Children's Choirs, conducted by Dr. R. Vaughan Williams.
Dedication: To L.H.M.C. Children's Division.
Publication: London, O.U.P. (© 1930), collectively as Oxford Choral

Songs series, No. 1034, individually as O.C.S., Nos. 1031–33. Orchestral parts on hire.

5. SONGS OF PRAISE FOR BOYS AND GIRLS. Edited by the Rev. Percy Dearmer, R. Vaughan Williams and Martin Shaw. Contains the following original tune by R.V.W. especially written for this volume:

95. Marathon ('Servants of the great adventure'). Adaptation of Processional Chorus in Parabasis (section 12) from *The Wasps* (vocal score of incidental music, p. 74). (© 1928 R.V.W.)

The following arrangements by R.V.W. are included. Those starred are of English traditional melodies.

* 1. Hardwick ('So here hath been dawning').
* 5. Horsham ('Through the night thy angels kept').
* 8. Shipston ('Jesus, tender Shepherd, hear me').
* 9. Tavistock ('Matthew, Mark and Luke and John').
13. Banbury ('The year's at the spring'), 17th century melody.
* 23. Rodmell ('When Christ was born in Bethlehem').
27. Come, Faithful People ('Come, faithful people, come away'). Arrangement of melody by the Rev. C. Bicknell (1842–1918).
* 29. (i) Bridgwater ⎫
*   (ii) Langport ⎬ ('See Him in raiment rent').
33. Solothurn ('Around the Throne of God'), Swiss traditional.
* 56. Monk's Gate ('He who would valiant be').
57. Pleading Saviour ('Heavenly Father, send Thy blessing'). Arrangement from Plymouth Collection (New York 1855).
* 58. Stowey ('How far is it to Bethlehem? Not very far').
* 60. East Horndon ('I think, when I read that sweet story of old').
* 64. Herongate ('It is a thing most wonderful').
65. Quem pastores laudavere ('Jesu, good above all other'). 15th century German melody.
* 69. Eardisley ('Lord, I would own Thy tender care').
* 72. Hambridge ('O dear and lovely brother').
* 76. St. Hugh ('Sing to the Lord the children's hymn').
* 80. Gosterwood ('The wise may bring their learning').
83. Epsom ('To Mercy, Pity, Peace and Love'). Arrangement from Arnold's *Compleat Psalmodist*, 1756.
93. Resonet in laudibus ('Who within that stable cries'). 14th century German carol.
94. Magdalena ('Remember all the people'). German traditional.
105. Magdalena ('We thank Thee, Loving Father'). German traditional.

*109. (i) St. Austin ⎱ ('O mother dear, Jerusalem').
*   (ii) Farnham   ⎰
Publication: London, O.U.P. (© 1929).

6. FANTASIA ON SUSSEX FOLK TUNES. For violoncello soloist and orchestra.

Unpublished.

Instrumentation: Solo cello, 2 flutes (2nd doubling piccolo), 1 oboe, 2 clarinets, 2 bassoons, 2 horns, 1 trumpet, timpani, strings.

First Performance : London, Queen's Hall, Royal Philharmonic Society Concert, 13 March 1930. Pablo Casals (cello). Orchestra of the Royal Philharmonic Society, conducted by John Barbirolli.

Dedication: To Pablo Casals.

Note: This work, completed in 1929, was based on the following folk songs:

1. Salisbury Plain. Collected by R.V.W. from Mr. and Mrs. Peter Verrall of Horsham.

2. The Long Whip. 'There was an old man who lived in the city.' Collected by R.V.W. from Mr. Beck at Rodmell, 10 January 1906.

3. 'Low down in the broom.' Collected by W. P. Merrick at Lods worth, near Midhurst, in 1900.

4. Bristol Town. Collected by Lucy Broadwood from Mr. Henry Burstow in Horsham, 1893.

5. 'I've been to France.' Collected by W. P. Merrick, 1900.

The work's title was changed from *Sussex Rhapsody*. Although the work was on hire for a time, eventually Vaughan Williams withdrew it, having never been satisfied with it. It is not a major work, but one regrets the ban he placed on its performance. It goes some way towards disproving Lambert's oft-quoted remark that there is nothing to be done with a folk song once it has been played except to 'play it over again and play it rather louder'. Despite Lambert's *mot*, Delius in *Brigg Fair*, Vaughan Williams in several works, not to mention Dvořák, Haydn, and Beethoven, have done a great deal with variants of folk song. Vaughan Williams's rhapsodic treatment of tunes which, by their strophic nature, do not lend themselves to symphonic development, has not received its proper due in appreciation. In the *Sussex Fantasia* the tunes are extended by the composer's skill into new tunes, with an amusing commentary on the quicker tunes from the woodwind section. What probably dissatisfied Vaughan Williams is the slightly uncomfortable rôle of the cello.

Whereabouts of MS. British Library. Full score (and piano reduction mostly in hand of Constant Lambert) (57471).

1930

1. HYMNS FOR TODAY, Missionary and Devotional. Contained two hymns by Vaughan Williams:
No. 36. Monk's Gate ('He who would valiant be') (arranged R.V.W.).
No. 79. Sine Nomine ('For all the saints').
Publication: London, The Psalms and Hymns Trust.

2. HYMNS FOR SUNDAY SCHOOL ANNIVERSARIES, and other special occasions. Edited by R. Vaughan Williams, Martin Shaw, the Rev. Percy Dearmer and Canon G. W. Briggs. Contains 14 hymns, with accompaniments, one by R.V.W.:
No. 12. Down Ampney ('Come down, O love divine').
Publication: London, O.U.P. 1930.

3. HYMN TUNE PRELUDE ON 'SONG 13' BY ORLANDO GIBBONS. For pianoforte. Composed 1928. *Andante tranquillo.*[1] G major. Tune occurs in *English Hymnal* to Nos. 314 and 413.
First performance: London, Wigmore Hall, 14 January 1930. Harriet Cohen (pianoforte).
Dedication: To Harriet Cohen.
Publication: London, O.U.P. (© 1930).
Other versions: (*a*) Arranged for organ by E. Stanley Roper. London, O.U.P. (© 1930).
(*b*) Arranged for strings by Helen Glatz. London, O.U.P. (Oxford Orchestral Series O.157). (© 1930).
Whereabouts of MS.: British Library (52287).

4. PRELUDE AND FUGUE IN C MINOR. For orchestra. *Allegro con fuoco. Allegro moderato.*
Instrumentation: 3 flutes, 2 oboes, 2 clarinets, 2 bassoons, 1 double bassoon, 4 horns, 3 trumpets, 3 trombones, tuba, timpani, percussion (2 players), organ, strings.
First performance: The Cathedral, Hereford, Three Choirs Festival, 12 September 1930, London Symphony Orchestra, conducted by Dr. R. Vaughan Williams.
Dedication: To Henry Ley [1887–1962].
Duration: 10 minutes.
Publication: Orchestral parts available on hire only from O.U.P.
Note: This work has been included in 1930 as date of first performance. The Prelude was composed in September 1921, revised July 1923 and March 1930. The Fugue was composed August 1921, revised July 1923 and March 1930.
Other version: Arrangement for organ. Published London, O.U.P. (© 1930).

[1] R.V.W. in letter to Miss Cohen in 1928 said: 'Play it not too quick; and calm, with sub-conscious emotion.'

Whereabouts of MS.: British Library. Full Score (50393).

5. JOB. A Masque for Dancing, founded on Blake's *Illustrations of the Book of Job*. Scenario by Geoffrey Keynes and Gwendolen Raverat. In nine scenes and an epilogue.

Instrumentation: 2 flutes (1 opt.), 1 bass flute, 2 oboes (1 opt.), 1 cor anglais, 3 clarinets (1 opt., doubled by bass clar.), bass clarinet (opt.), E flat saxophone (opt., may be doubled by bass clarinet player, bass clarinet notes being cued to 2nd clar. When sax. is doubled by bass clar., part should be omitted until Sc. VI), 2 bassoons, 1 double bassoon (opt.), 4 horns, 3 trumpets (1 opt.), 3 trombones, tuba, timpani, percussion (3 players: side drum, triangle, cymbals, bass drum, xylophone, glockenspiel, tam-tam; most of these opt.); 2 harps (1 opt.), organ (opt.), strings. Instrumentation for theatre orchestra by Constant Lambert: 2 flutes (2nd doubling piccolo), 1 oboe, 2 clarinets, E flat saxophone (played by 2nd clarinet), 2 horns, 2 trumpets, 1 trombone, timpani, percussion (3 players: cymbals, bass drum, xylophone, glockenspiel, tam-tam), 1 harp, strings.

First performance: Concert version, Norwich Festival, St. Andrew's Hall, Norwich, 23 October 1930. The Queen's Hall Orchestra, conducted by Dr. R. Vaughan Williams. First performance in London (broadcast in London Region from Savoy Hill): 13 February 1931, B.B.C. Symphony Orchestra, conducted by Dr. R. Vaughan Williams. First public performance: Queen's Hall, Royal Philharmonic Society Concert, 3 December 1931, orchestra of Royal Philharmonic Society, conducted by Basil Cameron.

Stage version: London, Cambridge Theatre, Sunday, 5 July 1931, by the Camargo Society with the following cast:

JOB	John MacNair.
HIS WIFE	Margery Stewart,
HIS THREE DAUGHTERS ..	Marie Nelson, Ursula Moreton. Doreen Adams.
HIS SEVEN SONS ..	William Chappell, Hedley Briggs, Walter Gore, Claude Newman, Robert Stuart, Travers Kemp, Stanley Judson.
THE THREE MESSENGERS ..	Robert Stuart, Claude Newman, Travers Kemp.
THE THREE COMFORTERS	William Chappell, Walter Gore, Hedley Briggs.
WAR, PESTILENCE AND FAMINE ..	William Chappell, Walter Gore, Hedley Briggs.
ELIHU	Stanley Judson.
SATAN	Anton Dolin.
JOB'S SPIRITUAL SELF	John Loftus.

THE CHILDREN OF GOD, SONS OF THE MORNING, etc.
Conductor: Constant Lambert. Scenery and costumes: Gwendolen
Raverat. Choreographer: Ninette de Valois. First performance by the
Sadler's Wells Company at the Old Vic Theatre was on 22 September
1931.
Dedication: To Adrian Boult.
Duration: 45 minutes.
Publication: London, O.U.P. Full Score © 1934, miniature score
© 1935; pianoforte arrangement by Vally Lasker © 1931. The
pianoforte score contains more detailed stage directions than are given
in the full score. It also has as frontispiece Blake's illustration 'Hast
thou considered my servant Job?' which was first published on
8 March 1825. Orchestral parts and pianoforte arrangement available
on hire.
Scenario: Vaughan Williams's scenario, or synopsis, printed in the full
score differs from Geoffrey Keynes's.[1] Both are given below, Keynes's
on the left, Vaughan Williams's on the right. In addition, I have incorporated into Vaughan Williams's some of the more important stage
directions from the pianoforte score and given the Biblical references'
chapter and verse:

Scene I

G.K.	R.V.W.
Job is sitting in the sunset of pros-perity with his wife, surrounded by his seven sons and three daughters. They all join in a pastoral dance. When they have dispersed, leaving Job and his wife alone, Satan enters unperceived. He appeals to Heaven, which opens, revealing the God-head (Job's Spiritual Self) en-throned within. On the steps are the Heavenly Hosts. Job's Spiritual Self consents that his moral nature be tested in the furnace of tempta-tion.	'Hast thou considered my servant Job?' (I:8). Introduction, Pastoral Dance, Satan's Appeal to God, Saraband of the Sons of God. Job and his family sitting in quiet con-tentment surrounded by flocks and herds. Scene as in Blake Illustra-tion I. Dance of Job's sons and daughters. The figures of this dance should take suggestions from the dances *Jenny Pluck Pears* and *Hunsdon House* also the dancing group in the 'Munich glyptothek'. Job stands up and blesses his children saying 'It may be my children have sinned' (I:5). Every-one kneels. Tableau as in Blake I. Angels appear at the side of the stage as in Blake II and V. Also

[1] Published in *Job and The Rake's Progress*, Sadler's Wells Ballet Books, No. 2
(The Bodley Head).

see Botticelli's Nativity (National Gallery) and Blake frontispiece. Enter Satan, who appeals to Heaven. Heaven gradually opens and displays God sitting in majesty surrounded by the Sons of God (as in Blake II). The line of angels stretches from earth to heaven. A light falls on Job. God regards him with affection and says to Satan 'Hast thou considered my servant Job?' Satan says 'Put forth thy hand now and touch all that he hath and he will curse thee to thy face' (I:11). God says 'All that he hath is in thy power' (I:12). Satan departs (see Blake V). The dance of homage begins again. God leaves his throne.

Scene II

Satan, after a triumphal dance, usurps the throne.

'So Satan went forth from the presence of the Lord' (I:12). *Satan's Dance of Triumph.* Heaven is empty and God's throne vacant. Satan alone on the stage. He dances, and climbs up to God's throne and kneels in mock adoration. The hosts of Hell enter running and kneel before Satan who has risen and stands before God's throne facing the audience. Satan in wild triumph and with a big gesture sits in God's throne.

Scene III

Job's sons and daughters are feasting and dancing when Satan appears and destroys them.

'Then came a great wind and smote the four corners of the house and it fell upon the young men and they are dead' (I:19). *Minuet of the Sons of Job and Their Wives.* Enter Job's sons and their wives and dance in front of the curtain. They hold golden wine cups in their left hands which they clash at points marked in the score. The dance should be formal, statuesque and slightly voluptuous. It should not be a minuet as far as choreography is concerned. For the clashing of the wine cups suggestions should be taken from the Morris Dance *Winster Processional*. See also Botticelli 'Marriage Feast'. The black curtain draws back and shows an interior as in Blake III. Enter Satan. The dance stops suddenly. The dancers fall dead. Tableau as in Blake III.

Scene IV

Job's peaceful sleep is disturbed by Satan with terrifying visions of War, Pestilence and Famine.

'In thoughts from the visions of the night . . . fear came upon me and trembling' (IV:13 . . . 14). *Job's Dream. Dance of Plague, Pestilence, Famine and Battle.* Job is quietly sleeping, as in Blake VI. [A note on the score after the 25th bar states that in the Blake illustrations Scene V (Messengers) follows here. Producers who wish to follow Blake's order exactly can make a pause at the double bar and go straight on to Scene V]. Job moves uneasily in his sleep and Satan enters. Tableau as in Blake VI. Satan stands over Job and calls up terrifying visions of plague, pestilence, famine, battle, murder and sudden death who posture before Job as in Blake XI. Each of these should be represented by a group of dancers. The dance should be wild and full of movement and the stage should finally be full. Suggestions may be taken from Rubens's 'Horrors of War' (National Gallery). The dancers headed by Satan make a ring round Job and raise their hands three times. The vision gradually disappears. [If Scene V has been taken before the dance in Scene IV, a pause should be made at the end of this scene to be followed by Scene VI Comforters. Otherwise there is no break between Scenes IV and V.]

(As Vaughan Williams separated the dance of the Messengers from that of the Hypocrites, the scene sequences are henceforward irregular.)

Scene V

Messengers come to Job with tidings of the destruction of all his possessions and the death of his sons and daughters. Satan introduces Job's Comforters, three wily hypocrites. Their dance at first simulates compassion, but this gradually changes to rebuke and anger. Job rebels: 'Let the day perish wherein I was born.' He invokes his vision of the Godhead, but the opening Heaven reveals Satan upon the throne. Job and his friends shrink in terror.

Scenes V and VI

'There came a messenger' (I:14). *Dance of the Messengers.* Job awakes from his sleep and perceives three messengers, who arrive one after the other, telling him that all his wealth is destroyed (see Blake IV). A sad procession passes across the back of the stage, culminating in the funeral cortège of Job's sons and their wives. Job still blesses God. 'The Lord gave and the Lord hath taken away, blessed be the name of the Lord.' (I:21). (When Scene V is taken before the dance in Scene IV, the music to follow the end of Scene V should be from the Allegro 10 bars before Cc to the end of the Allegro).

Scene VI: 'Behold, happy is the man whom God correcteth' (V:17). *Dance of Job's Comforters. Job's Curse. A vision of Satan.* Satan introduces in turn Job's three Comforters (three wily hypocrites). Their dance is at first one of pretended sympathy, but develops into anger and reproach (see Blake VII and X). Job stands and curses God. 'Let

the day perish wherein I was born'
(III:3). (See Blake VIII.) Heaven
gradually becomes visible, showing
mysterious veiled sinister figures
moving in a sort of parody of the
Sons of God in Scene I. Heaven is
now lit up. The figures throw off
their veils and display themselves as
Satan enthroned, surrounded by
the hosts of Hell. Satan stands. Job
and his friends cower in terror.
The vision gradually disappears.
There is no break between this
scene and the next.

Scene VI

There enters Elihu who is young
and beautiful. 'Ye are old and I am
very young.' Job perceives his sin.
The Heavens then open, revealing
Job's Spiritual Self again enthroned.

Scene VII

'Ye are old and I am very young'
(XXXII:6). *Elihu's Dance of Youth
and Beauty.* Enter Elihu, a beautiful young man. 'I am young and
ye are very old' (see Blake XII).
'Then the Lord answered Job'
(XXXVIII:1). *Pavane of the Sons
of the Morning.* Heaven gradually
shines behind the stars. Dim
figures are seen dancing a solemn
dance. As Heaven grows lighter,
they are seen to be the Sons of the
Morning dancing before God's
throne (see Blake XIV).

Scene VII

Satan again appeals to Job's Godhead, claiming the victory, but is
repelled and driven down by the
Sons of the Morning. Job's household build an altar and worship
with musical instruments, while
the Heavenly dance continues.

Scene VIII

'All the Sons of God shouted for
joy' (XXXVIII:7). *Galliard of the
Sons of the Morning.* Enter Satan.
He claims the victory over Job.
God pronounces sentence of ban-
ishment on Satan and the Sons of
the Morning gradually drive him
down (see Blake V and XVI).
Satan falls out of Heaven (Blake
XVI). 'My servant Job shall pray
for you' (XLII:8). *Altar Dance and
Heavenly Pavane.* Enter (on earth)

young men and women playing on instruments; others bring stones and build an altar. Others decorate the altar with flowers (see Blake XXI). Job must not play on an instrument himself. He blesses the altar (see Blake XVIII). The Heavenly dance begins again, while the dance on earth continues. There is no break between this scene and the next.

Scene VIII

Job sits a humbled man in the sunrise of restored prosperity, surrounded by his family, upon whom he bestows his blessing.

Scene IX

'So the Lord blessed the latter end of Job more than his beginning' (XLII:12). *Epilogue*. The same scene as the opening. Job, an old and humbled man, sits with his wife. His friends come up one by one and give him presents (see Blake XIX). Job stands and gazes on the distant cornfields. Job's three daughters enter and sit at his feet. He stands and blesses them (see Blake XX).

Scene I *Largo sostenuto—allegro piacevole—doppio più lento—andante con moto—largamente.*
   II *Presto (1 in the bar)—con fuoco—moderato alla marcia—presto.*
  III *Andante con moto.*
  IV *Lento moderato—allegro.*
   V *Lento—andante con moto—lento.*
  VI *Andante doloroso—poco più mosso—ancora più mosso—*tempo I*—andante maestoso.*
 VII *Andante tranquillo (tempo rubato)—allegretto—andante con moto.*
VIII *Andante con moto—allegro pesante—allegretto tranquillo—lento.*
  IX *Largo sostenuto.*

Whereabouts of MS.: British Library. Full score (54326). A few pages of 2-piano score (50411). Copy of piano II part of 2-piano arrangement (57286).

For 'The Voice Out of the Whirlwind' (motet adapted from *Job*) see 1947.

1931

1. **TWELVE TRADITIONAL COUNTRY DANCES.** Collected and

described by Maud Karpeles. Pianoforte arrangements by R. Vaughan Williams in collaboration with Maud Karpeles.[1]

Contents: Introduction; The Dance; Notation; Notes on the Tunes; The Tunes: (1) Corn Rigs; (2) Morpeth rant (D major) (Collected by M. Karpeles, arranged R.V.W.); (3) Soldier's joy (E major); (4) Roxburgh Castle (A major) (Collected and arranged by C. J. Sharp. © 1911 Novello); (5) The Sylph (tune, 'Off she goes', D major); (6) Long eight (tune, 'Haste to the wedding', C major) (Collected by M. Karpeles, arranged R.V.W.); (7) Three around three *or* Pleasures of the town (A major); (8) Steamboat (C major); (9) Piper's fancy (tune, 'The New Rigged Ship', A major) (Collected by C. J. Sharp, arranged R.V.W. and M.K.); (10) The tempest (F major); (11) The self (C major) (Collected by M. Karpeles, arranged R.V.W. and M.K. © 1931 M.K.); (12) Kitty's rambles (D major) (Collected by M. Karpeles, arranged R.V.W. and M.K. © 1931 M.K.).

Publication: London, Novello & Co. Ltd. for the English Folk Dance Society (15715).

Note: An orchestral arrangement of No. 10, made by R.V.W., was recorded on a 78 r.p.m. disc. Score and parts have not been traced.

2. SONGS OF PRAISE (Enlarged edition). 1925 edition enlarged by 207 hymns. Sections principally enlarged are: Advent; the weeks after Christmas and Epiphany; the six weeks after Easter; Special Occasions; General. All hymns written and arranged by R.V.W. in the 1925 edition are included except three:

226. Regina ('Dear Lord and Father of Mankind').

427. East Horndon ('I think when I read that sweet story of old'). (Both arranged from folk songs.)

330. Londonderry ('O son of man').

The following extra original tunes by R.V.W. are included:

126. Mantegna ('Into the woods my master went') (© R.V.W. 1931).

302. Marathon ('Servants of the great adventure') (Adapted from *The Wasps*) (© R.V.W. 1928).

319. (ii) Abinger ('I vow to thee my country') (© R.V.W. 1931).

432. Famous Men ('Let us now praise famous men') Canticle. (© 1923 J. Curwen & Son.)

489. White Gates ('Fierce raged the tempest') (© R.V.W. 1931).

The tune 'Salve Festa Dies' is set to new words by Percy Dearmer, 'Welcome Day of the Lord, the first and the best of the seven' (390). These had been asked for by the then Dean of Liverpool, Dr. Dwelly. The tune is unaltered except that in the third and 16th bars, instead

---

[1] Dr. Karpeles wrote to me on 12 December 1963: ' "In collaboration with M.K." must not be taken too literally. It amounted to little more than my saying that his first attempts would not do! He insisted on my name appearing, I think, mainly because he did not like the final result!'

of syncopation on the last two beats, it has the regular form of the rest. The following new arrangements by R.V.W. appeared for the first time in this edition:

59. Ah! think not, 'The Lord delayeth'. St. Olaf's Sequence. Norwegian church melody.

65. Lo He comes. Helmsley. *Descant* (© R.V.W. 1931).

164. (Appendix I) Sing, brothers, sing and praise your King! (Cobbold). 'From a melody by S.M.W.V.R.' (i.e. Shaw Martin Williams Vaughan Ralph). Cobbold was the maiden name of Shaw's wife Joan.

205. Hail, glorious spirits. Dorking. Joint arrangement with Martin Shaw.

232. Look up, by failure daunted. Oslo. Norwegian folk song.

353. Away in a manger. Cradle song. Arrangement of tune by W. J. Kirkpatrick (1838–1921).

393. City of Peace, our mother dear.

    (i) Stalham. Arrangement of English folk song collected by E. J. Moeran.

    (ii) Dunstan. English folk song ('The Lord of Life', collected by R.V.W. at Dunstan, August 1906).

Publication: London O.U.P. (1931).

3. CONCERTO IN C MAJOR FOR PIANOFORTE AND ORCHESTRA.

    I. Toccata. *Allegro moderato.*

    II. Romanza. *Lento.*

    III. Fuga chromatica, con finale alla tedesca.

Movements I and II were composed in 1926; III in 1930–1.

Instrumentation: Pianoforte, 2 flutes (2nd doubling piccolo), 2 oboes, 2 clarinets, 2 bassoons, 4 horns, 2 trumpets, 3 trombones, tuba, timpani, percussion (side drum, cymbals, bass drum, tam-tam), organ pedal (opt.), strings.

First performance: London, Queen's Hall, 1 February 1933. Harriet Cohen (pianoforte), B.B.C. Symphony Orchestra, conducted by Adrian Boult.

Dedication: To Harriet Cohen.

Duration: 25 minutes.

Composer's programme note: The first two movements of this Concerto were sketched in 1926, and the third movement in 1930. The work is dedicated to Miss Harriet Cohen.

There are three movements: (1) *Toccata* leading to (2) *Romanza* leading to (3) *Fuga chromatica con Finale alla Tedesca*. There is no break between the movements.

(1) *Toccata*. The pianoforte starts off with the following figure:

against which the orchestra plays the following theme:

Then follows this figure on the pianoforte:

a development of which leads in its turn to this:

Then the whole is repeated with slight modifications, the pianoforte and the orchestra as a rule changing places. After this comes a development of No. 3, which serves as an accompaniment to a new theme:

An extension of No. 2 leads to a shortened recapitulation, and the movement, which is quite short, ends with a version of No. 5 canonically treated by pianoforte and orchestra. A short *cadenza* for pianoforte leads to

(2) *Romanza*. The principal theme is as follows:

and is played by the pianoforte solo and repeated by the flute accompanied by pianoforte and strings. An additional theme is as follows (strings and muted horns):

There is an episode in 3-2 time founded chiefly on the following:

No. 8.

The opening themes are then heard again, but the movement is interrupted by the trombones, and a few bars of introduction lead to (3) *Fuga chromatica con Finale alla Tedesca*. The subject of the fugue is:

given out by the pianoforte. There is a counter-subject:

After various episodes a *stretto* on a dominant pedal is reached, built up chiefly on an augmentation of part of the fugue subject:

with which the subject and counter-subject of the fugue are combined. A *cadenza* for the pianoforte separates the fugue and the Finale, the subjects of which are the same as those of the fugue, but treated harmonically rather than contrapuntally, and finally there is another *cadenza* for the pianoforte, made up chiefly out of the episode (No. 8) in the slow movement. The *cadenza* ends with a quotation two bars long from a contemporary composer, added 'according to my promise'. Then a few bars of *Allegro* bring the Concerto to an end. R.V.W.

Publication: London, O.U.P. © 1936: Arrangement for two pianos (orchestral part arranged for second piano) by Vally Lasker. Orchestral material on hire. Full score including original solo piano part and 2-piano version, O.U.P. © 1973.

Other version: FOR TWO PIANOFORTES AND ORCHESTRA, made by Joseph Cooper in collaboration with the composer.

First performance: London, Royal Albert Hall, 22 November 1946, Cyril Smith and Phyllis Sellick (pianofortes); London Philharmonic and London Symphony Orchestras, conducted by Sir Adrian Boult.

Revisions: A quotation from Bax's Third Symphony at the end of the finale cadenza was removed after the first performance, although Ex. 8 is the Bax theme in disguise. Principal differences between the one and two-piano versions are at the end of the finale. A new solo for the two pianos is inserted between 49 and 50 of the old score, ten bars of ritornello are deleted and the work ends quietly with the fugue subject pizzicato in the strings, and a chord of B major (previous ending was in G).

Whereabouts of MS.: British Library.   Full score of original (50385).

1932

1. SONGS OF PRAISE FOR LITTLE CHILDREN (Full music edition). By the Rev. Percy Dearmer, R. Vaughan Williams, Martin Shaw and Canon G. W. Briggs (with prayers for little children). Arranged by R.V.W.:
14. Hardwick ('So here hath been dawning').

2. MAGNIFICAT. For contralto solo, women's choir (SA), solo flute and orchestra. Words adapted from the Bible. This work is not designed for liturgical use.
Instrumentation: 2 flutes, 2 oboes (1 opt), 1 cor anglais, 2 clarinets, 2 bassoons, 4 horns, 2 trumpets, timpani, harp, celesta (opt), percussion (2 players), organ (opt.), strings. *Or* 2 flutes, harp, celesta, strings. *Or* organ (or piano) with flute or violin obbligato.
First performance: The Cathedral, Worcester, Three Choirs Festival, 8 September 1932. Astra Desmond (contralto), women of Three Choirs Festival Chorus, London Symphony Orchestra, conducted by Dr. R. Vaughan Williams. First performance in London: Queen's Hall, 1 May 1934, Blodwen Caerleon (contralto), Philharmonic Choir, London Symphony Orchestra, conducted by C. Kennedy Scott.
Dedication: To Astra Desmond.
Duration: 12 minutes.
Publication: London, O.U.P. © 1932. V.S. (arrangement for flute obbligato and piano, chorus and contralto solo). Full score, orchestral material and solo flute part on hire.
Whereabouts of MS.: British Library. Two full scores (50451A and B).

3. CHORAL AND CHORAL PRELUDE. 'Ach, Bleib bei uns, Herr Jesu Christ' ('Now Cheer our Hearts this Eventide'), by J. S. Bach, freely arranged for pianoforte by R.V.W.
I. Choral. Lento. II. Choral Prelude. Andante tranquillo (quasi notturno). The melody of I is based on the alto part of a Choral by Seth Calvisius, 1594. The words of I, printed in the score, are by N. Selneccer, 1579, English adaptation by Robert Bridges in the *Yattendon Hymnal* (1899).
This work was a contribution to 'A Bach Book for Harriet Cohen', dedicated to her by the contributors who, besides Vaughan Williams, were Bantock, Bax, Berners, Bliss, Bridge, Goossens, Howells, Ireland, Lambert, Walton and W. Gillies Whittaker. All the contributions were pianoforte transcriptions of works by Bach.
Publication: London, O.U.P. © 1932.

1933

1. THE ENGLISH HYMNAL (Revised Edition). This edition contains all the tunes in the 1906 edition, with the addition or substitution of

126 tunes. The numbering of the hymns therefore remains as in 1906 edn. The Appendix of 1906 contained five plainsong tunes and 78 alternative tunes. The Appendix of 1933 has six plainsong melodies, 17 alternative tunes, and 49 transferred from the 1906 edition. The Plainsong was revised by J. H. Arnold.

Tunes and settings by R.V.W. added to 1933 edn. are:

18. (Modern tune) Rouen ('From East to West'). *Harmonization.*

58. (Modern tune) ⎫
59. (Modern tune) ⎬ O Invidenda Martyrum ('O Boundless
60. (Modern tune) ⎭ Wisdom'). *Harmonization.*

91. Valor ('Weary of earth'). From folk song.

157. Wicklow ('Our blest redeemer'). Irish traditional melody adaptation.

273. Magda ('Saviour, again to Thy dear name'). © 1925 R.V.W.

368. King's Weston ('At the name of Jesus'). © 1925 R.V.W.

541. White Gates ('Fierce raged the tempest'). © 1931 R.V.W.

638. (Part 3) Stalham ('Jerusalem, my happy home') or Dunstan.

Publication: London, O.U.P. 1933.

2. SONGS OF PRAISE FOR CHILDREN (Full Music Edition). Contains the following settings and arrangements by R.V.W.:

37. Resonet in Laudibus ('Who within that stable cries').

44. Forest Green ('O little town of Bethlehem').

45. Rodmell ('When Christ was born in Bethlehem').

68. Monk's Gate ('He who would valiant be').

87. Sine Nomine ('For all the Saints').

113. White Gates ('Fierce raged the tempest').

135. Hardwick ('So here hath been dawning').

147. Randolph ('God be with you till we meet again').

Amen (vi).

Settings to prayers for days of the week:

Tuesday (ii) 'Almighty God, whose service is perfect freedom.'

Wednesday (ii) 'O God, grant me this day.'

Thursday (i) 'Eternal Father, who hast called us.'

Publication: London, O.U.P. 1933.

3. THE RUNNING SET. Founded on Traditional Dance Tunes for medium Orchestra. *Presto.*

Instrumentation: 1 piccolo, 1 flute, 2 oboes (1 opt.), 2 clarinets, 2 bassoons, 2 horns (1 opt.), 2 trumpets (1 opt.), percussion (side-drum, triangle), pianoforte (opt.), strings. (Pianoforte part may be played on the harp in two specified sections only.)

First performance: National Folk Dance Festival, Royal Albert Hall, London, 6 January 1934; Orchestra conducted by Dr. R. Vaughan Williams. First concert performance: London, Queen's Hall, 27 September 1934, B.B.C. Symphony Orchestra, conducted by Dr. R. Vaughan Williams.

Duration: 5 minutes.

Note on score: 'The Running Set is a dance of British origin still performed in the remoter parts of the United States. When Cecil Sharp discovered it some years ago it had already lost its proper tune, if it ever had one, and was danceable to any appropriate tune or even to the mere thrumming of the bow on the fiddle. When Sharp introduced the dance into this country he used for it several traditional tunes from the British Isles which have since become closely connected with it. A few years ago a massed performance of the dance was arranged for the annual festival of the English Folk Dance Society. For this purpose several of the tunes were combined to make one continuous movement. At one point in the dance where a difficult new figure had to start, the director of the dance, Mr. Douglas Kennedy, asked that a well-known air should be introduced to guide the dancers. This was accordingly done. R.V.W.'

The tunes incorporated in this piece are 'Barrack Hill', 'The Blackthorn Stick', 'Irish Reel', and 'Cock o' the North'. 'The Blackthorn Stick' was collected by Elsie Avril from the fiddler of the Earsdon sword-dancers, Northumberland.

Publication: London, O.U.P. Full score © 1952. Arrangement for two pianofortes by Vally Lasker and Helen Bidder, © 1936. Orchestral material on hire.

Whereabouts of MS.: British Library, 2-piano score, full score and parts (50394-6).

4. PASSACAGLIA ON B.G.C., composed for the Bride. For organ.
Allegro moderato—doppio più lento—allegro moderato.
Unpublished.

This 95-bar piece was written for the marriage of Miss Barbara Lawrence to Alfred Gordon Clark (Judge Gordon Clark, Cyril Hare the novelist) on 9 September 1933.

Whereabouts of MS.: Formerly in possession of the late Mrs. Gordon Clark.

5. 'HENRY THE FIFTH'. Overture for brass band.
Introduces the following tunes: 'Agincourt Song', 'Magali' (Provençal folk song), 'Réveillez vous Piccars', 'The Earl of Oxford's March'.
Andante maestoso—allegro—andante sostenuto—allegro alla marcia—andante maestoso—moderato alla marcia.
Instrumentation: 5 cornets (soprano E flat, solo B flat, repiano B flat, 2nd and 3rd B flat); 1 flügel horn, B flat; 3 horns, E flat; 2 baritone saxophones, B flat; 2 trombones, B flat; 1 bass tuba, 1 euphonium, 2 basses (E flat and B flat), percussion, timpani (ad lib.). *Note.* The

bass drum and side drum are essential. The cymbals and timpani are ad lib.

Note on score: The tone of the cornets should approximate as far as possible to that of trumpets (indeed the composer would prefer the parts played on trumpets). In any case the vulgar sentimental vibrato which disfigures most brass-band performances should be strictly avoided.

First performance: Miami, Florida, Maurice Gusman Concert Hall, University of Miami, 3 October 1979, University of Miami Wind Ensemble, conducted by Frederick Fennell. First British performance: Thetford, Norfolk, Staniforth Road School, 3 May 1980, Desford Colliery Band, conducted by Howard Snell.

Publication: London, Boosey and Hawkes © 1981. Full score.

Whereabouts of MS.: British Library, full score and short scores (57288).

6. MARCH, 'THE GOLDEN VANITY'. For military band. *Allegro. Unpublished.*

Instrumentation: flute and piccolo in C; solo clarinet, B flat and 1st and 2nd B flat clarinets; alto saxophone, E flat; tenor saxophone, B flat; bassoon, solo B flat cornet and 3 B flat cornets, 1 trombone, euphonium, bass tuba, drums, piano–conductor.

Whereabouts of MS.: British Library. Full score (57288).

1934

1. FANTASIA ON 'GREENSLEEVES'. Adapted from the opera *Sir John in Love* and arranged for strings and harp (or pianoforte) with 1 or 2 optional flutes by Ralph Greaves. *Lento.* F minor. The folk tune 'Lovely Joan' is the basis of the middle section.

   First concert performance: London, Queen's Hall, 27 September 1934. B.B.C. Symphony Orchestra, conducted by Dr. R. Vaughan Williams.

   Duration: 5 minutes.

   Publication: London, O.U.P. © 1934. Full score. (Oxford Orchestral Series, O.102).

Other arrangements of 'Greensleeves' are given below. All are published by O.U.P.

The Fantasia:

(*a*) Pianoforte solo. (© 1937.)

(*b*) Pianoforte duet, arranged by Hubert J. Foss. (© 1942.)

(*c*) Two pianofortes (two copies under one cover), arranged by H. J. Foss. (© 1945.)

(*d*) Violin and pianoforte, arranged by Michael Mullinar. (© 1944.)

(*e*) Cello (or viola) and pianoforte, arranged by Watson Forbes (© 1947).

The Song:
(*a*) For solo voice and pianoforte. *Andante moderato.* F minor. (© 1934.)
Text modernized from *A Handefull of Pleasant Delites* (1584).

(*b*) Two-part women's voices and pianoforte. O.C.S. T.4. (© 1954.)

(*c*) Male voices (TTBB and tenor solo) unaccompanied. O.C.S. M.5.
(© 1957.)

(*d*) Mixed voices (SAT High Bar. B). Part-song. (© 1945.).
Dedication: To the Henley Choir.

(*e*) Organ solo, arranged by Stanley Roper. (© 1947.) Available separately and as No. 2 of *A Vaughan Williams Organ Album* (© 1964.)

(*f*) Medium orchestra, arranged by David Stone.
Instrumentation: 2 flutes (or descant and treble recorders), oboe,
2 clarinets, bassoon (or 3rd clarinet), 2 horns, guitar, pianoforte (or
harp), strings. © 1966.

(*g*) Guitar, arranged by Hector Quine. © 1973.

(*h*) Treble recorder(s) and pianoforte, arranged by Alan Frank. © 1969.

2. AN ACRE OF LAND. English folk song for male voices (TTBB)
with pianoforte accompaniment ad lib. *Molto moderato.* F major.
Publication: London, O.U.P. (© 1934.) Oxford Choral Songs,
No. 636.
Other versions:
   (*a*) For mixed voices (SATB) unaccompanied. O.U.P. (© 1934.)
   Oxford Folk Song Series, F.26.
   (*b*) Unison, with pianoforte accompaniment. From *Folk Songs of the
   Four Seasons.* O.U.P. © 1950.

3. JOHN DORY. English folk song arranged for mixed voices (SATB)
unaccompanied. From *Ballad Literature and Popular Music of the
Olden Time* by William Chappell (1879). *Allegro moderato.* D major.
Publication: London O.U.P. (© 1934.) O.F.S., F.25.

4. I'LL NEVER LOVE THEE MORE. For mixed voices (SATB)
unaccompanied. Words by James Graham, 1st Marquis of Montrose
(1612–50), 'Poem to his mistress'. Tune from Playford's *Dancing
Master. Andante moderato.* G major.
Publication: London, O.U.P. (© 1934.) O.F.S., F.27.

5. THE WORLD IT WENT WELL WITH ME THEN. Old
English air from Chappell's *Popular Music*, arranged for male voices
(TTBB) unaccompanied. *Allegro.* G minor.
Publication: London, O.U.P. (© 1934). O.C.S., No. 637.

6. TOBACCO'S BUT AN INDIAN WEED. Old English air from
Chappell's *Popular Music*, arranged for male voices (TTBB) unaccompanied. *Andante.* G major.
Publication: London, O.U.P. (© 1934.) O.C.S., No. 638.

7. **THE PLOUGHMAN.** English folk song, arranged for male voices (TTBB) with pianoforte accompaniment (ad lib.). *Allegro.* E modal minor.
Publication: London, O.U.P. (© 1934.) O.C.S., No. 639.

Other versions:
(*a*) For voice and pianoforte. No. 2 of *Six English Folk Songs.* O.U.P. © 1935.
(*b*) In *Penguin Book of English Folk Songs* (Ed. R.V.W. and A. L. Lloyd), 1959, p. 84.

8. **THE PILGRIM PAVEMENT.** Hymn for soprano solo, mixed chorus (SATB) and organ. Words by Margaret Ridgeley Partridge, written for and read at the dedication of the Pilgrims' Pavement in the Central Nave of the Cathedral of St. John the Divine, New York City, on 11 March 1934. *Andante moderato.* D modal minor.
First performance: New York, 10 February 1935. Choir of Cathedral of St John the Divine, conducted by Dr Norman Coke-Jephcott.

Publication: London, O.U.P. © 1934.

9. SIX TEACHING PIECES FOR PIANOFORTE. In Three Books.
Book I. Two 2-part Inventions.
　1. *Andante con moto.* G major.
　2. *Allegro moderato.* E flat major.
Book II. Valse Lente and Nocturne.
　1. Valse lente. *Moderato.* G modal minor.
　2. Nocturne. *Adagio.* A modal minor.
Book III. Canon and 2-part Invention.
　1. Canon. *Andante con moto.* C modal minor.
　2. Two-part Invention. *Moderato.* F major.
Publication: London, O.U.P. © 1934. Oxford Piano Series, Ed. A. Forbes Milne. Book I, Grade C–D, P. 208; Book II, Grade E, P. 209; Book III, Grade F, P. 210.

10. MUSIC FOR 'THE PAGEANT OF ABINGER'. The following were arranged by R.V.W.:
Triumphant Music; Latin hymn, 'Angelus ad Virginem'; Latin chant, 'Coelestis Urbs Hierusalem'; Sussex folk song, 'Twankydillo'; Country Dance, 'Gathering Peascods'; Metrical version of Psalm 68 'Let God Arise'; Country Dances, 'The Triumph', and 'Haste to the wedding'; Folk song, 'Seventeen come Sunday'; Folk song, 'The Sweet Nightingale'; Psalm 84, 'How Amiable are Thy Dwellings'; Hymn, 'O God our help in ages past'.
First performance: The Old Rectory Garden, Abinger, 14 July 1934. Band of the 2nd Bn. West Yorkshire Regiment (Prince of Wales's Own), conducted by David Moule Evans.

Whereabouts of MS.: British Library. Full score and piano arrangement, partly autograph (57289). Includes copy of programme-notes and narrator's speeches by E. M. Forster.

A permanent result of the pageant was:

10A. O HOW AMIABLE. Anthem for the dedication of a church or other Festivals (originally written for the Abinger Pageant, 1934), for mixed chorus (SATB) and organ. Words from Psalms 84 and 90. *Andante moderato.* E flat major.

Instrumentation: (as in original pageant version): piccolo, flutes, oboe, bassoon, clarinets, alto clarinet, bass clarinet, alto saxophones, tenor saxophone, baritone saxophone, trumpets, horns, trombones, baritones, euphonium, tubas, string bass, and timpani.

Dedication: To F.F. [Dame Frances Farrer.]

Publication: London, O.U.P. (© 1940). Oxford series of Modern Anthems (edited by Stanley Roper). A.94. Band accompaniment © O.U.P. score and parts on hire 19 3854856 AM.

Note on score: This was originally accompanied by military band. For open-air performance this is preferable.

11. SUITE FOR VIOLA AND SMALL ORCHESTRA.
Group I: Prelude; Carol; Christmas Dance.
Group II: Ballad; Moto perpetuo.
Group III: Musette; Polka mélancolique; Galop.

Instrumentation: 2 flutes (2nd doubling piccolo), 1 oboe, 2 clarinets, 2 bassoons; 2 horns, 2 trumpets, timpani, percussion (side drum, triangle), celesta, harp, strings.

First performance: London, Queen's Hall, 12 November 1934, Lionel Tertis (viola); London Philharmonic Orchestra, conducted by Dr. Malcolm Sargent.

Dedication: To Lionel Tertis.

Duration: 24 minutes.

Publication: London, O.U.P. Full score © 1963; with orchestral part arranged for pianoforte, © 1936.

Other versions:

(*a*) For viola and pianoforte, 1936, each group separate.

(*b*) Galop arranged for violin and pianoforte by Louis Persinger. © 1949.

(*c*) Carol and Musette arranged for organ by Herbert Sumsion.
   1. Carol: *Andante con moto*, E flat major.
   2. Musette: *Lento*, E flat major. O.U.P. © 1938. These arrangements also appear as Nos. 4 and 7 of *A Vaughan Williams Organ Album* © 1964.
   Duration of (*c*) approx. 7 minutes.

Whereabouts of MS.: British Library, Full score (3 parts) (50386).

12. FOLK SONGS FROM NEWFOUNDLAND. Collected and edited by Maud Karpeles, with pianoforte accompaniments by R. Vaughan Williams, Clive Carey, Hubert Foss and Michael Mullinar. Complete edition contains the following arrangements by R.V.W.

VOLUME I.

BALLADS

1. Sweet William's Ghost. *Moderato*, E flat major.
2. The Cruel Mother. *Allegretto*. D major.
3. The Gypsy Laddie. *Allegro vivace*. D major.
7. The Bloody Gardener. *Allegretto*. E modal minor.

SONGS

8. The Maiden's Lament. *Andante sostenuto*. C modal minor.
9. Proud Nancy. *Allegro moderato*. C modal minor.
10. The morning dew. *Andante*. E flat major.

VOLUME II.

BALLADS

1. The Bonny Banks of Virgie-O (The Bonny Banks o' Fordie). *Andante con moto*. E modal minor.
2. Earl Brand. *Moderato e maestoso*. D major.
3. Lord Akeman (Lord Bateman). *Moderato*.
7. The Lover's Ghost. *Andante moderato*. C major.

SONGS

8. She's like the swallow. *Lento non troppo*. C modal minor.
9. Young Floro. *Andante*. D modal minor.
10. The winter's gone and past. *Andante*. D modal minor.
11. The Cuckoo. *Andante con moto*. D modal minor.

Dedication: To Fred and Isabel Emerson of St. John's.
Publication: London, O.U.P. © 1934.

Re-published as FIFTEEN FOLK SONGS FROM NEW-FOUNDLAND, collected and edited by Maud Karpeles, with pianoforte accompaniments by R. Vaughan Williams. *Ballads* 1. Sweet William's Ghost. 2. The Cruel Mother. 3. The Gipsy Laddie. 4. The Bloody Gardener. 5. The Bonnie Banks of Virgie-O. 6. Earl Brand. 7. Lord Akeman. 8. The Lover's ghost. *Songs* 9. She's like the swallow. 10. The Maiden's Lament. 11. Proud Nancy. 12. The Morning Dew. 13. The Winter's gone and past. 14. The Cuckoo. 15. Young Floro. With notes on the collection. London, O.U.P. © 1968.

Other versions:

(*a*) Vol. II, No. 7: The Lover's Ghost. Arranged for SATB unaccompanied. (S. & B. 1562 © 1913.)

(*b*) Vol. II, No. 8: She's like the swallow. Unison, with pianoforte accompaniment. O.C.S. U.47.

13. SYMPHONY (No. 4) IN F MINOR. For Full orchestra. (Composed 1931–4.)

I. Allegro.

II. Andante moderato.

III. Scherzo: allegro molto.

IV. Finale con Epilogo fugato. Allegro molto.

Instrumentation: 3 flutes (1 opt.) (2nd doubling piccolo), 3 oboes (No. 2 opt. except in scherzo, No. 3 opt. in scherzo), 1 cor anglais, 2 clarinets, 1 bass clarinet (opt.), 2 bassoons, 1 double bassoon (opt.), 4 horns, 2 trumpets, 3 trombones, tuba, timpani (chromatic ad lib.), percussion (2 players: side drum, triangle, cymbals, bass drum), strings.

First performance: London, Queen's Hall, 10 April 1935, the B.B.C. Symphony Orchestra, conducted by Adrian Boult.

Dedication: To Arnold Bax.

Duration: 33 minutes.

Publication: London O.U.P. Full and Miniature Scores. © 1935.

Composer's programme note:

I

Two principal themes run through this Symphony:

 and: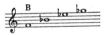

(Incidentally this is not the B A C H theme which in this key would run):

The (A) theme appears first as the tail-end of the opening subject of the first movement, thus:

Two other phrases complete the first group of subjects:

and the following version of (B):

Then follows a long *cantilena*, played by the upper strings, accompanied by repeated notes on the wind:

This leads to the key of D major and the following new theme:

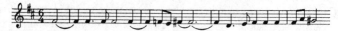

which is expanded for about forty bars and is interrupted by a passage founded on the opening subject which eventually transforms itself into the following version of (A):

There is no complete recapitulation of the first subjects, but after a few bars suggestive of the opening, the *cantilena* passage follows immediately, this time in the bass, with a counter melody in the treble. This works up to a *fortissimo*. The music then dies away, and ends with a soft and slow repetition of the D major theme, this time in D flat.

II

The second movement has for its introduction a passage suggested by (B). The principal theme which follows is played by first violins over a *pizzicato* bass:

Then follow two episodes, during the second of which the introductory passage is also heard:

The first half of the movement ends with this cadence figure:

Then after another episode there is a shortened recapitulation. The final cadence figure extends itself into a *cadenza* for the flute, under which (A) is heard on the muted trombones.

III

The principal theme of the Scherzo is:

played on the bassoons. This is of course a version of (B). (A) is also heard in the course of the movement. Then over the following rhythmical accompaniment:

comes a theme which eventually takes this form:

The trio of the Scherzo is a *fugato* on this subject:

After a re-capitulation of the Scherzo a long *crescendo* on a pedal leads direct to the Finale.

IV

This opens with a more energetic version of the cadence figure from the second movement:

This has, as a dependent theme, a melody for the wind over what is known in professional circles as an 'oompah' bass:

A further theme is the following:

which grows into this:

Instead of a development there is a long passage founded on the first three bars of the 'dependent' theme. Then a suggestion of the end of the first movement, and then another long pedal leading back to the recapitulation.

The subject of the fugal epilogue is (A), played first on the trombones and then heard both in its original form and inverted, combined with the other subjects of the finale. The work ends with a reference to the opening bars of the first movement.

The Symphony was sketched in the end of 1931 and the beginning of 1932, and was completed in 1934. It is dedicated to Arnold Bax. R.V.W.

Revisions: Early piano scores of the work show that in the first movement the meno mosso theme at four after ⑤ is a substitution for a repeated phrase in pentatonic harmony. Last bar was added in full score. Various other minor alterations are of no significant account. In second movement bars 5 to 11 after ⑨ are a compression of 17 bars of expository matter, and further cuts are to be found in the Scherzo. The finale has much alteration, the 'real' themes replacing 'made-up' ones, as was said by R.V.W. to Holst; for example, the repetition twice of bar 12 after 32 was scrapped for the present eight eventful bars. The fugue theme at ㉓ was originally six bars as it now appears for trombones at bars 7–12 after ㉓. The revision in the late 1950s of the last note of the flute solo at the end of the slow movement is best explained by quoting the composer's letter to Bernard Naylor:

'The note was originally F, but I always felt it was wrong, and I have taken 20 years trying to find the right note, and in the new parts and the large MS. scores it is altered to E, but of course not in the old gramophone record.'

Whereabouts of MS.: British Library. Full score (Add. 50140); Two-pianoforte score (50370).

1935

1. FOLK SONGS, Volume II. A selection of thirty-three less-known folk songs, arranged by Cecil Sharp, R. Vaughan Williams and others for voice and pianoforte. Compiled by Cyril Winn. Collected and arranged by R.V.W.:

    No. 7. The Bold 'Princess Royal'. (Norfolk.) *Moderato.* G major.
    18. The Jolly Ploughboy. *Allegro risoluto.* G major.
    32. Ward the Pirate. (Norfolk.) *Moderato alla marcia.* D major.

Publication: London, Novello & Co. Ltd.; N.Y., The H. W. Gray Co. © 1935.

Other versions:

(*a*) The Bold 'Princess Royal'. No. 11 of *Folk Songs of England*. Vol. II (Eastern Counties). Voice and pianoforte. (As above.)

(*b*) The Jolly Ploughboy.

   1. For male voices. Novello 1908.

   2. No. 18 of *Folk Songs for 'Schools*.

(*c*) Ward the Pirate.

   1. For male voices unaccompanied. Curwen (1912).

   2. Voice and pianoforte. Novello (1927) (as above).

   3. No. 9 of *Folk Songs of England*, Vol. II (Eastern Counties).

2. TWO ENGLISH FOLK SONGS. Arranged for voice and violin.

   1. Searching for Lambs. *Andante con moto*. A modal minor.

   2. The Lawyer. *Allegro vivace*. A modal minor.

Dedication: To Margaret Longman.

Publication: London O.U.P. (© 1935).

Note: 'The Lawyer' (No. 2), which was collected by Butterworth, was arranged by Vaughan Williams in the late 1920s for the English Singers (SSATBB unaccompanied) and first sung in London on 13 June 1927. It was recorded by them in America under the title 'It's of a lawyer fine and gay'. The words differ slightly from those in the voice and violin arrangement. The six-part version was turned into a unison setting and incorporated in 1949 into *Folk Songs of the Four Seasons* under the title 'The Green Meadow'. The text of this setting was again slightly varied.

3. SIX ENGLISH FOLK SONGS. Arranged for voice and pianoforte.

   1. Robin Hood and the Pedlar. *Andante con moto*. E modal minor. R.V.W. collection, sung by Mr. Verrall, Sussex.

   2. The Ploughman. *Allegro*. E modal minor. R.V.W. collection, sung by Mr. H. Burstow, Sussex.

   3. One man, two men. *Allegro ma non troppo*. G major. Hammond collection, sung by Mr. Moore, Dorset.

   4. The Brewer. *Allegro*. E modal minor. Hammond collection, sung by Mrs. Russell, Dorset.

   5. Rolling in the dew. *Allegretto*. D major. R.V.W. collection, sung by Mrs. Verrall, Sussex.

   6. King William. *Allegretto*. G major. Hammond collection, sung by Mr. Roper, Dorset.

Publication: London, O.U.P. (© 1935).

Whereabouts of MS.: British Library. Vocal Score (50480).

Other versions:

   1. In *The Penguin Book of English Folk Songs*, edited by R.V.W. and A. L. Lloyd (Penguin Books, 1959), p. 88.

2. Arranged for TTBB with optional accompaniment. O.U.P. 1934.

4. MY SOUL PRAISE THE LORD. Hymn arranged for chorus (SATB) and unison singing with descant, and organ (or strings and organ). Words from the Old Metrical Version (slightly adapted). *Maestoso.* C major.

Publication: London, S.P.C.K. (© 1935 R.V.W.); by O.U.P. (© 1947). (String parts on hire.)

5. FIVE TUDOR PORTRAITS. A Choral Suite in five movements, with soli for contralto (or mezzo soprano), baritone, mixed chorus (SATB) and orchestra, founded on poems by John Skelton (Laureate), 1460–1529, sometime Rector of Diss in Norfolk. The work was 'rough-finished' by 20 June 1935. The text used is based on the edition of *The Complete Poems of John Skelton, Laureate,* edited by Philip Henderson (London, 1931). The numbers given below in square brackets refer to the page in this edition.

1. The Tunning of Elinor Rumming. [p. 99.] Ballad. For contralto solo, mixed chorus and orchestra. *Allegro pesante.*

2. Pretty Bess. [p. 268.] (From *Speak Parrot.*) Intermezzo. For baritone solo, mixed chorus and orchestra. *Allegretto grazioso.*

3. Epitaph on John Jayberd of Diss. [p. 454.] Burlesca. For male chorus and orchestra. *Allegro.*

4. Jane Scroop (Her Lament for Philip Sparrow). [p. 59.] Romanza. For mezzo-soprano (or contralto) solo, women's chorus and orchestra. *Lento doloroso.*

5. Jolly Rutterkin. [p. 37 and p. 200.] (From 'Jolly Rutterkin' and 'Magnificence'.) Scherzo. For baritone solo, mixed chorus and orchestra. *Allegro moderato.*

Instrumentation: 3 flutes (3rd doubling piccolo), 2 oboes, 1 cor anglais, 2 clarinets, 2 bassoons, 1 double bassoon, 4 horns, 2 trumpets, 3 trombones, tuba, timpani (chromatic ad lib.), percussion (2 players), harp, strings. The following are cued in but should not be omitted if it is possible to obtain them (in order of importance): tuba, oboe 2, flute 2, horns 3 and 4, double bassoon, percussion 2. The harp part should be played on a pianoforte rather than be omitted.

First performance: 34th Norwich Triennial Festival, St. Andrew's Hall, Norwich; 25 September 1936; Astra Desmond (contralto), Roy Henderson (baritone); The Festival Chorus, The London Philharmonic Orchestra, conducted by Dr. R. Vaughan Williams;[1] First

---

[1] It should be stressed that the composer *did* conduct this performance. The printed programme shows the conductor as Dr. Heathcote Statham, and this is repeated by Edwin Evans in the *Musical Times.* The fact is, however, that the composer conducted. Dr. Heathcote Statham prepared the choir and tells me that it was always intended that the composer should conduct.

London performance, Queen's Hall, 27 January 1937, Astra Desmond (contralto), Roy Henderson (baritone), Croydon Philharmonic Society, B.B.C. Chorus, B.B.C. Symphony Orchestra, conducted by Sir Adrian Boult.

Duration: 42 minutes.

Composer's note:

In making a choral suite out of the poems of Skelton, I have ventured to take some liberties with the text. Certain omissions have been made necessary, partly by the great length of the original, partly from the fact that certain passages did not lend themselves to musical treatment, and partly that certain lines that look well when read cannot conveniently be sung.

I have occasionally, for musical reasons, changed the order of the lines; this seems to me legitimate, as there does not appear to be an inevitable sequence in Skelton's original order.

The first movement is a ballad telling of a certain Elinor Rumming who kept an alehouse in Leatherhead. The inn is still there ('The Running Horse') and a portrait of Elinor hangs on the outer wall.

The ballad is divided into five sections. The first describes Elinor herself, the second tells of the guests who came to the inn and the various shifts they were put to to obtain their ale till they are at length driven out by the angry hostess. Then follows the episode of a visit of 'drunken Alice' (represented by a contralto). She succeeds apparently in obtaining a free drink, then she falls into a drunken slumber. The fourth section introduces still another party of guests who join in a drinking chorus: 'With hey and with ho, sit we down a row.' Finally a few lines tell us that

'Thus endeth the geste
Of this worthy feast'.

The second movement is an Intermezzo, a love-song in praise of 'Pretty Bess', sung by the baritone solo, accompanied by the chorus.

The third (Burlesca) is a satirical epitaph on John Jayberd, the parish clerk of Diss, who was probably well known to Skelton and evidently cordially disliked by him. The words are written chiefly in monkish Latin with sudden unexpected interjections in English. The setting is for men's voices only.

The fourth movement (Romanza, for contralto solo and chorus of women's voices) is a lament sung by Jane Scroop, a pupil at the Abbey School of Carrow, near Norwich, for Philip, her sparrow, which had been killed by 'Gib, our cat'.

First there is a dialogue between Jane and her companions who may be supposed to enter in procession bearing the coffin and chanting the office. At first Jane laments her sparrow and cries for vengeance on all cats, wild and tame; then she summons all the birds of the air to take their part in the funeral ceremony; the robin to sing the requiem, the parrot to read the gospel, the peacock to sing the grail, and as a climax the phœnix to bless the hearse. Lastly the chorus sing their final fare-well to Philip, while Jane softly murmurs portions of a Latin office for the dead.

There is no justification, I think, for describing these touching words as a 'parody'. Jane saw no reason, and I see no reason, why she should not pray for the peace of her sparrow's soul.

The last movement is entitled 'Scherzo' and is made up out of two poems, 'Jolly Rutterkin', and a song out of the play 'Magnificence'. This fusion is, I hope, justified by the fact that the character who sings the song in the play has immediately before quoted a line from 'Jolly Rutterkin'. The setting is for baritone solo and chorus.

R.V.W.

Note on score: A preface to the score, by R.V.W., summarizes the above. After the first sentence he has added, 'In doing this I am aware that I have laid myself open to the accusation of cutting out somebody's "favourite bit". If any omissions are to be made this, I fear, is inevitable. On the whole I have managed to keep all my own "favourite bits".'

Publication: London, O.U.P. (© 1935). Vocal score; orchestral parts and arrangement for strings and pianoforte available on hire. V.S. con-tains text with glossary and free translation of the Latin epitaph in (3). Full score O.U.P. © 1971.

Origins: A Sixth Portrait, 'Margery Wentworth', was abandoned, a setting in G major beginning 'With marjoram gentle, the flower of goodli-head'. It was for baritone and chorus. The finale of 'Jolly Rutterkin' was extended after early sketches by 20 bars. The baritone's 'Hoyda' four bars after $\boxed{12}$ was answered by the chorus with 'Like a rutter Hoy-da', the final syllable being strongly accented as in the present ending.

Whereabouts of MS.: British Library. Sketches, including 'Margery Wentworth' (50455), Vocal score (50456), Full score, two parts (50457 A and B).

6. LITTLE CLOISTER (Hymn 262). Hymn tune for voices in unison and organ. Words by the Rev. Percy Dearmer. 'As the disciples, when thy Son had left them.' (Hymn 262 in *Songs of Praise*, enlarged edition where two melodies for it are given.) This extra tune for this hymn was composed in 1935 but has not been incorporated into the hymn book.
Publication: London, O.U.P. (© 1935).

7. FLOURISH OF TRUMPETS FOR A FOLK DANCE FESTIVAL (founded on the 'Morris Call', collected by C. J. Sharp in Gloucester-shire).
Instrumentation: Soprano cornet, E flat; solo cornet, B flat; 3 repiano

cornets, B flat; flügel horn, B flat; solo horn, E flat; 2 horns, E flat; 2 trombones, B flat; 1 bass trombone, side drum, cymbals.
First performance: London, Royal Albert Hall, International Folk Dance Festival, 17 July 1935.
Unpublished.
28 bars. *Allegro.* This work was recorded in 1937 by the Morris Motors Band, conducted by S. V. Wood, on Columbia DB1671 (78 r.p.m.).

1936

1. NOTHING IS HERE FOR TEARS. Choral song (unison or SATB) with accompaniment for pianoforte, organ, or orchestra. Composed upon the death of King George V. Words adapted from *Samson Agonistes* by John Milton (1608–74). *Moderately slow.* C major.
Instrumentation: 2 trumpets, 3 trombones, tuba, timpani, percussion, organ, strings. *Or* 2 flutes, 2 oboes (1 opt.), 2 clarinets, 2 bassoons, 4 horns (2 opt.), 2 trumpets, 3 trombones (opt.), tuba (opt), timpani, percussion, organ (opt), strings. *Or* strings and pianoforte.
First performance: London, broadcast concert, 26 January 1936. The B.B.C. Singers, conducted by Sir Walford Davies.
Publication: London, O.U.P. (© 1936). Vocal score. Orchestral parts on hire.
Whereabouts of MS.: British Library,   vocal score and full score (50458 A and B).

2. THE DAILY SERVICE. Prayers and hymns for schools. Editors: Prayers, Canon G. W. Briggs; hymns, the Rev. Percy Dearmer, R. Vaughan Williams, Martin Shaw, G. W. Briggs. Contains the following tunes or arrangements by R.V.W.:

  50. Forest Green ('O little town of Bethlehem').
  51. Rodmell ('When Christ was born in Bethlehem').
  90. Wicklow ('Our blest Redeemer').
  91. Down Ampney ('Come down, O Love Divine').
  97. Sine Nomine ('For all the saints').
124. White Gates ('Fierce raged the tempest').
148. Hardwick ('So here hath been dawning').
155. Magda ('Saviour, again to thy dear name').
164. Randolph ('God be with you till we meet again').
Amen VI.
Prayers: 1. Almighty God, whose service is perfect freedom.
        2. O God, grant me this day.
        3. Eternal Father, who hast called us.
        4. Unto Him that loved us.
Publication: London, O.U.P. 1936 Melody Edition; two later editions 1938; with supplement 1939; full music edition.

3. SONGS OF PRAISE: THE CHILDREN'S CHURCH. An order
of morning and evening prayer with *Songs of Praise for Children*.
Editors as in (2) above. Contains three hymns by R.V.W.:
  87. Sine Nomine ('For all the saints').
  113. White Gates ('Fierce raged the tempest').
  147. Randolph ('God be with you till we meet again').
  Amen VI.
Publication: London O.U.P. 1936 melody edition.

4. THE POISONED KISS, or The Empress and the Necromancer.
A Romantic Extravaganza, with spoken dialogue, written by Evelyn
Sharp (1869–1955), adapted from a story by Richard Garnett for
12 soloists, mixed chorus and orchestra. Composed 1927–9, revised
1934–5, revised again 1936–7, further revision 1956–7.
Instrumentation: 2 flutes (2nd doubling piccolo), 1 oboe, 1 cor anglais
(cued in), 2 clarinets, 1 bassoon, 2 horns, 2 trumpets, 1 trombone,
timpani, percussion (2 players if available), harp (or pianoforte),
strings.
Characters:

Angelica, Tormentilla's maid and companion	Soprano
Gallanthus, the Prince's attendant	Baritone
Hob, Gob and Lob, the Magician's hobgoblins	Tenor, baritone, bass
Dipsacus, a professional magician	Bass
Amaryllus, the Prince, son of the Empress	Tenor
Tormentilla, the Magician's daughter	Soprano
1st, 2nd and 3rd Mediums, the Empress's ⎱ assistants in amateur magic .. .. ⎰	Soprano, mezzo-soprano, contralto
An attendant	Speaking Part
Empress Persicaria, reigning sovereign in Golden Town ⎱ and amateur magician .. .. ⎰	Contralto
A physician	Speaking Part

Chorus.
Act. I. The magician's haunt in the forest.
Act II Tormentilla's apartment in Golden Town (a week later).
Act III. Room in the Empress's Palace (next day).
First performance: Arts Theatre, Cambridge, 12 May 1936, with the
following cast:

TORMENTILLA	Mabel (Margaret) Ritchie
DIPSACUS	Frederick Woodhouse
ANGELICA	Margaret Field-Hyde
AMARYLLUS	Trefor Jones
THE EMPRESS	Meriel St. Clair
GALLANTHUS	Geoffrey Dunn
HOB, GOB AND LOB ..	Herbert Sharp, Robert Tong, Eric Moss

MEDIUMS   ..   Marie Howes, Ena Mitchell, Barbara Digby

Costumes designed by Gwen Raverat. Producer, Camille Prior.

Conductor, C. B. Rootham.

First performance in London: Sadler's Wells Theatre, 18 May 1936, with cast as above, conducted by Dr. R. Vaughan Williams.

Note on score: 'The audience is requested *not* to refrain from talking during the overture. Otherwise they will know all the tunes before the opera begins. R.V.W.'

Duration: About 2 hours.

Publication: London, O.U.P. 1936 Vocal Score. (Vocal score, chorus and orchestral parts on hire.) Version with spoken dialogue by Ursula Vaughan Williams was first performed at Royal Academy of Music, 11 July 1957. For this revival the composer cut 10 songs: Act I, No. 9 (portion), 11, 13 and 14. Act II, Nos. 24, 26 and 30. Act III, Nos. 36, 40 and 43.

Whereabouts of MS.: British Library, Full score (50415 A–C); Sketches, including a notebook and some sketches in full score (50412). 'Never too late' quartet (57293).

4A. OVERTURE, 'THE POISONED KISS'.

Instrumentation as above.

Duration: 7 minutes.

Parts on hire from O.U.P.

Whereabouts of MS.: British Library, Full score (50413).

4B. INTRODUCTION AND SCENE FROM 'THE POISONED KISS'. For tenor, mixed chorus (SATB) and orchestra. (Now withdrawn.)

Instrumentation: 2 flutes (2nd doubling piccolo), 1 oboe, 2 clarinets, 1 bassoon, 2 horns, triangle, harp (or pianoforte), strings.

First performance: (Overture, Introduction Act II and Scene for Amaryllus): Three Choirs Festival, Gloucester, Shire Hall, 8 September 1937. Trefor Jones (tenor), London Symphony Orchestra, conducted by Dr. R. Vaughan Williams.

Duration: 12 minutes.

Whereabouts of MS.: British|Library, Full score (50414).

5. DONA NOBIS PACEM. A Cantata for soprano and baritone soloists, mixed chorus (SATB) and orchestra. Text compiled from various sources, as given below:

I. Agnus Dei. *Lento.* From the Liturgy. For soprano and chorus.

II. Beat! beat! Drums! *Allegro moderato.* From *Drum Taps*, by Walt Whitman. For chorus.

III. Reconciliation. *Andantino.* From *Drum Taps*, by Walt Whitman. For baritone, soprano and chorus.

IV. Dirge for two veterans. *Moderato alla marcia.* From *Drum Taps*, by Walt Whitman. For chorus. Composed in 1911.

V. (*a*) The Angel of Death. *L'istesso tempo.* Speech by John Bright (1811–89) in the House of Commons, 23 February 1855, during the Crimean War. For baritone and soprano.

(*b*) We looked for peace. *Poco animato.* Jeremiah, Ch. VIII, 15–22. For chorus.

(*c*) O man, greatly beloved. Daniel, Ch. X, 19. For baritone.

(*d*) The glory of this latter house. Haggai, Ch. II, 9. For baritone.

(*e*) Nation shall not lift up a sword against nation, etc. *Andante— poco animato—poco più lento.* Adapted from Micah IV, 3; Leviticus XXVI, 6; Psalms LXXXV, 10, and CXVIII, 19; Isaiah XLIII, 9, and LXVI, 18–22; Luke II, 14. For soprano and chorus.

Instrumentation: 3 flutes (3rd doubling piccolo), 2 oboes, 2 clarinets, 2 bassoons, 1 double bassoon, 4 horns, 4 trumpets (2 opt.), 5 trombones (2 opt.), tuba, timpani, percussion, bells, harp, organ (opt.), strings. *Or* strings and piano.

First performance: Huddersfield, The Town Hall, 2 October 1936. Renée Flynn (soprano), Roy Henderson (baritone), The Huddersfield Choral Society, The Hallé Orchestra, conducted by Albert Coates. First public performance in London: Queen's Hall, 5 February 1938, Elsie Suddaby (soprano), Redvers Llewellyn (baritone), The Royal Choral Society, London Philharmonic Orchestra, conducted by Dr. Malcolm Sargent. (Vaughan Williams conducted a broadcast performance in London on 13 November 1936, with Renée Flynn, soprano, Roy Henderson, baritone, the B.B.C. Chorus and B.B.C. Symphony Orchestra.)

Duration: 36 minutes.

Publication: London, O.U.P. (© 1936). Full score O.U.P. © 1971.

Whereabouts of MS.: British Library, Vocal score (50453); full score (50454).

6. RIDERS TO THE SEA. By J. M. Synge (1871–1909) Set to music by R. Vaughan Williams in one act, for five soloists, women's chorus and orchestra. Composed 1925–32.

Characters:

Maurya, an old woman	Contralto
Bartley, her son	Baritone
Cathleen, her daughter	Soprano
Nora, her younger daughter	Soprano
A woman	Mezzo-soprano

Chorus of women on-stage and off-stage (each with parts for solo voices). Man and woman (non-singing).

Instrumentation: 2 flutes (2nd doubling piccolo), 1 oboe, 1 cor anglais, 1 bass clarinet, 1 bassoon, 2 horns, 1 trumpet, timpani, bass drum, sea-machine, strings (not more than 6–6–4–4–2). Where bass clarinet is not available it can be replaced by special parts for clarinet and bassoon.

First performance: London, Royal College of Music, Palmer Fund for Opera Study, 30 November 1937 (private dress rehearsal); first public performance, 1 December 1937, with following cast:

MAURYA	Olive Hall
CATHLEEN	Janet Smith-Miller
NORA	Marjorie Steventon
BARTLEY	Alan Coad
A WOMAN	Grace Wilkinson
SOLO VOICES off-stage	Grace Wilkinson (contralto), Marjorie Skuffham (soprano)

CHORUS of 20 women's voices.

Producer, Clive Carey; Conductor, Dr. Malcolm Sargent.

Duration: 37 minutes.

Publication: London, O.U.P. (© 1936). Vocal score; orchestral parts on hire. Full score O.U.P. © 1972.

Whereabouts of MS.: British Library. Rough full score (50416); Full score (50417).

7. TWO HYMN-TUNE PRELUDES. For small orchestra.

1. Eventide (W. H. Monk, 1823–89). *Lento sostenuto.* G major.
2. Dominus regit me (J. B. Dykes, 1823–76). *Andante con moto.* B flat major.

Instrumentation: 1 flute, 1 oboe, 1 clarinet, 1 bassoon, 1 horn, strings.

First performance: Hereford, The Cathedral, Three Choirs Festival, 8 September 1936, London Symphony Orchestra, conducted by Dr. R. Vaughan Williams.

Duration: 6½ minutes.

Publication: London, O.U.P. Full score (© 1960).

Other versions: Arrangement for organ by Herbert Sumsion, O.U.P. (© 1938.)

Whereabouts of MS.: British Library. Full score (50397).

1937

1. FLOURISH FOR A CORONATION. For mixed chorus (SATB) and orchestra. Words from various sources, as below.

1. Allegro moderato. 'Let the priest and the prophet anoint him King . . . thou art exalted as head above all.' I Kings, 1, vv. 34, 40; II Chronicles, V, v. 13; Psalm CXXXVI, vv. 1, 3–5, etc.

2. Lento ma non troppo. 'O prince, desire to be honourable. . . .'

By Geoffrey Chaucer from 'L'Envoy to King Richard' from *Lake of Stedfastnesse*.

3. Lento ma non troppo—Tempo I. 'Now gracious God he save our King. . . .' From the Agincourt Song, MS. in possession of Trinity College, Cambridge.

Instrumentation: 4 flutes, 2 oboes, 3 clarinets, alto saxophone, 2 bassoons, double bassoon, 8 horns, 6 trumpets, 3 trombones, euphonium, tuba, timpani, percussion (2 players), glockenspiel, bells, 2 harps, organ, pianoforte, strings. *Or:* 2 flutes, 2 oboes, 2 clarinets, 2 bassoons, 4 horns, 2 trumpets, 3 trombones, tuba, timpani, strings.

First performance: London, Queen's Hall, Royal Philharmonic Society Concert, 1 April 1937, The Philharmonic Choir, London Philharmonic Orchestra, conducted by Sir Thomas Beecham.

Duration: 13 minutes.

Publication: London, O.U.P. (© 1937.) Vocal score, full score and parts on hire only.

Whereabouts of MS.: British Library. Full score and two leaves of sketch (50460).

3. FESTIVAL TE DEUM IN F MAJOR. Founded on traditional themes. For mixed chorus (SATB) and organ or orchestra. Words from the Book of Common Prayer. *Andante risoluto.*

Instrumentation: 3 flutes (1 opt.), 3 oboes (1 opt.), 2 clarinets, 1 bass clarinet (opt.), 2 bassoons, 1 double bassoon, 4 horns, 3 trumpets (1 opt.), 3 trombones, 1 tuba, timpani, percussion (2 players), organ, strings. *Or* organ.

First performance: London, Westminster Abbey, 12 May 1937, Coronation of King George VI, for which it was composed. Special Choir and Orchestra, conducted by Sir Adrian Boult.

Duration: 9 minutes.

Publication: London, O.U.P. (© 1937). Vocal Score (Oxford Church Music, edited by Harold Darke, No. 477); parts on hire.

Whereabouts of MS.: British Library, full score (50459).

Other version: Mixed chorus (SATB), accompanied by brass and percussion, adapted by John Bavicchi. © O.U.P. 1978. Score and parts for hire 19 385585 2 AR.

3. TE DEUM BY ANTONIN DVOŘÁK (first published 1892). For soprano and bass, mixed chorus (SATB) and orchestra. Vocal score by Josef Suk, revised by Franz Terwal. English adaptation by R. Vaughan Williams.

Publication: Leipzig, N. Simrock (© 1937) (15289). This adaptation was made for the Leith Hill Festival.

4. MUSIC FOR ENGLISH FOLK DANCE SOCIETY MASQUE.

Unpublished.

Instrumentation: 2 flutes (2nd doubling piccolo), 1 oboe, 2 bassoons, 1 horn, 1 trumpet, timpani (ad lib.), triangle, strings.

Overture. *Moderato.* Full score with parts in MS.

Also MS. of *An E.F.D.S. Medley,* possibly written earlier.

First performance: London, Royal Albert Hall, English Folk Dance and Song Society's New Year Festival, 9 January 1937. Orchestra of E.F.D.S.S., conducted by Dr. R. Vaughan Williams.

1938

1. ENGLAND'S PLEASANT LAND. Music for a pageant, by various composers including R.V.W. For mixed chorus (SATB) and military band.

Instrumentation: 1 concert flute, 1 oboe, 1 E flat clarinet, solo B flat clarinet, 3 repiano B flat clarinets, 1 bassoon, 1 E flat saxophone, 1 B flat saxophone, 2 horns in F, 2 cornets, 3 trombones, 1 euphonium, basses, percussion.

First performance: Milton Court, Westcott, Surrey, 9 July 1938. Band of the 2nd Bn., the Duke of Cornwall's Light Infantry, conducted by A. Young.

Act II, Scene 1, contained music by R.V.W.

1. Exit of the Ghosts of the Past. *Lento.*
2. The Funeral March for the old order. *Lento maestoso.* In this item the chorus sang the following translation by Vaughan Williams from the Latin of Horace (*Odes* II, XIV 1).

Eheu fugaces . . .
Swiftly they pass, the flying years,
No prayers can stay their course,
Here is the road each man must tread
Be he of royal blood or lowly birth.
Vainly we shun the battles' roar,
The perilous sea, the fever-laden breezes,
Soon shall we reach our journey's end
And trembling cross the narrow stream of death.
Land, house and wife must all be left,
The cherished trees be all cut down,
Strangers shall lord it in our home
And squander all our store.

This work is of unusual interest because in it he tried out some of the music of the Fifth Symphony. The Funeral March opens with the principal material of the first movement of the symphony (in a different key) and the setting of the Horace is linked to the symphony by certain of its phrases. The Exit of the Ghosts contains much of the subsidiary material of the Preludio and the chorale-like tune which occurs on the horns in the central section of the Scherzo.

Whereabouts of MS.: British Library. Autograph full score with copies of instrumental parts. Includes R.V.W.'s contribution, his scoring of Holst's 'I vow to thee', and John Ticehurst's music (57290). Also sketch of setting of Old Hundredth in A flat 'for pageant Scene 4' which may have been intended for this pageant or that in 1934 at Abinger (50455).

2. SERENADE TO MUSIC. For 16 solo voices (4s, 4c, 4t, 4b) and orchestra. Words from *The Merchant of Venice* (William Shakespeare), Act V, Scene 1.

Instrumentation: 2 flutes (2nd doubling piccolo), 1 oboe, 1 cor anglais, 2 clarinets, 2 bassoons, 4 horns, 2 trumpets, 3 trombones, 1 tuba, timpani, percussion, harp, strings, *Or* strings and pianoforte.

First performance: London, Albert Hall, 5 October 1938, Jubilee Concert of Sir Henry Wood. Isobel Baillie, Stiles Allen, Elsie Suddaby, Eva Turner (sopranos); Margaret Balfour, Muriel Brunskill, Astra Desmond, Mary Jarred (contraltos); Parry Jones, Heddle Nash, Frank Titterton, Walter Widdop (tenors); Norman Allin, Robert Easton, Roy Henderson, Harold Williams (basses). B.B.C. Symphony, London Symphony, London Philharmonic and Queen's Hall Orchestras, conducted by Sir Henry Wood.

Dedication: Composed for and dedicated to Sir Henry Wood on the occasion of his jubilee, in grateful recognition of his services to music.

Duration: 14 minutes.

Publication: London, O.U.P. Vocal score (© 1938); Full score 1961. The initials of the original singers appear against their parts in the full score. Orchestral parts on hire.

Other versions: Although written for 16 solo singers, the work may be performed by four soloists (sctb) with chorus, or all the solo parts may be sung in chorus.

Orchestral version:

Instrumentation: 2 flutes, 1 oboe, 1 cor anglais, 2 clarinets, 2 bassoons, 4 horns, 2 trumpets, 3 trombones, tuba, timpani, percussion, harp, solo violin, strings.

First performance: London, Queen's Hall, 10 February 1940, London Symphony Orchestra, conducted by Sir Henry Wood.

Duration: 14 minutes.

Publication: London, O.U.P. Parts on hire.

Whereabouts of MS.: London, Royal Academy of Music (Original version).

3. LITURGICAL SETTINGS OF THE HOLY COMMUNION (Editor, J. H. Arnold). I. Traditional, with *Benedictus* and *Agnus Dei* by R.V.W. All those parts of the service which belong to the congregation are set to traditional melodies.
Publication: London, O.U.P. (© 1938).

4. ALL HAIL THE POWER. To the Hymn Tune 'Miles Lane', by W. Shrubsole (1760–1806), arranged for unison (congregation), mixed chorus (SATB) with organ or orchestra. Words by Edward Perronet (1726–92). *Largo maestoso.* A major.
Instrumentation: 2 flutes, 2 oboes (1 opt.), 2 clarinets, 2 bassoons, 1 double bassoon (opt.), 4 horns (2 opt.), 3 trumpets (1 opt.), 3 trombones, 1 tuba (opt.), timpani, percussion, organ (opt.), strings.
Dedication: To Ivor Atkins.
Publication: London, O.U.P. (© 1938) V.S. Orchestral parts on hire.
Whereabouts of MS.: British Library. Full score (50461). Vocal score (57914).

5. DOUBLE TRIO. For string sextet.
    I. Fantasia.
    II. Scherzo Ostinato.
    III. Intermezzo (Homage to Henry Hall).
    IV. Rondo.
Composed in 1938. Unpublished in this form.
First performance: London, Wigmore Hall, 21 January 1939. The Menges Sextet (Isolde Menges, Beatrice Carrelle (violins); Jean Stewart, Alfred de Reyghere (violas); Ivor James, Helen Just (violoncellos). Revised version, first performance: London, National Gallery, 12 October 1942. The Menges Sextet (Isolde Menges, Beatrice Carrelle (violins); Jean Stewart, Alfred de Reyghere (violas); Ivor James, Helen Just (violoncellos).
The work was then withdrawn, and again rewritten in 1946–8 with a completely new finale (Fantasia) when it became:

5A. PARTITA FOR DOUBLE STRING ORCHESTRA.
Instrumentation: Orchestra I: At least four violins, two violas and two violoncellos; Orchestra II: At least four violins, two violas, two violoncellos, two double basses. These numbers refer to players.
First performance: B.B.C. Third Programme, 20 March 1948, B.B.C. Symphony Orchestra, conducted by Sir Adrian Boult. First public performance: London, Royal Albert Hall, Promenade Concert, 29 July 1948, B.B.C. Symphony Orchestra, conducted by Dr. R. Vaughan Williams.
Dedication: To R. Müller-Hartmann.

Duration: 21 minutes.

Publication: London, O.U.P. (© 1948). Parts on hire.

6. THE BRIDAL DAY. A Masque by Ursula Wood (Ursula Vaughan Williams). Founded on *Epithalamion*, by Edmund Spenser (1552–99). For baritone soloist, speaker, dancers, mimers, mixed chorus (SATB). Composed 1938–9. Revised 1952–3.

Characters: The Bride.
    The Bridegroom.
    Juno.
    Bridesmaids, groomsmen.
    Bride's parents, bridegroom's parents.
    Nymphs of Sea, River and Forest.
    The Three Graces.
    Bacchus.
    Priests and acolytes.
    Minstrels, bell-ringers.
    The Hours.
    The Evening Star.
    The Winged Loves.
    Juno's attendants.

Instrumentation: 1 piccolo, 1 flute, pianoforte, 2 violins, viola, violoncello, double bass, *Or* flute and pianoforte only.

 I. *Andante con moto—allegretto* (Nymphs' dance). Speaker.

 II. *Allegretto* (Bridesmaids' dance). Baritone soloist and chorus. Speaker.

 III. *Allegro moderato* (Dances of Groomsmen and Bridesmaids)—*poco animato—lento—andante maestoso—allegro vivace.* Speaker and chorus.

 IV. *Moderato* (Grotesque dance)—*poco animato* (Graces' dance).

 V. *Allegro* (General dance)—*molto vivace—lento—andante con moto* (Bell-ringers' dance)—*andante sostenuto.* Speaker.

 VI. *Andante sostenuto* (Dance cf the hours)—*poco animato* (Evening Star's dance)—*Tempo I.* Baritone soloist and chorus.

 VII. *Andante sostenuto—tranquillo.* Speaker, baritone soloist and chorus.

 VIII. *Allegretto—poco animando.* Speaker.

 IX. *Lento.*

 X. *Molto adagio—allegro.* Chorus.

 XI. *Andante maestoso.* Chorus.

First performance: Projected first performance was for Cecil Sharp House, Autumn 1939. The cast was to have included Ursula Wood as the Bride and Thora Jaques as Juno. At first play-through on 27 April 1939 Vaughan Williams conducted, and sang the baritone part. Joseph

Cooper was the pianist, Eve Kisch, flautist, and Leighton Quartet (Ruth Pearl, Irene Richards, Jean Stewart and Vera Canning). Cancelled by war. Actual first performance: London, 5 June 1953, B.B.C. Television, with following cast:

NARRATOR	Cecil Day Lewis
BARITONE	Denis Dowling
THE BRIDE	Sheila Shand Gibbs
THE BRIDEGROOM	Guy Verney
JUNO	Yvonne Marsh
BACCHUS	Roy Evans
EVENING STAR	Judith Whitaker

Settings designed by John Clements; choreography by David Paltenghi; produced by Christian Simpson. Chorus and Wigmore Ensemble, with Michael Mullinar (pianoforte), conducted by Stanford Robinson.

This work was composed in the winter of 1938–9. Originally the only vocal movements were 'Ah, when will this long weary day have end?' and the 'Io Hymen' Chorus. Revised 1952–3 when additions included 'Love Song of the Birds' (II) and 'Now, welcome Night' (VII). Music of 'But let still silence' (VII, 41B) quotes from 'Incarnatus est' of Mass in D by Beethoven.

Publication: London, O.U.P. (© 1956 V.S.). Full score and parts on hire.

Whereabouts of MS.: British Library, Full score (50421).

For EPITHALAMION, a Cantata based on *The Bridal Day*, see under 1957.

1939

1. SERVICES IN D MINOR. For unison voices, mixed choir (SATB) and organ.

Morning Service
   I. Te Deum. *Con moto.*
  II. Benedictus. *Andante.*
 III. Jubilate. *Allegro.*

Communion Service
   I. Kyrie. *Andante* (Latin words as alternative).
  II. Responses. *Andante.*
 III. (*a*) Before the Gospel. *Moderato.*
     (*b*) After the Gospel. *Moderato.*
 IV. Creed. *Con moto.*
  V. Sursum Corda. *Moderato.*
 VI. Sanctus. *Andante sostenuto.*
VII. Benedictus qui venit. *Andante.*
VIII. Agnus Dei. *Lento non troppo.*

IX. Gloria. *Moderato.*
Evening Service
   I. Magnificat. *Andante.*
   II. Nunc dimittis. *Largo.*
Words from the *Book of Common Prayer.*
Dedication: Written for and dedicated to Dr. C. S. Lang and his singers at Christ's Hospital.
Note on score: 'This service is designed for college chapels and other churches where there is, besides the choir, a large body of voices who also wish for a share in the musical settings of the service. The part allotted to these voices is entirely in unison or octaves. The part for the choir is, it is hoped, reasonably simple. Special care has been taken with the tenor part. It will seldom be necessary for the tenor singers to rise above E.'
Publication: London, O.U.P. (© 1939). (Oxford Church Music, Nos. 492, 493, 494. Congregational part available separately.)

2. FIVE VARIANTS OF 'DIVES AND LAZARUS'. For strings and harp (2 if possible).
   Introduction and theme. *Adagio.* B modal minor.
   Variant I. B modal minor.
   Variant II. *Allegro moderato.* B modal minor.
   Variant III. D modal minor.
   Variant IV. *L'istesso tempo.*
   Variant V. *Adagio.* B modal minor.
   First performance: New York (World Fair), Carnegie Hall, 10 June 1939, New York Philharmonic-Symphony Orchestra, conducted by Sir Adrian Boult. First performance in England, Bristol, Colston Hall, 1 November 1939, B.B.C. Symphony Orchestra (Section A), conducted by Sir Adrian Boult.
   Duration: 13 minutes.
   Note on score: 'These variants are not exact replicas of traditional tunes, but rather reminiscences of various versions in my own collection and those of others.'
   Publication: London, O.U.P. (© 1940). Full score. The parts for the viola and violoncello are not identical, one set belonging to desks 1, 3, 6, and the other to desks 2, 4, 5. By this arrangement the work can be played by any orchestra which possesses four or more violas and violoncellos.

3. SUITE FOR PIPES. For treble, alto, tenor and bass pipes. Composed 1938 or 1939.
   I. Intrada. *Moderato maestoso.* D major.
   II. Minuet and Trio. *Allegro moderato.* A major. Trio, B minor.
   III. Valse. *Lento.* B major.

IV. Finale. Jig. *Presto.* G major.

First performance: Chichester, Pipers' Guild Summer School, August 1939, by Pipers' Guild Quartet (Dorothy Barnard, treble; Gertrude Enoch, alto; Kay Connel, tenor; Annie Miller, bass).

Dedication: The Pipers' Guild Quartet.

Duration: 11 minutes.

Publication: London, O.U.P. Miniature Score (© 1947). The notation must be read an octave higher than printed.

Whereabouts of MS.: British Library. Full scores (50400).

Other version: For recorders. © O.U.P. 1980.

4. THE WILLOW WHISTLE. Song for voice and pipe. Words by M. E. Fuller. Undated, but possibly contemporary with the Suite. *Whereabouts of MS.:* British Library. MS. (50480).

5. A HYMN OF FREEDOM. Written in this time of war, 1939. For unison voices with pianoforte or organ. Words by Canon G. W. Briggs (1875–1959.) *Andante maestoso.* D major.

Publication: London, O.U.P. (© 1939). This hymn first appeared in the *Daily Telegraph* of 20 December 1939, when it was stated that publication by the O.U.P. would be 'immediate'. It later became No. 1 of *Five Wartime Hymns* (see 1942).

6. FLOURISH FOR WIND BAND. Composed 1939 as overture to pageant in Royal Albert Hall and scored for military band with numerous clarinets, cornets, saxophones, and euphoniums. Score was then lost, but reappeared in 1971 and was adapted by Roy Douglas for the wind instruments (with double basses and drums) of a symphony orchestra. This version was performed by the Tunbridge Wells Symphony Orchestra in 1974.

Instrumentation: Flute, E flat clarinet, B flat clarinets, alto clarinet, contra-alto clarinet, bass clarinet, contrabass clarinet, bassoon, alto saxophones, B flat saxophones, baritone saxophone, horns, cornets, trumpets, trombones, euphonium, basses, string bass, timpani, percussion.

First performance: London, Royal Albert Hall, 1 April 1939.

Duration: 1½ minutes.

Publication: London, O.U.P. © 1973. Score and parts.

Whereabouts of MS.: British Library (57489).

Other versions:

(*a*) Adapted for orchestral wind, double basses, percussion, and timpani by Roy Douglas. O.U.P. © 1972. Hire only.

(*b*) Arranged for brass band by Roy Douglas.

    Instrumentation: Soprano in E flat, 3 solo cornets in B flat, 1 repiano in B flat, 2 cornet 2 in B flat, 2 cornet 3 in B flat, 1 flugel in B flat, 1 solo horn in E flat, 1 horn 1 in E flat, 1 horn 2 in E flat, 1 baritone

1 in B flat, 1 baritone 2 in B flat, 1 trombone 1 in B flat, 1 trombone 2 in B flat, 1 bass trombone in C, 1 euphonium 1 in B flat, 1 euphonium 2 in B flat, 2 E flat bass, 2 B flat bass, timpani (opt.), bass drum (opt.), side drum, cymbals.
O.U.P. © 1981. Condensed score in B flat. Parts.

1940

1. SIX CHORAL SONGS—TO BE SUNG IN TIME OF WAR.

For unison voices with pianoforte or orchestra. Words by Percy Bysshe Shelley (1792–1822).

1. A Song of Courage (from 'There is no work', line 7 et seq.). *Allegro moderato*. E flat major.
2. A Song of Liberty (from *Hellas*, first words of semi-chorus). *Andante alla marcia*. D modal minor.
3. A Song of Healing (from *Prometheus Unbound*, IV, line 557). *Andante con moto*. A major.
4. A Song of Victory (last lines of *Prometheus Unbound*, line 576 being incomplete). *Andante con moto*. C modal minor.
5. A Song of Pity, Peace, and Love (from *Revolt of Islam*. Canto V, lines 2197–2211). *Andante moderato*. E flat major.
6. A Song of the New Age (from *Hellas*, final chorus, verses 3, 4 and 6 omitted). *Andante moderato*. A modal minor.

Instrumentation: 2 flutes, 2 oboes, 2 clarinets, 2 bassoons, 1 double bassoon, 4 horns, 2 trumpets, 3 trombones, 1 tuba, timpani, percussion, harp, organ, strings.
First performance: Broadcast concert, 20 December 1940, B.B.C. Chorus, B.B.C. Symphony Orchestra, conducted by Leslie Woodgate. (A projected performance during the 1940 Promenade season, for which rehearsals had taken place, was cancelled because of air raids.)
Publication: London, O.U.P. (© 1940). V.S. Parts on hire.
Whereabouts of MS.: British Library. Full score (50463): V.S. of 4, 5 and 6 (50462).

2. VALIANT FOR TRUTH.

Motet for mixed chorus (SATB) unaccompanied, or with organ or pianoforte. Composed in November 1940. Words from *The Pilgrim's Progress*, by John Bunyan (1628–88). *Lento*. D minor.
First performance: London, St. Michael's Church, Cornhill, 29 June 1942. St. Michael's Singers, conducted by Dr. Harold Darke.
Publication: London, O.U.P. (© 1941).

3. MUSIC FOR FILM '49TH PARALLEL'.

Composed 1940–1. Produced and directed for Ortus Films by Michael Powell.
Instrumentation: 2 flutes, 1 oboe, 1 cor anglais, 2 clarinets, 2 bassoons, 1 double bassoon, 4 horns, 2 trumpets, 3 trombones, tuba, timpani, percussion, harp, strings.

A suite from the film music is said to have been played in Prague in 1946. Its items were: (1) Prelude; (2) Warning in a dance hall; (3) Hudson's Bay (*a*) Un canadien errant, (*b*) L'alouette; (4) Nazis on the prowl; (5) The Hutterite settlement; (*a*) Anna's volkslied 'Lasst uns das Kindlein Wiegen', (*b*) The wheatfield; (6) Indian festival; (7) The lake in the mountains; (8) Nazis on the run; (9) Epilogue. Film first shown at Odeon Cinema, Leicester Square, 8 October 1941. Music played by the London Symphony Orchestra, conducted by Muir Mathieson. Stars of the film included Glynis Johns, Leslie Howard, Laurence Olivier, Raymond Massey, Eric Portman, and Anton Walbrook. The following items were published:

1. (*a*) PRELUDE, '49TH PARALLEL'.

   Instrumentation: 2 flutes, 2 oboes, 2 clarinets, 2 bassoons, 4 horns, 2 trumpets, 3 trombones, tuba, timpani, cymbals, harp, strings.

   Duration: 2 minutes.

   Publication: London, O.U.P. (© 1960). All parts fully cued by Roy Douglas so that all except strings are optional.

   (*b*) PRELUDE, arranged for string orchestra by Roy Douglas.
   Publication: London, O.U.P. (© 1960).

   (*c*) PRELUDE, arranged for brass band by Roy Douglas.
   Instrumentation: Soprano in E flat, 3 solo cornets in B flat, 1 re-piano in B flat, 2 cornet 2 in B flat, 2 cornet 3 in B flat, 1 flugel in B flat, 1 solo horn in E flat, 1 horn 1 in E flat, 1 horn 2 in E flat, 1 baritone 1 in B flat, 1 baritone 2 in B flat, 1 trombone 1 in B flat, 1 trombone 2 in B flat, 1 bass trombone in C, 1 euphonium 1 in B flat, 1 euphonium 2 in B flat, 2 E flat bass, 2 B flat bass, timpani, cymbals.

   Publication: London, O.U.P. © 1981. Condensed score in B flat. Parts. Full scores hire only.

2. PRELUDE: 'THE NEW COMMONWEALTH.' Arranged for organ by Christopher Morris.
   Publication: London, O.U.P. (© 1960) and as No. 6 of *A Vaughan Williams Organ Album* (1964).

3. SONG: 'THE NEW COMMONWEALTH.' Words by Harold Child (1869–1945). Music adapted from the Prelude to *49th Parallel*. For unison voices with pianoforte accompaniment or orchestra. *Moderato.* F major.
   Instrumentation: 2 flutes, 2 oboes, 2 clarinets, 3 bassoons, 4 horns, 3 trumpets, 3 trombones, tuba, timpani, percussion, harp, organ, strings. *Or* strings and pianoforte.
   Publication: London, O.U.P. (© 1943. V.S.). Parts on hire.

Other versions of this song:

(*a*) Two-part song (for SA or SS) with accompaniment as above. O.U.P. (© 1943).

(*b*) For male voices (TTBB) unacc. B flat. O.U.P. © 1943).

(*c*) For mixed voices (SATB) unaccompanied, in G major, *or* with following instrumentation: 2 flutes, 2 oboes, 2 clarinets, 2 bassoons, 2 horns, 2 trumpets, 3 trombones, timpani, cymbals, harp, pianoforte, strings. All optional except strings.

Publication: O.U.P. (© 1943). V.S. Parts on hire.

Whereabouts of MS.: British Library. Film music, full scores (including suite) and miscellaneous pianoforte scores and nine notebooks (50422–3); *The New Commonwealth* F.S. (50480).

For *The Lake in the Mountains*, for pianoforte, see 1947, No.4.

4. HOUSEHOLD MUSIC; THREE PRELUDES ON WELSH HYMN TUNES. For string quartet, or alternative instruments, and horn ad lib. These Preludes, composed in 1940–1, were designed principally for string quartet, but the composer envisaged their being played by almost any combination of instruments which may be gathered together. For the strings may be substituted oboe, clarinet, flute, saxophone, or cornet; or their equivalents at different pitches: bassoon, bass clarinet, recorder, B flat saxophone, and euphonium.

  I. Crug-y-bar (Fantasia) (Tune from 'Moliant Seion', 1883). *Andante sostenuto.*

  II. St. Denio (Scherzo) (Tune known in Wales as 'Joanna', based on folk tune). *Allegro vivace.*

  III. Aberystwyth (Eight variations). Theme, *Lento—allegro vivace—* tempo I. (Tune composed or adapted by Joseph Parry, 1879.)

First performance: London, Wigmore Hall, 4 October 1941. Blech String Quartet.

Duration: 17 minutes.

Publication: London, O.U.P. (© 1943) F.S. Parts published for violin I and viola; violin II and cello; violin III and cello II (to be used in absence of viola); clarinet I and III; clarinet II; alto saxophone and B flat saxophone; horns I and II.

Other versions:

(*a*) For medium orchestra. *Instrumentation:* 2 flutes, 1 oboe, 2 clarinets, 2 bassoons, 2 horns, 2 trumpets, timpani, percussion (side drum, triangle), strings. Parts on hire.

(*b*) Variations on 'Aberystwyth', arranged for organ by Herbert Byard. O.U.P. (© 1949).

Whereabouts of MS.: British Library. Full score (50398), parts (50399). Another F.S. (by courtesy of Harry Blech) (Add. 50862).

1941

1. ENGLAND, MY ENGLAND. Choral song, for baritone soloist, double choir, unison voices and orchestra, or with pianoforte. Words by W. E. Henley (1849–1903) from 'For England's Sake' III. Pro rege nostro. *Moderato maestoso.* D major.
   Instrumentation: 2 flutes, 2 oboes, 2 clarinets, 3 bassoons, 4 horns, 2 trumpets, 3 trombones, tuba, timpani, percussion, organ, strings.
   First performance: Broadcast concert, 16 November 1941, Dennis Noble (baritone), B.B.C. Chorus, B.B.C. Symphony Orchestra, conducted by Sir Adrian Boult.
   Publication: London, O.U.P. (© 1941). V.S. Parts on hire.
   Other versions: For unison voices with pianoforte (or orchestra as above) and optional descant for last verse. O.U.P. (© 1941). V.S. Parts on hire.
   Whereabouts of MS.: British Library. Two full scores (for orchestra and military band) and vocal score (50464).
2. A CALL TO THE FREE NATIONS. Hymn for choral or unison singing. Words by Canon G. W. Briggs. *Allegro moderato.* C minor— E flat major.
   Publication: London, O.U.P. (© 1941). Issued in 1942 as No. 2 of *Five Wartime Hymns.*

1942

1. MUSIC FOR THE FILM 'COASTAL COMMAND'. Produced by Ian Dalrymple, for Crown Film Unit. Music for the following episodes: Title; Island Station in the Hebrides; Taking off at night; Hudsons take off from Iceland; Battle of Beauforts; Sunderland goes in close (quiet determination); JU88 attacks; finale (no title).
   Film first shown at Plaza Cinema, Piccadilly Circus, 16 October 1942. Music played by the R.A.F. Symphony Orchestra, conducted by Muir Mathieson.
   SUITE (seven movements) from the film music, arranged by Muir Mathieson.
   Instrumentation: 2 flutes, 2 oboes, 1 cor anglais, 2 clarinets, 2 bassoons, 4 horns, 2 trumpets, 3 trombones, tuba, side drum, triangle, cymbals, tenor drum, bass drum, gong, timpani, harp, strings.
   First performance: Manchester, broadcast concert, 17 September 1942, B.B.C. Northern Orchestra, conducted by Muir Mathieson. (Six movements only.)
   Duration: 12 minutes.
   Publication: O.U.P. Parts on hire.
   Whereabouts of MS.: British Library. Incomplete full score of film music and sketches in four notebooks (50424); full score of Suite (50425); photostats of copy of full score of Suite (50426).

Note: Some of the music was also used for a radio feature *See the Vacant Sea*, about the work of Coastal Command. Its chief interest is that for this performance the composer marked the 'Quiet Determination' theme 'nobilmente', his only use of Elgar's favourite direction.

2. FIVE WARTIME HYMNS. For unison voices with pianoforte or organ, by R. Vaughan Williams, Martin Shaw, and Ivor Atkins. Words by Canon G. W. Briggs republished in revised form in *Songs of Faith* (O.U.P. 1945). Settings by R.V.W.:
   1. A hymn of freedom. *Andante maestoso.* D major.
   2. A call to the free nations. *Allegro moderato.* C minor—E flat major.
   Publication: London, O.U.P. 1942 (© 1939, 40 and 41).

3. THE AIRMEN'S HYMN. Unison song with pianoforte or organ. Words by 2nd Earl of Lytton (1876–1947). *Moderato maestoso.* E flat major.
   Publication: London, O.U.P. (© 1942).
   Whereabouts of MS.: British Library. Full score and V.S. (50465).

4. NINE CAROLS FOR MALE VOICES. For TTBB unaccompanied (baritone or bass).
   1. God rest you merry. *Allegro.* F minor.
   2. As Joseph was a-walking (*Cherry Tree Carol*). *Allegretto.* C major.
   3. Mummers' carol. *Very slow.* A major. (Words from *English Traditional Songs and Carols*, by Lucy Broadwood.)
   4. The First Nowell, baritone solo and chorus (TBar.B). D major.
   5. The Lord at first. *Andante moderato.* F minor.
   6. Coventry Carol. *Slow.* B minor.
   7. I saw three ships. Baritone solo and chorus (TBar.B). *Allegro.* F major. (May be sung in higher key.)
   8. A Virgin most pure. *Moderato.* G major. (Tune by permission of Maud Karpeles.)
   9. Dives and Lazarus. *Moderately slow.* E minor.
   Publication: London, O.U.P. (© 1942). Separate publications in Oxford Choral Songs, Nos. 665–673. Nos 2 and 3 and 5 and 6 are printed under one cover.
   Other versions:
   1. For SATB unaccompanied in *Twelve Traditional Carols from Herefordshire* (S. & B. 2042).
   8. In *Oxford Book of Carols*, Appendix I.
   9. In *Oxford Book of Carols* (57) and for SATB unaccompanied in *Twelve Traditional Carols from Herefordshire.* (S. & B. 2042.)

5. INCIDENTAL MUSIC FOR 'THE PILGRIM'S PROGRESS'. Composed in 1942 for B.B.C. production of an adaptation of Bunyan's book by Edward Sackville-West, with acknowledgements to W. Nugent

Monck, in which John Gielgud spoke the part of Christian. Produced by John Burrell.

First broadcast: 5 September 1943 (repeated 26 December 1943).

Instrumentation: 1 flute (doubling piccolo), 1 oboe, 1 clarinet, 1 bassoon, 1 double bassoon, 2 horns, 2 trumpets, 3 trombones, tuba, timpani, percussion, harp, strings.

First performers: B.B.C. Symphony Orchestra and B.B.C. Chorus, conducted by Sir Adrian Boult. Margaret Godley (soprano); Margaret Rolfe (contralto); Bradbridge White (tenor); Stanley Riley (baritone).

There were 38 sections of incidental music. Its principal interest is its relationship to the completed Morality. As at Reigate in 1906, the hymn-tune York was used as Prelude and Epilogue. Fuller use was made of the *Tallis Fantasia*, several pages of its opening being quoted verbatim after the words 'That I may show thee the words of God'. 'Who would true valour see', with slightly different notation, is as it appears in the Morality. The waltz for Madam Wanton (for two violins and orchestra) and the introduction to the Vanity Fair scene are largely as they were incorporated into Act III, Scene 1, of the Morality. The 'nasty fanfare' (the composer's title) at 'Guilty of death' is followed by what the composer identifies as a 'marche au supplice' (moderato alla marcia) which also went into the Morality in a fuller version. The beginning of Act IV, Scene 1, in the Morality was 'Dawn music' for the broadcast version. The Woodcutter's Boy's 'He that is down' was composed for the broadcast, with clarinet accompaniment. The final scene in the broadcast was much altered and elaborated for the final scene of the Morality.

Whereabouts of MS.: British Library. Full score (50419).

6. THE BLESSING OF THE SWORDS. Arranged for mixed chorus (SATB) and orchestra from *The Huguenots* by Jacob Meyerbeer (1791–1864). Text in English, freely adapted from the French. *Poco andante.* A flat major.

Publication: London, O.U.P. (© 1942).

1943

1. A WINTER PIECE (FOR GENIA). New Year's Day, 1943. For pianoforte solo. *Molto lento.*
Unpublished.

2. SYMPHONY (No. 5) IN D MAJOR. For full orchestra. (Composed 1938–43.)

   I. Preludio. *Moderato.*

   II. Scherzo. *Presto.*

   III. Romanza. *Lento.*

   IV. Passacaglia. *Moderato.*

Instrumentation: 2 flutes (2nd doubling piccolo), 1 oboe, 1 cor anglais, 2 clarinets, 2 bassoons, 2 horns, 2 trumpets, 3 trombones, timpani, strings.

First performance: London, Royal Albert Hall, Promenade Concert, 24 June 1943. The London Philharmonic Orchestra, conducted by Dr. R. Vaughan Williams.

Dedication: To Jean Sibelius, without permission.

Duration: 37 minutes (approx.).

Publication: London, O.U.P. Full score (© 1946). Orchestral parts on hire. Revised full score, published 1961.

Revision: The composer revised the score in 1951, in time for the first LP recording which was issued in 1954. His alterations were mainly modifications of dynamics, one change of harmony, corrections of misprints and several clarifications of texture—all directed to seeing that 'the tune comes through'. He was adamant that he did not want the two horns to be doubled. He had temporarily authorized doubling but regretted it. These corrections were inserted in the reprint copy of the score in 1961. Early piano scores show the symphony as 'in G'. This confirms the anecdote that the composer himself was always uncertain about this work's tonality!

Note: Details of this symphony's connection with the morality *The Pilgrim's Progress* are given under that entry in 1951.

Whereabouts of MS.: British Library, early sketches, 2-pianoforte scores (50371). Full score, partly autograph (50372).

3. MUSIC FOR THE FILM 'THE PEOPLE'S LAND'. Founded on traditional melodies. This film dealt with the work of the National Trust and is now in the Gaumont British Film Library. The music consists chiefly of folk songs—'John Barleycorn', 'The Springtime of the Year', 'Love will find out the way', and 'Chairs to mend'— linked by two motives illustrating the White Cliffs and the Lake District. Composed 1942. Made for British Council by Strand Films (produced and directed by Donald Taylor).

Film first shown: Ministry of Information (private screening), 17 March 1943. Music played by Section of London Symphony Orchestra, conducted by Muir Mathieson.

Instrumentation: 2 flutes, 1 oboe, 1 cor anglais, 2 clarinets, 2 bassoons, 1 double bassoon, 4 horns, 2 trumpets, 3 trombones, tuba, timpani, percussion, harp, strings.

Note: It is possible that work on this score began as early as 1941. At Elstree in September 1942 Mr. Roy Douglas was given some cans of music-tracks containing film music by R.V.W. which he fitted to a film called *Young Farmers*. This music was perhaps some 'left-over' from *The People's Land*.

Whereabouts of MS.: British Library. Three notebooks of pianoforte sketches (50427), full score (50428).

4. MUSIC FOR THE FILM 'FLEMISH FARM'. A Two Cities Film, produced by Filippo del Giudice and written and directed by Jeffrey Dell. The music to this wartime film about a Belgian flag buried on a Flemish farm, rescued in face of the enemy and taken to England to the Belgian Squadron of the R.A.F., survives only in the rarely-played Suite. Its chief interest is that two of the themes, which were not used in the film as finally shown, were said by the composer to be the germs of two themes in the Sixth Symphony which he began to sketch in 1944.

Film first shown: London, Leicester Square Theatre, 12 August 1943. Music played by London Symphony Orchestra, conducted by Muir Mathieson.

SUITE (Story of a Flemish Farm).

Instrumentation: 2 flutes, 2 oboes, 1 cor anglais, 2 clarinets, 2 bassoons, 1 double bassoon, 4 horns, 2 trumpets, 3 trombones, tuba, timpani, percussion (side drum, triangle, cymbals, bass drum, glockenspiel, large gong), harp, strings.

(I) The Flag flutters in the wind. (II) Night by the sea. Farewell to the Flag. (III) Dawn in the barn. The Parting of the Lovers. (IV) In a Belgian café. (V) The Major goes to face his fate. (VI) The dead man's kit. (VII) The wanderings of the Flag.

First performance: London, Royal Albert Hall, Promenade Concert, 31 July 1945. The London Symphony Orchestra, conducted by Dr. R. Vaughan Williams. *Duration:* 26 minutes.

Publication: London, O.U.P. Full score and parts on hire only.

Whereabouts of MS.: British Library. Rough full scores (50429); full score and 'control' condensed score (50430).

5. FANTASIA ON 'LINDEN LEA'. For oboe, clarinet, bassoon. Written in 1942–3 for John Parr of Sheffield.

Whereabouts of MS.: Formerly in possession of the late Max Hinrichsen.

6. A WEDDING TUNE FOR ANN, 27 OCTOBER 1943. For organ. *Andante con moto—poco animato—Tempo I.* Written for wedding of Miss Ann Pain, daughter of Mrs. Frances Pain, to Mr. Anthony Wilson at St. James's Church, Shere, Surrey.

Publication: Edited by Christopher Morris as No. 1 of *A Vaughan Williams Organ Album*, London, O.U.P. (© 1964).

Whereabouts of MS.: In private possession.

1944

1. CONCERTO IN A MINOR FOR OBOE AND STRINGS.

I. Rondo Pastorale—*Allegro moderato.* A minor.

II. Minuet and Musette—*Allegro moderato*. C minor.

III. Finale (Scherzo)—*Presto—doppio più lento—lento—presto*. E minor.

First performance: Liverpool, Philharmonic Hall, 30 September 1944. Léon Goossens (oboe), Liverpool Philharmonic Orchestra, conducted by Dr. Malcolm Sargent. First performance in London: Wigmore Hall, 4 May 1945, Léon Goossens (oboe), Bromley and Chislehurst Orchestra (string section), conducted by Marjorie Whyte.

Dedication: To Léon Goossens.

Duration: 20 minutes.

Publication: London, O.U.P. (© 1947), with orchestral part arranged for pianoforte by Michael Mullinar (for rehearsal only). Orchestral material on hire. Full score, O.U.P. © 1967.

Whereabouts of MS.: British Library. Early sketches (50387). F.S (50388).

2. STRING QUARTET (No. 2) IN A MINOR. FOR JEAN ON HER BIRTHDAY.

I. Prelude. *Allegro appassionato*. A minor.

II. Romance. *Largo*. G minor.

III. Scherzo. *Allegro*. F minor.

IV. Epilogue. Greetings from Joan to Jean. *Andante sostenuto*. D minor.

First performance: London, National Gallery, 12 October 1944. The Menges String Quartet (Isolde Menges, Lorraine du Val (violins); Jean Stewart (viola); Ivor James (violoncello)). (The quartet was played twice in one concert.)

Dedication: For Jean on her birthday. [This dedicatory line is required to be printed in programmes. (Jean = Jean Stewart (Mrs. George Hadley).)]

Duration: 20 minutes.

Publication: London, O.U.P. (© 1947). F.S. and parts.

Note: The first two movements were composed in 1942–3, the last two in 1943–4, with later revision. The main theme of the Scherzo is taken from *49th Parallel* (being marked in the score 'Theme from the *49th Parallel*') and that of the finale from music intended for a film about Joan of Arc which never materialized.

Whereabouts of MS.: British Library (52290).

3. INCIDENTAL MUSIC FOR 'RICHARD II'. Composed early 1944 for a broadcast performance of Shakespeare's play, but not used. There are 34 timed items to cover 15 scenes.

Instrumentation: 1 piccolo, 1 flute, 2 oboes, 2 clarinets, 2 bassoons, 4 horns, 3 trumpets, 3 trombones, timpani, percussion, harp, strings.

Whereabouts of MS.: British Library, Full Score (50432). Some sketches in private possession.

4. THANKSGIVING FOR VICTORY (later renamed A SONG OF THANKSGIVING). In B flat major. For soprano solo, speaker, mixed chorus (SATB), and orchestra. *Allegro moderato—andante sostenuto—alla marcia—andante sostenuto—largamente—moderato—maestoso.* Words selected from: 'Song of the Three Holy Children', vv. 29, 30, 31 and 33; Shakespeare's *Henry V*, Act IV, Scene 8; I Chronicles XXIX, v. 2; 'Song of the Three Holy Children', v. 67; Isaiah LXI, vv. 1–3; Isaiah LXII, vv. 10–12; Isaiah LXI, v. 4; Isaiah LX, v. 18; Children's Song from *Puck of Pook's Hill* by Rudyard Kipling; Isaiah LX, v. 20.

Instrumentation (reduced by Roy Douglas): 2 flutes, 2 oboes, 2 clarinets, 1 bass clarinet (opt.), 2 bassoons, 1 double bassoon (opt.), 4 horns (2 opt.), 3 trumpets (1 opt.), 3 trombones, 1 tuba (opt.), 2 (or 3) timpani (may be doubled if another player is available), percussion (side drum, triangle, cymbals, bass drum), harp or pianoforte (optional), organ (opt.), strings. If no organ, the orchestra should play all organ cues. (The original scoring included 6 trumpets, 6 clarinets, 6 timpani (2 players), 2 harps.)

First performance: London, B.B.C. Studio, 5 November 1944, when it was recorded for use when victory in the 1939–45 war was achieved. Recording was transmitted in special Thanksgiving Service between 9.30 and 10.30 a.m. on Sunday, 13 May 1945. Elsie Suddaby (soprano), Valentine Dyall (speaker), B.B.C. Chorus, Choir of Children from the Thomas Coram Schools, George Thalben-Ball (organ), B.B.C. Symphony Orchestra, conducted by Sir Adrian Boult. First concert performance: London, Royal Albert Hall, Promenade Concert, 14 September 1945. Elsie Suddaby (soprano), Valentine Dyall (speaker), B.B.C. Choral Society, Croydon Philharmonic Society, Choir of Children from the Thomas Coram Schools, B.B.C. Symphony Orchestra, conducted by Sir Adrian Boult.

Duration: 15 minutes.

Note on score: 'This work was originally designed for broadcasting. For concert and church use certain modifications are necessary. This is especially the case in the accompaniment to the speaker's voice. For broadcasting this should be performed poco forte, but "faded down" so as to form a background to the voice. In the concert room this must be represented by the softest pianissimo so that the speaker's voice may absolutely dominate.

'The soprano part should be sung by a powerful dramatic voice, but there must be no vibrato. On no account should the part be sung by a single boy's voice, though in the case of necessity it may be sung by several boys' voices in unison.

'The children's part must be sung by real children's voices, not sophisticated choir boys. The work was originally scored for large orchestra including six trumpets and six clarinets. If necessary trumpets 4, 5, and 6 and clarinets 4, 5, and 6 may be omitted and, to meet the needs of even smaller resources, the score has been extensively "cued in".

'Owing to the chronic scarcity of tenors the tenor line should be strengthened by a few high baritones. Where the tenor line divides, the higher notes should be taken by the real tenors and the lower by the baritones.'

Note: The work was renamed in 1952 when it was recorded by Parlophone. Copies of the work were overprinted with the new title, and the new title was printed on the reprint in 1956.

Publication: London, O.U.P. (© 1945 V.S.) Orchestral material on hire.

Whereabouts of MS.: British Library. F.S. (50466) separate sketch (50371).

Separate arrangements:

'Land of our birth' (Children's Song, by Kipling).

(*a*) For unison voices, with optional descant, accompanied by strings and pianoforte. O.U.P. (© 1946). Material on hire. Moderato. D major.

(*b*) For women's voices (SSA), accompanied by pianoforte or by strings and pianoforte. Latter version on hire. O.U.P. (© 1950).

(*c*) Arranged for organ by S. de B. Taylor. O.U.P. (© 1961). Available separately and as No. 8 of *A Vaughan Williams Organ Album* (1964).

5. FILM MUSIC FOR 'STRICKEN PENINSULA'. Ministry of Information film made for the Department of Psychological Warfare and dealing with rehabilitation of Southern Italy by Allied occupation forces. Produced and directed by Hans Nieter.

Note: The film was made in 1944 and shown to the trade in October 1945. It was 'shot' mostly around Naples by Paul Fletcher. The music, nothing of which survives, made use of Italian folk music, 'used merrily for an Italian brass band which appeared in the film,' Mr. Nieter tells me. The music was recorded by Ken Cameron and was played by a section of the London Symphony Orchestra, conducted by Muir Mathieson. It was scored for about 35 players.

1945

1. TWO CAROLS. Arrangements of traditional melodies. For SATB, unaccompanied.

1. Come love we God. (Old German Carol.) Words from the *Oxford Book of Carols*, adapted from the Shann MSS. by Ursula Wood. (O.B.C. 10.) *Moderately slow.* A flat major.

2. There is a flower (Es ist ein' Ros'). Melody set by Michael Praetorius. (O.B.C. 76.) Words freely translated by Ursula Wood. *In moderate time.* F major.
Publication: London, O.U.P. (© 1945).

2. CHANT FOR PSALM 67, *DEUS MISEREATUR.* Specially composed for St. Martin's Church, Dorking.
Unpublished. MS in possession of Dr. William Cole.
First performance: Dorking, St. Martin's Church, 14 October 1945.

1946

1. INTRODUCTION AND FUGUE FOR TWO PIANOFORTES. *Moderato.* G minor.
    I. Introduction.
    II. Fugue.
First performance: London, Wigmore Hall, 23 March 1946, by Cyril Smith and Phyllis Sellick.
Dedication: For Phyllis and Cyril.
Publication: London, O.U.P. (© 1947). Two copies are required.

2. MUSIC FOR THE FILM 'THE LOVES OF JOANNA GODDEN' (Ealing Studios). Produced by Michael Balcon, directed by Charles Frend. Music composed for following episodes: Main Titles; Funeral; Arthur goes away; Waking Ellen; Arthur in trap; Sheep; Farm montage; Lamb's foster-mother; Marriage banns; Driving to Dungeness; Martin drowning; Ram montage; Ellen arriving home; Ellen sketching; Fairground sequence; Fair music; Arthur on horseback; Night scene; Seasons montage; Sunrise; Ellen riding; Foot and mouth; Sheep burning; End music; End titles.
Instrumentation: 2 flutes, 2 oboes (2nd doubling cor anglais), 2 clarinets, 2 bassoons, 4 horns, 2 trumpets, 3 trombones, 1 tuba, timpani, percussion, harp, strings, and small women's chorus.
Film first shown: London, New Gallery Cinema, 16 June 1947. Music played by the Philharmonia Orchestra, conducted by Ernest Irving. Completed by December 1946.
Items preserved on a gramophone recording were: Romney Marsh; Joanna Godden; Sheepshearing; Work on the Farm; The Fair; Martin drowned at Dungeness; Ellen and Harry Trevor; Adoption of motherless lamb; Burning of the Sheep; Reunion.
Whereabouts of MS.: Piano score, full score, piano score of music for gramophone record, British Library (52288).

1947

1. THE SOULS OF THE RIGHTEOUS. Motet for treble (or soprano), tenor, baritone soloists and mixed chorus (Treble, ATB or SATB),

unaccompanied. Words from The Wisdom of Solomon, Ch. III, vv. 1–5.

First performance: London, Westminster Abbey, 10 July 1947, at dedication of the Battle of Britain Chapel, for which occasion it was composed. First concert performance: London, Wigmore Hall, 30 April 1948. The Tudor Singers, conducted by Harry Stubbs (Dorothy Langmaid, soprano; Frederick Freeman, tenor; George Blackford, baritone).

Duration: 3½ minutes.

Publication: London, O.U.P. (© 1947).

2. THE VOICE OUT OF THE WHIRLWIND. Motet for mixed chorus (SATB) and organ or orchestra. Adapted from *Galliard of the Sons of the Morning* (*Job*, Scene VIII). Words from The Book of Job (Ch. 38, vv. 1–11, 16–17; Ch. 40, vv. 7–10 and 14) *Andante con moto—moderato e pesante.*

Instrumentation: 2 flutes (2nd doubling piccolo), 2 oboes, 2 clarinets, 2 bassoons, 1 double bassoon (opt.), 4 horns, 3 trumpets, 3 trombones, tuba, timpani, percussion, harp, organ, strings.

First performance: London, Church of St. Sepulchre, Holborn Viaduct, St. Cecilia's Day Festival Service, 22 November 1947. Choir drawn from H.M. Chapels Royal and Canterbury Cathedral, St. Paul's Cathedral and Westminster Abbey, conducted by Dr. J. Dykes Bower, with Dr. William McKie (organ). First performance of version with orchestra: Dorking, The Dorking Halls, 16 June 1951. Surrey Philharmonic Orchestra and Leith Hill Festival Choir, conducted by Dr. R. Vaughan Williams.

Publication: London, O.U.P. (© 1947).

Whereabouts of MS.: British Library. Full Score (50467).

3. SYMPHONY (No. 6) IN E MINOR. For full orchestra. Composed 1944–47.

　　I. Allegro.

　II. Moderato.

　III. Scherzo. Allegro vivace.

　IV. Epilogue. Moderato.

Instrumentation: 3 flutes (3rd doubling piccolo), 2 oboes, 1 cor anglais, 2 clarinets, tenor saxophone in B flat, 1 bass clarinet (may double with sax.), 2 bassoons, 1 double bassoon, 4 horns, 4 trumpets (1 opt.), 3 trombones, 1 tuba, timpani, percussion, 3 players: side drum, bass drum, triangle, cymbals, xylophone; harp (doubled if possible), strings.

First performance: London, Royal Albert Hall, Royal Philharmonic Concert, 21 April 1948. The B.B.C. Symphony Orchestra, conducted by Sir Adrian Boult.

Dedication: To Michael Mullinar.

Duration: 37 minutes.

Composer's programme note: This Symphony was begun probably about 1944 and finished in 1947. It is scored for full orchestra including saxophone. There are four movements: Allegro, Moderato, *Scherzo* and Epilogue. Each of the first three has its tail attached to the head of its neighbour.

First Movement—Allegro. The Key of E minor is at once established through that of F minor, A flat becoming G sharp and sliding down to G natural at the half bar thus:

Ex. 1

The last three notes of (1) are continued, rushing down and up again through all the keys for which there is time in two bars, all over a tonic pedal.

Two detached chords

Ex. 2

lead to a repetition of the opening bar, but this time the music remains in F minor and the rush up and down is in terms of the first phrase. While strings and wind remain busy over this the brass plays a passage which becomes important later on

Ex. 3

The fussy semiquavers continue in the bass while the treble has a new tune in the cognate key of C minor.

Ex. 4

Then the position is reversed and the treble fusses while the bass has the tune. This leads us back to our tonic pedal and the instruments

rush around as at the beginning. Thus ends the first section of the
movement. The next section starts with this persistent rhythm:

Over this trumpets, flutes and clarinets play a tune in cross-rhythm
which starts thus

This continues for a considerable time with some incidental references
to Ex. 3 and is followed by a new tune while the persistent rhythm
persists.

Ex. 7
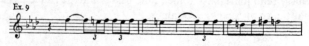

Then we are given a further instalment of Ex. 6. The brass now plays
Ex. 7 very loud and this brings us to what I believe the professional
Annotator would call the "*reprise* in due course". As a matter of fact
this *reprise* is only hinted at just enough to show that this is a Symphony
not a symphonic poem. But I am not sure that the "due course" is well
and truly followed when we find the tune Ex. 7 played for yet a third
time (this time in E major) quietly by the strings accompanied by harp
chords. To make an end and just to show that after all the movement
is in E minor, there is an enlargement of the opening bar.

Second Movement—Moderato. This leads on from the first movement
without a break. The principal theme is based on this rhythm

sometimes "straight" and sometimes in cross-rhythm. A flourish
follows, first on the brass loud, then on the woodwind loud and then
soft on the strings.

Ex. 9

Between each repetition there is a unison passage for strings

Ex. 10

The strings continue softly, but before they have finished the trumpets enter with this figure taken from the opening theme

Ex. 11

The trumpets start almost inaudibly, but they keep hammering away at their figure for over forty bars, getting louder and louder. Meanwhile the rest of the orchestra have been busy chiefly with the melody though not the rhythm of the opening theme. Having reached its climax the music dies down. The cor anglais plays a bit of Ex. 10 and this leads direct to the Third Movement.

Third Movement—Scherzo. This may be possibly best described as fugal in texture but not in structure. The principal subject does not appear at the beginning. Various instruments make bad shots at it and after a bit it settles down as

Ex. 12

With this is combined a trivial little tune, chiefly on the higher woodwind.

Ex. 13

An episodical tune is played on the saxophone and is repeated loud by the full orchestra.

Ex. 14

(Constant Lambert tells us that the only thing to do with a folk tune is to play it soft and repeat it loud. This is not a folk tune but the same difficulty seems to crop up.)

When the episode is over, the woodwind experiment as to how the fugue subject will sound upside down but the brass are angry and insist on playing it the right way up, so for a bit the two go on together and to the delight of everyone including the composer the two versions fit, so there is nothing to do now but to continue, getting more excited till the episode tune comes back very loud and twice as slow. Then once more we hear the subject softly upside down and the bass clarinet leads the way to the last movement.

Fourth Movement—Epilogue. It is difficult to describe this movement analytically. It is directed to be played very soft throughout. The music drifts about contrapuntally with occasional whiffs of theme such as

with one or two short episodes such as this, on the horns

and this on the oboe

At the very end the strings cannot make up their minds whether to finish in E flat major or E minor. They finally decide on E minor which is, after all, the home key.

The composer wishes to acknowledge with thanks the help of Mr. Roy Douglas in preparing the orchestral score. R.V.W.

Publication: London, O.U.P. (© 1948). F.S. Orchestral parts on hire. Revised impression, incorporating scherzo alterations, 1950.

Revisions: The manuscript versions in the British Museum show how consistently the composer kept to his original ideas on this symphony, but no sketch-books survive to show stages before full score. A different saxophone tune in the first movement and rhythmical changes in the trumpet part in the second movement are the most interesting to students. The scherzo was revised in 1950. Certain points of balance were altered—flutes and violins strengthened by trumpet and xylophone at bars 3 to 5 after 33 ; clarinets are reinforced by flutes, and a fourth trumpet part (optional) is added, for the restatement of the saxophone theme at 39 . A new brass theme is inserted at five points in the score.

Whereabouts of MS.: British Library. Full score (58072); 2-piano score and sketches (50373–4).

4. THE LAKE IN THE MOUNTAINS. Pianoforte solo. *Andante tranquillo.*

Dedication: To Phyllis Sellick.

This work is based on an episode from the music to *49th Parallel.*

Publication: London, O.U.P. (© 1947).

5. A WEDDING CANON (2 in 1 infinite). For organ. For Nancy, 30 May 1947, with love from Uncle Ralph. *Andante sostenuto.* Written for the wedding of Miss Nancy Harvey to Mr. Carol Elias.

Whereabouts of MS.: In private possession.

1948

1. PRAYER TO THE FATHER OF HEAVEN. Motet for mixed chorus (SATB), unaccompanied. (Pianoforte for rehearsal only.) *Andante sostenuto.* Words by John Skelton.

First performance: Oxford Festival of Music, Sheldonian Theatre, 12 May 1948. Oxford Bach Choir (Cantata Section), conducted by Dr. Thomas Armstrong.

Dedication: To the memory of my master Hubert Parry not as an attempt palely to reflect his incomparable art, but in the hope that he would have found in this motet (to use his own words) 'something characteristic'.

Duration: 4 minutes.

Publication: London, O.U.P. (© 1948).

2. MUSIC FOR THE FILM 'SCOTT OF THE ANTARCTIC' (Ealing Studios). Produced by Michael Balcon, directed by Charles Frend.

Film first shown: Royal Film Performance, Empire Theatre, Leicester Square, London, 29 November 1948; publicly, Odeon Theatre, Leicester Square, 30 December 1948. Music played by The Philharmonia Orchestra, conducted by Ernest Irving.

Vaughan Williams wrote more music than was included in the film. Music was composed for the following scenes (bracketed number indicates 'not used in film'):

1. Titles. Heroism. 2. Titles. Prologue. (What R.V.W. called 'the terror and fascination of the Pole'). [3]. Oriana (Wilson's wife). [4]. Doorn (Oriana's first meeting with Scott). [5] and [6]. Scott leaves Oriana. 7. Sculpture scene (Kathleen Scott and her husband). 8. Departure from Ross Island. 9. Ice floes. 10. Iceberg (two versions). 11. Penguins. 12. Ross Island. 13. Aurora. 14. Pony march. 15. Parhelion. [16]. Pony march. 17. Pony march and blizzard. 18. Distant glacier. 19. Climbing glacier. 20. Scott on the glacier. 21. Scott's decision on how many men to take to the Pole. 22. Polar party leaves. 23. Amundsen's flag at the Pole. 24. The return. 25. Death of Evans. 26. Death of Oates. [27]. Only 11 miles. 28. Final shots.

Whereabouts of MS.: British Library. Draft full score and piano score

(52289), autograph full score (59537). (See 1952, *Sinfonia Antartica*.)

4. HYMN FOR ST. MARGARET ('ST. MARGARET'). Composed January or February 1948. Words by Ursula Wood (Ursula Vaughan Williams). Unison. Appears as No. 748 in *Hymnal for Scotland, incorporating The English Hymnal* with first line 'Praise God for Margaret'. The St. Margaret is St. Margaret, Queen of Scots. She married Duncan's son Malcolm (the Malcolm of *Macbeth*).
Publication: London, O.U.P. (© 1950).
Whereabouts of MS.: British Library. Vocal Score, (50480).

5. PARTITA FOR DOUBLE STRING ORCHESTRA. See 1938, Entry No. 5A.

1949

1. FOLK SONGS OF THE FOUR SEASONS. A Cantata, based on traditional folk songs, for women's voices (SSAA) and orchestra.
PROLOGUE: To the Plough Boy. (All voices with descant for semi-chorus; R.V.W.'s collection, 1904.)
SPRING: Early in the Spring (for three voices, unaccompanied). The Lark in the Morning (for two voices, accompanied. R.V.W.'s collection, 1905). May Song (for full chorus and semichorus descant, accompanied. Part from Lucy Broadwood's *English County Songs*).
SUMMER: Summer is a-coming in and The Cuckoo (full chorus and semichorus, accompanied. The Cuckoo from Cecil Sharp collection). The Sprig of Thyme (for full chorus, with descants. R.V.W.'s collection, 1904). The Sheep Shearing (for two voices unaccompanied. Cecil Sharp collection). The Green Meadow (unison, accompanied. George Butterworth collection. Sometimes known as 'It's of a lawyer fine and gay').
AUTUMN: John Barleycorn (for two-part semichorus, with full chorus, accompanied. Sharp collection). The Unquiet Grave (for three voices, unaccompanied. Merrick and R.V.W. arr.). An Acre of Land (unison, accompanied. R.V.W. collection, 1904).
WINTER: Children's Christmas Song (in two-part harmony. Version from Hooton Roberts, Yorkshire). Wassail Song (unison with descant. Gloucestershire Wassail. R.V.W. collection, 1908). In Bethlehem City (for three voices unaccompanied). God Bless the Master (unison, with descant, accompanied).
Instrumentation: 2 flutes, 2 oboes (1 opt.), 2 clarinets, 2 bassoons (1 opt.), 4 horns, 2 trumpets, 3 trombones, tuba, timpani, percussion (2 players), harp, celesta, organ, strings. (Horns 3 and 4 are optional if there are 3 trombones and tuba, and vice versa.) Or 2 flutes, 1 oboe, 2 clarinets, 1 bassoon, 2 horns, 2 trumpets, timpani, harp, organ (opt.), strings. *Or* strings and pianoforte.

First performance: London, Royal Albert Hall, 15 June 1950. National Singing Festival of National Federation of Women's Institutes. Massed choirs (three classes drawn from 59 districts), London Symphony Orchestra, conducted by Sir Adrian Boult.

Duration: 45 minutes.

Composer's note: 'When I undertook to write a Folk Song Cantata for the Women's Institutes I set my mind to work to find some unifying idea which would bind the whole together. It was not long before I discovered the necessary link—the calendar. The subjects of our folk songs, whether they deal with romance, tragedy, conviviality or legend, have a background of nature and its seasons.

'When the lovers make love the plough boys are ploughing in the Spring and the lark is singing. When May comes round the moment is appropriate to celebrate it in song. The succession of flowers in the garden provides symbols for the deserted lover. The festivity of the Harvest Home is celebrated in the allegory of "John Barleycorn". The young maiden meets her dead lover among the storms and cold winds of autumn; and the joy of Christmas is set in its true background of frost and snow.

'The songs which I have chosen come from various sources. Many of them are from my own collection, others from Cecil Sharp's *Folk Songs from Somerset*. I have been kindly allowed to use others from the collections of Lucy Broadwood and Fuller Maitland.

'One of the tunes perhaps requires special notice: "The Round"—or "Rota"—"Summer is a-coming in" is not nominally a folk tune. It is supposed to have been composed in the thirteenth century by a monk —John of Forncete. It has long been a puzzle how this beautiful melody made its appearance amongst its clumsy contemporary monkish companions. The truth, I am sure, is that this is a folk tune and owes its freedom and grace to the fact that it was not bound by theoretical restrictions. At all events, I feel justified in including it in a collection of folk tunes.

'We can imagine Brother John's delight when he discovered one day that this tune—(just like "Early, early in the Spring" in this volume)— "went in canon". R.V.W.'

Publication: London, O.U.P. (© 1950). V.S. and Voice Part. Orchestral material on hire.

Whereabouts of MS.: British Library. Full score (50468). Rough score formerly in possession of the late Dame Frances Farrer.

Separate issues:

For unison voices with pianoforte (or orchestra as above).

   (*a*) An acre of land.

   (*b*) The Green Meadow. *Allegro.*

For unison voices with two-part semichorus (SA), accompanied.

(c) John Barleycorn. *Allegro moderato.*

For unison voices and semichorus (SSAA), accompanied.

(d) Summer is a-coming in and The Cuckoo. *Allegro—andante sostenuto.*

For unison voices with descant, accompanied.

(e) The sprig of thyme. *Andante sostenuto.*

For unison voices with optional descant, accompanied.

(f) May Song. *Andante moderato.*

(g) God Bless the Master of this House. *Lento maestoso.*

For two-part (SA), accompanied.

(h) The Lark in the Morning. *Moderato tranquillo—grazioso.*

(j) Children's Christmas Song. *Allegro moderato.*

For two-part (SA), unaccompanied.

(k) The Sheep Shearing. *Lento.*

For three-part (SSA), unaccompanied.

(l) Early in the Spring. *Andante.*

(m) The Unquiet Grave. *Slow.*

(n) In Bethlehem City. *Andante tranquillo.*

Publication: London, O.U.P. (© 1950).

1A. SUITE, FROM THE CANTATA FOLK SONGS OF THE FOUR SEASONS. Arranged for small orchestra, by Roy Douglas.

(I) To the Ploughboy and May Song; (II) The Green Meadow and An Acre of Land; (III) The Sprig of Thyme and The Lark in the Morning; (IV) The Cuckoo; (V) Wassail Song and Children's Christmas Song.

Instrumentation: 2 flutes (2nd doubling piccolo), 2 oboes (2nd doubling cor anglais), 2 clarinets, 2 bassoons, 2 horns, 2 trumpets, 3 trombones, timpani, percussion (side drum, triangle, cymbals, bass drum, glockenspiel), harp, strings. All parts are fully cued. The Suite may thus be played by strings and pianoforte only, or with any available wind added.

Duration: 13½ minutes.

Publication: London, O.U.P. (© 1956). Full score on hire only.

Note: a few necessary linking passages were composed by Roy Douglas, whose idea the suite was.

2. AN OXFORD ELEGY. For Speaker, small mixed chorus (SATB) and small orchestra. Words adapted from *The Scholar Gipsy* and *Thyrsis,* by Matthew Arnold (1822–88). (In order of verses in *Oxford Elegy*: *Scholar Gipsy,* verse 1, part of verse 2, verse 3; *Thyrsis,* 2 lines of verse 2, 1 line of verse 3; *Scholar Gipsy,* part of verse 4, part of verse 6, part of verse 7, part of verse 8, line of verse 12, verse 13, part of verse 14, line of verse 15, 2 lines of verse 18; *Thyrsis,* part of

verse 1, part of verse 2, part of verse 3, part of verse 4, part of verse 6, verse 7, part of verse 8, 2 lines of verse 11, part of verse 12, line of verse 13, part of verse 14, part of verse 15, part of verse 20, part of verse 24.) *Instrumentation:* 1 flute, 1 oboe, 1 cor anglais, 2 clarinets, 1 bassoon, 2 horns, strings. *Or* strings and pianoforte (arr. Denis Williams).

First performance: (Private) Dorking, The White Gates, 20 November 1949. Steuart Wilson (speaker), The Tudor Singers, Schwiller String Quartet and Michael Mullinar (pianoforte), conducted by Dr. R. Vaughan Williams. First public performance: Oxford, the Queen's College, 19 June 1952. Sir Steuart Wilson (speaker); the Eglesfield Musical Society. Chamber Orchestra, conducted by Bernard Rose. First performance in London: St. Martin-in-the-Fields, 22 March 1953. Clive Carey (speaker); St. Martin's Cantata Choir and Orchestra, conducted by John Churchill.

Duration: 25 minutes.

Publication: London, O.U.P. (© 1952). V.S. Orchestral parts on hire. *Whereabouts of MS.:* British Library. Voice parts and vocal scores (50473); incomplete full score (50474); full score (50475). Full score also in Bodleian Library, Oxford.

3. FANTASIA (QUASI VARIAZIONE) ON THE 'OLD 104TH' PSALM TUNE. For pianoforte solo, accompanied by mixed chorus (SATB) and orchestra. Metrical version of text attributed to Thomas Sternhold and John Hopkins. *Maestoso—largamente—poco animato— tranquillo—poco animato—tranquillo—poco animando—allegro—largo —poco animato.*

Instrumentation: Solo pianoforte, 2 flutes (2nd doubling piccolo), 2 oboes, 2 clarinets, 2 bassoons, 4 horns, 2 trumpets, 3 trombones, 1 tuba, timpani, percussion, organ (optional, except when there are no woodwind), strings. *Or:* Solo pianoforte, strings, 2 trumpets, 3 trombones, organ. *Or:* Solo pianoforte, strings and organ.

First performance: (Private) Dorking, The White Gates, 20 November 1949. Michael Mullinar (pianoforte), The Tudor Singers, The Schwiller String Quartet, conducted by Dr. R. Vaughan Williams. First public performance: Gloucester, The Cathedral, Three Choirs Festival, 6 September 1950. Michael Mullinar (pianoforte), Three Choirs Festival Chorus, London Symphony Orchestra, conducted by Dr. R. Vaughan Williams. First performance in London: Royal Albert Hall, Promenade Concert, 15 September 1950. Michael Mullinar (pianoforte), The Royal Choral Society, B.B.C. Symphony Orchestra, conducted by Sir Malcolm Sargent.

Duration: 15 minutes.

Publication: London, O.U.P. (© 1950). V.S. (includes solo pianoforte part). Full score O.U.P. © 1973. Orchestral parts on hire.

Whereabouts of MS.: British Library. Full score (50469). British Library also has sketches for a setting of Psalm 104 (50371 and 50427) and for another setting (50455).

4. MUSIC FOR THE FILM 'DIM LITTLE ISLAND'. This Central Office of Information film, produced and directed by Humphrey Jennings in 1949 for Wessex Film Productions and distributed by Grand National Pictures, was a 10-minute 'documentary', in which four narrators—John Ormiston, industrialist, Osbert Lancaster, artist, James Fisher, naturalist, and Vaughan Williams, musician—spoke of England's past achievements in relation to her future. The music consisted of a short prelude based on two folk songs, one of which is 'Pretty Betsy' and the other 'The pride of Kildare', both from Vaughan Williams's manuscript collection. A folk singer sings 'Dives and Lazarus' unaccompanied, and the statement of the tune from the Five Variants is used as background. Vaughan Williams described the 'pyramid' of British musical life—the folk singer, the amateur choirs, the professionals, the 'star' conductors—and was characteristically optimistic about music's growing popularity in Britain, stimulated by wartime concerts. The film was first shown at the 1949 Edinburgh Film Festival, and the music was (probably) conducted by John Hollingsworth. The assistant director was Harley Usill and the film was edited by Bill Megarry.

There is a curious episode connected with this film which may puzzle future biographers. During 1955–6, the *Musical Times* printed lists of corrections to and omissions from the fifth edition of Grove's *Dictionary of Music and Musicians*, submitted by its readers. Mr. Gerald Cockshott pointed out the omission of *Dim Little Island* from Vaughan Williams's film music. This brought a rejoinder from Vaughan Williams who wrote (February 1956, p. 89): 'I have never heard of this film nor, I need hardly say, had I spoken part of the commentary of it.' Mr. Cockshott very gracefully (March 1956, p. 147) stuck to his point, testifying that 'Dr. Vaughan Williams's name appears on the screen, while his voice is heard on the sound-track. . . . If Dr. Vaughan Williams was not personally concerned in the production, the makers certainly used recordings of his voice and music in such a way as to suggest that he was.'

Mr. Cockshott was right. The voice is Vaughan Williams's and his part of the narration is so characteristic of his beliefs and of his style that he must either have written it or revised it to his own requirements. His memory was always remarkable, and it is odd, unless the film's name was changed, that he had completely forgotten this film. But simply that and nothing else seems to be what happened. It is probable, too, that his part of the commentary was pre-recorded, perhaps at his home. Mr. Lancaster told me that Vaughan Williams was not present when he recorded his contribution. He confirmed the elusiveness of this film by adding, 'Until you had reminded me of it, I had forgotten all about the film . . . and, even now . . . I can recall absolutely nothing about it.'

1950

1. CONCERTO GROSSO. For string orchestra; in five movements.
   I. Intrada.
   II. Burlesca Ostinata.
   III. Sarabande.
   IV. Scherzo.
   V. March and Reprise.

Instrumentation: Three groups of strings.
   1. Concertino. A group of skilled players (6.6.4.4.2.).
   2. Tutti. All those who can play in the 3rd position, and simple double stops.
   3. Ad lib. Less experienced players. Two such parts for violins, and one each for viola and cello; also parts for violin, viola, cello, bass, for those players who prefer to use only open strings.

First performance: London, Royal Albert Hall, 18 November 1950. Massed orchestra (400 players) of the Rural Music Schools Association, conducted by Sir Adrian Boult.

Duration: 14 minutes.

Publication: London, O.U.P. (© 1950) F.S. Pianoforte condensation of the concertino and tutti parts is for rehearsal only.

Note on score: 'The composer wishes to thank Miss Gertrude Collins, Miss Edwina Palmer and Mr. Arthur Trew for much advice and help in preparing his score. Indeed, the ad lib. parts have been written entirely under their direction.'

2. MUSIC FOR THE FILM 'BITTER SPRINGS'. (Ealing Studios.) Produced by Michael Balcon, directed by Ralph Smart.

Film first shown: Gaumont Cinema, Haymarket, London, 10 July 1950. Music played by the Philharmonia Orchestra, conducted by Ernest Irving.

Instrumentation: 2 flutes, 2 oboes, 2 clarinets, 1 bass clarinet, 2 bassoons, 2 horns, 2 trumpets, 3 trombones, tuba, percussion, harp and pianoforte, strings.

This film, in which 'Chips' Rafferty and Tommy Trinder were the leading actors, was about a trek in the Australian Outback. Among scenes illustrated by music were: Main Titles and Opening Music. Incidents on The Trek: Extrication of wagons from (*a*) rocky defile, (*b*) mudhole. Dry desert: no water for sheep. Night trek: thirsty sheep in dust. Arrival at Bitter Springs: smoke signal (aborigines). The music was arranged and orchestrated by Ernest Irving from thematic material supplied by Vaughan Williams. In a letter to Irving dated 5 July 1950, Vaughan Williams wrote: 'I never thanked you for the records [studio records of the music]. I think they are fine and what marvels you have done with my silly little tune.'

There is also the following: '16 July 1950. To The Editor of *Radio Times*. Dear Sir. One of the speakers in the "Critics" section of your programme of July 16th (Home Service 12.10 p.m.) praised the "Kangaroo" music in the film "Bitter Springs". This portion of the music was composed by my collaborator, Mr. Ernest Irving.

Yours faithfully, R. Vaughan Williams.'

Whereabouts of MS.: British Library. Full score (52383). This plainly shows which sections were jointly composed. Several besides the Kangaroos were written wholly by Irving. With the score is the autograph of R.V.W.'s sketch (the 'silly little tune') for the Main Titles. He called this 'Irving's March' and wrote at the end: 'If you want any more you must sing it yourself.'

3. THE SONS OF LIGHT. A Cantata for mixed chorus (SATB) and orchestra. Composed in 1950. Poem by Ursula Wood (Ursula Vaughan Williams). 'In the musical setting of this poem the composer has, with the leave of the author, made a few verbal alterations.'

    I. Darkness and Light. *Allegro maestoso—allegro alla marcia— tranquillo—allegro moderato.*

    II. The Song of the Zodiac. *Allegretto pesante.*

    III. The Messengers of Speech. *Maestoso—maestoso alla marcia.*

Instrumentation: 2 flutes, 2 oboes (2nd doubling cor anglais), 2 clarinets, 2 bassoons, 1 double bassoon, 4 horns, 3 trumpets, 3 trombones, tuba, timpani, percussion, xylophone, glockenspiel, celesta, harp, strings. (A piano condensation is available for glockenspiel, celesta and harp.) *Or* 2 flutes, 2 oboes (1 opt.), 3 clarinets (1 opt.), 2 bassoons (1 opt.), 2 horns, 3 trumpets (1 opt.), 3 trombones (bass opt.), tuba (or eupho- nium), 3 saxophones (opt.), timpani, celesta (cued to pianoforte), percussion as available, pianoforte, strings. *Or:* strings and pianoforte (arr. by Arnold Foster).

First performance: London, Royal Albert Hall, 6 May 1951. Massed Choir of 1,150 voices from the Schools' Music Association of Great Britain (from 25 counties), London Philharmonic Orchestra, con- ducted by Sir Adrian Boult.

Dedication: To Bernard Shore. (H.M. Staff Inspector in Music, Ministry of Education, who commissioned this work for the S.M.A.'s second national (non-competitive) festival.)

Duration: 25 minutes.

Publication: London, O.U.P. (© 1951). V.S. Orchestral material on hire.

Whereabouts of MS.: British Library. Vocal score and sketches (50470); two full scores (50471–2).

3A. SUN, MOON, STARS, AND MAN. A cycle of four songs for unison voices with accompaniment for strings and/or pianoforte. Based on sections of the cantata *The Sons of Light.* Poems by Ursula Vaughan Williams.

    I. Horses of the Sun. *Allegro alla marcia.*

    II. The Rising of the Moon. *Lento.*

    III. The Procession of the Stars. *Allegro moderato.*

    IV. The Song of the Sons of Light. *Maestoso alla marcia.*

First performance: Birmingham, The Town Hall, 11 March 1955. City of Birmingham Symphony Orchestra, and choir of 450 voices from Secondary Schools in Birmingham North District, conducted by Dr. Desmond MacMahon.

Publication: London, O.U.P. (© 1954). V.S. Material for strings and pianoforte on hire.

Whereabouts of MS.: British Library. Full score (50478). Another is in the Library of Congress, U.S.A.

4. SOLEMN MUSIC FOR THE MASQUE OF CHARTERHOUSE. (FINAL SCENE.) Composed in 1950.

Instrumentation: 3 flutes, 2 oboes, 3 clarinets, 2 bassoons, 3 horns, 4 trumpets, 2 trombones, tuba, timpani, percussion. A drum-roll heralds the Solemn Music in which a theme from Scene 1 of the Masque (composed in 1911 by E. D. Rendall) is combined with rhythms from the *Carmen Carthusianum.* An orchestral version of the *Carmen* leads to a setting of the hymn itself.

First performance: Founder's Court, Charterhouse School, Godalming, 12 July 1950, Charterhouse School Choir and Orchestra, conducted by J. W. Wilson.

Whereabouts of MS.: Charterhouse.

5. THE MAYOR OF CASTERBRIDGE. Incidental music for radio serial based on novel by Thomas Hardy (1840–1928). See 1952, entry No. 5.

    I. Casterbridge.

    II. Intermezzo.

    III. Weyhill Fair.

Instrumentation: 2 flutes, 1 oboe, 2 clarinets, 1 bassoon, 2 trumpets, 2 trombones, 2 horns, timpani, strings.

First performance: First episode transmitted 7 January 1951 (10 weekly parts) on B.B.C. Home Service. (Repeated July–September 1953.)

B.B.C. West of England Light Orchestra, cond. Reginald Redman. *Whereabouts of MS.:* British Library. Full score (50433). For *Prelude on an Old Carol Tune* see 1952, No.5.

1951

1. THE PILGRIM'S PROGRESS. A Morality, in a Prologue, four Acts and an Epilogue, founded on John Bunyan's Allegory of the same name. German translation by R. Müller-Hartmann, with additions by Genia Hornstein. Libretto adapted by R. Vaughan Williams, with interpolations from the Bible and verse by Ursula Wood (Ursula Vaughan Williams).

Date of composition: Of all Vaughan Williams's works, this is the hardest to date with any accuracy. The following may be taken as the nearest to the truth:

First sketches and ideas	1909
Shepherds' episode	1921
Considerable parts of Acts I and II	1925–36
Further revision concerned with B.B.C. broadcast ..	1942
Sustained revision and additions	1944–9
Work completed and translated	1949
Addition of extra song	1951
Expansion of 'Vanity Fair'	1951–2

For 34 soloists (many parts can be doubled or trebled, and 11 soloists are sufficient), mixed chorus (SATB) and orchestra.

Instrumentation: 2 flutes (2nd doubling piccolo), 2 oboes (2nd doubling cor anglais), 2 clarinets, 2 bassoons, 1 double bassoon (opt.), 4 horns, 2 trumpets, 1 trumpet on stage (opt.), 3 trombones, 1 tuba, 1 euphonium (opt.), timpani, percussion (side drum, tenor drum, bass drum, cymbals, gong, triangle, xylophone, glockenspiel, bells), harp, celesta (opt.), strings. In the Intermezzo the celesta part must be played on the pianoforte if no celesta is available. The pianoforte must not be substituted elsewhere.

First performance: London, Royal Opera House, Covent Garden, 26 April 1951, with the following cast in order of appearance:

Prologue

JOHN BUNYAN (bass-baritone)	Inia te Wiata
THE PILGRIM (baritone)	Arnold Matters

Act I. Scene 1

EVANGELIST (bass) .. ..: ..	Norman Walker
THE FOUR NEIGHBOURS:	
PLIABLE (tenor)	Ernest Davies

OBSTINATE (bass) ..	..	..	..	Rhydderch Davies
MISTRUST (baritone)	..	..	..	Dennis Stephenson
TIMOROUS (tenor) ..	..	..	..	..	David Tree

Scene 2

THREE SHINING ONES:

Soprano ..	..	..	..	..	..	Adèle Leigh
Mezzo-soprano ..	..	..	..	..	Patricia Howard
Contralto ..	..	..	..	..	Vera Hoddinott

THE INTERPRETER (tenor) ..   ..   Edgar Evans

CHORUS of Men and Women of the House Beautiful.

Nocturne (Intermezzo)

WATCHFUL, the Porter (high baritone)   ..   ..   Bryan Drake

Act II. Scene 1

A HERALD (high baritone) ..   ..   Geraint Evans

CHORUS of 'certain persons clothed in gold'.

Scene 2

| DOLEFUL CREATURES | .. | .. | .. | Chorus and Dancers |
| APOLLYON (bass) .. | .. | .. | .. | .. Michael Langdon |

TWO HEAVENLY BEINGS:

| Soprano .. | .. | .. | .. | .. | Elisabeth Abercrombie |
| Contralto .. | .. | .. | .. | .. | .. Monica Sinclair |

Act III. Scene 1

CHORUS of Traders in Vanity Fair

LORD LECHERY (tenor buffo)	..	..	Dennis Stephenson
A JESTER ..	..	..	..	..	Keith MacMillan
DEMAS (baritone) ..	..	..	..	Hubert Littlewood
JUDAS ISCARIOT (baritone) ..	..	..	.. Ronald Firmager
SIMON MAGUS (bass)	..	..	..	.. Andrew Sellars
WORLDLY GLORY (high baritone) ..	..	.. Thomas Fletcher
MADAM WANTON (soprano)	..	..	.. Audrey Bowman
MADAM BUBBLE (mezzo-soprano) ..	..	.. Barbara Howitt
PONTIUS PILATE (bass)	..	..	..	.. Basil Hemming
USHER (tenor buffo) ..	..	..	..	..	David Tree
LORD HATE-GOOD (bass) ..	..	..	Rhydderch Davies
MALICE (soprano) ..	..	..	..	.. Leah Roberts
PICKTHANK (contralto)	..	..	..	.. Jeanne Bowden
SUPERSTITION (tenor)	..	..	..	.. Andrew Daniels
ENVY (bass) ..	..	..	..	..	.. John Campbell

(*Scene* 2 is The Pilgrim's alone.)

Act IV. Scene 1

A WOODCUTTER'S BOY (soprano or boy treble) ..	Iris Kells
MISTER BY-ENDS (tenor buffo)	Parry Jones
MADAM BY-ENDS (contralto)	Jean Watson

Scene 2

THREE SHEPHERDS*

Tenor	William McAlpine
Baritone	John Cameron
Bass	Norman Walker

(* The Shepherds are not differentiated by name, as they are in the one-act episode.)

THE VOICE OF A BIRD (soprano)	Adèle Leigh
A CELESTIAL MESSENGER (tenor)	Edgar Evans

Scene 3

THE ANGEL OF THE LORD (non-speaking)	Olga Frei
CHORUS in the Celestial City	
CHORUS on earth	

(*Epilogue* is Bunyan alone)

Chorus Master: Douglas Robinson. Producer: Nevill Coghill. Designer: Hal Burton. Covent Garden Orchestra and Chorus, conducted by Leonard Hancock.

SYNOPSIS

Prologue: Bunyan in Bedford Gaol.

Act I, Sc. 1: The Pilgrim meets Evangelist (background of curtains).

Sc. 2: The House Beautiful. At the Wicket Gate.

Intermezzo: As Scene 2, stage darkened. (Only to be played if Acts I and II are performed without a break.)

Act II, Sc. 1: The Arming of the Pilgrim. An Open Road.

Sc. 2: The Pilgrim meets Apollyon. The Valley of Humiliation, a narrow gorge.

Act III, Sc. 1: Vanity Fair. A street in Vanity Fair, at night, the scene being brightly lit by flares.

Sc. 2: The Pilgrim in Prison. Interior of a prison, with large gates beyond which lies the Pilgrim's Way.

Act IV, Sc. 1: The Pilgrim meets Mister By-Ends. The edge of a wood. The Pilgrim's Way stretches into the distance, with the Delectable Mountains far off.

Sc. 2: The Delectable Mountains. Just before sunset.

Sc. 3: The Pilgrim reaches the end of his journey. The Pilgrim's Way leads up to the Golden Gates.

Epilogue: Bunyan in front of the curtain.

Duration:				
Prologue	..	..	3½ mins.	
Act I, Sc. 1	..		10 mins.	
	Nocturne		6 mins.	
	Sc. 2	..	13 mins.	
Act II, Sc. 1	..		10 mins.	These timings
	Sc. 2	..	14 mins.	are, of course,
Act III, Sc. 1	..		17 mins.	approximate.
	Sc. 2	..	10½ mins.	
Act IV, Sc. 1	..		11 mins.	
	Sc. 2	..	17 mins.	
	Sc. 3	..	3 mins.	
Epilogue	..	.:	4 mins.	
Total	..	..	1 hr. 59 mins.	

The first performance of the revised version of Act III, Sc. 1, was given at the Royal Opera House, Covent Garden, on 12 February 1952. The part of Hylas was personified by Johaar Mosaval.

Composer's Note: For the Cambridge production in February 1954, before giving a summary of the story, Vaughan Williams wrote this explanatory note:

'The libretto of this Morality is a free adaptation of Bunyan's allegory. The text is chiefly from Bunyan, with additions from the Psalms and other parts of the Bible. The words of Lord Lechery's song in Act III are by Ursula Wood.

'For stage purposes a good deal of adaptation and simplification of the original has been necessary: thus, the Pilgrim's early domestic happiness has been omitted, his two companions, Faithful and Hopeful, do not appear, there are only three Shepherds; while Mr. By-Ends has been provided with a wife. In Act II the House Beautiful and the House of the Interpreter have been merged into one, and an elaborate scene of initiation is built up from Bunyan's few hints. No explanation is given in the original as to how the Pilgrim escapes from Vanity Fair; the author merely says that "he that overrules all things . . . so wrought it about that Christian, for that time, escaped them and went his way". For this purpose the libretto has utilized the escape described later from Doubting Castle. Incidentally, the name Pilgrim is used throughout the libretto, as being of more universal significance than Bunyan's title. R.V.W.'

Publication: London, O.U.P. (© 1952. V.S.) Orchestral parts, vocal scores and chorus parts on hire. Chorus parts and libretto on sale.

Whereabouts of MS.: British Library. Full score (50420). Autograph vocal score in possession of Michael Kennedy, Esq.

Revisions: The vocal score, an astonishing patchwork of fitted-together fragments, pasted-over revisions, crossings-out, transpositions, and numerous alterations, is eloquent testimony of the composer's struggle to bring the work into the required shape. The handwriting shows the gap of years between one part and another.

An early introduction to Act I, based on what became the opening of the Romanza of the Fifth Symphony, led straight into Pilgrim's cry of 'What shall I do?' The episode of Bunyan in gaol was an after-thought of later date. Pilgrim's song of deliverance after the fight with Apollyon was longer, but was cut evidently for the sake of realism. The original manuscript of the Intermezzo is a moving document. Hastily scribbled notes (on a train journey) are succeeded by a rapid working-out which even on the cold page still emits something of the tension of genius at high pressure.

A notebook of sketches includes music for the Slough of Despond and various versions of 'Who Would True Valour See'.

Acts III and IV have fewer revisions except for the extension of Vanity Fair after 1951. The vocal score makes it clear that the beautiful orchestral epilogue to Pilgrim's escape from prison was one of the earliest parts to be composed.

After the first performance, E. J. Dent wrote a series of letters to Vaughan Williams making detailed suggestions about ways of improving the production. These are of such interest that I reproduce them here with Vaughan Williams's surviving reply:

27 April 1951
Dear Vaughan Williams,

'I hope you were pleased with the performance of the *Pilgrim* last night, and with the way in which the audience were completely absorbed by it and gave it the tribute of a definite silence at the end. I felt very conscious all the time of the audience's tense concentration on the work. As I have myself a deep-rooted inherited Quakerism (though I have never been able to live up to it!) I can very willingly make a complete surrender to a work of that kind, although most of my friends would not think it possible. The performance last night was a great deal better than the rehearsal the day before. What impressed me very deeply was the complete sense of what the Germans call "Weihe" on the stage—a thing they know well and respect in the theatre, whereas Italians have no sense of it at all and Viennese hardly any; it is the utter self-surrender and self-dedication of all the performers to a great work of art. English people are fully capable of it, but we only get it in the theatre at Oxford and Cambridge, never (until last night) in the professional Opera House.

It has a practical and technical result too, for it produced really beautiful singing from everybody and a surprisingly clear and intelligent enunciation of the words, such as I have never heard at Covent Garden before. I felt indeed thankful to escape from the influences of Milan and Vienna!

Leonard Hancock managed his job with great skill and understanding, I thought; he made the whole orchestra *sing*—which is always very necessary in your music—and never go for orchestral virtuosity. He reserved that for the one moment of Apollyon where the brass blared out with ostentatious brilliance very appropriately. The other brass ensembles such as the opening hymn had a noble sonority and dignity which few conductors of today seem to understand. Leonard seems to have a very good sense of rhythm and continuity; he always kept the music moving on and never let it become static, however slow, and I thought him extremely skilful in his management of those horribly difficult moments so characteristic of yourself where there is nothing but an oboe and a solo viola, or something like that—very beautiful thoughts, but most difficult to make clear to an audience and hold their interest with them.

I expect the management is wise not to give more than three performances; people will run no risk of getting tired of the work and will realize that it is a thing to hear as something apart from the general repertory, and they will want to hear it again next year and I hope for many years after that.'

2 May 1951

'I am very glad to hear that you are firmly determined to reserve the *Pilgrim* for the theatre and not to allow it to be performed as an oratorio. I agree entirely with everything that you say. I have only seen the last dress rehearsal and the first performance, but I was completely convinced by it as a work for the stage, and I accept your music whole-heartedly, though I dare say you will eventually make alterations such as you yourself suggest. Newman said it wanted the environment of a cathedral, but I am sure he is quite wrong; that is just what a conventional-minded critic *would* say. I am sure it would be dreadfully boring as an oratorio, and hard pews would make it unbearable! It does not want a cathedral environment, because Bunyan stands for "pure" religion without the external decorations of a church. Of course the architectural environment of Covent Garden auditorium is definitely hostile to it, but it is a technical matter of lighting and stage-management to get over that, and I have seen far worse cases of mental and optical conflicts between stage and auditorium—e.g. *Wozzeck* in the old opera house at Berlin, where the huge area of fresh gilding on pilasters and pediments, brilliantly lit up by the light reflected from a hundred music desks in the orchestra, was a horrible foreground to an opera which is all blood and soot both visually and auditively.

I can understand people saying that your music is "undramatic", but it is the function of the stage to provide action and colour to complete the work as an *opera*; if it was to be an oratorio it would need much more "operatic" music to supply what could not be presented to the eye. I did not find that your music ever obstructed the stage, or kept the action waiting; that *would* have been undramatic. Hancock kept it moving and understood where to get climaxes; a cathedral conductor probably would not have had the insight for that. . . .

As to your suggested alterations: Vanity Fair would certainly bear enlarging; it is over too soon to make its full effect. The trouble is that you have a lot of minor characters (Judas, Pilate, etc.) who have very little to sing and are gone before one has realized who they are or what they are talking about. Boito did the same thing in *Nerone* (which I saw at Milan—and I have studied the libretto carefully too); he was so soaked in his period that he knew all these characters personally and their complete histories, but on the stage he had only time to give them 4 or 5 bars apiece, sometimes "off" and they were lost in the crowd. Britten did much the same in *Peter Grimes*, though good casting and clever production (at Budapest) did much to bring them out more vividly. . . . *Traviata* is a similar case; Verdi treated the minor parts (Baron, Marquis, Doctor) very scurvily, but Guthrie at C.G. (on my advice) placed them where they could be well seen and make their effect, besides emphasizing them in dress and make-up. The stage people could do a lot more to help Vanity Fair; but it certainly would help still more if *you* could make their parts more individual and give them more time to impress themselves on the audience. After all, Judas and Pilate are not people everybody knows by sight like Don Quixote or Napoleon, and not people one would expect to meet at a fair—unless one had read Bunyan beforehand. Most of us have read him in childhood and forgotten details; and I have lost my own copy—so I was grateful for your gift of a libretto.

I can't form a judgment on the Apollyon scene if so much of the music was cut; it certainly did not come off very well. I expect your own idea of the gigantic shadow was far better, and I should have thought it was not impossible to carry out.

Designer and producer certainly had a new and strange problem to tackle, so I must not be unkind to them. Nobody could enter completely into your music and your idea until they were saturated with it and knew it as a complete whole (as Hancock of course did); and non-musicians would be so distracted by their own technical problems at rehearsals that they could only grasp the music vaguely. I had the impression that they just did all the most obvious things which, though not positively wrong, were just rather inadequate and unimaginative. With a well-known opera they would not have had that difficulty; they would have seen stock performances and said to themselves "Well, I can do better than that if I get the chance". But with this work—it is only now that it is actually on the stage that they can go into the auditorium and watch it all comfortably and then begin to see how much better they could do the job if they could start all over again. I expect it will not be possible to make drastic alterations now, but it ought to be possible to re-study the opera and re-plan the stage pretty completely next season or next year. And if they are willing, there is probably a good deal that can be done now and bit by bit, without any great expenditure of money, time or labour, but with a good deal of expenditure of *ingenuity* on the part of designer and producer. I hope they won't refuse to do that.

Anyway, the music is all safe enough, and the stage presentation not disastrous, but workable and respectable enough to carry it through, though not as good as it ought to be. The singers and orchestra will all improve steadily as the performances go on and even at the first performance, they gave the impression of being completely "convinced" of their parts.'

6 May 1951

'I am more and more convinced by the music, and more and more certain that it must be an Opera on the stage and not an oratorio. I have read several criticisms and think them mostly stupid and unintelligent. I think I know more about Opera than all the lot of the critics put together, and I have a more analytical mind than any of them; I am a complete unbeliever and generally a scoffer but I have no difficulty or reluctance to surrender wholeheartedly to Bunyan and to your music.

Vanity Fair, Apollyon, and By-Ends stand out as the three "exciting" scenes of contrast with the general "mystical" atmosphere, and want very careful working-up. V.F. is certainly too short and might easily be lengthened; the opera was over last night by 9.35 and it can safely last till 10, though preferably not longer. (There was a good audience, except for the Grand Tier, and a crowded gallery; a great crush in the foyer, but the intervals were adequate for refreshment, so I think we may take the timing as normal.)

If I make suggestions for you yourself, I expect they can't be considered until after June, and for the present nothing drastic can be done.

Could you enlarge V.F. a little *before* the P. comes on? to get the audience well into the atmosphere of vanity? and also to let us make the acquaintance of Judas etc quite clearly before the P. does? Some of the actual stage effects suggested possibilities; the jester and tumblers, also the people with old musical instruments. Not a *set ballet* on Playford (I have just had to arrange a six-minute Playford Suite for the Arts Council concert in June, so Playford is in my head!) but fragmentary suggestions. You might also enlarge the friends of Lord Hate-Good—very good figures to look at, especially the Jesuit or whatever he is, and there is an elderly female who might be made more of—I don't know who she is but a harsh mezzo-soprano part would be effective.

I can't tackle Apollyon etc until I have studied the score. But the stage and the music don't seem to agree (see Notes). Can we have more chorus singing, even if "off" because of impossibility of changing costumes? Chorus off, and more ballet on. I could not understand the functions of the "creatures" and thought they ought to be more *active* and even more frightening to the P. Mood starting perhaps with Limbo and Despair, but working up to a *crescendo* and *accelerando* of sound and movement to the blaze of the brass for Apollyon. I don't feel happy about those long speeches of Apollyon on one note—my own stupidity, no doubt, but your intention does not reach me somehow. The collapse of the P. after the fight was not very convincing, but I don't know what ought to be done. More intelligent use of lighting would help here a great deal. The scene of the ministrations is a little long, especially after the singing stops. I should hate to cut a note of the music but the producer has not solved that problem.

I enjoy what I call the "By-Ends" scene immensely, but it is not quite right yet. The Boy is a delightful character, and the music for the By-Ends couple really admirable. Congratulations to Parry Jones for managing to make a Covent Garden audience laugh! Could the Boy sing his hymns a little faster?

Could you allow Hancock a little more liberty of tempo? So much of the music goes at a steady four miles an hour (good Pilgrim's pace!) and even in V.F. where there is an illusion of quickness the conductor's beat—which is that of the music—goes on at a pretty steady 4/4 or 3/4 crotchet about 80 to 84. An almost imperceptible quickening of the tempo at certain definite changes of mood would help a great deal. The orchestra sometimes needs keeping down a little more where the harmony is pretty full, and elsewhere perhaps more nuance in individual instruments; all that will come gradually, I am sure. I will not admit that the music is monotonous, as some critics find it; but it does need all the help and sensitivity that it can get.

York is the making of the whole opera (how Alan Gray would have been thrilled by it! he had a deep devotion to that tune). I find it indescribably uplifting, every time it comes in, and more and more; it sets the whole mood of the opera at the start (and how beautifully you have orchestrated the wind there) and I felt I should never have got to Paradise if I didn't hear York there! The Epilogue music rounds off the whole work quite perfectly. I don't know if you were there last night; there was quite a long silence when the curtain fell.

I think it is stupid of the critics to talk about your symphonies in connection with the opera; they may use the same themes but in this connection they are perfectly irrelevant. If the critics want to make comparisons they should compare the *Pilgrim* with your other *Operas* (and after all, York comes into *Hugh!*).

As regards *tempo*: I notice that practically all opera-singers tend to drag, though almost imperceptibly (and critics don't notice it, because it happens so often and they accept it as normal) through the fact that they are taking pains to sing well—even the really good singers. All the more in the P. because they sincerely want to do their best to be "impressive". But in very slow music, like much of yours, it tends to become tedious. It ought to improve as they get to know the music better and sing it with more ease, and so get more sense of long rhythms, and if they can understand that the singer (as in Monteverdi) must create the rhythmic impulse *himself*, instead of leaving it to the conductor. But that is the mark of really supreme singing, like Messchaert (you will remember him, I expect).

All the difficulties of the *Pilgrim* are purely technical and can be solved by skill, intelligence and ingenuity.' [Dent then added the following section:]

PILGRIM'S PROGRESS
Notes on Production

'The Main Curtain (with GR embroidery) ought never to come down except at the end of an ACT, so as to indicate an Interval. The plain red curtain ought to be used to divide the scenes, if necessary; it looks very well, especially when lights were flashed on it.

The Landscape scenes were very English—I suppose intentionally; but if so they showed English weather at its worst. The best was the Delectable Mountains; the others were often clumsily lit. There was little sense of "England's green and pleasant land", at least in the lighting.

The producer and choreographer seem to have done all the most "obvious" things, without penetrating to the real moral background. The *House Beautiful* actions are too ecclesiastical, and some costumes too; the atmosphere required is surely not Priestly Authority, Penance, formal Worship and Reverence, but Kindness and Friendliness, Love and Sympathy, *Helpfulness* on the part of all the heavenly beings (including Evangelist and Interpreter).

There is an enormous lot of *kneeling* all through the opera, which becomes monotonous and its emotional value gets cheapened.

Apollyon Scene: The Ballet was not impressive or at all frightening; we are too familiar with dancers lying on their backs and kicking their legs about. I wish the "shadow" idea could have been carried out, and more made of the combat.

Vanity Fair: some dresses rather too Hogarthian? suggestive of the Beggar's Opera? In any case the width of the dresses of Lechery and Co. takes up so much room on the stage that the thinner characters are crowded out and lost. The minor characters such as Judas and Pilate have so little to sing and are visually so inconspicuous that it is difficult to realize who they are before they have vanished into the shadows.

Soldiers who arrest the Pilgrim might be made to look more cruel and terrifying.

Prison scene, like a photograph frame descending into a wood landscape looks very ugly and clumsy, and the wood seen on right and left of it takes away the dramatic effect of the view seen when the door is unlocked (which is too narrow for picturesque effect).

Act I. Pilgrim's black luggage is much too neatly packed; if it represents his sins it ought to be more awkward and untidy, like a sack of potatoes or coals, something very uncomfortable and fatiguing to carry; he might even drag it or shift it sometimes; it never suggests an unbearable burden.

At House B. the libretto says they bring in a faldstool, but they carried in (very ceremonially) a small red hassock or kneeler, which looked rather ridiculous when put on the floor.

I wish the designer could have done more to suggest that the whole story is "*a dream*" but I suppose this would have been technically too difficult; the opera is much cut up into bits by curtains falling. Every time a curtain falls one is made conscious of Covent Garden auditorium.

Bunyan in Epilogue: too much ceremony, waving book to right and left etc, and kneeling: I suggest that he should be more simple and almost statuesque, with as little movement as possible, a complete contrast to the reality of the Pilgrim. Or else something more to suggest his persecution and imprisonment; but perhaps that would fall flat after the imprisonment of the Pilgrim.

As in all operas, the "poor people" are all too neat and tidy; they never give the impression of real poverty and suffering.

House Beautiful: surely the Pilgrim ought to enter through the "wicket gate" between the two posts with lanterns? not through the wings further back.

Act II: "arming" scene—this reproduces almost exactly the previous "robing" scene; I suggest that the Pilgrim should be dressed standing, not kneeling.

Watchman: (I hear that this was inserted at the last moment to cover change of scenery) I don't like his singing it at the prompter's box like a concert aria, but I don't see how to avoid it.

Apollyon Scene: the stage action and the music do not seem to agree, and I don't understand it. The ballet is insignificant and meaningless. Ought not the whole scene to be much more *frightening*? More and more "creatures", crescendo of movement and crowding to suggest terror and oppression; the whole scene seems to go slowly.

After the ministrations of the Heavenly Beings there is a long piece of orchestra music during which the characters make indecisive movements. I suggest 3 possible alternatives—

(1) shorten the music (but only in the *very last* resort; I don't want to do that at all).

(2) keep the characters absolutely motionless as a pictorial composition with gradual fading out.
(Rather risky, considering length)

(3) let them all gradually move off the stage as if the Beings were showing P. the way to his next trial and giving him encouragement and help.

Vanity Fair: this seemed to have been improved by May 5; lighting better, more light at the sides, and characters thus given more chance. Judas gets well forward, but he is over-weighted with a voluminous skirt and a huge "vanity-bag". I suggest something more like Leonardo's picture (which everybody knows and can recognize at once; more conspicuously *red* wig and beard (even if quite unnatural) fewer clothes, to suggest more *activity* and the familiar money-bag.

Simon Magus insignificant, and looks like a conjurer at a village entertainment, an improvised dress-up.

Hate-Good is excellent, and also the Jesuit (or Anglo-Catholic?).

Prison: will do as long as flanked by neutral curtains, but quite dreadful after the door opens and the landscape is seen *on each side* of the ruined walls. (It is an ugly landscape anyway with a very ugly and hard line formed by the united wings and top border.) Could the prison be painted on a cloth which will look quite transparent when lit from behind? and then be taken up almost imperceptibly like a gauze? This has been done in other operas at C.G.

All through, the lighting is the weak spot (sometimes too much the "strong spot"!); the beam from the auditorium ceiling is a most dangerous toy, and has been the ruin of many C.G. operas. I do not see a "long-term policy" in the lighting; it generally seems to work from bar to bar, without any sense of a scene—much less of an Act or of the whole Opera—as a complete whole.

I suggest to the Producer the German system of dividing scenes into "Stimmungen", first, second, third etc as required. Points in the score are settled where the *Stimmung* definitely changes (often with definite change of tempo or orchestral colour in the music), and the stage shows a change (which may be sudden or gradual) of lighting, or of grouping or movement, but always moving forward to a foreseen end.

There is far too much self-conscious "reverence" throughout. There must be about three dozen or more "kneel-downs" and two-thirds of them ought to be taken out, as they become horribly *cheap* as the opera goes on. Movements and gestures all hieratic. The shepherds' movements suggest curates rather than rustics. Surely Bunyan meant all the human beings (including Evangelist and Interpreter) to be real human people with *human* kindliness and helpfulness, when on the "good" side. On the other hand the Angel with the Arrow (Shepherds' Scene) ought to be more definitely celestial and *radiant* in appearance—costume too dark in colour, unless he is meant to symbolize Death, in which case he is not dark enough. It is only the halo which distinguishes him in appearance from Evangelist etc. and the halo was not at all effective. Could it be made as a spider's web of gold wire, with an irregular surface that would catch light and glitter more? It looks too much like a mere brass plate. (Always a difficult costume problem on any stage.)

Pilgrim has a great many changes of costume, none very satisfactory. I recall the Bristol production of 1927 in which he appeared most impressively as a Cromwellian soldier after the Civil War was over. Or did Bunyan imagine him wearing the traditional "pilgrim" dress with cockleshell hat and staff? In any case I think a hat and staff would often help to suggest *pilgrimage*; he sometimes looks too "ecclesiastical" without them.

Epilogue: a second sight of the opera confirms me strongly in what I have already said, especially in view of the very beautiful music and the tune York; he ought to symbolize himself as a great national immortal classic here, instead of offering his book to the Royal Box.

I wish *my* printers and publishers would do their work as quickly as his seem to have done theirs!'

17th May, 1951

'Dear Dent

I have been a long time answering your most interesting and helpful letters. I am now sending some comments on your notes, together with a copy of the vocal score in case you have not got one. If you have already got one you can pass this one on to anyone you think would like to have it.

I will take your notes on production first.

I agree that the main curtain should only come down between the Acts and not even then when, as in Act I and Act II, they are joined together. I was told that it was necessary to have the House curtain down between Acts I and II or the noise of the changing scenery would be heard, but as a matter of fact they used the Red curtain, which was very effective.

As regards the Religious aspect of the H.B., I like the landscape backcloths on the whole. In "House Beautiful" what we want is a scene of initiation, which I have made by expanding two sentences in Bunyan.

I agree there is too much kneeling. On the other hand you must remember that the Opera is to be acted almost like a ritual and not in the ordinary dramatic sense.

The "Apollyon" scene I admit is unsatisfactory at present. I still believe that my shadow scheme can be carried out and I am keeping it in the score but perhaps as an alternative.

On the whole I like the ballet, and therefore do not agree with you over this. I think it was right to stress the dolefulness, not the terror.

As regards "Vanity Fair", both you and Coghill have told me that I ought to enlarge the scene when Judas Iscariot &c come on. Here I cannot agree. They are mere momentary incidents and it does not much matter if people do not recognize them. If we "establish their characters" we should upset the whole balance, to my mind, and when they have said their little say they, quite rightly, retire to the background and once again become one of the chorus.

The "Prison" scene I admit is a difficulty and you will see from my stage directions it is not quite what I meant, but it is partly my own fault because I insisted that the road into the distance must be seen from all parts of the house.

Incidentally they did not carry out quite what I meant either there or in the Armoury scene.

I wanted the backcloth to represent a road stretching straight out into the distance. This, for some reason they said could not be done—I never quite understood why, because the same effect was produced very effectively in the last Act of Bliss's opera ["The Olympians"].

To go back for a minute. I agree that "Vanity Fair" is too short, but I am not prepared to lengthen the Judas Iscariot scene. Instead I am adding a song for Lechery and a little more for Madam Bubble and Madam Wanton and also am enlarging the scene of the witnesses. I think that will make the difference to Act III.

As regards Pilgrim's burden, it is usually represented by that in all the illustrated editions I have seen, even the quite early ones.

In the "House Beautiful" we tried a faldstool but it looked rather painfully like a commode, so we dropped it and had a cushion instead.

I agree about Bunyan in the Epilogue. I do not like all his gestures.

Act II. Here and elsewhere there is, I admit, too much kneeling and I never wanted the characters from "House Beautiful" to reappear. He ought not to be armed by three young women, but by a lot of soldiers, I think. Of course the end of the scene was a last minute affair. You will see in the score that the original idea was that the Pilgrim should go off singing and his voice be gradually lost in the distance after which there would be a black-out and a curtain (not the House curtain), but we found that on the large Covent Garden stage his voice could not be heard as soon as he got "off-stage" and so we had to alter it at the last minute, but it is not meant to be a curtain in the conventional sense of the word. I am, however, altering it. I am cutting out his exit and putting a short shout for the chorus to bring the curtain down.

I had great difficulty over the "Watchful" scene. My instructions were that the house curtain must come down or the noise of the shifting scenery would be heard; also that it must come down while Watchful was singing, otherwise half the audience would applaud and the rest go out to the bar. So I had to arrange that he came right down stage and sang his song in front of the house curtain. I did not like it, but after all it is done in Mozart—at all events in Glyndebourne, although I know that is not much of a recommendation to you.

The end of Act II where the Evangelist appears I think ought to be all right if they will keep quite still. I always feel a long silence, if properly held, is very effective. Originally the Pilgrim's dress is put on during that end, but we felt it was too fussy and cut it out. Anyway there is almost too much dressing and undressing of the Pilgrim throughout, but I can put an optional cut in the music in case the Producer finds that his actors cannot hold their tableau.

You say, I think rightly, that in Act II, Scene 2 on page 42 of the vocal score, the 2 young women have difficulty in filling out the music. You will note that there is a repeat—I begged Coghill to cut it, but he said he wanted it all—so what was I to do?

I have already dealt with the prison scene and it is largely my fault.

You refer a good deal to Bunyan, but remember that this is not Bunyan but only adapted from Bunyan. He would certainly have had a fit at some of the things that I do!

What we have got to decide is whether it is good and effective drama without any reference to Bunyan.

As regards Hancock's *tempi*, I hardly interfered with him at all except that he was inclined to get a little bit too slow in places. Perhaps that was the singers' fault—they were apt to drag a bit, I know.

Of course the Opera suffers from what people call "the Eternal Andante", but I do not see how it can be helped short of rewriting the Opera which I must leave my successor to do.

I may think of some more later on in which case I shall worry you again.

Yours gratefully
R. Vaughan Williams.

Relationship to Fifth Symphony: It may be thought useful to have a list of those sections of music which appear in the D major symphony and in

The Pilgrim's Progress. Their treatment is in the two cases quite different, the symphony's development being strikingly independent.

Symphony.

First movement: The three-note figure which is the basis of the Preludio's development section (full score, p. 12) is to be found in the introduction to Act II, Scene 2, when Pilgrim meets Apollyon.

The second subject, with its wonderful change into E major (full score, p. 7), occurs in the morality (Act I, Scene 1, vocal score, p. 10) while Evangelist tells Pilgrim to go to the Wicket Gate, and recurs while the Interpreter welcomes Pilgrim (vocal score, p. 26) and later describes to him the room prepared for him (vocal score, p. 30).

Third movement (Romanza): The opening of this movement, and its cor anglais theme (full score, p. 70) occur at the beginning of Act I, Scene 2 (vocal score, p. 21). The cor anglais theme is set in the morality (vocal score, p. 24) to some of the words which were originally inscribed above the slow movement of the symphony: 'He hath given me rest by his sorrow and life by his death.'

The climax of the Romanza's animato section (full score, p. 81) on the brass may be referred to Pilgrim's 'Save me' (vocal score, p. 24) and some of the woodwind phrases (full score, p. 80) derive from the meno mosso accompaniment (bar 2 vocal score, p. 26) and culminate in the violin solo (full score, p. 88).

Fourth movement (Passacaglia): The basis of the passacaglia theme (full score, p. 90) occurs in the morality in the accompaniment to Pilgrim's inquiries to the Interpreter (vocal score, p. 29 and p. 30, at 'andante sostenuto'). The tenth bar of p. 30 of the morality vocal score is a link with the scherzando section of the symphony movement (full score, p. 98)—see oboe and trumpet parts especially—and 'Who would true valour see' is a derivative from, or parent of, the brass paeans in the symphony (full score, pp. 100–2).

Separate issues:

1A. SEVEN SONGS FROM 'THE PILGRIM'S PROGRESS'. For voice with pianoforte accompaniment.

1. Watchful's Song (Nocturne); for baritone. Words from the Book of Psalms and the Book of Isaiah. *Lento moderato.*
   Dedication: To Bryan Drake.

2. The Song of the Pilgrim (Bunyan); for baritone. *Allegro moderato e maestoso.*
   Dedication: To Douglas Robinson and the members of the chorus at Covent Garden.

3. The Pilgrim's Psalm; for baritone. Words adapted from the Epistles of St. Paul and the Book of Psalms. *Moderato alla marcia.*
   Dedication: To Arnold Matters.

4. The Song of the Leaves of Life and the Water of Life; soprano solo or duet. Words adapted from the Book of the Revelation. *Andante sostenuto.*
   Dedication: To Elisabeth Abercrombie and Monica Sinclair.

5. The Song of Vanity Fair; for baritone. Words by Ursula Vaughan Williams. *Allegro moderato.*
   Dedication: To whoever shall first sing it.[1]

6. The Woodcutter's Song (Bunyan); for soprano. *Andante.*
   Dedication: To Iris Kells.

7. The Bird's Song; for soprano. Words from the Book of Psalms. *Andante tranquillo.*
   Dedication: To Adèle Leigh.
   Duration: 21 minutes.

Note: On each song is a note pointing out that it is a concert version and differs either slightly or considerably from the original version.
Publication: London, O.U.P. (© 1952).
Whereabouts of MS.: British Library. |Vocal Score (50481).

1B. THE TWENTY-THIRD PSALM. Arranged by John Churchill for soprano solo and SATB chorus unaccompanied, or SSATB if no soloist. *Andante tranquillo.*
Publication: London, O.U.P. (© 1953).

1C. PILGRIM'S JOURNEY. A Cantata for soprano, tenor and baritone soloists, with mixed chorus (SATB) and orchestra (organ), devised in 1962 by Christopher Morris and Roy Douglas from the Morality *The Pilgrim's Progress.*

I. Cast Thy Burden Upon The Lord; for tenor and baritone soloists, semichorus (SSA) and chorus (SATB). *Moderato—lento —andante—lento—andante sostenuto—lento moderato—andante sostenuto—poco animato—andante—andante sostenuto—tranquillo.*

II. Into Thy Hands, O Lord (Watchful's Song); for baritone soloist. *Lento—poco meno lento—lento.*

III. Who Would True Valour See; for soprano and baritone soloists and chorus (SATB). *Allegro moderato e maestoso— largamente—moderato alla marcia.*

IV. Unto Him That Overcometh; for women's chorus (SS or SA). *Andante con moto—tranquillo.*

V. Vanity Fair; for tenor and baritone soloists and chorus (SATB). *Allegro pesante—moderato.*

VI. He That is Down; for soprano solo. *Andante.*

[1] The first singer of the song in the Morality was Thorsteinn Hannesson; of the concert version, John Cameron.

VII. The Lord is My Shepherd; for chorus (SSATB). Unaccompanied if preferred. *Andante tranquillo* (The voice parts are based on John Churchill's arrangement—see 1B, above.)

VIII. Alleluia; for soprano, tenor and baritone soloists and double chorus. *Allegro moderato—maestoso.*

Instrumentation: 2 flutes (2nd doubling piccolo), 2 oboes (2nd doubling cor anglais), 2 clarinets, 2 bassoons, 4 horns, 2 trumpets, 2 tenor trombones, 1 bass trombone, timpani, percussion (side drum, triangle, cymbals, bass drum, gong, glockenspiel and xylophone— the last three opt.), harp (or pianoforte), strings. *Or:* strings and pianoforte, with optional addition of any or all of the following: 2nd pianoforte, flute, trumpet and timpani. *Or:* organ only.

First performance: Dorking, Leith Hill Musical Festival, 26 April 1963, Iris Kells (soprano), Kenneth Bowen (tenor), John Noble (baritone), Leith Hill Festival Chorus and Orchestra, conducted by Dr. William Cole.

Duration: 36 minutes.

Note in vocal score by composer's widow: '*Pilgrim's Progress*, a morality founded on Bunyan's allegory of the same name, was written for the stage, and the composer refused to allow church or concert performances of the complete work. But as he had prepared a short cantata, *In Windsor Forest*, from his opera *Sir John in Love* and authorized *A Cotswold Romance*, Maurice Jacobson's concert version of *Hugh the Drover*, it seemed that there were good precedents for making some of the music of *Pilgrim's Progress* available in similar form. My thanks go to the Rev. G. J. Cuming for the initial suggestion that this cantata be devised, to Mr. Christopher Morris for drawing up the scheme and preparing the vocal score, to Mr. Eric Gritton for arranging the organ accompaniment, and to Mr. Roy Douglas for preparing the full score from the original orchestration and arranging the alternative strings and piano accompaniment. U.V.W.'

Publication: London, O.U.P. (© 1962). V.S. Orchestral parts and vocal scores on hire.

1D. THE WOODCUTTER'S SONG (He that is down). Arranged by Brian Judge for oboe solo or organ.
Publication: London, O.U.P. © 1975.

2. FLOURISH FOR THREE TRUMPETS. Specially written for Staffordshire schools in the year of the Festival of Britain.
Unpublished.
First performance: Stafford, Borough Hall, 19 March 1951, conducted by Maude Smith.

Whereabouts of MS.: Music Department, William Salt Library, Stafford.

3. THREE SHAKESPEARE SONGS. For mixed chorus (SATB), unaccompanied.

    1. Full fathom five. Words from *The Tempest*, Act I, Scene 2. *Andante misterioso.*

    2. The Cloud-Capp'd Towers. Words from *The Tempest*, Act IV, Scene 1. *Lento.*

    3. Over hill, over dale. Words from *A Midsummer Night's Dream*, Act II, Scene 1. *Allegro vivace.*

First performance: London, Royal Festival Hall, 23 June 1951, at British Federation of Music Festivals National Competitive Festival. Test piece for mixed voice choirs. Sung by combined mixed voice choirs, conducted by Dr. C. Armstrong Gibbs.

Dedication: To C. Armstrong Gibbs.

Duration: 7 minutes.

Publication: London, O.U.P. (© 1951).

Whereabouts of MS.: British Library. Vocal score (50481).

Other versions:

    2. The Cloud-Capp'd Towers. Arranged for women's voices (SSAA), unaccompanied, by Douglas Guest.
    London, O.U.P. (© 1955) (O.C.S.W17).

    3. Over hill, over dale. Arranged for women's voices (SSAA), unaccompanied, by Douglas Guest.
    London, O.U.P. (© 1956) (O.C.S.W18).

4. ROMANCE IN D FLAT FOR HARMONICA. Accompanied by an orchestra of strings and pianoforte. *Andante tranquillo—poco animando—allegro moderato.*

First performance: New York, Town Hall, 3 May 1952. Larry Adler (harmonica), Little Symphony Orchestra, conducted by Daniel Saidenberg. First performance in England: Liverpool Stadium, 16 June 1952, Larry Adler (harmonica), Liverpool Philharmonic Orchestra, conducted by Hugo Rignold. First performance in London: Royal Albert Hall, Promenade Concert, 6 September 1952, Larry Adler (harmonica), B.B.C. Symphony Orchestra, conducted by Sir Malcolm Sargent.

Dedication: To Larry Adler.

Duration: 6 minutes.

Publication: London, O.U.P. (© 1953), arrangement for harmonica and pianoforte. Orchestral parts on hire.

Whereabouts of MS.: British Library. Full Score (50389).

1952

1. IN THE SPRING. Song for voice and pianoforte. Words by William

Barnes (1801–86), from *Poems of Rural Life in the Dorset Dialect*.
Lento moderato.
Dedication: To the members of the Barnes Society.
Publication: London, O.U.P. (© 1952).
Whereabouts of MS.: British Library. Vocal Score (50480). Presented
by Shaftesbury Museum from the Barnes Society Collection.

2. SINFONIA ANTARTICA. For full orchestra, soprano soloist and
women's chorus, in five movements. Composed 1949–52.

    I. Prelude. *Andante maestoso.*

> 'To suffer woes which hope thinks infinite,
> To forgive wrongs darker than death or night,
> To defy power which seems omnipotent,
> Neither to change, nor falter, nor repent:
> This . . . is to be
> Good, great and joyous, beautiful and free,
> This is alone life, joy, empire and victory.'
> —from *Prometheus Unbound* (P. B. Shelley),
>   Act IV, l. 570.[1]

    II. Scherzo. *Moderato—poco animando.*

> 'There go the ships
> and there is that Leviathan
> whom thou hast made to take his pastime therein.'
>   —Psalm CIV.

    III. Landscape. *Lento.*

> 'Ye ice falls! Ye that from the mountain's brow
> Adown enormous ravines slope amain—
> Torrents, methinks, that heard a mighty voice,
> And stopped at once amid their maddest plunge!
> Motionless torrents! Silent cataracts!'
>   —from *Hymn before Sunrise in the Vale of
>   Chamouni* (S. T. Coleridge).

    IV. Intermezzo. *Andante sostenuto.*

> 'Love, all alike, no season knows, or clime,
> Nor hours, days, months, which are the rags of time.'
>   —from *The Sun Rising* (John Donne).

    V. Epilogue. *Alla marcia moderato (ma non troppo).*

> 'I do not regret this journey; we took risks, we knew we took
> them, things have come out against us, therefore we have no
> cause for complaint.'
>   —from *Captain Scott's Journal.*

---

[1] These same lines, it is worth noting, were set to music by Vaughan Williams as
No. 4 of the *Six Choral Songs to be sung in Time of War*. See 1940, No. 1.

Instrumentation: 3 flutes (3rd doubling piccolo), 2 oboes, 1 cor anglais, 2 clarinets, 1 bass clarinet, 2 bassoons, 1 double bassoon, 4 horns, 3 trumpets, 3 trombones, 1 tuba, timpani, percussion (3 or 4 players: triangle, cymbals, side-drum, bass drum, gong, bells, glockenspiel, xylophone, vibraphone, wind machine), harp, celesta, pianoforte, organ (opt.), soprano solo, small SSA chorus, strings.

First performance: Manchester, Free Trade Hall, 14 January 1953, The Hallé Orchestra, Margaret Ritchie (soprano), women of the Hallé Choir, conducted by Sir John Barbirolli. First performance in London: Royal Festival Hall, Royal Philharmonic Society concert, 21 January 1953, by the same artists.

Dedication: To Ernest Irving.

Duration: 39 minutes.

Composer's programme note: This work was suggested by the film *Scott of the Antarctic* which was produced by Ealing Studios a few years ago. Some of the themes are derived from my incidental music to that film. The Musical Director was Ernest Irving (he indeed composed three bars of the music himself). The *Sinfonia* is therefore gratefully dedicated to him.

A large orchestra is used, including a vibraphone, a wind machine and women's voices used orchestrally. There are five movements— *Prelude, Scherzo, Landscape, Intermezzo* and *Epilogue.* Each movement is headed by an appropriate quotation [not repeated here].

I. *Prelude*

The opening subject starts as follows:

No. 1.

This theme is used as a whole or in parts throughout the work. Then a few antarctic shimmerings form a prelude to a soprano solo without words, accompanied by a chorus of sopranos and altos.

No. 2.

This is followed by other themes of minor importance which lead up to a theme accompanied by deep bells, which was supposed in the film to be 'menacing'. It also is used frequently throughout the work. Then, after a repetition of the soprano solo, a trumpet flourish

introduces the coda which is built up largely on the opening theme.

II. *Scherzo*

The opening theme is as follows:

This is followed by another little wisp of theme:

No. 5.

Then we get down to business with a *motif*, which as it is 'representative', must be thus designated. Those who wish may take it as representing whales

The next section would, I suppose, be called by the official analyst the 'trio'. Its tune was used in the film to suggest penguins.

No. 7.

Trumpet   Trombone

The music ends softly on an indefinite chord for muted brass and celesta.

III. *Landscape*

The music here is chiefly atmospheric, but the following themes may be noted:

In this movement there is a part for the organ (if there is one and at the right pitch). It leads without break to

IV. *Intermezzo*

There are two main themes:

Towards the end of the movement the bell passage reappears followed by some very soft music connected in the film with the death of Oates.
V. *Epilogue*
The *Epilogue* starts with another flourish:

Then follows a march tune, obviously suggested by the opening of the Prelude (Ex. 1).

Other themes follow leading to a big climax. The bell passage comes in again, suddenly very soft. The voices are heard again and the opening flourish, first loud and then soft, leads to a complete repetition of the beginning of the *Prelude*. Then the solo singer is heard again and the music dies down to nothing, except for the voices and the Antarctic wind. R.V.W.

Publication: London, O.U.P. (© 1953). Full score. Orchestral parts on hire.

Whereabouts of MS.: British Library, sketches, parts of pianoforte score (50375); full score (on loan to B.L. from Royal Philharmonic Society), Royal Philharmonic Society MSS., Supplement VI.

Revisions:

1st movement—First 25 bars are an expansion of original sketch. At figure 15 in score 31 bars were cut from the full score (a further development of the opening theme). Movement originally ended tragically, or pessimistically.

2nd movement—Trivial revisions, chiefly harp replacing side-drum in early bars.

3rd movement—Some of the organ part was an afterthought.

4th movement—The episode of the bells (3 bars after 6) originally led directly to a recapitulation of bar 13 after 7. The interlude of Oates's death at 7 was inserted.

5th movement—Poetic superscription was originally 'Their bodies are buried in peace, but their name liveth for evermore' (Ecclesiasticus, XLIV, v. 14). The movement originally ended five bars after $\boxed{17}$ with rich G major chords. Episode between $\boxed{11}$ and $\boxed{12}$ replaced a further development of the theme in bars 1 and 2 of $\boxed{10}$.

3. O TASTE AND SEE. Motet for unaccompanied mixed choir (S (or Treble) ATB) with an organ introduction. Composed November–December 1952. Words from Psalm XXXIV, v. 8. *Andante sostenuto.*

First performance: London, Westminster Abbey, 2 June 1953, Coronation of Queen Elizabeth II. Sung by Choristers during the Queen's Communion, conducted by Sir William McKie.

Duration: 1¾ minutes.

Publication: London, O.U.P. (© 1953).

Other version: Arranged for women's voices (SSA) unaccompanied, by the composer. O.U.P. (© 1953).

4. LE PARADIS. French folk song arranged for voice and harp (or pianoforte).

Unpublished.

First performance: London, Institut français du Royaume-Uni, 17 November 1952, Sophie Wyss (soprano), Maria Korchinska (harp).

Whereabouts of MS.: In possession of Miss Sophie Wyss.

5. PRELUDE ON AN OLD CAROL TUNE (Founded on incidental music written for *The Mayor of Casterbridge* by Thomas Hardy (1840–1928)).

Instrumentation: 2 flutes, 1 oboe, 2 clarinets, 1 bassoon, 2 horns, 2 trumpets, 2 trombones, timpani, strings.

First performance: B.B.C. broadcast, 18 November 1952, B.B.C. West of England Light Orchestra, conductor Reginald Redman. First public performance: King's Lynn Festival, 31 July 1953. The Boyd Neel Orchestra, conducted by Dr. R. Vaughan Williams.

Duration: 8 minutes.

Note: The old carol tune is 'On Christmas Night the joy-bells ring'.

Publication: London, O.U.P. (© 1953). Orchestral parts on hire.

Whereabouts of MS.: British Library. Full Score (50401).

1953

1. SILENCE AND MUSIC. For mixed chorus (SATB), unaccompanied. Words by Ursula Vaughan Williams. *Lento.* Composed as No. 4 of *A Garland for the Queen,* in which ten British composers and ten poets paid tribute to Queen Elizabeth II in the year of her coronation.

First performance: London, Royal Festival Hall, 1 June 1953, Cambridge University Madrigal Society and the Golden Age Singers, conducted by Boris Ord.

Dedication: To the memory of Charles Villiers Stanford, and his Blue Bird.

Duration: 5 minutes.

Publication: London, O.U.P. (© 1953).

2. THE OLD HUNDREDTH PSALM TUNE (All People That On Earth Do Dwell). Arranged for mixed choir (SATB), congregation, orchestra and organ. Completed February 1953. Text by W. Kethe (Daye's Psalter, 1560–1). *Very slow.* Verse 1, congregation and choir in unison; verse 2, congregation; verse 3, choir unaccompanied, with trumpet descant; verse 4, choir and orchestra; verse 5, congregation and choir in unison.

Instrumentation: 3 flutes, 3 oboes, 3 clarinets, 3 bassoons, 4 horns, 3 trumpets, 3 trombones, tuba, timpani, percussion, organ, strings. (The score is marked 'All available trumpets'.) Extra 'fanfare' instrumentation: 4 trumpets, 3 trombones, side drum. The brass mostly doubles the orchestral brass, and the side drum is cued into the full orchestra.

First performance: London, Westminster Abbey, 2 June 1953, Coronation of Queen Elizabeth II. Special Coronation Choir and Orchestra, with trumpeters of Royal Military School of Music, Kneller Hall, conducted by Sir William McKie. First concert performance: Manchester, Free Trade Hall, 27 October 1957; the Hallé Choir and Orchestra, conducted by Sir John Barbirolli.

Duration: 5½ minutes.

Note: The notation is in crotchets and minims instead of the customary minims and semibreves and does not imply a quicker pace. The metronome timing of $\downarrow$ = 66 should never be exceeded. In cathedrals and other large buildings the pace should be even slower. The opening flourish is adapted from the composer's setting of The Hundredth Psalm. The harmonization of verse 2 is taken from *Songs of Praise.* The faux-bourdon in verse 4 is by John Dowland (1621).

Publication: London, O.U.P. (© 1953). V.S. Orchestral parts on hire. *Whereabouts of MS.:* British Library. Vocal Score and Full Score (50476).

Other versions:

(*a*) Arranged by Roy Douglas for mixed choir (SATB) with 'normal symphony orchestra' instrumentation without organ: 2 flutes, 2 oboes, 2 clarinets, 2 bassoons, 4 horns, 3 trumpets, 3 trombones, tuba (opt.), timpani, percussion, and strings. O.U.P. © 1965, on hire.

(*b*) Arranged by Roy Douglas for mixed choir (SATB) with 3 trumpets, organ, and timpani (opt.). O.U.P. © 1965, on hire.

(*c*) Re-scored by David Stone for mixed (SATB) or unison voices and orchestra: 2 flutes, oboe, 2 clarinets, bassoon, 2 horns, 2 trumpets, timpani, percussion, and strings. O.U.P. © 1972.

(*d*) Arranged by Robert Washburn for mixed voices and wind band: flutes, oboes, bassoons, clarinets, alto clarinet, bass clarinet, contra-alto clarinet, contrabass clarinet, alto saxophones, tenor saxophone, baritone saxophone, trumpets (cornets), horns, trombones, baritones, euphonium, tubas, string bass, timpani, percussion, and organ. O.U.P. © 1975.

(*e*) Re-scored by Roy Douglas for mixed voices and brass ensemble: 4 trumpets (opt.), trombone, tuba (in lieu of trombone 3), timpani, and organ. O.U.P. © 1969.

1954

1. TE DEUM AND BENEDICTUS. Set to well-known metrical psalm tunes for unison voices (boys, men or women) or mixed voices (with occasional optional harmony) with accompaniment of organ, harmonium or pianoforte.

    I. TE DEUM. *Moderato maestoso—poco tranquillo.* Psalm tunes employed: Old 104th, Song 13, Croft's 136th.

    II. BENEDICTUS. *Andante con moto.* Psalm tunes employed: Song 22, Magdalen College.

Publication: London, O.U.P. (© 1954). V.S.

Whereabouts of MS.: British Library. V.S. in note book (50452).

2. CONCERTO IN F MINOR FOR BASS TUBA AND ORCHESTRA.

    I. Allegro moderato.

    II. Romanza—*andante sostenuto.*

    III. Finale—*rondo alla tedesca.*

Instrumentation: solo bass tuba, 2 flutes (2nd doubling piccolo), 1 oboe, 2 clarinets, 1 bassoon, 2 horns, 2 trumpets, 2 trombones, timpani, percussion (2 players, side drum, triangle, bass drum, cymbals), strings.

First performance: London, Royal Festival Hall, L.S.O. Jubilee Concert, 13 June 1954. Philip Catelinet (tuba), London Symphony Orchestra, conducted by Sir John Barbirolli.

Duration: 13 minutes.

Dedication: To The London Symphony Orchestra.

Composer's programme note: 'The form of this concerto is nearer to the Bach form than to that of the Viennese School (Mozart and

Beethoven) though the first and last movements each finish up with an elaborate cadenza which allies the concerto to the Mozart-Beethoven form. The music is fairly simple and obvious and can probably be listened to without much previous explanation. The orchestration is that of the so-called theatre orchestra consisting of woodwind, two each of horns, trumpets and trombones, timpani, percussion and strings. R.V.W.'

Publication: London, O.U.P. (© 1955). Arrangement for tuba and pianoforte. Full score O.U.P. © 1979. Orchestral parts on hire.

Note: The Romanza may also be played by euphonium, bassoon or violoncello and pianoforte. A B flat treble clef part for euphonium is published by O.U.P.

Whereabouts of MS.: British Library. Full Scores, 50391–2. Sketches in notebooks (50390 and 50482A).

3. THIS DAY (HODIE). Composed 1953–4. A Christmas Cantata for soprano, tenor and baritone soloists with mixed chorus (SATB), boys' voices, organ (opt.) and full orchestra.

    I. Prologue. *Allegro vivace—moderato maestoso.* For chorus and orchestra. Words from the Vespers for Christmas Day.

   II. Narration. *Moderato con moto.* For trebles and organ, and tenor soloist and orchestra. Words from St. Matthew I, vv. 18–21, and St. Luke I, v. 32.

  III. Song. *Poco meno mosso (andante sostenuto).* For soprano soloist, women's voices (SA) and orchestra. Words from *Hymn on the Morning of Christ's Nativity* (John Milton, 1608–74).

  IV. Narration. *Moderato con moto.* For trebles and organ. Words from St. Luke II, vv. 1–7.

   V. Choral. *Andante sostenuto.* For mixed chorus, unaccompanied. Words by Miles Coverdale (1488–1568) after Martin Luther (1483–1546).

  VI. Narration. *Moderato con moto—allegro alla tedesca—lento sostenuto—allegro vivace—tranquillo—Tempo I.* For trebles and organ, tenor soloist, and orchestra, soprano soloist, mixed chorus and orchestra. Words adapted from St. Luke II, vv. 8–17, and the Prayer Book.

 VII. The Oxen. *Andante sostenuto.* For baritone soloist and orchestra. Words by Thomas Hardy.

VIII. Narration. *Moderato con moto—alla tedesca ma tranquillo.* For trebles and organ, women's voices (SA), and orchestra. Words from St. Luke II, v. 20.

  IX. Pastoral. *Allegretto tranquillo.* For baritone soloist and orchestra. Words by George Herbert.

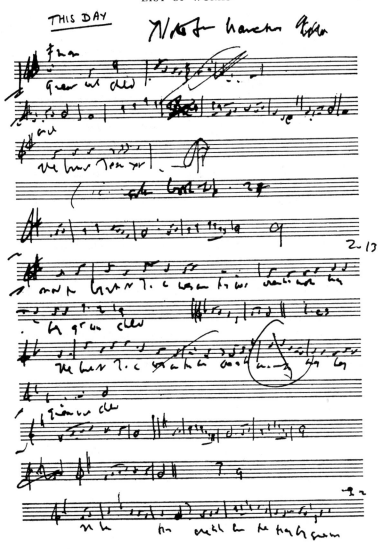

An MS page of 'Notes for Narration' for Hodie

X. Narration. *Moderato con moto.* For trebles and organ. Words from St. Luke II, v. 19.

XI. Lullaby. *Andante sostenuto.* For soprano soloist, women's voices (SA), and orchestra. Words by William Ballet.

XII. Hymn. *Allegro maestoso*. For tenor soloist and orchestra. Words by William Drummond (1585–1649).

XIII. Narration. *Moderato con moto*. For trebles and organ, male voices (TB), and orchestra. Words adapted from St. Matthew II, vv. 1, 2 and 11.

XIV. The March of the Three Kings. *Maestoso alla marcia—tranquillo*. For soprano, tenor, baritone soloists, mixed chorus, and orchestra. Words by Ursula Vaughan Williams.

XV. Choral. *Lento*. For mixed chorus and orchestra. Words: Verse 1, Anon; Verse 2, Ursula Vaughan Williams.

XVI. Epilogue. *Moderato—allegro maestoso—poco animato—moderato*. For baritone, tenor and soprano soloists, mixed chorus, and orchestra. Words adapted from St. John I, vv. 1–14, and Milton's *Nativity Hymn*.

Instrumentation: 3 flutes (1 opt.) (3rd doubling piccolo), 2 oboes (1 opt.), 1 cor anglais, 2 clarinets, 2 bassoons, 1 double bassoon (opt.), 4 horns (2 opt.), 3 trumpets (1 opt.), 3 trombones, tuba, timpani, percussion, celesta, harp (opt.), pianoforte, organ (opt.), strings.

First performance: Worcester Cathedral, Three Choirs Festival, 8 September 1954, Nancy Evans (mezzo-soprano); Eric Greene (tenor); Gordon Clinton (baritone); Festival Chorus, London Symphony Orchestra, conducted by Dr. R. Vaughan Williams. First performance in London: Royal Festival Hall, 19 January 1955, soloists as above; B.B.C. Chorus and Choral Society, boys of Watford Grammar School, B.B.C. Symphony Orchestra, conducted by Sir Malcolm Sargent.

Duration: 55½ minutes.

Dedication: To Herbert Howells. 'Dear Herbert, I find that in this Cantata I have inadvertently cribbed a phrase from your beautiful *Hymnus Paradisi*. Your passage seems so germane to my context that I have decided to keep it. R.V.W.' [Professor Howells has said that he and Vaughan Williams later searched for the passage in question and could not find it![1]]

Publication: London, O.U.P. (© 1954). V.S. with pianoforte arrangement by Roy Douglas. Full score. O.U.P. © 1967. Orchestral and choral parts on hire.

Whereabouts of MS.: British Library. Full Score (50477).

Separate arrangements:

1. Lullaby.
    (*a*) For women's voices (SSA) with pianoforte accompaniment. O.U.P. (© 1954).

---

[1] The *Sunday Times*, 31 August 1958.

(*b*) For soprano solo, women's chorus (SA), harp (opt.) and strings, arranged Christopher Finzi (hire only). O.U.P. (© 1954).

2. Two Chorals.
(*a*) The Blessed Son of God. ⎫ For mixed chorus
(*b*) No sad thought his soul ⎬ (SATB) unaccompanied.
affright. O.U.P. (© 1954). ⎭

4. SONATA IN A MINOR. For violin and pianoforte.

I. Fantasia—*allegro giusto.*

II. Scherzo—*allegro furioso ma non troppo.*

III. Tema con Variazione—*andante*—*allegro* (six variations).

First performance: B.B.C. Home Service broadcast, 12 October 1954, Frederick Grinke (violin), Michael Mullinar (pianoforte). First public performance: Rochester, New York, U.S.A., Rochester Civic Music Association, 14 November 1955, Josef Szigeti (violin) and Carlo Bussotti (pianoforte). First public performance in England: London, Wigmore Hall, Institute of Contemporary Arts, 20 December 1955, Frederick Grinke (violin) and Michael Mullinar (pianoforte).
Duration: 23 minutes.
Dedication: To Frederick Grinke.
Note: The theme of III comes from the Pianoforte Quintet in C minor (see 1903, No. 13).
Publication: London, O.U.P. (© 1956).
Whereabouts of MS.: In possession of Frederick Grinke, Esq. Sketches in notebook are in British Library (50482A).

5. HEART'S MUSIC. Song for mixed chorus (SATB), unaccompanied. Words by Thomas Campion (1567–1619) from the 'Book of Ayres'.
Andante sostenuto.
First performance: London, Church of St. Sepulchre, Holborn Viaduct, 25 November 1954. St. Thomas's Hospital Choir, conducted by Wilfrid Dykes Bower.
Dedication: Written for Wilfrid Dykes Bower and the St. Thomas's Hospital Musical Society.
Publication: London, O.U.P. (© 1955). (O.C.S. X8).

6. MENELAUS ON THE BEACH AT PHAROS. Song for medium voice and pianoforte. Composed summer, 1954. Words by Ursula Vaughan Williams. Poem and music were written in one day after the composer and his wife had been reading T. E. Lawrence's translation of the Odyssey. *Andante moderato.*
First performance: New York, Cornell University, 14 November 1954, Keith Falkner (baritone), Christabel Falkner (pianoforte). First performance in England: London, Wigmore Hall, 26 May 1955, Keith Falkner (baritone), Michael Mullinar (pianoforte).

Dedication : To Keith Falkner.
Publication: London, O.U.P. (© 1960. (See *Four Last Songs,* 1958, Entry No. 2.)
Whereabouts of MS. : In possession of Sir Keith Falkner.

7. THREE GAELIC SONGS. Arranged for mixed voices (SATB) unaccompanied. Gaelic and English words (English version by Ursula Vaughan Williams).

1. Dawn on the hills (S'tràth chuir a'ghrian). A milking song from Eigg. (Sung by Janet Anderson, nurse at Bracadale Manse, 1861, who learned it in Eigg). Slow.
2. Come let us gather cockles (An téid thu bhuain mhaoraich). Lively.
3. Wake and rise (Mhnàthan a'ghlinne so!). Commemorative of a cattle raid. Flowing, not too fast.

The melodies and Gaelic words of these songs were published in the Folk Song Society's *Journal,* 1911. These arrangements were made at Santa Barbara, California, between 21 and 26 October 1954.
Publication: London, O.U.P. (© 1963) (O.C.S. X109, Staff and Solfa notation).
Whereabouts of MS.: In possession of Mrs. Eila Mackenzie.

1955

1. SONG FOR A SPRING FESTIVAL. Words by Ursula Vaughan Williams. *Allegro moderato.* For mixed chorus (mostly voices in unison). Written for and given to the Leith Hill Musical Festival, in April 1955, by the author and composer, to be performed nowhere else.
First performance: Dorking, The Dorking Halls, Leith Hill Musical Festival, 15 April 1955, conducted by Dr. R. Vaughan Williams.
Privately printed by the Oxford University Press. Not for sale.

2. PRELUDE ON THREE WELSH HYMN TUNES. For brass band.
Instrumentation: E flat soprano cornet, B flat solo cornet and 1st and 2nd cornets, B flat flügel horn, E flat solo tenor or sax horn and 1st and 2nd tenor or sax horns, B flat 1st and 2nd baritones, B flat solo euphonium, B flat 1st and 2nd tenor trombones, G bass trombone, E flat bass tuba, B flat bass tuba, snare drum, cymbals, timpani.
The hymn tunes used in this prelude are (1) Ebenezer; (2) Calfaria; (3) Hyfrydol.
First performance: In private during February 1955; first (broadcast) performance in B.B.C. 'Listen to the Band' series, 12 March 1955, International Staff Band of Salvation Army, conducted by Bernard Adams; first public performance, London, Regent Hall, Oxford Street, 19 March 1955, by same artists.
Duration 9 minutes.
Publication: London, Salvationist Publishing and Supplies Ltd.

in *The Salvation Army Brass Band Journal Festival Series*, July, 1955
(© 1955).
Whereabouts of MS.: British Library. Full score and printed copy
(50402).

3. SYMPHONY No. 8 IN D MINOR.[1] For full orchestra. Composed
   1953–5, slight revision of finale, 1956.

   I. Fantasia (Variazioni senza Tema). *Moderato—presto—andante
   sostenuto—allegretto—andante non troppo—allegro vivace—andante
   sostenuto—Tempo I ma tranquillo.*

   II. Scherzo alla marcia (per stromenti a fiato). *Allegro alla marcia—
   andante—Tempo I (allegro).*

   III. Cavatina (per stromenti ad arco). *Lento espressivo.*

   IV. Toccata. *Moderato maestoso.*

Instrumentation: 2 flutes (2nd doubling piccolo), 2 oboes, 2 clarinets,
2 bassoons (3rd bassoon opt. in II), 2 horns, 2 trumpets, 3 trombones,
timpani, percussion (five players: side drum, triangle, cymbals, bass
drum, vibraphone, xylophone, glockenspiel, tubular bells, 3 tuned
gongs as used in Puccini's *Turandot*), celesta, 2 harps (1 opt.), strings.
The gongs are not absolutely essential, but their inclusion is highly
desirable. The tubular bells glissandi in the last movement can be
obtained by a rapid alternation of the left-hand hammer sweeping
across the top of the bells (above the bar) from right to left, and the
right-hand hammer across the centre (below the bar) from left to right.
First performance: Manchester, Free Trade Hall, 2 May 1956, The
Hallé Orchestra, conducted by Sir John Barbirolli; first performance in
London: Royal Festival Hall, 14 May 1956, by same artists.
Dedication: To John Barbirolli. [This is the inscription on the score.
When the composer presented Sir John with the autograph full score,
Sir John asked all the players in the first performance to sign it. At the
head of the list the composer wrote: 'For glorious John with love and
admiration from Ralph'.]
Duration: Approximately 28 minutes. (In my list of timings, Sir John
Barbirolli is shown as taking 26¾ minutes, and Sir Adrian Boult 29½
minutes.)
Composer's programme note: The symphony is scored for what is known
as the 'Schubert' orchestra: with the addition of a harp. Also there is a
large supply of extra percussion, including all the 'phones and 'spiels
known to the composer.
The *first movement*, as its title suggests, has been nicknamed 'seven

---

[1] This was the first of his symphonies which Vaughan Williams allowed to be given a
number. He originally called it 'Symphony in D' (minor was added later) but when it
was pointed out to him that this might cause confusion with the Fifth, he reluctantly
agreed to its being called No. 8.

variations in search of a theme'. There is indeed no definite theme. The opening section contains only a few isolated figures which are developed later, but that is all: here is a list of them.

The second section is played presto, and (*a*), (*b*), and (*c*) are juggled with alternately by wind and strings.

In the third section a choral-like melody appears on the strings and harp which proves to be a descant of (*a*).

This leads to a cantabile phrase for oboe and solo violoncello which seems to be another variation of (*a*).

There is also another phrase suggested by (*c*).

The fourth section, Allegretto 6/8, also starts with a variation of (*a*).

This gives way to still another variant of (*a*).

There is also a reference to (*c*).

The fifth section consists chiefly of the lengthening out of (*a*), starting with the violoncello and harp, the other instruments gradually joining in.

with another suggestion of (*c*).

We return to quick tempo in the sixth section which is chiefly occupied with (*a*) and a perversion of (*b*).

The seventh and last section is a repetition on a larger and more grandiose scale of the third section; starting softly, the music rises to a climax and then sinks down to softness, and the whole movement finishes with a reference to the opening.

I understand that some hearers may have their withers wrung by a work being called a symphony whose first movement does not correspond to the usual symphonic form. It may perhaps be suggested that by a little verbal jugglery this movement may be referred to the conventional scheme. Thus, the first section may be called the first subject; the second (presto), section can become the 'bridge passage'; the third section, starting at (*d*), may be described as the second subject. Sections four and five we will call the development, the allegro will be the reprise of the first subject, though this, I admit, will be skating over rather thin ice: but there will be no difficulty in referring the final section to the recapitulation and coda. Thus all wounds will be healed and honour satisfied.

The *second movement* (*Scherzo*) is, as its title suggests, for wind instruments only, namely, flute, piccolo, two oboes, two clarinets, three bassoons (third ad lib.), two horns, two trumpets and three trombones.

Under an accompaniment of repeated chords the bassoons have a tune, starting thus:

This is repeated by flute and piccolo while the bassoons have occasional scales. This leads to another tune, on the trumpet:

with a sequel played by the higher wind instruments.

A figure out of this section suggests a fugato which is started by the bassoons and carried on with various devices, such as stretto, augmentation, etc., by the rest of the band.

There is a short trio in 6/8 time.

There is no complete recapitulation of the scherzo, its place being taken by a short stretto and a few bars of coda. I think I may claim precedence for this idea of the truncated recapitulation in the third movement of Brahms's Clarinet Quintet.

In the *third movement* (*Cavatina*) the strings take over, thus giving the wind a well-earned rest. The violoncello start off with a cantilena twelve bars long, which begins thus:

This leads to a short episode of which we shall hear more later.

Then the violins take up (*a*) again, with occasional pizzicato scales in the bass: this leads to an important second section in triple time.

A development follows founded on this figure.

This development also contains a cadenza-like passage for the solo violin. Then comes the orthodox recapitulation of the opening theme, this time given to violas, cellos and basses, which leads to a shortened version of (*c*), and an arpeggio figure, based on (*d*), for a solo violoncello ends the movement.

The *fourth movement, Toccata,* besides full strings and wind, commandeers all the available hitting instruments which can make definite notes, including glockenspiel, celesta, xylophone, vibraphone, tubular bells and tunable gongs. These last are ad lib.: according to the score they are 'not absolutely essential but highly desirable'.

After a short, rather sinister exordium,

the trumpet gives out the principal theme, surrounded by all the tunable percussion.

There are thus two sections, each of which is repeated by full orchestra. Then comes another tune, given to strings and horns.

This returns us safely to the principal theme: indeed, we shall soon discover that this movement is a modified rondo. Music (*b*) and (*c*) recur at intervals, surrounded by episodes. The first episode is built up on this theme.

The second is characterized by the voice of the xylophone, and the third episode introduces vibraphone and celesta. The fourth episode consists of a resumption of (*d*) accompanied by glissandi on all the available percussion instruments. This leads to a final, and perhaps rather portentous statement of (*b*) and (*c*)—the symphony ends with a reference to the sinister exordium. R.V.W.

Publication: London, O.U.P. (© 1956). F.S. Parts on hire.

Separate items: Scherzo alla marcia (second movement) for wind instruments. O.U.P. (© 1958). Score and parts. Cavatina for strings (third movement). O.U.P. (© 1958). Score and parts.

Whereabouts of MS.: British Library. Full score (57338). Sketches (50376 and 50390) and incomplete rough full score (50377).

Revisions: I. Sketches have a fragment of folk-dance-like music headed 'opening string tune', which was abandoned, and a 'second subject' in F major. The 'andante sostenuto' and 'andante non troppo' variations were originally marked 'lento'. There is an early score showing a fairly complete version of variations 2–5 and possibly explaining the composer's remark about variations in search of a theme, for these were written first.

II. Originally scored without trombones. The final section (18 bars in final version) was considerably shorter. Minor alterations in instrumentation.

III. The chief alteration of any account is the discarding of 10 bars in a modal D major. Bars 6 and 7 after ⑨ were an afterthought. There are several versions of the final cello solo.

IV. Bars 8 and 14 of final version were insertions. Doubling of woodwind by celesta, not violins, at bars 8–10 after ② was discarded. A two-bar modulation from E flat to D after the third bar of ㉒ was abandoned in favour of the abrupt change to D at the largamente.

4. MUSIC FOR THE BRITISH TRANSPORT COMMISSION FILM 'THE ENGLAND OF ELIZABETH'. Composed autumn 1955. Music recorded 18 January 1956. Film produced by Ian Ferguson

(executive producer Edgar Anstey), directed by John Taylor.

Instrumentation: 2 flutes (2nd doubling piccolo), 1 oboe, 1 cor anglais, 2 clarinets, 1 bassoon, 2 horns, 2 trumpets, 3 trombones, timpani, percussion, harp, celesta, pianoforte, strings.

Film first shown: London, Leicester Square Theatre during the first week of March 1957. Music played by The Sinfonia of London, conducted by John Hollingsworth.

The music was continuous, but Vaughan Williams headed the sections: Titles, Street Scenes, Countryside, Tudor Houses, Portraits, Elizabeth, Hatfield, Henry VIII, Tintern, Books, Seamen, Dance, Wedding Procession, Country Dance, London, Theatres, Cradle, Map, School, Charlcote, Deer Park, Road to London, Armada, Battle, Waves, Aftermath, More maps, Treasures, New houses, Yeoman's Cottage, Shakespeare Song, Shakespeare's Tomb, King's College Introduction, Conclusion. During the recording at Beaconsfield of the music for this film, a short film of Vaughan Williams at work was made. This is now deposited in the National Film Archive.

Whereabouts of MS.: British Library. Full score and short score (60392). Original title on MS.: *The Elizabethan Age.*

4A. THREE PORTRAITS from 'THE ENGLAND OF ELIZABETH' Suite adapted for concert use by Muir Mathieson.

    I. Explorer. *Allegro maestoso—allegro animato.* (Based on the 'Titles' music of the film.)

    II. Poet. *Largo—andante tranquillo—allegro scherzando—lento—allegretto—largamente.*

    (The *allegro scherzando* and *allegretto* sections are, respectively, orchestral treatments of the sixteenth-century songs 'It was a lover and his lass' and 'The wind and the rain'. The *largo* opening, based on the film's 'Tintern' sequence, includes a theme which also occurs in *The Solent, A Sea Symphony,* and the Ninth Symphony).

    III. Queen. *Allegro maestoso—andante tranquillo—allegro maestoso—largo sostenuto.* (Based on film episodes 'Elizabeth', etc.)

Instrumentation: 2 flutes (2nd doubling piccolo), 1 oboe, 1 cor anglais, 2 clarinets, 1 bassoon, 2 horns, 2 trumpets, 3 trombones, timpani, percussion (side drum, triangle, cymbals, bass drum, glockenspiel, tubular bells in C, D, and E (E is opt.), vibraphone (opt.), tuned gong in E (opt.)), celesta (opt.), harp, strings. (Four players are needed for the full percussion scoring, but the work can be performed with two players only, omitting triangle and bass drum, etc., when necessary.)

Duration: 16½ minutes.

Publication: London, O.U.P. (© 1964). F.S. Parts available on hire.

4B. TWO SHAKESPEARE SKETCHES from 'THE ENGLAND
OF ELIZABETH'. Adapted for concert use by Muir Mathieson.
  I. *Allegro moderato.* ('The wind and the rain'.)
  II. *Allegretto—largamente.* ('It was a lover and his lass'.)
  (These are arrangements of two sections from 'Poet' in 4A.)
Instrumentation: 2 flutes (2nd doubling piccolo), 1 oboe, 2 clarinets,
1 bassoon, 2 horns, 2 trumpets, 3 trombones, timpani, percussion
(tabor, side drum, triangle), pianoforte, harp, strings. (All instru-
ments optional except strings.)
Publication: London, O.U.P. (© 1964). F.S. Music for Amateur
Orchestras Series. Parts on sale.

5. HANDS, EYES AND HEART. Song for medium voice and piano-
forte, *Andante tranquillo.* Composed early 1955 (completed by 7
March). Words by Ursula Vaughan Williams.
First performance: Christchurch, New Zealand, recital broadcast by
New Zealand Broadcasting Corporation, 21 December 1956, Keith
Falkner (baritone), Christabel Falkner (pianoforte).
First performance in England: B.B.C. Home Service, 3 August 1960,
Pamela Bowden (contralto), Ernest Lush (pianoforte).
Publication: London, O.U.P. © 1960 (See *Four Last Songs*, 1958,
entry No.2).
Whereabouts of MS.: In possession of Sir Keith Falkner.

6. 'DIABELLERIES' (Variations by various composers for 11 instru-
ments on a theme 'Oh! Where's my little basket gone?' attributed to
Alfred Scott-Gatty). As its punning title implies, this was a compo-
site work by R.V.W. (who suggested it), Howard Ferguson, Alan
Bush, Alan Rawsthorne, Elizabeth Lutyens, Elizabeth Maconchy,
Gerald Finzi, Grace Williams, and Gordon Jacob.
Unpublished: Instrumentation of R.V.W.'s variation (an orchestra-
tion of the theme): Flute, oboe, B flat clarinet, bassoon, horn, trum-
pet, 2 violins, viola, cello, double bass.
First performance: London, Arts Council, 4 St. James's Square,
16 May 1955, ensemble conducted by Iris Lemare.
Whereabouts of MS.: British Library. Full score and parts (some
autograph, others in hands of Anne Macnaghten and Richard Rodney
Bennett) (59809).

1956

1. A VISION OF AEROPLANES. Motet for mixed chorus (SATB)
and organ. Words from Ezekiel, Chapter I. *Moderato—alla marcia—
più lento.*
First performance: London, St. Michael's Church, Cornhill, 4 June

1956, St. Michael's Singers, conducted by Dr. Harold Darke, John Birch (organist).
Dedication: To Harold Darke and his St. Michael's Singers.
Duration: 10 minutes.
Publication: London, O.U.P. (© 1956).
Whereabouts of MS.: Formerly in possession of the late Dr. Harold Darke.

2. A CHORAL FLOURISH. For mixed chorus (SAT and high Bar. B) with introduction for organ or two trumpets. Words from Psalm XXXII (Authorized Version, Psalm XXXIII). Original setting is for Latin words, with English version as alternative.
First performance: London, Royal Festival Hall, 3 November 1956, 21st anniversary of National Federation of Music Societies. Royal Choral Society, Bach Choir, Croydon Philharmonic Society, St. Michael's Singers, conducted by Dr. Reginald Jacques.
Dedication: To Alan Kirby.
Publication: London, O.U.P. (© 1956). V.S.

3. TWO ORGAN PRELUDES. Founded on Welsh folk songs.
   I. Romanza ('The White Rock'). *Andante sostenuto.*
   II. Toccata ('St. David's Day'). *Allegro.*
Publication: London, O.U.P. (© 1956). II also published as No. 3 and I as No. 5 of *A Vaughan Williams Organ Album* (1964).
Whereabouts of MS.: British Library (50403).

4. GOD BLESS THE MASTER OF THIS HOUSE. From the Sussex Mummers' Carol, arranged for mixed chorus (SATB), unaccompanied. *Lento maestoso.*
Publication: London, O.U.P. (© 1956). (Oxford Folk Song Series, No. 52.)
Whereabouts of MS.: British Library. Vocal Score (50480).

5. 'SCHMÜCKE DICH, O LIEBE SEELE'. By J. S. Bach, arranged for violoncello and strings by R. Vaughan Williams. *Unpublished.*
First performance: London, Friends' House, Euston Road, 28 December 1956, London Bach Group concert in honour of Casals Birthday Fund (Casals's 80th birthday was on 29 December 1956). Anthony Pini (cello), Collegium Musicum Londinii, conducted by John Minchinton.
Whereabouts of MS.: In private possession.

6. FEN AND FLOOD. Cantata for male chorus (TTBar.B) and orchestra by Patrick Hadley (1899–1973), arranged for soprano and baritone soloists, mixed chorus (SATB) by R. Vaughan Williams. Libretto by Charles Cudworth, dealing with the history of the Fen Country from primeval times to the great flood of 1953.
First performance: Cambridge, Hall of Gonville and Caius College,

12 June 1955. Caius Chorus, conducted by Professor Patrick Hadley, with score reduced for two pianofortes ('and,' the composer says, 'odd instruments in addition which happened to be available'), Anne Keynes (soprano), Malcolm Hossick (baritone). First performance of SATB version: King's Lynn Festival, St. Nicholas's Chapel, 27 July 1956, B.B.C. Midland Chorus and Orchestra, conducted by Stanford Robinson, with Jennifer Vyvyan (soprano), Gillian Martin (soprano, a schoolgirl who sang only *Walsingham*), Hervey Alan (baritone) and Fred Calvert (baritone). Mr. Calvert was the King's Lynn Superintendent of police who directed rescue operations in the 1953 floods. He sang in Part II, section from K to N. The words are those which he used during the rescue work.

Publication: London, O.U.P. 1956 (SATB version only).

1957

1. EPITHALAMION. A Cantata founded on the Masque, *The Bridal Day*, for baritone, mixed chorus and small orchestra. Words chosen by Ursula Vaughan Williams from Spenser's *Epithalamion* (from stanzas 2, 3, 5, 7, 8, 9, 10, 12, 14, 15, 18, 20, 22 and 78. The extracts from 9 and 10 do not occur in *The Bridal Day*).

Instrumentation: 1 flute (doubling piccolo), pianoforte, strings.

    I. Prologue. Chorus. *Andante con moto—allegretto.*

    II. 'Wake Now.' Baritone solo and chorus. *Allegretto.*

    III. The Calling of the Bride. Chorus. (Over 50 bars of new material.) *Allegro moderato.*

    IV. The Minstrels. Chorus. *Allegro.*

    V. Procession of the Bride. (Chorus.) ('Procession of relatives' in *The Bridal Day*.) *Andante maestoso.*

    VI. The Temple Gates. (Chorus.) *Adagio—allegro.*

    VII. The Bellringers. (Chorus.) (10 bars of new material.) *Andante con moto.*

    VIII. The Lover's Song. (Baritone and chorus.) *Andante sostenuto—poco animato.*

    IX. The Minstrel's Song. (Baritone and chorus.) *Andante sostenuto—tranquillo.*

    X. Song of the Winged Loves. (Women's chorus.) *Allegretto.*

    XI. Prayer to Juno. (Baritone and chorus.) *Molto adagio—allegro—andante maestoso.*

First performance: London, Royal Festival Hall, New Era Concert Society, 30 September 1957. Gordon Clinton (baritone), Goldsmiths' Choral Union Cantata Singers, Royal Philharmonic Orchestra, conducted by Richard Austin.

Duration: 37 minutes.

Publication: London, O.U.P. (© 1957). V.S. Parts and vocal scores on hire.

Whereabouts of MS.: British Library. Vocal and full scores, in nine notebooks (50479).

For THE BRIDAL DAY *see* 1938, No. 6.

2. VARIATIONS FOR BRASS BAND. *Andante maestoso*; Variation I, *Poco tranquillo*; II, *Tranquillo cantabile*; III, *Allegro*; IV, (Canon), *Allegro*; V, *Moderato sostenuto*; VI, *Tempo di Valse*; VII (Arabesque), *andante sostenuto*; VIII, *Alla Polacca*; IX, *Adagio*; X (Fugato), *Allegro moderato*; XI (Chorale).

Instrumentation: E flat soprano cornet, solo B flat cornet, Repiano B flat cornet and flügel horn, 2 B flat cornets, solo E flat horn and 2 E flat horns, 2 B flat baritone saxophones, 2 B flat trombones and bass trombone, 1 B flat euphonium, 2 bass tubas, drums, timpani.

First performance: London, Royal Albert Hall, 26 October 1957, National Brass Band Championship of Great Britain, where it was the test piece for 21 bands. Winner was Munn and Felton's (Footwear) Band of Kettering. At Festival Concert that evening the work was played by the Massed Bands (Fairey Aviation Works, Carlton Main Frickley Colliery, Clydebank Burgh, C.W.S. (Manchester), Morris Motors and Munn and Felton's Works Bands), conducted by Dr. Karl Rankl.

Duration: 12 minutes.

Publication: London, Boosey and Hawkes (© 1957) (Brass Band *Journal*, No. 867).

Whereabouts of MS.: British Library. Full Score and sketches (50404–5).

Orchestral version: VARIATIONS FOR ORCHESTRA. Arranged by Gordon Jacob (with revision by Frank Wright).

Instrumentation: 2 flutes (2nd doubling piccolo), 2 oboes, 2 clarinets, 2 bassoons, 4 horns, 2 trumpets, 3 trombones, 1 tuba, timpani, percussion (2 players), strings.

First performance: Birmingham, Town Hall, 8 January 1960, City of Birmingham Orchestra, conducted by Sir Adrian Boult. First performance in London: Royal Festival Hall, 5 May 1960, London Philharmonic Orchestra, conducted by Sir Adrian Boult.

Duration: 12 minutes.

Parts on hire from O.U.P.

3. FLOURISH FOR GLORIOUS JOHN. From R.V.W. For full orchestra. Unpublished. (59 bars). *Moderato maestoso.*

Instrumentation: 2 flutes (2nd doubling piccolo), 2 oboes, 1 cor anglais, 2 clarinets, 1 bass clarinet, 2 bassoons, 1 double bassoon, 4 horns,

3 trumpets, 3 trombones, 1 tuba, timpani, percussion (side drum, bass drum, cymbals, glockenspiel, tubular bells), harp, organ, pianoforte, strings.

First performance: Manchester, Free Trade Hall, 16 October 1957. The Hallé Orchestra, conducted by Sir John Barbirolli. (Opening of the Orchestra's 100th Season, for which occasion it was specially written.)

Duration: 3 minutes (approx.).

Whereabouts of MS.: British Library. Full score (57339). MS. of piano reduction in private possession.

4. SYMPHONY No. 9 IN E MINOR. For full orchestra. Composed 1956–7. Revised between 21 March and 2 April 1958.

I. Moderato maestoso—tranquillo.

II. Andante sostenuto—moderato tranquillo—poco animato ma pesante—moderato sostenuto—Tempo I.

III. Scherzo: *Allegro pesante.*

IV. Andante tranquillo—poco animato—andante sostenuto—poco meno mosso—ancora poco animando—poco animato $\downarrow = 112$ ma pesante—largamente.

Instrumentation: 3 flutes (3rd doubling piccolo), 2 oboes, 1 cor anglais, 2 clarinets, 1 bass clarinet, 2 bassoons, 1 double bassoon, 2 E flat saxophones, 1 B flat saxophone, 4 horns, 1 flügel horn in B flat, 2 trumpets, 3 trombones, tuba, timpani, percussion (5 players: glockenspiel, xylophone, side drum, bass drum, tenor drum, cymbals, triangle, very large (deep) gong, tam-tam, deep bells), 2 harps, celesta, strings. The first E flat saxophone is indispensable, the other two 'nearly so' and can be dispensed with by playing the cues chiefly in bassoon and clarinet parts. The flügel horn is very important, but if one is unobtainable, the part may be played in the tutti on a 3rd trumpet, some solo passages being cued in for 1st trumpet or 1st horn. The flügel horn part must never be played on a cornet; a real flügel horn mouthpiece must be used.

First performance: London, Royal Festival Hall, Royal Philharmonic Society Concert, 2 April 1958. The Royal Philharmonic Orchestra, conducted by Sir Malcolm Sargent.

Dedication: To The Royal Philharmonic Society.

Duration: 36 minutes.

Composer's note: This symphony was begun, except for a few vague sketches, early in 1956, and was finished, so far as a composition ever is finished,[1] in November 1957. It was written chiefly in London, but partly

---

[1] This phrase illustrates one of R.V.W.'s profound beliefs. When I stayed with him in August 1958, he came into his study in the morning and began to play the first movement of the Ninth Symphony on his upright pianoforte. One section seemed to be

in Majorca and partly at Ashmansworth, the home of Gerald and Joyce Finzi. It is dedicated to the Royal Philharmonic Society, and was first played at a concert on 2 April 1958 by the Royal Philharmonic Orchestra conducted by Sir Malcolm Sargent.

The usual symphony orchestra is used, with the addition of three saxophones and flügel horn. This beautiful and neglected instrument is not usually allowed in the select circles of the orchestra and has been banished to the brass band, where it is allowed to indulge in the bad habit of vibrato to its heart's content. While in the orchestra it will be obliged to sit up and play straight. The saxophones, also, are not expected, except possibly in one place in the scherzo, to behave like demented cats, but are allowed to be their own romantic selves. Otherwise the orchestration is normal, and is, the composer hopes, sound in wind and strings.

There are four movements, as is usual in a symphony. The first movement, *Allegro Moderato*, is not in strict sonata form but obeys the general principles of statement, contrast and repetition, which is the basis of all musical form.

The opening subject is this:

It is played by the trombones and tuba, and then repeated a fifth higher by the other brass, surrounded by an E pedal in four octaves. This theme occurred to the composer after playing some of the organ part of the opening of Bach's St. Matthew Passion. Those who are curious about these matters can doubtless trace the connection. This section finishes with a cadential passage founded on the Neapolitan sixth played by the saxophones against a minor tonic chord on the strings.

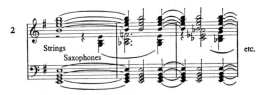

The opening is repeated, with a counter-theme after this pattern.

---

troubling him and I asked the reason. He replied that in the night he had dreamed of a new tune for this movement but could not now remember just where it had 'fitted'. After a time he stopped, saying: 'Well, never mind, it will come back if it's really needed.'

Then follows what is apparently a second subject, played on three clarinets.

Surely there is something wrong here? The second subject should be in G major? But all will be explained before long. This theme, 4, gradually unfolds itself with passing references to 1, till G major is reached. The correct key for the second subject at last; but, oh dear, it is not a new subject at all but a version of 4, developed and extended. Never mind, Haydn often does much the same, and what is good enough for the master is good enough for the man. We now successfully return to the home key, E, but major this time, not minor. But alas, there is no sign of the first subject, instead another version of 4 develops into a rhapsodical passage on the solo violin accompanied by harp and pizzicato strings. Surely there is something wrong again, here? Well, it's Joseph Haydn to the rescue once more: the fact is the composer had forgotten all about the first subject, so he adds it now, very softly, hoping it doesn't intrude. This is the end of the movement, except for the saxophone cadence, *à la Napolitaine*.

The second movement, *Andante Sostenuto*, seems to have no logical connection between its various themes. This has led some people to think it must have a programme since apparently programme music need not be logical. It is quite true that this movement started off with a programme, but it got lost on the journey—so now, oh no, we never mention it—and the music must be left to speak for itself—whatever that may mean.

Here is the opening theme:

It is played on the flügel horn (senza vibrato!).

There is a footnote in the score that it must never be played on the cornet, and if the flügel horn unfortunately is not available, the passage must be played on the French horn. This theme is borrowed from an early work of the composer's,[1] luckily long since scrapped, but changed so that its own father would hardly recognize it.

[1] The tone-poem *The Solent*. See 1903, No. 12.

The episode which follows is a strong contrast; a barbaric march theme:

against which there is a counter-theme:

A sudden modulation to B flat minor brings back a version of 5, followed by a romantic episode in triple time, played chiefly by the strings.

followed by another theme:

and

Then a menacing stroke on the gong brings back a reminiscence of 5. Why is a gong in the orchestra always supposed to be menacing? To the unmusical hearer a note on the gong means dinner; this perhaps often is menacing enough, as a well-known parody of a hymn reminds us. Anyhow, the gong stroke gives a sinister aspect to this theme. Then a quick crescendo leads to a re-statement of 6, played by the full force of the orchestra, which dies down again to softness, and the flügel horn and its tune are once more heard, this time with a counter subject below it on the clarinet.

The third movement, *Allegro Pesante*, is a scherzo. After a few preliminary side-drum taps the opening theme is announced on three saxophones:

A repetition of this in a higher octave leads to a new theme:

and then to

Indeed, this is a movement of juxtaposition, not of development. A cadenza-like passage on the three saxophones leads to the most important of the subsidiary themes:

The composer, to his delight, discovered that by a little jugglery this tune could be made to go in canon; he could not resist the temptation. For some time the music has been loud; it now dies down to introduce the recapitulation, which is not exact, but takes the form of a fugato on this theme:

The various subsidiary themes are introduced in turn as counterpoints to the fugue subject. All well mannered orchestral fugues must be interrupted by a choral; this duly happens, thus:

(This is where the demented cats come in.)
The well-mannered choral, after its first statement, should of course be combined with the fugue subject. The composer tried this, but found the result so dull that he scrapped it and substituted a simple repetition of the choral with rather fuller instrumentation. Then, as a climax, comes a re-statement of the opening theme, 11, at half the speed, for full orchestra, thus:

This leads to another saxophone cadenza, and lastly, the first saxophone plays its little tune very softly accompanied by the side drum. When the tune is finished the side drum goes on by itself and quietly taps itself to death.

Only a very short pause separates the scherzo from the last movement, *Andante Tranquillo*. This final movement is really two movements, played without break, and connected by three short phrases which recur throughout:

We start off with a long cantilena played by the violins,

It is answered by the violas and a florid counterpoint on the clarinet adds its quota. This leads to the first of the before-mentioned connecting phrases.
This in its turn leads to another new tune:

It is played on the horn, to an accompaniment of Verdi-like arpeggios on the woodwind. This is repeated and extended and leads to a loud repetition of 18, which in its turn leads to the two other connecting links, 19 and 20, both soft. Then 'all that again' as Purcell would say, but differently coloured. This leads to a loud statement of 20 which, however, soon softens down and is followed by an episode, 23, which divides the two sections of the movement.

The second half starts with this tune played on the violas, under a high pedal G.

This tune develops itself, at first it is soft, but gradually wakes up and becomes loud and contrapuntal. The three connecting themes are also heard, then 24 is blared out by the full orchestra in two-part harmony, we hear a suggestion of 19, and the movement ends with the saxophones once more in their Neapolitan vein, but this time with the final chord of E major. R.V.W.

Publication: London, O.U.P. (© 1958). F.S. Parts on hire.

Whereabouts of MS.: British Library. Sketches for each movement (50378–81); pianoforte score and Roy Douglas's queries (50382); early full score (50383); final full score (50384). One of the sketches in 50378, is marked 'Wessex Prelude', a pointer to the original programmatic basis of the symphony.

Revisions: A study of the very fully documented genesis of this work is possible from the British Library manuscripts. The principal changes are in a constant urge towards compression. An important change is at the end of the first movement where the coda was originally based on the second subject, not the first.

II. The present first tune is a complete substitution for the original sketch.

III. The two bars after ⌧36⌧ were a late interpolation. The 'cats' choral' episode was also a late evolution of an early sketch. In one of the early versions, the second theme (3 bars after ⌧2⌧) is missing and the tune which now occurs at ⌧5⌧ is inscribed 'Georgia'.

IV. The composer made cuts in this movement, originally entitled 'Landscape', after the first play-through on 21 March 1958. The actual ending of the work was extensively worked over. The present bars 1–3 after ⌧14⌧ are the relics of 25 bars of a G major episode which was deleted when the score was in preparation by the publisher, hence the absence of rehearsal figure ⌧15⌧. A sketched version in E of the theme at ⌧16⌧ was inscribed 'Introibo ad altarem Dei', a relic of the symphony's original 'Salisbury' programme.

5. TEN BLAKE SONGS. For voice and oboe. Composed Christmastide, 1957. Words by William Blake.
1. Infant Joy (Songs of Innocence) (tenor or soprano). *Andante con moto.*
2. A Poison Tree (Songs of Experience) (tenor). *Lento ma moderato.*
3. The Piper (S. of I.) (tenor or soprano). *Allegro moderato.*
4. London (S. of E.) (tenor). *In free time* (oboe silent).
5. The Lamb (S. of I.) (tenor). *Andante con moto.*
6. The Shepherd (S. of I.) (tenor or soprano). *Allegretto* (oboe silent).
7. Ah! Sunflower (S. of E.) (tenor). *Moderato.*
8. Cruelty has a human heart (S. of E.) (tenor or soprano). *Moderato.*
9. The Divine Image (S. of I.) (tenor or soprano). *Semplice* (oboe silent).
10. Eternity (Miscellaneous Poems) (tenor or soprano). *Andante sostenuto.*

These songs were written for the film *The Vision of William Blake*, produced and directed in 1958 by Guy Brenton and made by his company, Morse Films, for the Bi-centenary Committee of the Blake Society. They were performed by Wilfred Brown (tenor) and Janet Craxton (oboe) and only eight were used in the film (Nos. 2 and 3 were excluded). The rest of the music of the film was extracts from *Job*. The film was first shown at the Academy Cinema, London, on 10 October 1958, having previously been shown privately to the Blake Society.

First concert performance: B.B.C. Third programme, 8 October 1958, Wilfred Brown (tenor), Janet Craxton (oboe). First public performance: London, Arts Council, 4 St. James's Square, 14 November 1958, Macnaghten Concert, by the same artists.
Dedication: To Wilfred Brown and Janet Craxton.
Duration: 19 minutes.
Note: The oboe parts may, in case of necessity, be played on a violin or (by transposing the songs down a tone) on a B flat clarinet—but neither of these expedients is advisable. R.V.W.
Publication: London, O.U.P. (© 1958).
Whereabouts of MS: British Library (50481).

1958

1. THREE VOCALISES. For soprano voice and B flat clarinet.
I. Prelude. *Moderato.*
II. Scherzo. *Allegro moderato.*
III. Quasi menuetto. *Moderato.*

First performance: Manchester, Free Trade Hall, 8 October 1958, Margaret Ritchie (soprano); Keith Puddy (clarinet). First London

performance: B.B.C. Home Service, 22 December 1958, Margaret
Ritchie (soprano), Gervase de Peyer (clarinet).
Dedication: To Margaret Ritchie.
Duration: 5 minutes.
Publication: London, O.U.P. (© 1960).
Note: It is probable that the composer would have added more dyna-
mic indications had he been able to revise the work before publication.
No dynamics other than those which appear in the MS. have been
added.
Whereabouts of MS.: British Library   (52614 and 50481).

2. FOUR LAST SONGS. For medium voice and pianoforte. Composed
between 1954 and 1958. Words by Ursula Vaughan Williams. These
songs were the completed parts of two projected song-cycles. All are
suitable for mezzo-soprano and Nos. 1, 2 and 4 for baritone. (1) Procris.
(1958) *Andante sostenuto.* (2) Tired. (1956) *Andante sostenuto.* (3)
Hands, Eyes and Heart. (1955) *Andante tranquillo.* (4) Menelaus.
(1954) *Andante moderato.* Nos. 3 and 4 were first sung separately (see
1955, entry No. 5, and 1954, entry No. 6).
First performance of cycle: B.B.C. Home Service, 3 August 1960,
Pamela Bowden (contralto), Ernest Lush (pianoforte); first performance
of songs nos. 1 and 2: London, Arts Council, 4 St. James's Square,
Macnaghten Concert, 27 November 1959, John Carol Case (baritone),
Daphne Ibbott (pianoforte).
Duration: 12 minutes.
Note: Dynamic marks in parentheses in the printed score were sug-
gested by Roy Douglas.
Publication: London, O.U.P. (© 1960).
Whereabouts of MS: In private possession.

3. THE FIRST NOWELL. A Nativity play for soloists, mixed chorus
(SATB) and small orchestra. Libretto adapted from medieval pageants
by Simona Pakenham. Music composed and arranged from traditional
tunes by R. Vaughan Williams, with additions after R.V.W.'s death by
Roy Douglas.
Speaking parts: Creator, Gabriel, Mary, Elizabeth, Joseph, Caspar,
Melchior, Balthazar.
Singing parts: Soprano soloist, baritone soloist, angels (chorus
SATB).
Speaking and singing parts: 1st Shepherd (baritone or bass); 2nd Shep-
herd (tenor); 3rd Shepherd (tenor or treble).
Instrumentation: 2 flutes, 1 oboe, 2 clarinets, 1 bassoon, 2 horns, 2
trumpets, tenor trombone, bass trombone, timpani, harp, strings.
   1. Prelude. Baritone solo and chorus. *Andante sostenuto—moderato
   —andante sostenuto.*

2. Orchestra and speaker. *Andante con moto.*

3. Soprano solo. *Allegretto.*

4. (completed by Roy Douglas) Chorus. *Allegretto.*

5. Soprano solo. *Allegretto.*

6. Chorus. *Andante con moto.*

7. (slightly revised by R.D.) Soprano solo. *Andante tranquillo.*

8. Soprano (or baritone solo in concert version) and chorus. *Andante.*

9. Women's chorus. *Andante tranquillo.* Oboe solo 'It's a rosebud in June'.

10. Oboe solo. *Lento.*

11. Horn solo.

12. Tenor I (or Treble), Tenor II, Bass. *Allegro.* Dance (added by R.D.)

13. Chorus off-stage. *Lento—andante sostenuto—con moto.* Viola solo 'It's a rosebud in June'.

14. Tenor I (or Treble). *Allegretto.*

15. (adapted by R.D.) Baritone solo and chorus. *Allegretto.*

16. (added by R.D.) Tenor I (or Treble), Tenor II, Bass. *Allegretto.*

17. (Constructed from sketches, by R.D.) Chorus. *Maestoso con moto.* (Translation of words by R.V.W.)

18. (added by R.D.) Orchestra.

19. (Constructed from sketches, by R.D.) Chorus. *Maestoso con moto.* (Translation by R.V.W.)

20. (completed by R.D.) Full. *Andante sostenuto—poco più mosso.*

Note in score 2 bars before $\boxed{H}$ says: 'At this point the original manuscript full score ends; the remainder of this section has been constructed and developed, by R.D., from the composer's fragmentary sketches'. Alternative ending provided by R.D.

Note: For concert version, following numbers should be included: 1, 3, 4, 6, 7, 8, 9, 15, 16, 17, 18, 20. Nos. 2, 5 and 12 may also be included if wished.

The following traditional tunes are included: 'God rest you merry', 'God bless the master', 'This is the truth sent from above', 'Angelus ad virginem', 'The Salutation Carol', 'Eia Mater Domini', 'The Cherry Tree Carol', 'As Joseph was a-walking', 'O, Joseph being an old man truly', 'In Bethlehem City', 'It's a rosebud in June', 'Bring us in good ale', 'On Christmas Night', 'The First Nowell'. Also used is the 'Gloria in Excelsis' from Taverner's 'Western Wynde' Mass, chosen by R.V.W. and edited by R.D. from *Tudor Church Music* (O.U.P.).

First performance: London, Theatre Royal, Drury Lane, 19 December 1958 (as part of St. Martin-in-the-Fields Christmas matinée) with following cast:

CREATOR   ..   ..   Peter Coke

GABRIEL	John Westbrook
MARY	Thea Holme
ELIZABETH	Molly Rankin
JOSEPH	Eric Dodson
CASPAR	Kenneth Fortescue
MELCHIOR	Raf de la Torre
BALTHAZAR	Edric Connor
1ST SHEPHERD	Anna Pollak
2ND SHEPHERD	Andrew Downie
3RD SHEPHERD	George Rose
SOPRANO SOLOIST	Eileen Poulter
BARITONE..	Geraint Evans

St. Martin-in-the-Fields Concert Orchestra and Singers, conducted by John Churchill. Produced by Noel Iliff and Geraldine Stephenson.
Duration: Stage version, 50 minutes; concert version, 30 minutes.
Publication: London, O.U.P. (© 1959), Vocal score and libretto. Material and vocal scores on hire, also arrangement of accompaniment for strings and organ (or pianoforte).
Whereabouts of MS: In possession of Roy Douglas Esq.
Separate publication: THREE CHRISTMAS TUNES from *The First Nowell*, adapted for brass quartet by Roy Douglas, 1. As Joseph Was A-Walking. 2. On Christmas Night. 3. How brightly shone the Morning Star. O.U.P. © 1977.

OTHER POSTHUMOUS PUBLICATIONS

1. THE PENGUIN BOOK OF ENGLISH FOLK SONGS. Edited by R. Vaughan Williams and A. L. Lloyd. Specimen accompaniments by R.V.W. to 'Salisbury Plain', 'Banks of Green Willow' and 'The Basket of Eggs', but the editors urge that the best way to sing folk songs is unaccompanied. The volume contains 70 songs. The following are from R.V.W.'s collection (date of collection in brackets):
'All Things are quite silent' (Sussex, 1904). 'The Basket of Eggs' (Sussex, 1903). 'The Blacksmith' (Herefordshire, 1909). 'The Broom-field Hill' (Herefordshire, with Mrs. Leather, 1910). 'The Devil and the Ploughman' (Sussex, 1903). 'Fare thee well, my dearest dear' Sussex, (1904). 'The Green Bed' (Hampshire, 1909). 'Lovely Joan' (Norfolk, 1908). 'The Man of Burningham Town' (Norfolk, 1908). 'On Monday Morning' (Hampshire, 1909). 'The Outlandish Knight' (Norfolk, 1908). 'Oxford City' (Norfolk, 1905). 'The Ploughman' (Sussex, 1904). 'Ratcliffe Highway' (Norfolk, 1905). 'Robin Hood and the Pedlar' (Sussex, 1906). 'A Sailor in the North Country' (Sussex, 1904). 'Salisbury Plain' (Sussex, 1904). 'The Young and Single Sailor' (Surrey, 1904). 'Young Edwin in the Lowlands Low' (Hampshire, with Charles Gamblin, 1907).

Publication: Penguin Books 1959. © A. L. Lloyd and the representatives of R. Vaughan Williams, 1959.

UNDATABLE POSTHUMOUS PUBLICATION

1. ROMANCE FOR VIOLA AND PIANOFORTE. *Andante—poco animato—Tempo I.*
First performance: London, Arts Council, 4 St. James's Square, Macnaghten concert, 19 January 1962. Bernard Shore (viola) and Eric Gritton (pianoforte).
Note: There is no information about the date of this work. It may have been intended for Lionel Tertis.
Publication: London, O.U.P. (© 1962). Viola part edited by Bernard Shore; pianoforte part edited by Eric Gritton.
Whereabouts of MS: British Library. Copy by Adeline Vaughan Williams (Add. 50863).

WORKS LEFT INCOMPLETE

1. CONCERTO FOR VIOLONCELLO AND ORCHESTRA. Sketches and fair copies of this work seem to date first from 1942–3. It was intended for Casals, and the composer was 'looking at it' again from 1953 onwards. There are three movements:
    I. Rhapsody. *Andante con moto.*
    II. Lento.
    III. Finale. *Allegro moderato.*
Sketches of a scherzo were abandoned.
Some of the themes are:
Opening of first movement:

First tutti:

Opening of slow movement:

Opening of finale:

Whereabouts of MS.: British Library (57292).

2. THOMAS THE RHYMER. An Opera in 3 Acts.
   Libretto by Ursula Vaughan Williams, based on two ballads, *Thomas the Rhymer* and *Tam Lin*. This was the principal work on which Vaughan Williams was engaged when he died. The work is completed in pianoforte and vocal score, but he had not begun to score it fully or to revise it. Since it cannot be known what further changes he and the librettist might have made, it is not fair to his memory to reproduce examples of what was still an embryonic work.

3. SKETCHES. Among incomplete works in Vaughan Williams's late sketchbooks were proposed settings of Robert Graves's 'Star Talk', Chesterton's 'In Praise of Wine,' themes for a string quartet and more notes for his 'Belshazzar' opera. There were sketches of a 'Vibraphone piece', *Exsultate Jubilate* for double choir; 'London Calling'; and a Romance for organ. Some 'Notes' for the vibraphone piece are in the British Library (50378) and some belong to me. Other sketches in the British Library are of R.V.W.'s pianoforte continuo for four numbers in Bach's *St. Matthew Passion* (50378), an introduction to a masque (50378), folk songs, organ prelude, military march, and symphony (57294D), folk songs (57294F), and sketches for a symphony (57294G).

BY OTHER EDITORS

1. A YACRE OF LAND. Sixteen folk songs from the manuscript collection of Ralph Vaughan Williams. Edited by Imogen Holst and Ursula Vaughan Williams. Arranged for unison voices and pianoforte or for unaccompanied part-singing by Imogen Holst.
   1. A Yacre of Land (1904) SAB
   2. John Reilly (1904) SAB
   3. The Week Before Easter (1904) SAB
   4. Willie Foster (1906) SAB
   5. The Jolly Harin' (1904) SAB or TBB
   6. Nine Joys of Mary (1907) SAB
   7. Joseph and his Wedded Wife (1905) SATB
   8. The Lord of Life (1906) SSA or SSAB
   9. Over the hills and mountains (1906) SSA

10. The Foxhunt (1905) SSA
11. Come all you young ploughboys (1906) SSA
12. A Bold Young Sailor (1905) SA or SAT
13. The Pretty Ploughboy (1904) SA
14. Seventeen Come Sunday (1907) SA
15. It was one Morning (1905) SA
16. My coffin shall be black (1906) SA

Names of singers and dates of collection are given in the score. (They may be discovered on pages 261–95 of this book.)
Publication: London, O.U.P. (© 1961). Full edition and melody and words edition.

2. A VAUGHAN WILLIAMS ORGAN ALBUM.
Contains the following:
1. A Wedding Tune for Ann. *Andante con moto.* Edited by Christopher Morris. (See 1943, No. 6.) (© 1964.)
2. Greensleeves. *Andante moderato.* Arranged by Stanley Roper. (© 1947.)
3. Toccata ('St. David's Day'). *Allegro.* Originally No. 2 of *Two Organ Preludes founded on Welsh Folk Songs.* (© 1956.)
4. Carol. *Andante con moto.* Arranged by Herbert Sumsion from *Suite for Viola.* (© 1938.)
5. Romanza ('The White Rock'). *Andante sostenuto.* Originally No. 1 of *Two Organ Preludes founded on Welsh Folk Songs.* (© 1956.)
6. Prelude ('The New Commonwealth'). *Andante con moto.* Arranged by Christopher Morris. (© 1960.)
7. Musette. *Lento—poco animato—Tempo I.* Arranged by Herbert Sumsion from *Suite for Viola.* (© 1938.)
8. Land of Our Birth. *Moderato—maestoso.* Arranged by S. de B. Taylor from *Song of Thanksgiving.* (© 1961.)
Publication: London, O.U.P. (© 1964).

3. NINE ENGLISH FOLK SONGS FROM THE SOUTHERN APPALACHIAN MOUNTAINS. For voice and pianoforte.
These arrangements were made by Vaughan Williams in about 1938 and given to Maud Karpeles. References in parentheses below are to versions of the songs in *English Folk Songs from the Southern Appalachians*, collected by Cecil J. Sharp, edited by Maud Karpeles (London, O.U.P. 1952).
1. The Elfin Knight, or The Lovers' Tasks (1A). *Andante*
2. Lord Randal (7H). *Lento moderato*
3. Lord Thomas and Fair Ellinor (19M). *Allegro*
4. Fair Margaret and Sweet William (20L). *Moderato*

5. Barbara Allen (24M). *Andantino*
6. The Daemon Lover, or The House Carpenter (35M). *Andante con moto*
7. The Rich Old Lady (55A). *Allegro*
8. The Tree in the Wood (206B). *Allegro*
9. The Ten Commandments, or The Twelve Apostles (207D). *Allegro*

Note: The tempo indications are those originally assigned by R.V.W.
Publication: London, O.U.P. © 1967.
Separate publications: Arranged for unison voices with pianoforte accompaniment. 1. The Rich Old Lady. 2. The Tree in the Wood. 3. The Twelve Apostles. London, O.U.P. (© 1968). Oxford Unison Songs U.135, U.136, and U.137.

FOLK SONGS: Sketchbooks of Vaughan Williams's folk song collections held in the British Library are catalogued as Additional MSS. 54187–91, 59535, 59536, and 57294 D and F.

Folk Songs collected by
Vaughan Williams

WHAT follows is a chronological list, as complete as surviving documentation will allow, of Vaughan Williams's manuscript collection of folk songs and variants, compiled from his notebooks. Names of the original singers are given where known, with quotations from R.V.W.'s biographical notes about them. The size of the list tells of the labour involved; to read through it is to recall a vanished England, and its bare comments on where the songs were collected—'at the level crossing', 'in the workhouse', 'in the inn'—are eloquent in themselves. It is possible to recapture something of the zeal of the young collector—a journey to one village to collect one song, a convivial evening in a country inn where one singer has started his companions off so that they then went through their repertoire. The singers themselves have their place in English musical history and it is well that their names are recorded in Vaughan Williams's and others' collections. These are men (and women) from whom our ways begin, but in their case, fortunately, it is not true to add

       'There is silence, there survives
       Not a moment of your lives.'

Some attained fame in their lifetimes. Henry Burstow, a bootmaker, of Horsham, sang to Lucy Broadwood and to Vaughan Williams. He knew 420 songs of various kinds, and refused to sing the words of 'Salisbury Plain' to Miss Broadwood as he did not consider them fit for a lady's ears. He was born in 1826 and died at the end of January 1916. In his *Reminiscences of Horsham*, published in 1911 (and actually written by William Albery), he described how he sang to Vaughan Williams 'such songs as he asked for, all of which he recorded by his phonograph. This was the first time I had seen or heard one of these marvellous machines, and I was amazed beyond expression to hear my own songs thus repeated in my own voice'.

Burstow was a bellringer at Horsham Church for sixty-five years, but never attended a service. He was convinced of the truth of Darwinism. To their credit, successive vicars of Horsham refused to take any action against him when outraged church officers protested about his presence among the ringers. Strange that in his eightieth year he sang his Sussex songs to Darwin's great-nephew in the Darwin-Wedgwood stronghold at Leith Hill Place.

Nothing can now adequately convey what must have been the sheer tedium of many of the folk-song collectors' forays. But tedium is soon forgotten, and what remained in Vaughan Williams's recollection was this kind of experience which he had with Mrs. E. M. Leather among the Herefordshire gipsies:

'It was a cold, clear September night[1] and we stood by the light of a blazing fire in the open ground of the gipsy encampment; the fire had been specially lighted to enable us to note down tunes and words in the growing darkness. Then, out of the half light, there came the sound of a beautiful tenor voice singing "The Unquiet Grave".'[2]

1903

Place and date	Name of song (as noted by R.V.W. at the time)	Name of singer
4 December (Ingrave)	Bushes and Briars (also sung to Willy of the Waggon Train)	Charles Pottipher (labourer, aged 75 in 1904).
„	The Storm	„
„	Princess Royal	„
„	Here comes little David (hunting song)	„
„	The cruel father and the affectionate lover	„
„	The Sheffield Apprentice	„
„	It's of a fair young damsel (Banks of Sweet Dundee)	Mr. George Sewell (aged about 40).
„	Fair Phebe	Mrs. Horsnell and her daughter. Cottager at Ingrave who came originally from Willingale-Doe. Mrs. Horsnell's mother 'knew a song called "The Red Barn" about a young man and woman who were murdered. Her mother knew the man and the woman and the barn, but she would not teach this song to Mrs. Horsnell but said she would keep it to herself till she died.'
„	The tarry sailor	
„	There was a fearless highwayman	
„	With her cheeks as red as roses (Chorus only of 'The stream of Lovely Nancy')	

[1] 10 September 1912. The singer was Alfred Pryce Jones.
[2] *Journal of Folk Song Society*, No. 32. Vol. VIII, part 2.

Place and Date	*Name of Song*	*Name of Singer*
4 December (Ingrave)	The Farmer's daughter In Jesse's city	A servant at Ingrave Rectory who came from Chigwell where she learnt the songs from neighbours.
,,	My shoes are made of Spanish	Tune for a game-song sung by Ingrave schoolchildren.
,, ,, ,, ,, ,,	Died for love Ever so poor Young Jimmy, or Into the Deep In Sheffield Park On the banks of Invaree	Mr. Broomfield, woodcutter, of West Horndon. Well known as a singer 'and has been known to go on for hours when well primed. I should think he sang these songs in the traditional manner, shutting his eyes tight and *speaking* the last line at the end of the song'.
Surrey 7 December (Leith Hill Place) ,, ,, ,, ,,	The Basket of Eggs It was just against the Chasher gate Creeping Jane (racing song) Convict's lamentation ('I was born in the land called England') The Devil he came to an old man at plough (with whistling) Irish girl's lament Bristol Town (new version) (see Folk Song Journal, Vol. I, No. 4 (4)) The Sheffield Apprentice (new version) (see F.S.J., Vol I, No. 4 (32).	Mr. Henry Burstow of Horsham, Sussex. Sung to R.V.W. at Leith Hill Place.
27 December (Broadmoor, near Leith Hill)	The dark-eyed sailor The Poachers	Mr. Isaac Longhurst of Broadmoor.

Place and Date	Name of Song	Name of Singer
December but no specific date	The Ploughboy's Dream	Mr. Garman, labourer, aged about 60, of Forest Green, nr. Ockley, Surrey. 'Mr. G. used to sing to the Rev. John Broadwood who would give half a crown to hear The Ploughboy's Dream. He learnt the Health Song at suppers at Lyne.'
"	The Child's Dream	
"	Hunting Song	
"	The cruel father	
"	The dragoon and the lady	
"	Health song at Harvest Home	

1904

Essex

22 February (Herongate)	Died for love	Mr. Broomfield, of West Horndon, at the Cricketers Inn, Herongate.
	On the banks of Invaree	
"	Never sail no more	
"	Ever so poor	
"	Down in a valley (Lost lady found)	
"	A nutting we will go	
"	The green mossy banks of the Lea	
(Ingrave)	Spencer the Rover	Mr. Pottipher. (It was on this occasion that Pottipher made his remark: 'If you can get the words, the Almighty sends you a tune.')
	The pretty ploughboy	

Westminster, Barton Street

24 March	William and Phillis	Three men selling ballad sheets in Barton Street.
Undated, but probably 24 March	Water-cress cry	

Essex

14 April (Fyfield)	The Farmer's Boy	Mrs. Charles White.
	Sweet Primroses (Four versions)	1. By Mrs. White. 2. In The Bell Inn, Willingale-Doe. 3. ditto. 4. Mr. Sam Chiles, of Willingale-Doe.

Place and Date	*Name of Song*	*Name of Singer*
14 April (Fyfield)	Poacher's Song On Monday morn	In The Bell, Willingale-Doe. Singer unspecified.
,,	How old are you, my pretty maid	
,,	'Twas down in a valley	Mr. Chiles, of Willingale-Doe.
15 April (Ingrave)	The Irish Girl The Constant Farmer's Son	Mr. and Mrs. Ratford, of Ingrave.
,,	Green bushes	
16 April (Little Burstead)	Down in our village The spotted cow	Mr. Harris, farmer.
,,	Three weeks before Easter	Mr. Ted Nevill.
,,	The jolly harin' (herring)	
,,	I am a rover	
(Ingrave)	John Barleycorn	Mr. Peacock, at The Cricketers Inn, Ingrave.
18 April	The farmer's boy	Rob. Johnston (aged 15) who heard it from George Sewell.
21 April (East Horndon)	The painful plough The thresher and the nobleman	Mr. James Punt, of East Horndon.
,,	Bold Turpin	
,,	Lovely Nancy	
,,	Three butchers	
,,	The gallant Hussar	
,,	The lost lady found	
,,	I am a stranger	
19 April (Little Burstead)	All round my hat	Mr. Harris, who heard it sung by a clown at Chelmsford Races about 1840.
22 April (East Horndon)	Silvery, silvery Van Dieman's Land	Mr. Broomfield, at The Dog, East Horndon.
,,	The factory girl	
,,	New garden fields	
,,	The nobleman's daughter	Mr. Peacock, at The Dog.
,,	The Angel Inn at Manchester	Mr. Thomas Ellis, of East Horndon.

Place and Date	Name of Song	Name of Singer
23 April (East Horndon)	New garden fields	
	Newport Street	
,,	Courtship	
,,	The fisherman	
,,	Admiral Benbow	
,,	Long life to young Jimmy	Mr. Punt.
,,	Jacky Robinson (dancing song)	
,,	The cobbler	
,,	Died for love	
,,	The sprig of thyme	
25 April (Ingrave)	The golden glove	
	Tarry Trowsers	
,,	Poacher's Song (tune of Constant farmer's son)	
,,	Come buy me a hawk and a hound (sung by Mrs. Humphreys' grandfather who died aged 76 in about 1837)	Mrs. Humphreys, of Ingrave, aged 72. She learnt it from her grandmother, Ann Smyth, born at Blackmore, 1794.
,,	The saucy sailor boy	
,,	I'm a stranger	
,,	Silvery, silvery	
,,	The cambric shirt	
25 April (Billericay (Union)	The Indian lass	
	Robing Wood (Robin Hood) and Little John	
,,	The Smuggler's boy	
,,	The bonny blue handkerchief	
,,	The little oyster girl	Mr. John Denny, aged 65, of Nevinton, Essex
,,	The farmer's daughter	
,,	The old-fashioned farmer	
,,	The farmer's boy	
,,	Lord Bateman	
,,	The shady green tree	
,,	The bold young farmer	
Surrey		
May (date unspecified)	The Lads of Kilkenny	Mrs. Berry, of Leith Hill Farm.

Place and Date	Name of Song	Name of Singer
May (date unspecified)	With your gun on your shoulder	Mr. Ansfield, gamekeeper, Leith Hill Place.
,,	The brave ploughboy Epsom Downs The birds in the Spring	Mr. Isaac Longhurst, of Forest Green.
,,		
Sussex 24 May (Horsham)	A sailor in the North Countree	
,,	Banks of the Nile	
,,	I've lived in service	
,,	An alderman lived in the city	Mrs. Harriet Verrall, of Nuthurst Road, Monk's Gate.[1] (Aged about 50.)
,,	Covent Garden (Cupid's Garden?)	
,,	The lark in the morning	
,,	On Christmas night	
,,	Unnamed carol	
Surrey 25 May (Forest Green)	The Bold Fisherman Young Collins	
,,	The little ploughboys	Mr. Garman, of Forest Green.
,,	Hunting song	
,,	Cabin boy	
Sussex 28 May (Hollycombe)	I once was a bold fellow Shipcrook and black dog	Mr. Stacey, cowman, aged about 80. He learnt most of his songs from his father and knew about 50. He and a friend used to go wassailing.
,,	It was one morning in the Spring	
,,	The tarry sailor	
,,	As I walked out	
Berkshire and Buckinghamshire 23 June (Maidenhead)	The greasy butcher boy	Mr. Parsons, an old cow-doctor, in the workhouse at Maidenhead.

[1] In the Sussex Directory of 1905, the place was spelt 'Monksgate'. The modern spelling seems to be consistently Monk's Gate, and this form has been adopted in this book. This famous folk singer died in 1918 aged about 63. She is buried in an unmarked grave in Hill's Cemetery, Horsham. Her husband died a few years after her. In about 1905 they moved from Monk's Gate to a cottage, 34 North Street, Horsham. This was pulled down and they moved to Stanley Street. They had three children.

Place and Date	*Name of Song*	*Name of Singer*
Unspecified date in June (Bourne End)	Her father dragged to a stake	Mr. Wetherill, tailor, who heard them in inns at Farnham and Hedgerley.
„	Lord Bateman	
	I had one man, I had two men	
(Cookham Dean)	The pride of Kildare	Mr. Copas, son of the landlady of the Chequers, Cookham Dean.
Yorkshire 13 July (Westerdale)	Forty miles	Mr. Willy Knaggs, sexton, at the Duncombe Arms, Westerdale. 'I found it difficult to take down the words as they were broad Yorkshire.'
	There was an old man	
„	Young William	
„	The miller and his three sons	Mr. Greenwood, school-master, at the Duncombe Arms.
„	A yacre of land	
22 July (Robin Hood's Bay, Fylingdales)	In Fylingdales parish	Mr. John Newton, butcher, aged about 80. He said 'In Fylingdales parish' was invented, words and music, by his father-in-law, John Jilson, in 1811.
	Billy O'Rooke	
	I married a wife	
23 July (Westerdale)	The farmer's daughter (same tune as Sweet Dundee)	Thomas Bowes, of Westerdale, at the Duncombe Arms.
„	The farmer's boy	
„	A brisk young farmer (contains a 'now my apron's up to my chin' verse)	
Unspecified date	?Dance tune, Katherine Osie	Perhaps by Mr. John Mason, fiddler of Dent, Yorks.

Place and Date	Name of Song	Name of Singer
10 August (Dent)	Carless Solly (reel)	Mr. John Mason, who learnt the reels from two old fiddlers (Bainbridge and Firby) some by heart and some from a book of which the notes had been 'pricked out by hand by Mr. Bainbridge'.
	Hornpipe (no name)	
,,	Butter'd pease (learnt from Firby, of Hawes)	
,,	The devil's dream	
,,	Tarry Woo'	
Wiltshire		
27 August (Ramsbury)	The lost lady	Mr. Woolford, aged about 70, of Ramsbury.
	All serene	
,,	The young Indian lass	
,,	Mossy banks of the Lea	
,,	Erin's lovely home	
31 August (Stratford Tony, near Salisbury)	Bizzoms (sung to Brice at Crewkerne by an old fiddler called Blind Jimmy, who 'could make the fiddle speak')	Mr. Brice, carter, aged about 45.
,,	The farmer boy	
31 August (Coombe Bissett)	The waggoner	A man called 'Pardner' in the Fox and Goose, Coombe Bissett. He lived in a shepherd's hut in the summer, went to London in the winter.
,,	An acre of land	Frank Bailey, ex-soldier, aged about 50, in the Fox and Goose.
1 September (Salisbury)	Erin's lovely home	Mr. Smith, from Durrington, near Amesbury, then settled in Britford and is now in St. Nicholas' Hospital, Salisbury.

Place and Date	Name of Song	Name of Singer
1 September (Salisbury)	Come all you young ladies I am a rover	Mr. Seers or Shears of Winterslow, now in Salisbury Union.
„ „	The bonny bunch of roses	Maria Pearce, about 75, in Salisbury Union.
„	Ground for the floor	Elias Coombes, shoemaker, in Salisbury Union
„	The Irish convict	Mr. Blake, in Salisbury Union.
„	Lord Bateman	Mr. Mitchell, about 60, in Salisbury Union, formerly of Coombe Bissett.
2 September (Coombe Bissett) „	One man shall mow Tuesday morning	F. Bailey, at the Fox and Goose.
„ „	What's the life of a man ("I doubt if it's a folk song, he learnt it 30 years ago. R.V.W.") The blackbird	Mr. J. W. Wright.
(Salisbury)	Good people all	Mr. Smith in St. Nicholas' Hospital.
September (date unspecified) (Salisbury) „	The buffalo The battle of Waterloo	Mr. Leary, formerly of Hampshire, in Alms Houses, Castle Street, Salisbury
Dorset September (date unspecified) (Farnham)	The bailiff's daughter	Mr. Adams, carrier, and his daughter, of Farnham.

Place and Date	*Name of Song*	*Name of Singer*
Sussex 8 October (Horsham)	As I walked out Cupid the pretty ploughboy It was one summer morning The young servant man Salisbury Plain The jolly thresherman Young jockey The gallant rainbow The powers above Come all you young ploughboys Henry Martin The red barn	Mr. Peter Verrall and his wife Harriet.
,, ,, ,, ,, ,, ,, ,, ,, ,, ,,		
Sep. or Oct. (Leith Hill Place) ,, ,, ,, ,,	The jolly thresherman Spencer the rover 'Twas on a Sunday morning The ranter parson	Mr. Earle, labourer at Leith Hill Place, formerly of Highlands, near Leatherhead, aged 61, learnt most of his songs off "ballets" or from his father.
Essex 26 October (East Horndon) ,, ,, ,,	Good people of England Merry broom green fields Lay still (The Lark in the Morning) Fountain's flowing (Our captain calls)	Mr. James Punt. Mr. Kemp, about 77, of Herongate.
,, ,,	Ingatestone Hall As I walked out	Mr. Broomfield, of Herongate.

Place and Date	Name of Song	Name of Singer
Surrey		
21 December		
(Forest Green)	The drums do beat	
,,	Our ship she lays in harbour	Mr. Baker, senr., of Forest Green, formerly of Petworth, aged about 70.
,,	Banks of Invary	
,,	Some rival	
,,	The brisk young lively lad	
,,	Cold blows	
Sussex		
22 December		
(Horsham)	Boney's in St. Helena	
,,	Dream of Napoleon	
,,	Deeds of Napoleon	
,,	Grand conversation of Napoleon	
,,	The new deserter	
,,	Battle of America	
,,	Green mossy banks	Mr. Henry Burstow.
,,	In Essex there lived	
,,	It's of a sailor	
,,	Effects of love	
,,	Newport street	
,,	Down in those meadows	
,,	Peggy Bain	
,,	Pretty wench	
,,	London apprentice	
,,	Gosport beach	
,,	No name (see Jolly Thresherman and Golden Glove)	
,,	The mole catcher	
,,	Abroad as I was walking	
,,	I once loved	
,,	Our captain calls (new)	Mrs. Verrall.
,,	Fare thee well my dearest dear	
,,	Oxford City	
,,	As a sailor was walking	
,,	An outlandish rover	
,,	The ship's carpenter	

Place and Date	*Name of Song*	*Name of Singer*
(Lower Beeding)		Mr. Ted Baines, labourer, aged about 70, of Plummers Plain near Lower Beeding.
,,	All things are quite silent	
,,	Young Sandy	
,,	The lawyer	
23 December (Kingsfold)	Come all you jolly ploughmen	Sung at the Wheatsheaf, Kingsfold, at a sing-song, by W. Chennell.
,,	Golden Glove	ditto by J. Chennell.
,,	Horn Fair	,, by Ted Gill.
,,	Handfuls of roses	,, (singer unknown)
,,	The week before Easter	,, ,,
,,	Maria Martin	,, by Booker.
,,	Salisbury Plain (same tune as Verralls', with variants)	,, by J. Chennell.
,,	William and Sally	,, by Knight.
,,	The ship's carpenter	,, by Booker.
,,	The trees they do grow high	,, ,,
26 December (Plaistow)		Mr. Cooper, at the Sun Inn, Plaistow, near Dunsfold.
,,	Adieu to lovely Nancy	
Kent 31 December (Gravesend)	John Reilly	
,,	Orange and blue	
,,	Robin Hood and the pedlar	Mr. and Mrs. Truell of Perry Street, Gravesend.
,,	Foggy dew	
,,	Cupid's garden	
,,	Spencer the rover	
,,	Tom Block	

1905

Norfolk 7 January (Tilney All Saints)	Lord Bateman	Mr. J. Whitby, sexton, of Tilney All Saints, near King's Lynn. Aged about 50.
	It was one morning	
,,	Bold carter	

Place and Date	Name of Song	Name of Singer
(Tilney St. Lawrence)	The foxhunt	Mr. Stephen Poll, labourer, of Tilney St. Lawrence. Aged about 80. He learnt the dances at Lynn Fair. He used to fiddle for dances—the old country dances made more money for him because each couple as they got to the top gave him a penny.
,,	Trip to the cottage (dance)	
,,	Gipsies in the wood ,,)	
,,	Low backed car (,,)	
,,	Ladies triumph (,,)	
8 January (Tilney All Saints)	Lord Lovel	Mr. J. Whitby.
	The red barn	
	The streams of lovely Nancy	
,,	As I was a-walking	
,,	Green bushes	
,,	The Yorkshire bite (Lincolnshire Farmer)	
,,	Young Jocky	
9 January (King's Lynn)	Deeds of Napoleon	Mr. Carter, fisherman, about 70, at North End.
	The captain's apprentice	
,,	Ward the Pirate	
,,	As I was a-walking one midsummer's morning	
,,	The dragoon and the lady	
,,	The basket of eggs	Mr. Anderson, fisherman, aged about 70, of Lynn.
,,	The Yorkshire farmer	
,,	John Reilly	
,,	Van Dieman's Land (or Young Henry the Poacher)	
,,	Erin's lovely home	
,,	Sheffield apprentice	
,,	Dream of Napoleon	Mr. Crist, sailor, at the Lynn Union.
,,	On board a '98	Leatherday, sailor, at the Lynn Union.

Place and Date	Name of Song	Name of Singer	
9 January (King's Lynn)	Napoleon's farewell (This is doubtful because he was very hoarse. R.V.W.)	Woods, sailor, at the Lynn Union.	
,,	Spurn Point	Leatherday	Ditto.
,, ,,	Princess Royal Loss of the Ramillies	Crist	Ditto.
10 January (King's Lynn)	Erin's lovely home Raven's feather	Chesson	Ditto.
,,	Creeping Jane	Leatherday	Ditto.
,,	The Irish Girl	Cooper	Ditto.
,,	It's of an old lord	Elmer	Ditto.
,,	Hares in the plantation	Unknown singer	Ditto.
	John Raeburn	Crist	Ditto.
,, ,, ,, ,,	The bold robber A bold young sailor The nobleman and the thresherman As I was a-walking (Handfuls of roses)	Mr. Anderson.	
,,	The blacksmith (with variant from J. Bayley, 11 January)	Mr. Carter.	
10 and 11 January King's Lynn	Ratcliff Highway Our anchors weighed Sheffield apprentice	Mrs. Betty Howard, aged about 70, of King's Lynn.	
11 January (King's Lynn)	The Cumberland's crew	Crist, at Lynn Union.	
,,	The robin's petition	Tune Leatherday, words West, at Lynn Union.	
,,	The maids of Australia	Crist Ditto.	
,,	Spanish ladies	Crist and Leatherday at Lynn Union.	
,, ,,	Barbary Allen The farmer's daughter	Mrs. Larley (? Lolly) Bennefer of King's Lynn	

Place and Date	Name of Song	Name of Singer
11 January (King's Lynn)	It's of a shopkeeper The three butchers	} 'Elizabeth' of King's Lynn.
,,	I went to Betsy	Mr. John Bayley of King's Lynn.
12 January (Sheringham)	Come Nancy will you marry me?	} B. Jackson, at the level crossing.
,,	Near Scarborough Town	Mr. Enery at the Crown Inn.
13 January (King's Lynn)	Bold Princess Royal	Mr. Smith, sailor, of Lynn.
,, ,,	Bold Princess Royal Young Indian lass	} Mr. Anderson.
13 and 14 January (King's Lynn) ,, ,, ,, ,, ,, ,,	Paul Jones or The American frigate Fair Flora ('a Welsh song') Just as the tide was flowing Oxford city Poor Mary Captain Markee (?) Edward Gayen (?)	} Mr. Harper of King's Lynn.
,, ,, ,, ,, ,, ,, ,, ,,	Hills of Caledonia (John Raeburn) Pat Reilly Glencoe Spanish ladies Come all you young sailors Come all you gallant poachers Banks of Claudy	} Mr. Donger, ex-sailor and sailmaker of Lynn.
14 January	Betsy and William	Mr. Harper.
(King's Lynn)	The golden glove	Mr. Carter.
,,	My bonny boy	Mr. Harper.
Buckinghamshire June (date unspecified) (Cookham Dean)	No title	Mrs. Brooklyn of Cookham Dean.

Place and Date	*Name of Song*	*Name of Singer*
(Cookham Rise)	The green bushes	} Singer unknown.
(Hedgerly)	Geordie	

Sussex

November (date unspecified) (Horsham)	Duke William The North Fleet The 18th day of June (Sung to Burstow by J. Shoebridge, Rifle Brigade, who was in the Battle of Waterloo and, Burstow thought, learnt it there.)	} Mr. Burstow.
,,	County Tyrone	
,,	That landlady had a daughter	
,,	Come all you freemasons	

8 November (Horsham)	Fanny Blair Basket of eggs	Mr. and Mrs. Verrall at 34 South Street, Horsham, to which they had moved from Monk's Gate.
,,	It was one winter's evening	
,,	Captain Ward	
,,	The gown of green	
,,	The Royal George	

| 8 November (Kingsfold) | The trees they do grow | Mr. Booker. |

| 11 November (Horsham) | Lord Allanwater | Mr. E. A. Stears, at 34 South Street, Horsham. |

1906

Sussex

9 January (South Ease)	Come all you young ploughmen	Mr. Baker, shepherd, of Mad-Misery Farm,[1] South Ease, near Lewes.
,,	Young Collins	
,,	Blackberry Fold	

---

[1] This is how Vaughan Williams noted the farm's name, and he was much pleased, when the book *Cold Comfort Farm* appeared, to have gone one better. Leonard Woolf, in *Beginning Again*, the third volume of his autobiography, refers (p.146) to 'a building . . . known locally as Mad Misery Barn, a name which I always thought must be a corruption of Me Miserere.'

Place and Date	Name of Song	Name of Singer
10 January (Rodmell)	Cold blows the wind / Pretty Betsy	Singer unspecified, at The Inn, Rodmell.
„ / „	The ship's carpenter / Young Edwin	Mr. Norman, shepherd, of North Ease, at The Inn, Rodmell.
10 January (South Ease)	The bailiff's daughter	Mr. Baker
10 January (Rodmell) / „	Come all you worthy Christians / The long whip	Mr. Back, shepherd, at The Inn, Rodmell.
10 January (Telscombe) / „	Come all you jolly ploughmen / The painful plough	Mr. Wooler, shepherd, of Telscombe.

Essex

16 February (Herongate)	Murder of Mountnesson	
„	William and Mary	
„	The little dun mare	
„	Dick Turpin (a modern tune introducing well-known tunes, with dialogue)	Mr. Bell, bricklayer, of Herongate.
	A blacksmith courted me	
„	Come all you merry sportsmen	
„	Cold blow the winds	
„	Robin Hood	
„	The little town boy	

Northumberland

28 and 29 July (Howick)	The beggarman	
	Sixteen come Sunday	Mr. Urquhart of Howick, near Alnwick.
„	The four Maries	
31 July (Dunstan)	The beggarman	
	Hornpipe	Mr. and Mrs. Thompson of Dunstan, near Alnwick.
„	Hornpipe (Barley mow)	
7 August (Craster)	The lass o' Glenshee	
	The bonny banks o' Coquet	Mr. Mason, at The Fisherman, Craster.
„	Come all	
„	The bonny house of Airlie	

Place and Date	*Name of Song*	*Name of Singer*
(Dunstan)	Over the hills	
,,	Lullaby	
,,	Psalm tune (XXIII Ps.)	Mr. Thompson.
,,	(The Lord of Life)	
,,	Willy Foster	
,,	My coffin shall be black	Children's songs and games
,,	Here stands a lady	communicated by Mr. Kin-
,,	Roman soldiers	naird, schoolmaster, of
		Dunstan.

Cumberland

9 August	Bleckel Murry neet	
(Carlisle)	King Roger	
,,	Barberry Bell	
,,	A wife of Willy Miller	Mr. Carruthers of Carlisle.
,,	Rossler Fair	
,,	Geordie Gair	
,,	Rob Lowry	

Cambridgeshire

20 August	Sheffield Apprentice	Mr. Jim Austin, of Little
(Little	The Keeper	Shelford.
Shelford)	God rest you	
22 August	Abroad as I was walking	Mr. Llewellyn Malyon, of
(Fen Ditton)	Rosemary Lane	Fen Ditton.
,,	John Barleycorn	
25 August	The lousy tailor	Mr. Gothard, of Wilbur-
(Wilburton)	The lost lady	ton.
27 August	Little lowland maid	Mr. Pamplin, of Fen
(Fen Ditton)	Georgie	Ditton.
,,	Cold winter's night	
,,	Irish Molly	
,,	Maria Martin and Van	Mr. Harry Malyon, of Fen
	Dieman's Land	Ditton.
	(versions of same tune)	
,,	Plains of Waterloo	
,,	The cobbler	
,,	As I walked out	

Place and Date	*Name of Song*	*Name of Singer*
31 August (Wilburton)	Bobbing around	
	The gay ploughboy	
,,	As I walked out	Mr. Gothard.
,,	Twankydillo	

Norfolk

1 September (King's Lynn)	Lord Bateman	
	The 14th day of February (*not* Bold Princess Royal)	Mr. Elmer, in the Lynn Union.
,,	Kilkenny	
,,	Bold robber (Doubtful—R.V.W.)	
,,	Three butchers	Mr. Leatherday, in Lynn Union.
,,	Spanish ladies	Mr. Crist Ditto.
,,	A sailor was riding along	Mr. Carter.
,,	Chanty—Heave away	
,,	Shenandoah	Mr. Donger.
,,	Erin's lovely home	

Sussex

27 September (Kingsfold)	Golden glove	Mr. Chennell. (Not specified whether W. or J.)
,,	Joggin' along	Mr. Gutteridge of Kingsfold.
,,	Golden Vanity	Mr. A. Muggeridge of Kingsfold.
,,	A sailor's life	
,,	Clear away the morning dew	Mr. Attwater of Kingsfold.
,,	Green mossy banks	
,,	Seasons of the year	
,,	Seventeen come Sunday	Singer unspecified.
,,	Rambling Sailor	Mr. Booker.

1907

Sussex

2 May (Horsham)	Orton Town	Mr. and Mrs. Verrall
,,	The gown of green	
,,	The rambling sailor	Ditto (phonograph)
,,	Basket of eggs	

Place and Date	*Name of Song*	*Name of Singer*
2 and 4 May (Rusper	What hurricane wind	Mr. Penfold, landlord of the Plough Inn, Rusper, and others.
,,	Green broom	Mr. Penfold.
,, ,,	Unknown title Pull the string	} Unspecified singer.
,,	Henry Martin	Mr. Miles in the Plough. Notation and phonograph.
,, ,, ,,	The miller of the Dee The turtle dove The trees they do grow high	} Mr. Penfold (phonograph)
3 May (Kingsfold)	Seventeen come Sunday	Mr. Gutteridge.
Cambridgeshire 12 July (Fowlmere) ,, ,,	Lord Ellenwater May Song The lost lady The Yorkshire bite	} 'Hoppy' Flack, at Fowlmere.
22 July (Meldreth)	The trees they do grow high	} 'Ginger' Clayton.
30 July (Bassingbourne)	Lakes of Cold Fenn (?) Adieu my lovely Nancy	} Mr. Harmon, of Bassingbourne.
Hertfordshire 31 July (Royston)	Green bushes God rest you	} Mr. Wiltshire (of Fowlmere) at Royston Union.
Unspecified August dates (possibly 1 Aug. (Royston)	May Song Nine joys of Mary	} Mr. Wiltshire in Royston Union.
Cambridgeshire 3 August (Cottenham) ,, ,,	No title No title The cuckoo and the nightingale There is an alehouse	} Mrs. Dann of Cottenham.

Place and Date	*Name of Song*	*Name of Singer*
10 Aug. (Fowlmere)	Three days before Easter Golden glove (version of above) The red barn Shannon side	'Hoppy' Flack.
"		
"		
Unspecified August date (probably 10)	Geordie Rolling in the dew	Unspecified. Flack.
"	The Yorkshire Bite	Mr. Smith
(Fen Ditton)	Gilderoy	Mr. H. Malyon.
Surrey 13 August (Mitcham) "	Geordie High Germany The jolly sailor	Mr. Jeffries of 24 Queens Road, Mitcham, at Mitcham Fair. He learnt his songs from his father at Headcorn, Kent.
20 August (Lyne) " "	Salisbury Plain Robin Hood's men Robin Wood and the Pedlar Down by some river	Mr. Flint, shepherd, of Taylor's Farm, Lyne, aged 71. Came from East Grinstead.
Suffolk 31 August (Kersey)	The green mossy banks	Played on a penny whistle at The Bell, Kersey.
" " "	Basket of eggs Barbry Ellen I courted a dark girl (The false lover)	Mr. Ansell, in The Bell.
1 September (Hadleigh)	Eggleston Hall	Mr. Warner, in the Shoulder of Mutton, Hadleigh.
2 September (Hadleigh)	Our chief mate's name it was Ike Green (chanty)	Mr. Broome, of Hadleigh.

Place and Date	*Name of Song*	*Name of Singer*
3 & 4 Sept. (Hadleigh)	Baskets of eggs	
	Green lanes	
,,	The broadstriped trowsers (Tarry Trowsers)	Mr. Jake Willis, Crimean War and Indian Mutiny veteran.
,,	Vilikins and his Dinah	
,,	The baffled Knight (The dew is on the grass)	
,,	The milk pail	
,,	Green mossy banks	
3 and 4 Sept. (Hadleigh)	I hunted my merry dogs	Mr. Robert Clark, completed by Willis.
3 September	Silvy	The Clark Family.
(Hadleigh)		
,,	Come all you roaring boys	'A man from Stepney in the workhouse.'
3 September (Holton St. Mary)	I once loved a dark girl (The false lover)	Mrs. Tiffen, junior.
Yorkshire Sept., dates unspecified (Wickersley)	T'old Tup (part of a play of that name)	'A man in the inn at Wickersley.'
,,	The old horse	
Sept., dates unspecified (Theybergh)	A frolicsome sergeant	Mr. Drabbles of Theybergh.
	The two champions	
	Bold William Taylor	
,,	The silvery tide	
Sept. dates unspecified Braithwell	Seventeen come Sunday	A navvy from Lincolnshire in an inn at Braithwell.
Sept., dates unspecified (Stainton)	Poor Mary	Singing games heard at Stainton.
	Oats and beans	
	Wallflowers	
,,	Jolly sailor boys	

Place and Date	Name of Song	Name of Singer
Sept., dates unspecified (Hooton Roberts)	Milkmaids	
	O may he never prosper (tune very doubtful, R.V.W.)	A gipsy.
,,	Erin's lovely home (doubtful. R.V.W.)	
,,	I courted an old man	

Sussex

29 November (Godwicks, near Ifield)	Down by some river's murmur side	
	Merchant's daughter	
,,	The American	Mr. Harry Flint of God-wicks.
,,	High Germany	
,,	'Twas over hills and scraggy rocks (hunting song)	
,,	Our captain calls	
,,	The old miser	

1908

Norfolk

11 April (South Walsham)	Lovely on the water	Mr. Hilton, of South Wal-sham.
	When I was a bachelor	
	Joan's ale was new	
13 April (Acle)	Bonny bunch of roses	Mr. Christopher Jay, at Bridge Inn, Acle.
14 April (Ranworth)	Bonny blue handkerchief	Mr. Saunders, of Ran-worth.
	When Joan's ale was new	
,,	Derbyshire farmer	
14 April (Acle)	Jolly Waggoner	Mr. Rose, landlord, Bridge Inn.
,,	I'll go and 'list for a sailor	Mr. Walter (Skipper) Deb-bage at Bridge Inn.
,,	A bold young farmer	
,,	John Bull	
15 April (Acle)	Georgie	Mr. Walter Debbage at Bridge Inn.
	Fishes swim	
,,	Lovely Joan	Mr. Christopher Jay, at Bridge Inn.

Place and Date	Name of Song	Name of Singer
15 April (Hickling)	'Twas early one morning	Mr. Peter Knight, in inn at Hickling.
,,	Spurn Point Turkish lady	} Sung by Peter ?
16 April (Horning)	Wooden legged Parson Bold Princess Royal	} Sung at New Inn, Horning.
16 and 18 April (South Walsham)	She borrowed some of her mother's gold	
	Peggy Band	
,,	Young Johnson	
,,	Grand conversation of Napoleon	} Mr. Hilton, of South Walsham.
,,	Jew Pedlar	
,,	The mole catcher	
,,	Liverpool landlady	
,,	Captain Ward	
,,	Banks of the Clyde	
,,	Lancashire Farmer	
17 April (Horning)	Bold Princess Royal Brisk young farmer	
,,	Nancy	} Mr. Barlow, Ferry Inn.
,,	Shannon side	
17 April (Ranworth)	Title unknown So late it was	} Sally Brown, of Ranworth.
,,	John Barleycorn	
,,	Frog and mouse	} Mr. Walter Debbage at Ranworth.
,,	Polly Oliver	
17 April (Rollesby)	Flower of London Dark-eyed sailor	
,,	Just as the tide was flowing	} Mr. Locke, of Rollesby.
,,	It's of an old miser	
,,	Plymouth Sound	
,,	The man of Burningham town	

Place and Date	Name of Song	Name of Singer
18 April (Acle)	Pretty Nancy	Mr. W. Debbage at Bridge Inn.
,,	Lovely Joan	
,,	Mole catcher	
,,	Monday morning	Mr. Christopher Jay, at Bridge Inn
,,	Phoebe	
,,	John Reilly	
,,	Maria Martin	
,,	Foggy Dew	
,,	John Reilly	Another singer at Bridge Inn.
Unspecified date in Norfolk, probably coincident with above	Old Roger	
	All the boys	Children's singing games.
	Sally Walker	
	Wallflowers	

Suffolk

13 June (Orwell)	The lady looked out	
	When I was a young man	Mr. Billy Waggs at the Red Lion, Orwell.
,,	The red running rue	
August (Madley)	Green bushes	Mr. Mole, in Comet Inn, Madley.

Herefordshire
(with Mrs. Leather)

27 July	Angel Gabriel	
,,	Our Saviour's love	W. Hirons, of The Haven, Dilwyn
(Weobley)	Big bunch of roses	
,,	Carnal and crane	
28 July	A man shall live (The man that lives)	Mrs. Wheeler, of Weobley.
(Weobley)	Tom Sayers	Mr. Richards, of Weobley.
July or Aug. (undated) (Weobley)	Three jolly sailor boys	
	There stands a lady	Children's games.
	We a prisoner have got	
July or Aug. (undated)	A brisk young sailor	
,,	Highway robber (Outlandish Knight)	William Colcombe, Weobley.
,,	Sinner's dream	

Place and Date	*Name of Song*	*Name of Singer*
July or Aug. (undated)	God rest you (carol) Shannon side	} William Colcombe, Weobley.
Aug. (no place specified except 'Herefordshire')	Myrtle tree or Weaver came over the sea Blacksmith (2 'doubtful' versions)	
„	Green bushes	
„	Stockings and gown	
„	William Taylor	
„	Captain Evans (As I was riding over Galway mountains)	Mrs. Ellen Powell, prob-ably at Westhope, Canon Pyon.
„	O early, early Merry green broom fields	
„	Cold blows the wind	
„	Pretty Caroline	
„	All round my hat	
„	Dabbling in the dew	
„	A lady walking	Mr. Floyd.
„	Joys of Mary	} Mr. Griffiths.
„	The Saviour's love	

Surrey and Sussex

7 August (Lyne)	High Germany Salisbury Plain	} Mr. Flint.
8 August (Horsham)	Little cabin boy Rolling in the dew	
„	Good morning (see 'Abroad as I was walking' from V.H. (von Holst's) book, R.V.W.)	} Mr. and Mrs. Verrall.
„	Noble Lord Archer	
12 August (Lambs Green)	Down in the groves	Mr. Blundon at the inn, Lambs Green.
13 August (Rusper)	Hurricane wind	Mr. Penfold at the Plough.
„	Pretty ploughboy	'David' at the Plough.
„	O where are you going to? (Lord Rendel)	Mr. Miles Ditto.

Place and Date	Name of Song	Name of Singer
Aug., and some in April, dates unspecified (Capel)	An outlandish Knight Maria Martin Highland Jane Come all you valiant shepherds	Mr. Burrage, of 'Rushetts', Capel.
,,	A lady walking in a garden	
6 September (Horsham)	The London Prentice It's of an old couple	
,,	The little cobbler	Mrs. Verrall.
,,	My boy Billy (Where have you been)	
8 September (Horsham)	Cloddy (Claudy ?) banks Botany Bay	
,,	The squire in the North Countree	Mr. Verrall.
Derbyshire Month and date of 1908 unspecified (Castleton)	All you that are to mirth inclined On Christmas Day (And all in the morning)	Mr. J. Hall of Castleton.
,,	Down in yon forest	

1909

Herefordshire
(with Mrs. Leather)
July
(Pembridge)

,,	Blackberry fold	
,,	Awake, awake sweet England	Mrs. Caroline Bridges.
,,	Paddy's for Ireland	
,,	Green grow the rushes	
,,	Untitled	dance
,,	Work boys work	tunes
,,	Hornpipe	Mr. Goff.
,,	Hornpipe 2	
,,	The bold cripple	
,,	The false lover	songs
August (Pembridge)	Gloucestershire Wassail	Unspecified singer in the inn at Pembridge.

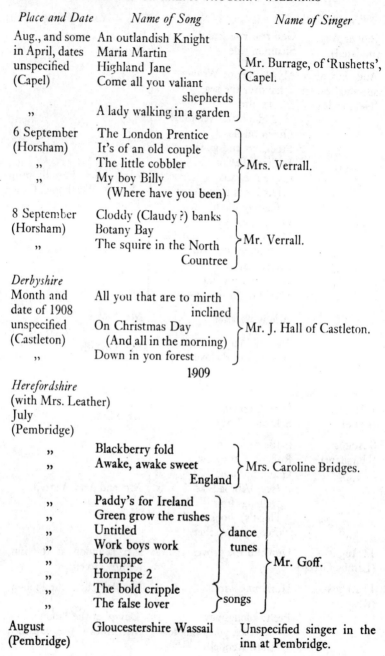

Place and Date	Name of Song	Name of Singer
August (Pembridge)	I'll sing you one O[1] (All rather doubtful as Dukes was in a great hurry. R.V.W.)	Mr. Dukes, in the inn at Pembridge.
"	Prickly briar	Mr. Bedford, in the inn at Pembridge.
" "	Apprentice boy	Mrs. Esther Smith Ditto.
August (King's Pyon)	Under the leaves (The seven virgins) Christ made a trance	Mrs. Harriet Jones, gipsy.
"	Shenfield apprentice	
"	The blacksmith	
"	The man that lives	Mr. Jenkins.
"	This is the truth sent from above	
August	There is a fountain	Gipsy, phonograph.
(Herefordshire)	There is a fountain	Mr. John Hancocks.
"	It's of a poor young girl	Gipsy, phonograph.
" (Weobley)	Johnny Dale Weobley Morris Dance— Sheepstring	Unspecified, but probably John Lock.
"	Hunt the squirrel	
Month and date of 1909 unspecified (Hardwick)	The turtle dove A virgin unspotted The moon shines bright Fountain of Christ's blood	Mr. G. Lewis of Hardwick, near Pembridge.

1910

Suffolk October (date unspecified) (Southwold)	Three jolly butchers Royal George When Jones' ale was new	Singer unspecified. Singer unspecified. Mr. Ben Hurr, of Southwold.
"	Bold Princess Royal	Mr. Robert Hurr.
"	Bold Princess Royal	Mr. William Hurr.
"	Liverpool hornpipe (concertina)	Mr. Robert Hurr.

[1] Contains the verse: 3 are the shiners,
   2 are the lily white boys Clothed all in green O.

Place and Date	Name of Song	Name of Singer
(Southwold)	It's of a rich old farmer (The Tinker)	Unspecified.
23 October (Southwold)	Tiresome wife In London town (Newry fields)	} Mr. Robert Hurr.
23 & 25 Oct. (Southwold)	Lovely Joan	Mr. William Hurr (Phonograph also).
24 October (Southwold)	The cobbler Isle of France	} Mr. Ben Hurr.
25 October (Southwold)	Loss of the London When I was bound apprentice	} Mr. William Hurr.
25 October (Reydon, Southwold)	Georgie	Mr. Newby in almshouses, Reydon
Norfolk 25 October (Rollesby)	New garden fields	Mr. Locke.
25 & 26 October (Filby) „ „	Captain's apprentice Irish girl Just as the tide was flowing Roger the miller	} Mr. George ("Chummy") Goble, of Filby.
25 October (Rollesby) „ „ „	Green mossy banks Bold fisherman Liverpool play Just as the tide was flowing Scarborough Town	} Mr. Locke.
Herefordshire Unspecified October date „ „ „	Come all you worthy Christians Dance tune (allegro) I can sing you one O A bold young farmer	} Phonograph. } Singers unspecified.

1911

Place and Date	Name of Song	Name of Singer
Chelsea 21 July	Lavender Cry (Used in *A London* *Symphony*)	Unspecified.
County Durham 30 August (Barnard Castle)	Greenbed Brennan on the Moor Abroad (for pleasure) as I was a-walking	
,, ,, ,,	Black frost Franklin's crew Banks of Shannon (Raven's feather)	Unspecified singer(s) in the Workhouse at Barnard Castle.

,,	Dumble down dèary
	    (Young Richard of
	    Taunton Dene)	

,,	Dumb wife	
Norfolk (with George Butterworth)		
19 December (Diss)	Words Unknown Cold Irons	Unspecified singer in the Workhouse.
,,	General Wolfe	Mr. Dade in workhouse
,, ,, ,,	Trot away Ratcatcher's daughter Hearts [*sic*] of Oak	Mr. Tuffs, senior, at Diss.
Date unspec. (Tibbenham, near Diss)	Untitled (Yorkshire bite) Untitled	Sung at the Horseshoes, Tibbenham. Sung by Noah Fisher at an inn in Long Row, Tibben- ham, in 'Dolly Vardon' style.
Date unspec. (near Diss)	Keys of heaven Miller and three sons	Unspecified. Mr. Tuffs, junior.
20 December (Diss)	Health song (rather doubtful, R.V.W.)	Mr. Dade in the Workhouse.
,, ,,	Mole catcher (doubtful, R.V.W.) Rose of Britain's isle	Mr. Tooke, in the Work- house.

Place and Date	Name of Song	Name of Singer
20 December (Diss)	John Reilly Coming down from Manchester	} Mr. Stevenson Ditto.
„	Isle of France (doubtful)	} Unspecified Ditto.
„	Butcher Boy	
20 December (Tibbenham)	Horse Race Song Jockey to the fair	} 'Blue' Fisher at inn at Tibbenham.
„	Poacher (Hares in the old plantation)	} Noah Fisher, at the Horse-shoes, Tibbenham.
20 Dec. (?) (Scole, near Diss)	'Sewing machine' (words no use—R.V.W.) Trot along	} Mr. Woodcock at the Greyhound, Scole.
21 December (Tibbenham)	Sweet Primeroses	Mr. Last, landlord of the Horseshoes.

1912

Herefordshire (with Mrs. Leather)

Sept. (few dates specified) (Sutton St. Nicholas) (near Weobley)	The holy well On Christmas Day Under the leaves	} Gipsies.
(same date or day after)	Under the leaves (another version)	} Alfred Pryce Jones.
„	Under the leaves (another version)	} Mrs. Whatton and daughters (gipsies).
„	Good people	Gipsies.
„	Good people (another version)	The Whattons.
„	God rest you merry, gentlemen	} Gipsies.
„	God rest you merry (another version)	} The Whattons.
10 September (Monkland)	There is an alehouse Claudy Banks	} Gipsy.

Place and Date	*Name of Song*	*Name of Singer*
10 September (Monkland)	Cold blows the wind (The Unquiet Grave) The Irish stranger	} Alfred Pryce Jones.
Unspecified (near Weobley) ,, ,,	Wassail song God rest you merry A virgin unspotted I will give you one-O	} Mr. Dukes.
,, ,,	Bitter Withy Come all you jolly seamen	} Mr. Morris.
,, ,,	Christ made a trance Shrewsbury gaol	} The Whattons.
,, ,, ,, ,, ,, ,, ,, ,, ,,	Gipsy Lord There was a lady lived in York Billy Taylor I'll burn my petticoat My mother sent me for some water Sheffield Park The unquiet grave Riding down to Portsmouth Molly Bawn	} Mrs. Esther Smith (*née* Whatton).
,,	The tiresome wife	J. Gardner, of Ludlow, in hop-fields near Weobley.
Herefordshire 16 September (Ashperton) ,, ,, ,, ,, ,,	**1913** Sylvie The trees (double version, i.e. they sang differently. R.V.W.) Cold blows the wind Butcher boy Birmingham town Green bed The holy well	} Mr. Saxton and Mr. Wildes at Poolend and Trumpet. Ditto (?) Loveridges (father and son).
Unspecified date (Ashperton)	Dives and Lazarus Christmas Day is drawing nigh at hand	} A waggoner.

Place and Date	*Name of Song*	*Name of Singer*
Unspecified date	It's of a farmer (Bruton Town)	Unspecified.
(Ashperton)	O who is that	Loveridge jnr., at camp near the Trumpet.
,,	The twelve apostles	} Mr. Wildes of Poolend
,,	The Saviour's love	} (came from Tipton, Staffs).
,,	Green bushes	}
,,	Croppy boy (rather doubtful)	} An Irishwoman at Poolend.
,,	New garden fields	}
,,	O who is that	Mr. Saxton.
16 September (Aylton, near Ledbury)	God made a trance	}
	Joseph was an old man	} Mr. Davies, hop-picking at Ball's hopgarden.
	Oxford city	}
,,	The holy well	}
,,	The trees they grow so high	}

1922

Herefordshire

8 September (Monkland)	Cold blows the wind (The unquiet grave)	Alfred Pryce Jones.

1955

Hampshire

27 August (Lyndhurst)	Raggle taggle gipsies	Juanita Berlin.

———

Phonograph reproductions (probably 1907)

Covent Garden[1]	Mrs. Verrall.
Moorfields (last verse)	Mr. Burstow.

No date, place or source

A blacksmith courted me.
Joseph and his wedded wife.
Come all you worthy people.

[1] In 1905 Mrs. Verrall won first prize in a competition to discover 'the best old Sussex songs' sponsored by the *West Sussex Gazette* (issue of 20 April 1905). Her entries were 'Covent Garden' and 'Salisbury Plain'. The judge was Lucy Broadwood. The account of the judging adds: 'Mrs. Verrall sends also a very good Christmas carol, with an excellent tune to it,' presumably 'On Christmas Night'.

The following folk songs for which MSS. survive either undated or in rough pencil versions appeared in the *Journal* of the Folk Song Society:

Place	Song	Singer
1902		
Bournemouth	Lord Thomas and Fair Eleanor	Mrs. Chidell
	(J.F.S.S. No 7, p. 106. Undated MS. survives)	
„	Long Lankin, or Young Lambkin	„
	(noted by Miss Chidell and R.V.W.	
	J.F.S.S. No. 7, p. 111–2)	
1905		
Wimbledon	Our Saviour tarried out (Bitter Withy)	Mr. Hunt
September	(J.F.S.S. No. 8, p. 205. Undated MS.)	
1906		
Rodmell	It's of an old farmer	'In the Inn'
January	(J.F.S.S. No. 8, p. 209)	
	As I walked over London Bridge	Mr. Thomas Deadman
	(J.F.S.S. No. 8, p. 208)	(1827–1920)
	MSS of above two songs in B.M. (50361)	
Horsham	Robing Wood and the Pedlar	Mr. P. Verrall
March 17	(J.F.S.S. No. 8, p. 156)	
1913		
Herefordshire		
September		
Poolend	Christmas now is drawing near	Mr. Wildes
	(J.F.S.S. No. 18, p. 10)	
Aylton	Awake, awake	Mr. Davies
	(J.F.S.S. No. 18, p. 16)	

Songs noted by R.V.W. in Herefordshire from phonograph recordings by Mrs. E. M. Leather:

1907		
January and	Dives and Lazarus	Mr. J. Evans, Dilwyn
March	The moon shines bright	G. Vaughan, Dilwyn
	The milkmaid's song	Mrs. E. Powell, Canon Pyon
	The tailor and the crow	
	The seasons of the year	Mrs. Beddoe
	Dilly Dove	Mrs. E. Goodwin, King's Pyon
	The mantle of green	
	Sailor Boy	Mrs. Bridges
	There is an alehouse	
	The trees they do grow high	Mr. Hirons, Haven
	The Unquiet Grave	
1908		
October	The holy well	Mrs. E. Goodwin
	The seven virgins	Angelina Whatton, Weobley
	There is a fountain	W. Hancock, Monnington
	another version	Mrs. Eliza Smith, Weobley
	There lived a lady in merry Scotland	Mrs. Loveridge, Dilwyn
1909		
January	The bitter withy	Mrs. Tristram, Withington
	another version	Mr. W. Holder, Withington

Songs collected by R.V.W. in Hampshire may be traced in J.F.S.S., but no MSS have come to light.

Bibliography of the Literary Writings of Ralph Vaughan Williams

Compiled by Peter Starbuck

I AM grateful to Mr Peter Starbuck for allowing me to incorporate into this book additions he has made to Part I of the bibliography which appeared in the first edition of this book. Mr Starbuck's complete bibliography, fully annotated, was submitted in 1967 as his thesis for Fellowship of the Library Association.

Mr Starbuck's original main sources were the libraries of London, particularly the Music Library of the University of London, and he received assistance from the British Library, the Royal College of Music, the Central Music Library of Westminster Public Library, and Mrs Vaughan Williams.

A few trivial letters to newspapers and periodicals have been omitted.

M.K.

1902

A School of English music.
(*The Vocalist*, Vol. I, No. 1, April 1902, p. 8.)
The Soporific finale.
(*The Vocalist*, Vol. I, No. 1, April 1902, p. 31.)
Palestrina and Beethoven.
(*The Vocalist*, Vol. I, No. 2, May 1902, pp. 36–7.)
Good taste.
(*The Vocalist*, Vol. I, No. 2, May 1902, p. 38.)
(*a*) *Reprinted in* VAUGHAN WILLIAMS, Ralph, & HOLST, Gustav. *Heirs and Rebels, etc.*, 1959, pp. 27–8.
Bach and Schumann.
(*The Vocalist*, Vol. I no. 3, June 1902, p. 72.)
(*a*) *Reprinted in* VAUGHAN WILLIAMS, Ralph, & HOLST, Gustav. *Heirs and Rebels, etc.*, 1959, pp. 29–33.

The Words of Wagner's music-dramas.
> (*The Vocalist*, Vol. I, No. 3, June 1902, pp. 94–6; No. 5, August 1902, pp. 156–9.)
> (*a*) *Extract reprinted* in VAUGHAN WILLIAMS, Ralph, & HOLST, Gustav. *Heirs and Rebels, etc.* 1959, as 'Librettos', pp. 33–6.

Brahms and Tschaikowsky.
> (*The Vocalist*, Vol. I, No. 7, October 1902, pp. 198–200.)

A sermon to vocalists.
> (*The Vocalist*, Vol. I, No. 8, November 1902, pp. 227–9.)

1903

'Ein Heldenleben'.
> (*The Vocalist*, Vol. I, No. 10, January 1903, pp. 295–6.) [A description of the work by Richard Strauss, with music examples.]

1904

Conducting.
> *In Grove's Dictionary of Music and Musicians.* 2nd ed. London, Macmillan, 1904–10. Vol. I,. pp. 581–89.
> (*a*) *Reprinted* in VAUGHAN WILLIAMS, Ralph, & HOLST, Gustav. *Heirs and Rebels, etc.*, 1959, pp. 36–7. (Extract.)
> (*b*) *Reprinted*, with omissions and revisions, in *Grove's Dictionary of Music and Musicians*, 3rd ed., London, Macmillan, 1927. Vol. I, pp. 697–700; in 4th ed. London, Macmillan, 1940, Vol. I, pp. 697–700; in 5th ed. London, Macmillan, 1954, Vol. II, pp. 397–9, 403–4.

Fugue.
> *In Grove's Dictionary of Music and Musicians.* 2nd ed. London, Macmillan, 1904–10. Vol. II, pp. 114–21.
> (*a*) *Reprinted* in *Grove's Dictionary of Music and Musicians*, 3rd ed. London, Macmillan, 1927, Vol. II, pp. 320–7; in 4th ed. London, Macmillan, 1940, Vol. II, pp. 320–7; in 5th ed. London, Macmillan, 1954, Vol. III, pp. 513–21.

1906

Preface (The Music) to The English Hymnal with tunes.
> London, Henry Frowde, 1906. pp. x–xix.
> (*a*) *Extract reprinted* as 'Hymn Tunes' in VAUGHAN WILLIAMS, Ralph, & HOLST, Gustav. *Heirs and Rebels, etc.*, 1959, pp. 37–8.

Preface, Journal of Folk Song Society, Vol. II, No. 8, pp. 141–2.

1910

The Romantic in Music. Course No. 2 – VIII. 'Some thoughts on Brahms'.

(*The Music Student*, Vol. 2, No. 8, April 1910, pp. 116–20.)

English folk song.

(*The Musical Times*, Vol. 52, No. 816, February 1911, pp. 101–4.)

[Report of lecture to Oxford Folk Music Society, 16 November 1910.]

1912

Who wants the English composer?

(*Royal College of Music Magazine*, Vol. 9, No. 1, Christmas **Term** 1912, pp. 11–15.)

(*a*) *Reprinted in* Foss, Hubert. *Ralph Vaughan Williams: a study*. London, Harrap, 1950, pp. 197–201.

(*b*) *Reprinted* in Danish in *Dansk Musiktidsskrift*, Vol. 33, 1958, pp. 80–2.

English folk songs (Lecture given at the Vacation Conference on Musical Education, 10 January 1912).

I (*The Music Student*, Vol. 4, No. 6, March 1912, pp. 247–8)

II (*The Music Student*, Vol. 4, No. 7, April 1912, pp. 283–4)

III (*The Music Student*, Vol. 4, No. 8, May 1912, pp. 317–8)

IV (*The Music Student*, Vol. 4, No. 9, June 1912, p. 347)

V (*The Music Student*, Vol. 4, No. 10, July 1912, p. 387)

VI (*The Music Student*, Vol. 4, No. 11, August 1912, pp. 413–4)

(*a*) English folk songs: a lecture given at the vacation conference on musical education, 10 January 1912. Publication in connection with the English Folk Dance Society, London, Joseph Williams, Ltd. [1912], 17pp. (This lecture in its printed form has undergone considerable revision and enlargement.)

(*b*) English folk songs. [London], The English Folk Dance Society, 1912? 16pp. (Abridged from a lecture.)

(*c*) *Reprinted* in Young, Percy Marshall. *Vaughan Williams*. London, Dennis Dobson Ltd., 1953, pp. 200–17.

1914

Influence of folk song on chamber music.

(*Chamber Music*, a supplement to the Music Student, No. 8, May 1914, pp. 69–71.)

(*a*) *Reprinted*, slightly revised, as 'Folk Song in Chamber Music' in Cobbett, Walter Willson, Ed. *Cobbett's Cyclopedic Survey of Chamber Music*. London, O.U.P., 1929, Vol. I, pp. 410–12.

(*b*) *Reprinted* in *Cobbett's Cyclopedic Survey of Chamber Music*, 2nd ed. London, O.U.P., 1963, Vol. I, pp. 410–12.

British music (Course no. 1 of the Home Music Study Union).
  I. The foundations of a national art. (*The Music Student*, Vol. 7,
     No. 1, September 1914, pp. 5–7.)
 II. British music in the Tudor period. (*The Music Student*, Vol. 7,
     No. 2, October 1914, pp. 25–7.)
III. The Age of Purcell. (*The Music Student*, Vol. 7, No. 3, November
     1914, pp. 47–8.)
 IV. British music in the eighteenth and early nineteenth centuries.
     (*The Music Student*, Vol. 7, No. 4, December 1914, pp. 63–4).

1918

Appreciation [of George Butterworth].
  In *George Butterworth 1885–1916*, ed. Sir Alexander Kaye Butterworth.
  York and London (private), 1918, pp. 92–4.
Sir Hubert Parry.
  (*The Music Student*, Vol. 11, No. 3, November 1918, p. 79.)

1919

Dance tunes.
  (*The Music Student*, Vol. 11, No. 12, Aug. 1919, pp. 453–7.)
  [With music examples.]

1920

The Letter and the spirit.
  (*Music and Letters*, Vol. I, No. 2, April 1920, pp. 87–93.)
  (*a*) *Reprinted* after revision in VAUGHAN WILLIAMS, Ralph.
      Some thoughts on Beethoven's Choral Symphony, etc. 1953, pp. 53–63.
  (*b*) *Reprinted in* VAUGHAN WILLIAMS, Ralph. *National Music and Other
      Essays*, 1963, pp. 121–28.
Gustav Holst.
  (*Music and Letters*, Vol. 1, No. 3, July 1920, pp. 181–90; pp. 305–17.)
  [With music examples.]
  (*a*) *Reprinted* in VAUGHAN WILLIAMS, Ralph.
      Some thoughts on Beethoven's Choral Symphony, etc. London,
      O.U.P., 1953, pp. 64–92.
  (*b*) *Reprinted in* VAUGHAN WILLIAMS, Ralph. *National Music and
      Other Essays*, 1963, pp. 129–51.

1921

Gervase Elwes.
  (*Musical News and Herald*, Vol. 60, No. 1504, 22 January 1921,
  pp. 107–8). [A tribute to his singing, especially of Gerontius and the
  Evangelist in Bach's *St. Matthew Passion*].

(a) *Reprinted*, shortened, in ELWES, Winefride, and ELWES, Richard, *Gervase Elwes, the Story of his Life*, London, Grayson and Grayson, 1935, pp. 294–6.

Sailor Shanties.
(*Musical News and Herald*, Vol. 61, No. 1553, 31 December 1921, pp. 683–4.) [Review of Richard Terry's collection of sea shanties, *The Shanty Book*.]

1923

Music for music's sake.
(*Musical News and Herald*, Vol. 64, No. 1610, 3 February 1923, p. 106.) [Summary of address to British Music Society conference in January 1923.]

1924

Charles Villiers Stanford, by some of his pupils.
(*Music and Letters*, Vol. 5, No. 3, July 1924, p. 195.
[A short tribute to his music.]

1926

How to sing a folk song.
(*The Midland Musician*, Vol. 1, No. 4, April 1926, p. 127.)

1927

The Late Mr. Frank Kidson.
(*Journal of the English Folk Dance Society*, 2nd Series. No. 1, 1927, p. 51.)

Lucy Broadwood: an appreciation.
(*Journal of the Folk Song Society*, Vol. 8, No. 31, Sept. 1927, pp. 44–5.)

1928

Ella Mary Leather.
(*Journal of the Folk Song Society*, Vol. 8, part 2, No. 32, December 1928, p. 102.) [Obituary containing reminiscence of folk-song collecting in Herefordshire.]

1929

Folk song [part of the article].
In Encyclopaedia Britannica. 14th ed. Chicago and London, Encyclopaedia Britannica, 1929. Vol. 9, pp. 447–8.

1931

Introduction to
HADOW, Sir William Henry.
English Music, London, Longmans, Green & Co., 1931, pp. vii–xiii.

1933

Cecil Sharp's accompaniments [Appendix B].
In STRANGWAYS, Arthur Henry Fox, and KARPELES, Maud, *Cecil Sharp*, London, O.U.P., 1933, p. 217.

Elizabethan Music and the modern world.
(*Monthly Musical Record.* Vol. 63, No. 752, Dec. 1933, pp. 217–8.)
[The substance of a speech delivered at the Dinner of the Tudor Singers and the Madrigal Summer School on 28 Oct. 1933.]

1934

National Music.
(The Mary Flexner lectures on the Humanities II). London, O.U.P., 1934, ix, 146 pp.

Contents: 1. Should music be national?

    2. Some tentative ideas on the origins of music.

    3. The folk song.

    4. The evolution of the folk song.

    5. The history of nationalism in music.

    6. Tradition.

    7. Some conclusions.

    8. The influence of folk song on the music of the church.

(*a*) Abridgement of two chapters reprinted as 'The Nature of and evolution of folk song'.
In SIEGMEISTER, Elie, *Ed.*
The Music lover's handbook. New York, Morrow, 1943, pp. 33–7.

(*b*) Extracts also reprinted in the above as 'The Folk song and the composer', pp. 40–4.

(*c*) Chapter I 'Should music be national?' reprinted as 'The composer speaks' in EWEN, David, ed. *The Book of Modern Composers*, New York, Knopf, 1943, pp. 286–90; in 2nd ed. 1950, pp. 286–90; in 3rd ed. revised and enlarged as *The New Book of Modern Composers*, 1961, pp. 419–23.

(*d*) Extracts reprinted under the titles 'Should music be national?' (pp. 3, 13, 129ff.), 'Historical aspects of nationalism in music' (pp. 98ff.), and 'Genius' (p. 92) in MORGENSTERN, Sam, ed. *Composers on Music: an anthology of composers' writings from Palestrina to Copland*, New York, Pantheon, 1956, pp. 362–8.

(*e*) *Reprint* of 1934 edition. London O.U.P., 1959, 164pp.

(*f*) Extract (pp. 114–30) from Chapter 8 'Some Conclusions' reprinted in WILSON, John, ed., *The Faith of an Artist*, London, Allen & Unwin, 1962, pp. 160–71.

(*g*) Reprint in a Danish translation of Chapter 1 'Should music be national?' as 'Bør Musik vaere national?' in VAUGHAN WILLIAMS, Ralph, *Essays om Musik*, Copenhagen, Steen Hasselbalchs Forlag, 1962, pp. 28–40.

(*h*) *Reprinted* in VAUGHAN WILLIAMS, Ralph. *National Music and Other Essays*. London, O.U.P., 1963 (Oxford Paperbacks, No. 76), pp. 1–82.

Introductory talk to Holst memorial concert. 4 pp.

(Broadcast in the National and Regional Programmes on Friday, 22 June 1934.)

[Script held by B.B.C. Scripts Registry; an appreciation of Holst both as a visionary and as a realist.] *Reprinted* in SHORE, Bernard. *The Orchestra Speaks*. London, Longmans, Green & Co., 1938, pp. 139–41.

Gustav Holst: man and musician.

(*Royal College of Music Magazine*, Vol. 30, No. 3, Dec. 1934, pp. 78–80)

(*a*) *Reprinted* in VAUGHAN WILLIAMS, Ralph. *Some thoughts on Beethoven's Choral Symphony, etc.* 1953. pp. 94–8.

(*b*) *Reprinted* in VAUGHAN WILLIAMS, Ralph. *National Music and Other Essays*, 1963, pp. 151–3.

1935

What have we learnt from Elgar?

(*Music and Letters*, Vol. 16, No. 1, Jan. 1935, pp. 13–19.)

['This is not an article really, but a few stray ideas set down without much method'—R.V.W. Some comments on Elgar's orchestration, with examples of phrases that influenced V.W.]

Happy days.

In Tales of a Field Ambulance 1914–1918, told by the personnel. Southend-on-Sea, Borough Printing and Publishing Co., 1935.

1937

Cecil James Sharp (1859–1924).

In Dictionary of National Biography, 1922–30. London, O.U.P., 1937, pp. 761–3.

1938

Ivor Gurney: the musician.

(*Music and Letters*, Vol. 19, No. 1, Jan. 1938, pp. 12–13.)

A Note on Gustav Holst.

In HOLST, Imogen.

Gustav Holst. London, O.U.P., 1938, pp. vii–ix.

Henry Wood.

(*The London Mercury*, Vol. 38, No. 228, Oct. 1938, pp. 497–501.)

Traditional Arts in the 20th century.
(*English Dance and Song*, Vol. 2, No. 6, June-July 1938, pp. 98–9.)

1939

A. H. Fox Strangways, AET. LXXX.
(*Music and Letters*, Vol. 20, No. 4, Oct. 1939, pp. 349–50.)
Making your own music.
(Broadcast talk in the Home Service—Sunday, 3 Dec. 1939, 8.45–9.0 p.m. Script held by B.B.C.'s Script Registry.) 6 pp.
Local musicians.
(*The Abinger Chronicle*, Vol. 1, No. 1, Christmas 1939, pp. 1–3.)

1940

The Composer in wartime.
(*The Listener*, Vol. 23, No. 592, 16 May 1940, p. 989.)
(*a*) *Reprinted* in VAUGHAN WILLIAMS, Ralph, and HOLST, Gustav. *Heirs and Rebels, etc.*, 1959, pp. 90–3.

1941

The justification of folk song.
(*English Dance and Song*, Vol. 5, No. 6, July-August 1941, pp. 66–7.)

1942

Let us remember. . . Early days.
(*English Dance and Song*, Vol. 6, No. 3, Feb. 1942, pp. 27–8.)

1943

Reprint of extracts from 'National Music'. (See 'National Music', 1934 (*a*) and (*b*).)
Composing for the films.
(*The Piping Times*, Vol. 4, No. 1, October 1943, pp. 4–5.)
[Short article from which 1944 'Film Music' was expanded.]

1944

Film music.
(*Royal College of Music magazine*, Vol. 40, No. 1, Feb. 1944, pp. 5–9.)
(*a*) Reprinted in HUNTLEY, John.
British Film Music. London, Skelton Robinson, 1947, pp. 177–82.
(*b*) *Reprinted* in VAUGHAN WILLIAMS, Ralph.
Some thoughts on Beethoven's Choral Symphony, etc. 1953, pp. 107–15, entitled 'Composing for the films'.
(*c*) *Reprinted in* BONAVIA, Ferrucio, *Ed.*
Musicians on music, London, Routledge & Kegan Paul, 1956, pp. 40–6.

(*d*) *Reprinted* in VAUGHAN WILLIAMS, Ralph.
National Music and Other Essays, 1963, pp. 160–5, entitled 'Composing for the films'.

1947

Gloria, Sanctus, and Agnus Dei from Mass in B minor – Bach.
In Leith Hill Musical Festival programme, 18 April 1947.

(*a*) *Reprinted* in VAUGHAN WILLIAMS, Ralph, *Some Thoughts on Beethoven's Choral Symphony, etc.* 1953, pp. 164–7, as 'The Mass in B minor in English: a programme note'.

(*b*) *Reprinted* in VAUGHAN WILLIAMS, Ralph, *National Music and Other Essays*, 1963, pp. 199–201.

1948

A Minim's rest.
In MILFORD, *Sir* Humphrey Sumner.
Essays mainly on the nineteenth century presented to Sir Humphrey Milford. London, O.U.P., 1948, pp. 113–6.

(*a*) *Reprinted* in *Some thoughts on Beethoven's Choral Symphony, etc.* 1953, pp. 116–21.

(*b*) *Reprinted* in *National Music and Other Essays*, 1963, pp. 166–9.
Lucy Broadwood, 1858–1929.
(*Journal of the English Folk Dance and Song Society*, Vol. 5, No. 3, Dec. 1948, pp. 136–8).

1949

Gustav Theodore Holst.
In Dictionary of National Biography 1931–1940. London, O.U.P., 1949, pp. 441–3.

First performances. Preface to prospectus of Henry Wood Promenade Concerts (B.B.C. publication), July 1949.

1950

Musical autobiography.
In FOSS, Hubert.
Ralph Vaughan Williams: a study. London, Harrap, 1950, pp. 18–38.

(*a*) *Reprinted* with slight revisions in VAUGHAN WILLIAMS, Ralph.
Some thoughts on Beethoven's Choral Symphony, etc. 1953, pp. 132–58.

(*b*) *Reprinted* in revised version in Danish translation as Musikalsk Selvbiografi in VAUGHAN WILLIAMS, Ralph, *Essays om Musik*, Copenhagen, Steen Hasselbalchs Forlag, 1962, pp. 41–61.

(*c*) *Reprinted* in VAUGHAN WILLIAMS, Ralph. *National Music and Other Essays*, 1964, pp. 177–94.

The Composer speaks.
Reprinted from 'National Music'.
In EWEN, David, *Ed.*
The Book of modern composers. 2nd ed. rev. and enlarged. New York, Knopf, 1950, pp. 286–90.
Bach the great bourgeois.
(Talk broadcast in July 1950. Script held by B.B.C.'s Scripts Registry.)
(*a*) *Printed* in *The Listener*, Vol. 44, No. 1123, 3 Aug. 1950, pp. 170–1.
(*b*) *Reprinted* in HINRICHSEN, Max, *Ed.*
Music book, Volume VII of Hinrichsen's Musical Yearbook. London, Hinrichsen's Edition Ltd., 1952, pp. 277–82.
(*c*) *Reprinted in* VAUGHAN WILLIAMS, Ralph.
Some thoughts on Beethoven's Choral Symphony, etc. 1953, pp. 122–31.
(*d*) *Reprinted* in Danish translation as Bach, den geniale Smaaborger in VAUGHAN WILLIAMS, Ralph, *Essays om Musik*, Copenhagen, Steen Hasselbalchs Forlag, 1962, pp. 20–7.
(*e*) *Reprinted* in VAUGHAN WILLIAMS, Ralph. *National Music and Other Essays*, 1963, pp. 170–6.
Appeal on behalf of the English Folk Dance and Song Society.
[Broadcast on Sunday, 24 Sept. 1950 in the Home Service; script held by the B.B.C.'s Scripts Registry.]

1951

Preface to
WHITE, E. A., compiler, *An Index of English Songs contributed to the Journal of the Folk Song Society 1899–1931 and its continuation the Journal of the English Folk Dance and Song Society to 1950*, ed. DEAN-SMITH, Margaret. London, English Folk Dance and Song Society, 1951, p. vii.
Foreword to
Arts Council of Great Britain commemorative book of eight concerts of Henry Purcell's music, ed., WATKINS SHAW, Harold. London, Arts Council of Great Britain, 1951, p. 7.
[A plea for more performances of Purcell's music.]
Verdi – a symposium
(*Opera*, Vol. 2, No. 3, February 1951, pp. 111–2.)
[Appreciation of Verdi's use of song to elucidate dramatic situations.]
(*a*) *Reprinted* in ROSENTHAL, Harold, ed. *The Opera Bedside Book.* London, Gollancz, 1965, pp. 193–4.
Arnold Schoenberg 1874–1951
(*Music and Letters*, Vol. 32, No. 4, October 1951, p. 322.)
[Pithy contribution to obituary tributes.]

Choral Singing.
Article in programme of Royal Choral Society concert, 9 June 1951.
Art and organization.
In STANDING CONFERENCE OF COUNTY MUSIC COMMITTEES.
Music and the Amateur: a Report. London, the National Council of Social Service Incorporated, 1951, p. 3.
[A short 'message', in a witty style, concerning the unfortunate necessity for administration in the field of art. 'Organization is not Art, but Art cannot flourish without it.']

1952

The Stanford centenary. 3 pp.
(Broadcast talk in the General Overseas Service, Tues., 30 Sept., Fri., 3 Oct., and Sat., 4 Oct. 1952.) Script held by the B.B.C. Scripts Registry.
Carthusian music in the 'eighties.
(*The Carthusian*, Vol. 21, No. 1, Dec. 1952, pp. 1–2.)

1953

Some thoughts on Beethoven's Choral Symphony with writings on other musical subjects.
London, O.U.P., 1953, 172 pp.
Contents: 1. Some thoughts on Beethoven's Choral Symphony. [Not previously printed.]
2. The Letter and the spirit.
3. Gustav Holst: an essay and a note.
4. Nationalism and internationalism. [Not previously printed.]
5. Composing for the films.
6. A minim's rest.
7. Bach the great bourgeois.
8. A Musical autobiography (Revised).
9. Charles Villiers Stanford [Reprinted from 'London Calling'].
10. The Mass in B minor: a programme note.
11. Shrubsole [Reprinted from the Manchester Guardian, 1943].
Reprinted in *National Music and Other Essays* [Paperback edition], London, O.U.P., 1963, pp. 83–204.
Address (To the 5th conference of the International Folk Music Council).
(*Journal of the International Folk Music Council*, Vol. 5, Jan. 1953, pp. 7–8.)

1954

Preface to
FRASER, Norman, *Ed.*
International catalogue of recorded folk music. London. O.U.P., 1954,
pp. iv, V.
[In French and English.]
Cecil Sharp: an appreciation.
In SHARP, Cecil James.
English folk song: some conclusions. Rev. by Maud Karpeles. 3rd ed.,
London, Methuen & Co. Ltd., 1954, pp. v–vi.
  (*a*) *Reprinted* in 4th (rev.) ed. prepared by KARPELES, Maud. London,
    Mercury Books, 1965, pp. vii–ix.
Preface to
FOSS, Hubert James, and GOODWIN, Nöel.
London Symphony: portrait of an orchestra. London, Naldrett Press,
1954, pp. iii–iv.
[A few reminiscences of the London Symphony Orchestra.]
Arnold Bax: 1883–1953.
  (*Music and Letters*, Vol. 35, No. 1, Jan. 1954, pp. 13–14.)
  [A short memoir among others.]
Ernest Irving: 1878–1953.
  (*Music and Letters*, Vol. 35, No. 1, Jan. 1954, pp. 17–18.)
  [A few reminiscences including one concerning the 'Sinfonia Antar-
tica'.]
Gustav Holst: a great composer.
  (*The Listener*, Vol. 51, No. 1318, 3 June 1954, pp. 965–6.)
  [A transcript of a broadcast talk in 'Music Magazine'.]

1955

The Making of music.
  Ithaca, New York, Cornell University Press, 1955, vii, 61pp. New
  edition 1965.
  (The substance of four lectures given at Cornell University, 1954.)
Contents: 1. Why do we make music?
       2. What is music?
       3. How do we make music?
       4. When do we make music?
       5. What are the social foundations of music?
       6. The folk song movement.
       Epilogue. Making your own music (adapted from a lecture
       given at Yale University, 1 December 1954).

(a) *Reprinted* in VAUGHAN WILLIAMS, Ralph. *National Music and Other Essays*, 1963, pp. 205–42.

Reminiscences of fifty years.

In *The Leith Hill Musical Festival 1905–1955:* a record of fifty years of music-making in Surrey. Epsom, Surrey, Pullingers Ltd., 1955, pp. 35–40.

Where craft ends and art begins.

(*Saturday Review*, Vol. 38, 26 March 1955, pp. 37–9 and 64–5.)

['Taken from his forthcoming book "The Making of Music" '.]

Sibelius.

(*Royal College of Music Magazine*, Vol. 51, No. 3, Sept. 1955, pp. 58–60.)

[A personal appreciation of his music written as a 90th birthday greeting.]

Sibelius at 90: greatness and popularity.

(*The Daily Telegraph & Morning Post*, No. 31,308, Thursday 8 December 1955, p. 6.)

The Teaching of Parry and Stanford.

14 pp.

[A shortened version of the lecture given at the Composers' Concourse, 1955, broadcast on Sunday, 1 Jan. 1956, in the Third Programme. Script held by the B.B.C. Scripts Registry.]

(a) *Reprinted* in

VAUGHAN WILLIAMS, Ralph, and HOLST, Gustav.
Heirs and Rebels, etc., 1959, pp. 94–102.

N.B. The date given there is 1957.

Martin Shaw

(*The [Ipswich] Diocesan Magazine*, Vol. 42, No. 6, December 1955, p. 85.)

[Address given on eightieth birthday of Martin Shaw in St Mary-le-Tower Church, Ipswich, 22 October 1955.]

1956

Preface to

CHAMBERS, George Bennett.
Folksong—Plainsong: a study in origins and musical relationships.
London, The Merlin Press, 1956, p. v.

The New Vaughan Williams Symphony.

(*Music and Musicians*, Vol. 4, No. 9, May 1956, pp. 8–9.)

[A 'pre-view' of the 8th symphony, with music examples.]

Some reminiscences of the English Hymnal.

In *The First Fifty Years: a brief account of the English Hymnal from 1906 to 1956*. Oxford, O.U.P., 1956, pp. 2–5.

Bernard Shaw as a music critic

(*The Listener*, Vol. 56, No. 1428, 9 August 1956, p. 205)
[Letter objecting to criticism by Tippett – influenced by Shaw – of Parry's *Job*.]
Sir Ralph Wedgwood
(*The Times*, No. 53,633, Tuesday, 11 September 1956, p. 11.)
[Obituary tribute.]
Mr Gerald Finzi: a many-sided man.
(*The Times*, No. 53,652, Wednesday, 3 October 1956, p. 11.)
[Obituary tribute.]

1957

Introduction to
CRANMER, Arthur.
The art of singing. London, Dennis Dobson, 1957.
Elgar today.
(*The Musical Times*, Vol. 98, No. 1372, June 1957, p. 302.)
[Contribution to Elgar centenary symposium.]
'Hands off the Third.'
(*Music and Musicians*, Vol. 6, No. 2, October 1957, p. 15.)
[Attack on proposed cuts and changes in B.B.C. Third Programme.]
'Local Tradition.'
(*English Dance and Song*, Vol. 22, No. 2, November-December 1957, p. 64.)

1958

The Music of my new ninth symphony: an analysis of this month's premiere.
(*Music and Musicians*, Vol. 6, No. 8, April 1958, p. 12–13.)
[With music examples. This is Vaughan Williams's programme note for the work.]
The English Folk Dance and Song Society.
(*Ethnomusicology*, Vol. 2, No. 3, Sept. 1958, pp. 108–12.)
The Diamond jubilee of the Folk Song Society.
(*Journal of the English Folk Dance and Song Society*, Vol. 8, No. 3, Dec. 1958, pp. 123–4.)
Translation into Danish of 'Who wants the English Composer?'.
Harpsichord or piano? A word to purists.
(*The Daily Telegraph & Morning Post*, No. 31,990, Thursday, 20 February 1958, p. 8.)
[Defence of his use of the piano as continuo instrument in Bach's *St. John Passion*.]

1959

Introduction to

VAUGHAN WILLIAMS, Ralph, and LLOYD, Albert Lancaster, eds. *The Penguin Book of English Folk Songs*. Harmondsworth, Penguin Books, 1959, pp. 7–10.

VAUGHAN WILLIAMS, Ralph, and HOLST, Gustav.

Heirs and rebels: letters written to each other and occasional writings on music. Ed. by Ursula Vaughan Williams and Imogen Holst. London, O.U.P., 1959, xiii, 111 pp.

Includes: Some of Vaughan Williams's early writings on music.

1. Good taste.
2. Bach and Schumann.
3. Librettos.
4. Conducting.
5. Hymn tunes.

> *also* The Composer in wartime.
> Talk on Parry and Stanford.

(*a*) Extracts reprinted in GAL, Hans, ed. *The Musician's World: great composers in their letters*. London, Thames and Hudson, 1965, pp. 418–28.

(*b*) Extracts reprinted in GAL, Hans, ed. *The Musician's World: letters of the great composers* (paperback title). London, Thames and Hudson, 1978, pp. 418–28.

National Music. Lithographic reprint of 1934 edition. London, O.U.P., 164 pp.

1962

Essays om Musik.

Paa Dansk ved Bent Olsen (Hasselbalchs Kultur-Bibliotek, Bind 211.) Copenhagen, Steen Hasselbalchs Forlag, 1962.

Contents: 1. Inledning (Preface) by OLSEN, Bent.

2. Aanden og Bogstaven (The Letter and the Spirit.)

3. Bach, den geniale Smaaborger (Bach, the great bourgeois.)

4. Bør Musik vaere national? (Should music be national?)

5. Musikalsk Selvbiografi (Musical autobiography.)

1963

National Music and Other Essays

(With Preface by Ursula Vaughan Williams.) London, O.U.P., 1963 (Oxford Paperbacks, No. 76), x, 246 pp.

Includes: National Music (1934).

Some Thoughts on Beethoven's Choral Symphonies, with writings on other musical subjects (1953).

The Making of Music (1955).

Index.

Index of Works

(U = Unpublished)

ARRANGEMENTS AND EDITIONS OF MUSIC BY OTHER COMPOSERS
(excluding harmonizations)

CHAMBER MUSIC

DANCING, WORKS FOR (MASQUES AND BALLETS)

FILM MUSIC
(unpublished in original form)

FOLK-DANCE ARRANGEMENTS

FOLK-SONG AND CAROL ARRANGEMENTS AND COLLECTIONS, BRITISH, FRENCH, AND GERMAN

HYMNALS AND HYMN-TUNES

(Tunes arranged or harmonized by Vaughan Williams will be found under the entries for *English Hymnal* and *Songs of Praise* in the Catalogue)

INSTRUMENTAL SOLOIST WITH ORCHESTRA

JUVENILIA (1878–95)
LEITH HILL PLACE, CHARTERHOUSE, R.C.M., AND CAMBRIDGE
(These works are unpublished with the exception of 'Cradle Song')

MISCELLANEOUS

ORCHESTRAL MUSIC
(A) BRASS BAND

ORCHESTRAL MUSIC
(B) FULL ORCHESTRA OR STRINGS ONLY

ORCHESTRAL MUSIC
(C) MILITARY AND WIND BAND

ORGAN WORKS AND ARRANGEMENTS

PAGEANTS

STAGE WORKS
(excluding masques and ballets)

VOCAL MUSIC
(Duets, Partsongs, etc., Unaccompanied or with Light Accompaniment; excluding Folk Songs)

General Index